The Sanctuary

Also by Emma Haughton

The Dark

Emma Haughton

The Sanctuary

HODDER &
STOUGHTON

First published in Great Britain in 2022 by Hodder & Stoughton
An Hachette UK company

1

Copyright © Emma Haughton 2022

The right of Emma Haughton to be identified as the Author of the Work has been
asserted by her in accordance with the Copyright, Designs and Patents Act 1988.

A CIP catalogue record for this title is available from the British Library

Hardback ISBN 978 1 529 35666 3
Trade Paperback ISBN 978 1 529 35667 0
eBook ISBN 978 1 529 35665 6

Typeset in Sabon MT by Hewer Text UK Ltd, Edinburgh
Printed and bound in Great Britain by Clays Ltd, Elcograf S.p.A.

Hodder & Stoughton policy is to use papers that are natural, renewable
and recyclable products and made from wood grown in sustainable
forests. The logging and manufacturing processes are expected to
conform to the environmental regulations of the country of origin.

Hodder & Stoughton Ltd
Carmelite House
50 Victoria Embankment
London EC4Y 0DZ

www.hodder.co.uk

For the usual suspects – including the three hairy ones

I

The heat wakes me. And the pain. I'm lying on my back, sweat pooling between my breasts, on my stomach, in the creases of my neck. My head is thumping so hard I feel nauseous.

Why is the apartment so infernally hot?

I push aside the sheet and try to drift back into unconsciousness. I'm almost there, almost slipping into the oblivion of sleep, when something sparks in my brain.

The quiet.

The usual medley of sounds of New York's East Village, the incessant blare of horns, of sirens, the low drone of planes headed to JFK or La Guardia – it's all gone. Nothing but an eerie silence, save for the background *beat-beat-beat* of my heart.

What the actual . . .?

I sit up, waiting for my eyes to focus. My heart rate faster now, more a gallop than a trot. Around me none of the mess I've made of my uncle's spare bedroom, the random piles of books and discarded clothing, the heaps of magazines and dirty mugs and plates. Gone is the IKEA unit and matching chest of drawers, the ornate gilt mirror Dan hung over the exposed brickwork, that ugly green bowl he picked up in a street market on Columbus Avenue, used as a dump for coins and keys.

This room has whitewashed walls surrounding a narrow bed. On one side a window, slightly ajar, the thin cream curtain wafting in the warm breeze. Opposite, a plain oak door with a single brass hook. To the right of it there's a large wardrobe, half with open shelves; in the middle sits a pile of what appears to be fresh underwear.

I glance down. Beside the bed is a small table, topped with a full bottle of water and a clean tumbler.

What the hell?

Where am I?

I close my eyes and count to five, praying this is all just a weird dream. But when I open them again, the room is still here, the air inside heavy with heat. The silence so thick, so cloying, it seems to have a density of its own.

What on earth happened last night? Gripped by rising panic, I try to recall, head throbbing with the effort. Drinks in the bar on Avenue A with Franny and Rocco and a handful of Rocco's friends. Then a few flashes from the club. Talking to a couple of guys who sat at our table. Drinking tequila. Not much more than that.

I kick off the sheet. Note, to my relief, I'm still wearing the ripped jeans and Ramones T-shirt I went out in. No sign though of my leather jacket; nor my favourite Doc Marten boots.

Or my phone or cigarettes, I realise, gazing around. I slide out of bed and walk to the window, feeling unsteady, my throat parched. As I pull back the curtain, shock jolts through me with a force that makes my legs tremble.

Nothing.

No streets or block houses. No towers in the distance. No cars, no taxis, no shops, no restaurants, no cafes. Just empty space as far as I can see. A desert, I realise. Dry red earth and cacti and scrubby little bushes.

Holy fuck. Where am I?

A wave of nausea hits as I let out a whimper of surprise and terror. Have I been ... *kidnapped?* Or am I hallucinating?

Maybe I've finally scrambled my brain and tipped over some kind of edge. But the hot breeze wafting through the window feels real enough. The air has an arid, earthy smell. And the fierce sunlight makes my eyes squint and my head wince with pain.

I glance around. Under the bed, I spot a pair of flip-flops. Slipping them on my feet, I try the door – to my relief, it opens easily.

Not imprisoned then.

I peer along the dark corridor, making out several closed doors. What is this place? Some sort of hostel?

I venture out and knock on the closest, but no one answers. I turn the handle. When the door opens, I glance inside. It's completely empty, save a bed with a bare mattress. I move down the passage and try the next, finding myself in a small shower room. I peer into the mirror above the sink.

Jesus. I look awful. Haggard, eyes smudged with mascara, my skin blotchy and pale, covered in a sheen of sweat. My hair is loose, grazing my shoulders, dark and matted. I press a finger to the base of my nose ring. It's red and swollen, tender to the touch.

As I drop my gaze I notice the mark on my jeans – a brown smear across the left thigh that looks like . . . oh God . . . dried blood.

My heart thumps harder as I roll down my jeans and check my leg. No sign of any injury. Pulling them back on, I examine my face, fingers exploring my scalp for cuts or bumps. Nothing.

I lean against the sink unit, breathing hard, stomach roiling.

What happened to me?

Where am I?

I stand there, gripping the basin, trying desperately to recall the night before. For a few moments there's a blank in my head where memory should be. Then a burst of sirens, of flashing lights. Hands pushing me into a car.

An overwhelming sense of fear, of distress.

Suddenly I'm so dizzy and thirsty I can barely stay upright. Staggering back to the room I woke up in, I gulp down the entire contents of the water bottle, then hover there, breathing hard, before venturing again into that gloomy corridor.

This time I head the other way. Passing through a stone archway, I find myself in a huge atrium filled with light. One side is a sheer wall of glass, giving an unspoiled view of the landscape, the miles of dirt and cacti stretching out to distant hills. A telescope is positioned in the corner, tilted towards the sky. At the other end of the room is a large stone fireplace, flanked by a pair of studded leather sofas and a heavy wooden coffee table topped with an enormous vase of fresh flowers. Above the fireplace hangs a massive oil painting, a desert scene in rich bold colours.

Polished flagstones cover the floor, and carefully tended indoor plants soften the space. Above my head, two massive wrought-iron chandeliers hang from the oak beams supporting the second-storey ceiling.

Jesus, this place is something else.

'Hello?' I call, tentatively at first, then louder. 'Hello? Is anyone here?'

No answer, but over in the far corner, I spy a wide curved stone staircase leading to the next level. I climb up, panting with the effort. The nearest door, also unlocked, reveals a beautiful room with a mahogany sleigh bed and a view over the rear of the property. Unlike the rooms downstairs, this one is clearly occupied. A white towelling dressing gown has been thrown across the bed, and a hairdryer lies on the dresser, along with a brush and make-up bag.

'Hello?' I call again, wondering if the room's occupant is in the en suite bathroom.

Silence.

It's the same story in the other rooms. All unlocked and empty, but clearly occupied. The last at the far end of the landing is the largest, with a sumptuous king-size bed and heavy wooden furniture polished to a high sheen. This one has an actual log fireplace, and a huge ceiling fan overhead. Windows on two sides offer panoramic views across the desert, a pair of double doors leading to a balcony.

I open them and lean over the ornate iron railings, hoping to spot houses or traffic. But there's no sign of any other buildings. This place appears to be literally in the middle of nowhere.

Closing the balcony doors again, I check out the huge bathroom, dominated by one of those fancy claw-foot tubs you get in high-end hotels. In the opposite corner, there's a wet room with a large circular head, the kind that showers you in warm rain. Every inch, even the vaulted arches in the ceiling, is tiled in stone mosaics.

This place is gorgeous, and reeks of money. If it weren't for the fact there are no locks on the doors, I'd assume it was an expensive hotel or luxury guest house.

I glance at the toiletries ranged around the sink. Kiehl's, Dior, Tom Ford. All men's stuff. Is this somebody's home then? Did I hook up with an insanely rich guy at the club?

Not that Unravel usually attracts Wall Street types, but who knows? Maybe someone fancied a walk on the scruffy side. Thought it might be amusing to slum it with a grungy girl as piss-poor as her attitude.

But that still doesn't make sense. This can't be anywhere near New York, and surely I wouldn't forget going to an airport or getting on a plane?

Anyway, why would I be stuck downstairs in that little box room with all my clothes on?

A fresh wave of frustration and anxiety floods my system. I hurry down the curved stairs, trying doors at random. One opens on a library, every wall lined with shelves crammed with books and magazines. The next reveals a spacious lounge, long leather sofas surrounding a marble-topped coffee table, the fireplace in the background stacked with freshly split logs. A third door turns out to be a store cupboard filled with brushes and hoovers and other cleaning stuff. Finally I discover a short passageway leading to another, plainer annex with more rooms – these, however, seem to be locked, and I don't bother trying more than a couple.

Backtracking and heading in the opposite direction, I find myself in a large courtyard, surrounded by buildings on all sides. I pause, taking it in. This place is idyllic. A long covered terrace shelters yet more sofas and wooden tables, interspersed with giant urns filled with plants. The floor is covered in beautiful old terracotta tiles, the walls painted in that traditional desert pinky-red. A series of stone archways separates the terrace from the garden, where a tall tree shades a neat patch of lawn, bordered by a large pond. All around, long beds are filled with dark green foliage and various jewel-bright flowers.

The air in this leafy courtyard is moist and several degrees cooler, and I'm loath to step back into the cloying indoor heat. But I need to find somebody. I have to discover where I am – and how I got here.

I retrace my steps through the house, this time turning left at the corridor that leads out of the atrium. All of a sudden I'm in a wide reception area, facing a pair of heavy wood and glass entrance doors. I make straight for them, dreading the moment

I find they're locked and discover I'm a prisoner in the world's most gorgeous gaol.

But a second later I'm standing in a covered porchway; when I step out of its shade, the heat hits me like a wall. I almost retreat from the intensity of it, half blinded by the fierce sun.

'Hello?' I yell, hand shielding my eyes from the glare. I look about me. This is surreal.

Where the fuck is everyone?

I force myself into the impossibly hot air, stumbling across the gravel in the borrowed flip-flops towards a scatter of outbuildings – three large sheds clad in pale wood, all with solar panel roofs, though I catch the low hum of a generator. One seems to be a carport, a single vehicle parked underneath. Some kind of jeep, designed for rugged, open country.

Plenty of that around here.

I gaze towards the low wall that surrounds the whole property, spotting a pair of heavy iron gates. I stop, bewildered.

There's nothing beyond. No sign of a road, or even a dirt track.

Returning to the carport, I try the door of the jeep. Locked. I shield my eyes again and peer inside, hoping at least to spot my phone. But the interior is empty, save for several five-gallon bottles of water in the boot.

I feel another sharp pulse of fear.

What the hell is going on? Am I completely alone here?

'HELLO!' I shout, as loudly as I can manage. But my voice carries away on the warm breeze and nothing comes back.

Ignoring the pain in my head, the pressure in my stomach, I set off around the whole complex. Built on top of a small rise, it turns out to be a series of buildings interconnected by walkways and hacienda-style arches, and in one place an actual bridge. Some have red-pink walls with traditional terracotta-tiled roofs, others are constructed in dark granite, including a tall round tower topped with a satellite dish and cockerel weathervane.

Surrounding the house, at intervals, are olive trees, their gnarled trunks topped with silvery foliage heavy with green fruit. Between them lurk various wild animals and birds, sculpted in metal and stone. Beyond, in the gardens that run down to the low wall, I spot fruit trees and a vegetable plot, along with every kind of flowering bush and plant this climate could sustain.

The vine-covered veranda wrapped around the main house gives unparalleled views of the arid vista beyond the boundary wall. I walk along it, studying the horizon in every direction, but can't spot a single dwelling or farm, not even a power line.

This place is an oasis. A gorgeous architect-designed haven in what appears to be unending wilderness.

It must have cost an absolute bomb to build.

As I round the far end of the main house, my attention is snagged by a soft splashing sound. I leave the shade of the veranda and hurry towards the beautiful rockery of stone and cacti and spiky green yuccas, where a small stream cascades over artfully-arranged rocks before disappearing into gravel at the base. Beyond is a large rectangular swimming pool, with one of those infinity edges where the turquoise water merges with the deep blue sky.

As I stand there, mesmerised, something brushes against my leg, making me squeal in surprise. I look down to see a small black-and-white cat staring up at me, purring, its tail and back arched. It opens its mouth in a silent greeting, then strolls off into the flowering shrubs on the other side of the pool.

I take a deep breath, trying to calm my racing heart, then walk up and peer into the water. It's flat and still, as intensely blue as the sky above. I gaze at my own shimmering reflection. I look ragged, desperate.

And horribly alone.

My stomach churns, provoking another intense surge of nausea. I close my eyes, disoriented, steadying myself. In a far-off part of my brain, something surfaces. A noise, impossibly loud, a persistent deafening buzz, followed by the sensation of lifting.

But everything is confused, soft around the edges. I grasp at the memory, struggling to bring it into focus, but it slides away, leaving only questions in its wake.

Did I set off on some crazy road trip? Perhaps Franny or Rocco took it into their heads to drive all the way out to New Mexico, or Arizona.

But that would take days, surely?

And how could I possibly forget a journey like that?

None of it makes sense. I'd never agree to leave New York. I'm supposed to be house-sitting my uncle Dan's apartment and his two highly strung Manx cats. I can't take off and leave them to fend for themselves.

Besides, I'm broke. I could work for ten years flat in one of my dead-end jobs and not have the money for a place like this.

Same goes for Rocco and Franny.

The relentless sun beats down on my face, my skin beginning to burn. I glance up at the sky. Not a cloud in sight.

At that moment I catch a distant sound, carried on the hot wind blowing off the desert, coming from beyond the boundary wall. I squint into the dazzling light, scanning the barren landscape, finally spotting what I'd previously missed, obscured by the outbuildings. Some two hundred yards away, on the flat plain below the house, is a large round tent, guy ropes radiating like sunrays, a triangular red flag fluttering from the top of the central pole.

And from it, faintly, a high-pitched, piercing noise.

The sound of a woman screaming.

2

I stand, paralysed, as screams pierce the silence. Every last brain cell is telling me to run, hide, barricade myself in that room. I hesitate for a second or two, jaw tensing with indecision, then scramble over the low stone wall and charge towards the marquee.

What the actual fuck are you doing? shouts a voice in my head.

Are you completely crazy?

Sweat pours down my face, my neck, my body as I pound across the parched desert soil, dodging stones and cacti. I'm gasping for breath, the heat sucking all the oxygen out of the air.

Seriously, Zoey, why are you doing this? What are you trying to prove?

I keep going.

As I draw closer, sobs are audible between the screams, interspersed with wild howls of protest. In the gaps, another voice.

Male. Angry.

I glance about for something I can use to defend myself. See nothing but prickly shrubs, their spines vicious, impossible to grasp. Frantic, I search until I spot a slackened guy rope, its large wooden peg lying on the ground. I pick it up, gripping it tightly in my fist. Then approach the entrance of the marquee.

'You're accusing me of making it up?' yells a woman, her words emerging in gasps. 'Are you trying to fucking kill me? Is that what you want?'

Her voice rises into a protracted wail of anguish. '*You want me to die?* Why not finish me off yourself, get it over with?'

I brandish the peg like a weapon, ready to strike. Another sliver of memory surfaces, from the club last night. My hand clutching something else, something smooth and heavy, as my body floods with anger and adrenalin.

I push it aside and burst into the tent. After the glare of the sun, it's black as pitch inside. I hesitate, blinking, and gaze around in confusion, waiting for my eyes to adjust.

A few seconds later, I see them. A dozen people, all sitting in a circle on folding chairs, stare back at me. Most look as shocked as I feel, but several appear merely amused.

'Hey, Riley, it's the cavalry,' sniggers a guy in a black beanie.

I stare at the young woman standing in the middle of the circle, her fists clenched, her small features rigid with distress. Despite the heat, she's dressed in a long-sleeved grey T-shirt and baggy blue joggers, her straight dark hair matted with sweat and the force of her emotion.

'Oh great,' she snarls at me. 'That's fucking priceless. Nice timing, asshole.' She slumps back onto an empty chair, swiping away furious tears.

'I'm sorry,' I stammer, gazing at all the seated faces. My head is reeling, and I can barely breathe. 'But what the fuck is going on here?'

A man with a tightly clipped beard gets to his feet. 'Hi, Zoey, glad you could make it.' His tone placatory as he reaches out and takes the tent peg from my hand. 'Have a seat,' he adds, gesturing at a vacant chair.

I don't move. I can't move. I gulp in air, head spinning, struggling to process what's happening.

'How do you know my name?' I try to say. '*Where the hell am I?*'

My lips formed the words, but no sound leaves my mouth. A moment later, the world goes black and I sink to the floor.

3

When I come round, I'm lying on an exam couch in what appears to be a plainly furnished clinic. A big double-door metal cabinet to the left of me, along with a stainless steel trolley containing boxes of tissues and rubber gloves and other medical stuff. On the other side of the room, a desk with a laptop.

A small, pretty Asian woman is slipping a blood pressure cuff onto my arm. 'Don't sit up yet,' she says in a soft Canadian accent, her hand gently pushing me back onto the couch. 'Give yourself a few minutes.'

I watch silently as she pumps up the cuff, eyeing the reading as it deflates. 'You're okay,' she says, removing the cuff and sticking a digital thermometer to my forehead. 'Your blood pressure's a little low, and your pulse is fast, but I think you're simply dehydrated and somewhat overwrought. How do you feel?'

'Awful,' I croak, my clothes tacky on my skin. 'My head is killing me.'

She checks the reading on the thermometer. 'Well, you don't have a fever. Your temperature is normal.'

'Where am I?' I ask. 'And who are you?'

'Don't you remember, Zoey?'

I shake my head. A burst of pain shoots through my skull, dwarfing the background thump of my headache.

'My name's Sonoya – Dr Sonoya Kimura – I'm the physician and psychotherapist here. I did introduce myself last night.'

I grope for the memory, but come up blank. Then I recall the girl in the tent. 'That woman who was screaming. Is she all right?'

'You mean Riley? Yes, she's fine.'

'So she's not hurt or anything?' I blink at Dr Kimura. 'Are you sure? She seemed pretty upset.'

'People occasionally get distressed in group therapy,' she smiles. 'In Riley's case, it was actually something of a breakthrough.'

I frown. 'Group therapy? What do you mean?'

'Rory and Mike will explain in a moment. Meanwhile, I'd like you to sit up and drink this.' She holds out a large glass full of lurid orange liquid, a plastic straw leaning over the side.

'What is it?' I heave myself upright and stare at it dubiously.

'Oral rehydration formula. It'll help restore your electrolyte balance.'

I gaze at Dr Kimura's serene expression, wondering if I can trust her. Then accept the glass and take a sip. It's not too bad, a vaguely orangey flavour, and pleasantly sweet. I gulp it down, and lie back, head pulsating.

'What is this place, and why is it so infernally hot?' I complain.

'The air conditioning has broken down,' Dr Kimura replies, ignoring my first question. 'That's why no one was around when you woke up – Mike and Alejandro were in the control shed trying to fix it.'

'Do you have any painkillers?' I ask as she puts away her equipment. 'My head really hurts.' God knows, this is shaping up to be the worst hangover in living history.

How much did I have to drink last night?

Not that much, surely?

'I'm afraid not,' Dr Kimura says. 'The head pain is probably a result of the alcohol you consumed, coupled with the dehydration. We tried to get you to drink plenty of water when you arrived, but you weren't very cooperative.'

'When I arrived where?' I snap, increasingly irritated. On top of everything else I'm dying for a cigarette. 'When are you going to tell me what's going on?'

'Wait a second.' The woman leaves the room. I stare up at the ceiling. If the orange drink is supposed to have any positive effect, I'm not aware of it; I can't remember when I last felt this terrible.

A few minutes later, Dr Kimura reappears. 'Zoey, if you'll come with me, Rory and Mike would appreciate a chat in the office.'

She holds the door open while I edge off the couch, legs wobbly, and follow her down a narrow corridor and across the reception area towards a room near the front entrance. Inside, a stocky man sits behind a large oak desk. Late forties, at a guess, dressed in a short-sleeved white shirt with damp patches under the armpits. His face is red and shiny with sweat.

'Have a seat, Zoey,' he says in a broad Brummie accent that seems completely out of place here. He sniffs, then gestures at the chair opposite. 'My name's Mike, I'm the centre director.'

Before I can ask what centre he's talking about, the door swings open and another man walks in. It's the guy who took the tent peg from me earlier, right before I passed out. He sits in one of the empty chairs, regarding me thoughtfully.

I stare back at him. Tall, attractive, mid thirties, dressed in cargo shorts and a rust-coloured polo shirt. His sandy hair and beard so neatly trimmed he must do them every day.

'I'll go check on Riley.' Dr Kimura disappears, closing the door behind her.

The man called Mike regards me for a moment or two, then clears his throat. 'We would like to apologise that no one was here when you woke up – Rory and Sonoya were in group, and Alejandro and I were busy in one of the sheds. We thought you'd be asleep longer, frankly, given the state you were in when you arrived.'

'The state I was in?' I echo, noticing now how hoarse my voice is, my throat sore and over-used. 'I've no idea what you're talking about. And what is this place? How do you all know my name?'

'As we explained last night, this is the Sanctuary,' says the other man. His accent is Australian, I think. Or maybe Kiwi.

'The Sanctuary?' I frown at him. 'Sanctuary from what? And who are you anyway?'

'My name is Rory, and I'm the programme manager here. The Sanctuary is a therapeutic refuge for clients to rebalance their lives and address any issues they might be experiencing.'

'A therapeutic refuge?' I gaze at the pair of them blankly. 'What the fuck's that? Some kind of rehab?'

'Yes, we are a registered rehabilitation centre,' Mike explains, using a cotton handkerchief to wipe the sweat from his face. 'We do support clients struggling with addictive patterns, but we don't take people who need medical help with detoxing.'

'We prefer to think of the Sanctuary as a radical alternative to conventional rehab,' Rory chimes in. 'A unique opportunity for profound healing and lifestyle readjustment. People come for a variety of reasons, not necessarily addiction. Some simply need space to reflect and regroup, to deal with the toll that everyday life can take on the body and spirit.'

I gaze at them. 'Sounds like complete bullshit. Anyway, what the hell am I doing here? I'm not an addict, and my lifestyle doesn't need readjusting.' I wince at a bolt of pain in my skull, close to throwing up.

'You sure about that?' Mike studies me with a knowing smile that makes me want to punch him on the nose.

'Just explain to me how I got here.'

'You really don't remember?' Rory frowns at me.

I shut my eyes to block out the dazzling sunshine streaming in through the window behind the desk. Another splinter of memory breaks through. Two men, in my room in Dan's apartment. Me arguing, pleading. They just stand there, implacable.

Then nothing. Blankness.

Were they real, or did I hallucinate them?

I groan, keeping my eyes squeezed closed. *Wouldn't be the first time, would it, Zoey, that you've imagined stupid shit when you were drunk?* Like when I was convinced somebody had broken into Dan's apartment, because I'd left it in such a mess. Or that super-embarrassing occasion when a large pizza turned up at the door and I insisted someone had stolen my credit card – I'd been too pissed to remember ordering it.

'I need some painkillers,' I rasp. 'And a cigarette. Seriously, I feel terrible.'

'I'm sorry, Zoey,' Mike clears the phlegm from his throat again, 'but the Sanctuary operates a no-drugs policy, and that includes alcohol, cigarettes and any prescribed medication that isn't purely for an existing physical disord—'

'All I'm asking for is some fucking paracetamol or Tylenol,' I snap back. 'My headache is totally slaying me and I can't think straight.'

'Pain is the price of freedom, Zoey.' Rory's sanctimonious expression makes me feel even queasier. 'We need to detoxify the body in order to detoxify the mind, and that includes the tendency to self-medicate our prob—'

'This is mental.' I jump up and nearly fall over as the blood rushes to my head. 'I went out for my friend Rocco's birthday.

A few drinks at a local bar, before going on to Unravel. And then I wake up in the middle . . .' I gesture out of the window '. . . in the middle of sodding nowhere.'

I'm close to crying, but I'm damned if I'll lose face in front of these idiots.

'Hey, Zoey,' Rory gets to his feet, 'stay calm. It won't help to get worked up again. Let's talk this through, shall we?'

All of a sudden my legs go so weak I nearly collapse. I sink back into the seat, swallowing down another rush of nausea.

'Unravel?' Mike asks. 'What's that?'

'A club in Tribeca.' I give him a once-over in his polyester shirt and office-grade trousers. 'I doubt it would be your scene.'

'So you were drinking? You sure that's all you did?'

'Yes,' I say, indignant.

'But you can't remember?'

I grit my teeth, but don't reply. I glance at the bloodstain on my jeans. The sweat in my armpits is beginning to stink. I must appear every bit as sordid as I feel right now.

'You don't take party drugs then?' Mike persists. 'GHB, methamphetamine, ketamine, stuff like that.'

'No,' I hiss, glaring at him. 'At least not often. I can't handle the comedown.'

'Marijuana?'

I force a sarcastic laugh. 'Are you seriously suggesting the occasional spliff should land you in rehab?'

Mike and Rory exchange a look.

'So how much *did* you drink last night?' Rory asks.

'I told you. I honestly can't remember. I'm not denying I'll have had a few tequilas. It was Friday night. It was my friend's *birthday*. But I don't understand why I ended up here – or how.'

'So you can't recall what happened at the club?' Mike asks. 'Or afterwards?'

I shake my head miserably. 'Nothing much. It's all so confused. But I do remember two guys, standing in my room.' I eyeball the pair sitting before me now. 'Were they real?'

Mike nods. 'We occasionally use freelance escorts to ensure people arrive here safely.'

'Escorts?' I gaze at him, incredulous. 'So, you . . . what . . . had me *kidnapped*? How is that even legal? I'm an adult. I have rights. And no way did I agree to come to . . .' I sweep my arm around again '. . . wherever the fuck this place is.'

'Actually, Zoey, you did.' Mike reaches into a drawer and pulls out a Manila file, handing me a document. My hands are shaking so much I can barely see the words, so I put it on the desk and lean forward to read it.

'This is your consent form and disclaimer, and this,' Mike turns it over, pointing to the bottom of the page, 'this is where you signed it.'

I study the squiggle of blue biro, and my chest tightens. A bit crooked, wobbly even, but definitely my signature.

'I don't understand,' I stammer. 'I'd never agree to this. And it's . . . what . . . free? Newsflash, I'm broke. I haven't got any money, if that's what this is all about.'

Mike coughs, followed by a small laugh. 'It's not free, no. But that's been taken care of.'

I frown. 'What do you mean?'

'Our charges have been covered by a third party.'

'Who?'

'I'm not at liberty to say.'

My frown deepens. 'You're kidding, right? Was it my father?' Unlikely, I realise, the moment the words leave my mouth. Though we've barely spoken in three years, I know his second divorce left him strapped for cash.

Dan then? But that doesn't seem likely either. My uncle has never given me grief about my lifestyle – God knows, he's partial to a few Jack Daniels himself. So why would he do this?

More to the point, how the hell could he afford it? Dan's got a good job, sure, but no savings, and a large mortgage on the apartment – and I can't imagine this place comes cheap.

That leaves Mum, which would make some sense at least – she's been nagging me for years to get my life together, to get a career, or even a proper job. And to stop smoking. But there's no way on earth she could afford anything like this; her position at the council barely covers her mortgage and living expenses.

'So your "escorts" brought me here.' I gaze out of the window at the flat desert landscape, the dull red earth. 'And where is here, exactly?'

'The Sonoran Desert,' Mike replies. 'Northern Mexico.'

'Mexico!' My mouth drops open so fast the back of my lip piercing chinks on my bottom teeth. 'You're shitting me. How the hell did I get here?' I rack my brains, but no memories come.

'Private plane from La Guardia to Hermosillo. Then a helicopter.'

Private plane? Helicopter?

I'm so gobsmacked I can't speak. But suddenly I know it's true. That loud whirring sound I recalled earlier must have been the rotor blades.

'How long am I expected to be here?' I rub my temples, praying it's only a couple of days.

'You signed up for the full ten-week programme,' Rory informs me.

I lift my head and stare at him. 'But I wouldn't have,' I protest. 'I'm supposed to be looking after my uncle's cats. I can't simply abandon them.'

'That's been dealt with,' Mike assures me. 'This was all explained to you at the time, Zoey, and it's in the legal waiver you signed. Nothing has been done without your consent.'

My head thumps, and I'm craving a cigarette so badly now I can't think straight. All I want is to get the hell out of here and find a bar or cafe where I can get a long cool drink and a packet of Camel Lights. Followed by a bus ride back to New York when I'm feeling more human.

'I withdraw my consent.' I rise to my feet, taking things slowly this time. 'I want to go home.'

'In which case I refer you to the small print on that piece of paper with your signature at the bottom.' Mike sniffs again, tapping the paragraph at the top of the second page. 'Should you withdraw, all the associated costs of bringing you here are chargeable to you. Along with the costs of your return. Not to mention the consequences you'll face back in the city.'

'*The consequences I'll face in the city?*' I ask, voice rising. 'What the fuck are you talking about?' I'm beginning to sound, I realise, like that hysterical girl in the tent.

Rory raises a hand to placate me. 'Listen, Zoey. I can see this is something of a shock, and I'm sorry if you feel that it's been sprung on you. I repeat, it was all spelled out to you during the initial intervention, and you agreed. I strongly suggest you give yourself time to reflect, and understand that you've been offered an invaluable opportunity. Don't squander it.'

'But I don't need treatment,' I protest. 'Seriously. It's ridiculous. I only drink when I go out, and that's no more than two, three times a week.'

'Like I said before, everyone can benefit from our programme,' Rory responds, undaunted. 'People pay an awful lot of money to come here – or have vulnerable family members brought here – and we have a very high success rate in terms of relapse.'

All at once, I burst into tears. My anger, my bravado evaporates, and I'm plain scared. This is surreal. Ridiculous. One moment I'm with my friends, hanging out in our favourite bar on Avenue A, looking forward to a fun-packed night; the next I wake up in some weird treatment centre in the heart of the Mexican desert.

'I want my phone,' I wail. 'And my passport.'

'No phones allowed, I'm afraid.' Rory rises to open the door. 'Rest assured we have it in safekeeping, along with your documents.'

I stare at him aghast. 'So how the hell am I expected to contact people? Let them know I'm here. You have computers, right? I can get online?'

Mike shakes his head, his finger tapping the piece of paper on the desk. 'This was all explained—'

'Oh fuck your waiver,' I explode, walking out of the door.

Rory catches up with me in a few long-legged strides. 'I suggest you lie down for a while, Zoey. You're tired, and it's obvious you're finding this difficult to process. I'll get some food sent to your room. Then this afternoon you can talk to Sonoya, when you feel less . . . agitated. She'll explain more about the programme, and what to expect from your stay.'

I open my mouth to object, but I haven't the strength.

I'll lie down and sleep, I decide, and when I wake up I'll be back in my bed in Dan's apartment on Seventh Street. I'll ring in sick and skip my shift at the grocery store, then call Franny and Rocco to meet up for brunch, and stuff my face with French toast and fries while I tell them all about this crazy nightmare I just had.

4

I strip to my underwear and crawl onto the narrow bed. Despite my exhaustion, I can't sleep. I'm too hot and itchy and desperate for a cigarette. Even with the window wide open, the air is so close and heavy it feels suffocating.

I lie there, head still pounding, trying to process everything that's happened since I woke in this stifling little room a few hours ago, but it's all so jumbled and confused. My attempts to piece together last night disintegrate into an ever-revolving merry-go-round of anxious thoughts – only not very merry. I picture Franny and Rocco back in New York, probably sitting in the Waverly Diner right now, facing off their hangovers with eggs and hash browns, with plenty of black coffee and fresh-squeezed orange juice to wash down their food.

Are they wondering where the hell I've got to, why I'm not returning their calls? Is Dan? Who's looking after Binx and ZeeZee while I'm stuck in this place? And what about the shifts I signed up to at the local grocery store? Has anyone told them I'm away?

I picture Mum at home in Guildford. Does she know I'm here? More to the point, does she know who did this to me? I feel a stab of betrayal. I'm still struggling to believe anybody would dump me in the back of beyond without so much as a heads-up.

Ugh. I close my eyes and push down another lurch of nausea, trying to focus on what in the world I can do. Assuming it's my signature on that form, it's not clear how I'll get out of here without incurring God knows how much in debt.

Surely that's illegal? Don't these places have to give a cooling-off period where you can change your mind?

Perhaps I could sue them. Insist I was in no fit state to consent to any of this.

What with? You're broke, Zoey. You haven't the money for lawyers, let alone court costs if you lose.

I clench my fists in frustration as the air around me shimmers and swims. I need my phone – I should have insisted they hand it over while I was in that office. What kind of bullshit is that anyway? Why cut people off entirely from the outside world?

A knock at the door makes me jump. Dr Kimura walks in, bearing a tray. 'Hey, Zoey.' She smiles. 'How are you doing?'

She places the tray on my bedside table. There's another of those luminous orange drinks, and a roll filled with salad and cheese. 'I wasn't sure what you'd like, so I made you a sandwich. You'll feel better if you eat.'

She takes my wrist in her hand, placing two fingers on my pulse. 'Rory says you're still having trouble remembering how you got here?' Her head cocks to one side. 'I thought perhaps we might have a chat in a while – we can discuss what happened and how to move forward.'

'There's nothing to discuss, Dr Kimura,' I retort. 'I've no intention of staying.'

She regards me, her expression set to blandly neutral. 'I understand you're coming down and rather confused by it all. And please, call me Sonoya – we all go by first names here.'

'I'm not fucking coming down from anything, *Sonoya*.' I force myself to sit up and my head swims alarmingly. 'I don't get it. This is way worse than a standard hangover. I feel really strange.'

A furrow appears in Sonoya's smooth brow, but she doesn't comment. 'Eat your sandwich and get some rest. Let's go through things this afternoon in your first therapy session. We can address your treatment plan and discuss your options then.'

'I don't need therapy or a treatment plan,' I protest again, but my voice sounds listless and unconvincing, even to me. Sonoya ignores my comment, checking the little silver watch on her wrist. 'Say, two thirty in the consult lounge? That's the room next to the main office.'

She opens the door on the wardrobe to reveal a neat stack of toiletries and clean clothes, even a sunhat and sunglasses and a pair of strappy leather sandals. 'You didn't bring much with you, so Elena picked out some clean clothes and items from storage. You can freshen up in the bathroom down the hallway.'

'You keep clothes here?' I ask, puzzled.

'Guests often leave things they no longer want or need. And yes, we keep spare sets of underwear, and other items people might have forgotten or run out of.'

With that, she's gone. Only, after Sonoya's left I realise that without my phone I have no way of knowing the time. I sit there, seething. Screw this. Screw bullshit and evasion and never answering a simple question.

I pick up the sandwich and start chewing. I'm not hungry but I'll need all my strength to get the hell out of here. And my passport, I realise. I'll demand my passport and phone and hike back to civilisation, then ring Dan and beg him to Paypal the fare for the bus ride to New York. Or call Rocco and persuade him to hire a car and drive down here; he's always up for an adventure – especially if it involves tequila.

It can't be far to the nearest town, I decide. Impossible to run a place like this without supplies – water, food, fuel for the generator, shit like that. And it's not as if they can stop me leaving, is it? What would they do? Arrest me?

And if sweaty Mike tries to stiff me for the cost of bringing me here, good luck with that – he'll only be throwing good money after bad. When I find out who did this, they can cough up.

After all, someone got me into this mess.

They can fucking well get me out of it.

5

'Hey, dude, you any idea what time it is?'

The guy ambling across the atrium turns at the sound of my voice. His dark hair is wet, slicked against his head, and he's wearing chino shorts, a black T-shirt, and an expression a shade above surly. He fixes me with a gaze so blank I wonder if perhaps he doesn't speak English. I tap my wrist and nod at the expensive-looking watch on his, one of those ridiculous chunky numbers with lots of complicated dials and knobs.

'Ten after two,' he says, in an educated West Coast accent, without even glancing at his swanky timepiece. I think I recognise him from the tent, sitting in the seat next to the one vacated by the screaming girl.

'Thanks,' I say.

He disappears up the curved staircase, leaving me feeling oddly slighted. Would it have killed him to be a bit more friendly? Forget it, I remind myself. You'll be out of here soon. Who cares about some random stranger?

Returning to my room, I fetch the toiletries from the cupboard and lock myself in the shower. I peer again into the mirror above the sink. A pale-faced ghoul gazes back at me. I look even worse than earlier. My dark hair is lank and matted with sweat, the skin around the piercings in my nose and lip red and sore. My cheeks are sheeny and blotchy, and dark circles ring my eyes. Zombie-punk Zoey. Grabbing a few sheets of loo roll, I wipe away the smeared mascara – it helps, but only a little.

I give my reflection the finger, then sit on the loo and try to pee. It takes an age, and what does come out is an odd colour, much more orange than usual.

Dehydration? Or a side effect of that luminous drink?

I flush the loo, then strip off, trying not to think about how much I want a cigarette. Surely somebody here must have some? Rob, the only person I've ever known go to rehab, managed to kick the coke addiction, but came back with a 20-a-day cigarette habit instead.

Climbing into the shower, I hose myself down and wash my hair. I swaddle up in a towel, grab my clothes, and hurry back to my room, then realise I needn't bother rubbing myself down – I'm dry in seconds, the little hairs on my arms and legs standing on end as the heat evaporates the moisture from my skin.

I gaze at the pile of sweaty clothes on the bed. I can't face putting them on again, so I check out the stuff in the wardrobe, relieved to discover my leather jacket on a hanger, my Doc Martens lined up underneath. I grab some white briefs and a matching bra – both brand new and still in their packets – then pick out a pair of loose cotton trousers with a drawstring waist and a pale blue top. I check the labels.

Bloody hell. The trousers are Ralph Lauren and the top is a brand I've never heard of, but it's obvious from its weight and quality that it didn't come from T.J. Maxx or Walmart.

I get dressed, then return my attention to my own clothes, hesitating. I'll need these later when I leave – no way I'm walking out of here in Ralph Lauren. Returning to the shower room, I dunk my jeans and Ramones tee in the basin with some shampoo, then rinse and drape them over the sill in the bedroom – in this heat, they'll dry in an hour.

Another knock at the door. That doctor therapist again. Her gaze is drawn immediately to the wet clothes on the window sill. 'There's a laundry by the staff annex,' she says. 'Ask anyone to show you.' She looks back at me. 'See you in five?'

She closes the door before I even have a chance to answer. I hover by the bed, undecided. All I want to do is lie down and gather enough energy for the hike into town. I still feel horrible; as if I have a really bad hangover, only worse somehow, more enervating and all-consuming.

But at the same time I'm curious, my head full of unanswered questions – no harm in seeing if I can actually get some answers.

A few minutes later I'm sitting in the consult lounge. In contrast to the opulence of the main house, it's surprisingly stark – just a pair of armchairs with a coffee table in between. I study the immaculate Sonoya as she arranges her phone, notepad, pen and a plain envelope folder in a tidy pyramid, then sits back and offers me another bland smile.

Little Miss Bloody Perfect, I think. I bet Sonoya sat at the front of the class at school, first to raise her hand whenever the teacher asked a question. How on earth does she manage in this infernal heat? She looks as if she never breaks a sweat. My clean blue top, on the other hand, is already sticking to the fresh layer of perspiration on my skin.

'When will they have the air con fixed?' I ask.

'Alejandro's installing a new control panel. It shouldn't be much longer.' She studies my desperate expression. 'You're probably sweating out the toxins in your body.'

I inhale, refusing to take the bait. 'So what's with the free clothes? Do people simply abandon stuff when they leave?'

'Yes.' Sonoya sighs. 'We encourage clients not to bring too many personal effects, but many ignore our advice.'

'Why?' I ask. 'I mean, why don't you want them bringing their belongings?'

She gives me an appraising look. 'We find it levels people, Zoey. Most of our clients are very wealthy, and come to rely on material possessions as a signifier of status, but also something they can hide behind. Or use as a crutch, a substitute for what they really need.'

'Such as?'

'Self-esteem. Genuine relationships with people. A sense of purpose. The opposite of addiction isn't sobriety, Zoey, it's an authentic connection with ourselves and others, with our own lives.'

I don't comment. Not much I can say, except that *not* possessing much of any material value hasn't exactly filled my life with purpose and connection either.

'That's why we insist people stay offline,' Sonoya adds, 'and it's a rule we rigidly enforce. If you want to make progress, you need to remove yourself from your normal environment, your usual routines, whether that's downing a couple of bottles of wine every evening, or spending hours browsing social media. Willpower alone won't break addictive patterns or help you deal with the aftermath of trauma – you have to build a lifestyle that supports new habits.'

I raise an eyebrow, unconvinced. 'So, there's literally nothing to do here?'

Sonoya's smile is indulgent, shallow creases appearing at the corner of her eyes that make me reappraise her age – not thirties, as I first imagined, but closer to forty. 'You'll find there's plenty to do here. As well as our thrice-weekly individual therapy sessions, we have group every day, plus Tamara and Rory offer a full programme of activities, including daily yoga and meditation. Plus you can swim, or use the gym. There's even a pool table in the games room across the courtyard.'

The swimming pool – fat use that'll be to me. Ditto the gym. My idea of exercise is walking a few blocks rather than getting the subway; luckily I have a metabolism that lets me get away with it.

'So how about you?' The therapist picks up the biro and notepad, turning to a fresh page. 'What do you feel you're lacking in your life, Zoey?'

'Right now, a cigarette, plus a bottle of cold beer. Oh, and my phone, passport and a one-way ticket out of here.'

Sonoya ignores my facetiousness. 'It sounds as if all this has come as something of a shock.'

'No kidding,' I say. 'Waking up in the middle of the desert with no memory of how on earth you got there. You could describe that as "something of a shock".'

'So you honestly don't recall anything about the events leading up to your arrival?' she asks, making a note in her pad.

'Not really.'

'The escorts reported you were very agitated when they collected you.'

'Perhaps that's because I was in the process of being kidnapped.' I glare at her, but Sonoya doesn't react.

'Zoey, you agreed to all this. It was explained to you at the time exactly what you were signing up to, and what the alternatives were.' She gazes at me, slowly revolving the pen in her small slim fingers. 'How about you run me through what you do remember, from the beginning of your evening out. And to reassure you, everything you tell me is strictly confidential.'

I sigh. Close my eyes, then open them again. 'It was Rocco's birthday. I met up with him, my friend Franny, and some of Rocco's friends at a Brazilian bar on Avenue A. We had a few beers, shared some nachos and French fries, then went on to Unravel – a club in Tribeca.'

'And do you recall what happened there?'

'Not much. I'm guessing I drank a few tequilas. Danced a bit. The usual.'

Sonoya's expression remains impassive. It occurs to me she might never have actually been to a nightclub.

'So you've no memory of later on?' she asks.

I frown. 'No. What do you mean?'

The therapist taps her teeth with the end of her biro then scribbles a quick note. I suppress the impulse to ask her what she's writing.

'Can I ask if you've ever had blackouts before, Zoey?'

I blink at her. Open my mouth and close it again. You didn't sign up for this, I remind myself; you don't have to participate in this bullshit.

'Reading your medical records, it seems this isn't the first time, is it?' the therapist prompts after a full minute of silence.

'I object to you reading those,' I say. 'How the hell did you get hold of them anyway?'

'As Mike explained earlier, you gave us permission in the waiver you signed, Zoey.'

I take a deep breath. 'Wouldn't you agree, *Dr Kimura*, that a person who has no recall of consenting to something has not, in fact, consented?'

Sonoya slides over my point as if I hadn't made it. 'It said in your records that when you were twenty, your mother found you unconscious in her house in England. She couldn't rouse you. You ended up having your stomach pumped in the emergency room and were kept in overnight.'

'I couldn't sleep, that's all,' I protest, my voice too loud. I force myself to speak more evenly. 'I'd left university and was having a hard time adjusting, so I took some of my mother's sleeping pills with a drink. They had a bad effect on me – you shouldn't mix them with alcohol, apparently.'

33

'How do you know that, Zoey?'

'It said so on the packet.'

'No, I mean you told the psychiatrist you had no memory of any of it. Even having your stomach pumped, which is a pretty distressing thing to undergo.'

'I worked it out. I put two and two together.'

'So it wasn't a suicide attempt?'

'I wasn't trying to kill myself,' I insist, my voice rising again. 'I'd never do that, not after . . .' I stop. Swallow. 'I really don't want to get into it.'

'Fair enough,' Sonoya says calmly. 'There's plenty of time for that later.'

'There's not going to be a later. I don't want to stay here. What do I need to sign so I can leave?'

The therapist regards me steadily. 'That's not anything we can arrange at the drop of a hat, Zoey. It was part of the agreement with the NYPD and the person you assaulted that you attend mandatory rehab for the full ten weeks. If you insist on returning to New York, we will have to inform the police department, and they may decide to pursue prosecution.'

I stare at her open-mouthed. The police? Prosecution?

The person I assaulted?

What the fuck is she talking about?

A tightness in my chest makes the air in the room even harder to breathe, but I resist the urge to ask more. It's clearly a bluff. A ruse to keep me here, and no way am I playing along with this charade – after all, if I'd done anything serious, the police would never have let me leave the country.

'Listen.' Sonoya leans forward, suspending her pen between the tips of each forefinger as she formulates what to say. 'I understand you're angry and confused, and probably experiencing all sorts of physical after-effects from last night. I get that. All I ask is that you don't do anything hasty. Give it a week or so and see how you feel.' She offers me another little smile. 'You never know, you might find you like it here.'

Never in a million years, I think, but stay mute.

'I truly believe you're being given a unique opportunity to turn your life around,' Sonoya continues, unfazed, 'and that's not something you should throw away lightly.' She leans further forward, forcing me to meet her gaze. 'Can you honestly say you don't have any issues you need to deal with?'

To my dismay, several tears edge down my cheeks. I swipe them away, mortified.

'Tell me you'll think about it, Zoey,' the therapist concludes, shutting her notebook and picking up the folder and her phone. 'Just for a few days. If you still want to leave at the end of the week, I promise we can discuss it.'

I nod, then hurry out before she sees me cry.

6

Another knock at my door, just as I'm finally falling into a doze. I groan in frustration, praying it's not Little Miss Perfect on my back again. I've spent several hours churning over what that therapist said to me earlier. About the police. About my alleged assault of someone. Trying to remember anything from last night.

It's bullshit, I've concluded. Crap they've made up to keep me here.

But instead of Sonoya, a pretty woman walks in, wearing a tight gym top and wide-legged yoga pants with 'Gucci' embroidered in large letters down the right leg. Mid thirties, maybe a year or two older than me, with beautiful bronze spiral curls and an enviable golden glow to her skin.

On her heels is the black-and-white cat I saw earlier. She picks it up as it jumps on my bed and puts it outside. 'Sorry,' she says, shutting the door and facing me, 'Simpkins gets everywhere, especially when you least want him. I'm Naomi Rivera. Rory sent me to see if you'd like some supper – we're eating in the dining hall next to the lounge.'

'Thanks.' I return her smile, but it's a paltry effort – while hers radiates friendliness and positivity, mine is all wariness and suspicion. 'I'll pass though. I'm really tired.'

'I didn't know they put guests in this part of the house,' Naomi says, glancing around. 'I thought it was empty. It's . . . umm . . . cosy, isn't it?'

I grimace. It's obvious what she's thinking – the contrast with this room and those I saw upstairs is pretty stark.

'Yeah, they reserve this bit for the charity cases,' I quip, immediately regretting it when I see the embarrassment on Naomi's face. But instead of making an excuse and leaving, she sits at the foot of my bed.

'You okay?'

'I guess,' I reply, staring at the sparkly studs in her ears, wondering if they're real diamonds. Naomi radiates the kind of wholesome good health only money can buy. She looks like an advert for Whole Foods Market or another high-end grocery store where you need to take out a mortgage for an organic kombucha and fresh salad.

'That was quite some entrance you made in the Top,' she giggles. 'Stopped Riley right in her tracks.'

'The Top?'

'It's what we call the tent because it resembles the Big Top you get in circuses. They're planning to build somewhere more permanent for group, but I rather like it.'

'Group?'

'Group therapy,' Naomi explains, her large brown eyes fixed on mine. 'That's what we were doing when you found us.'

'Okay.' Sounds like hell on earth – especially if Riley the screamer is anything to go by. 'Why was she so upset anyway?' I ask. 'Riley, I mean. She acted like she was being murdered.'

Naomi sighs. 'Riley's had a hard time. In life, that is. Lots of shit with her family, and some guy abused her when she was only fifteen.'

'Okay,' I repeat, though obviously it isn't.

'Plus she's devastated about Ed leaving so suddenly. She got on really well with him, so it's hit her hard. It's hit everyone hard, to be honest.'

'Who's Ed?'

'He was one of the other residents. He left when you arrived.'

'Why did this Ed leave?' I ask, more out of politeness than genuine curiosity.

'Nobody knows.' Naomi shrugs. 'He was doing so well, really loved this place. It was his second stay here – he told me the first time he did the programme, it completely changed his life and this next visit was the icing on the cake. But then out of the blue he packed up his stuff and got on the chopper last night.'

'The one that brought me in?'

'Yes.' Naomi fiddles with a ring on her finger, with a gorgeous pale blue stone set in the centre. 'That's what made it so odd – he just did a runner in the middle of the night. Anyway, Riley was distraught when she found out this morning. Ed was like a father figure to her – took her under his wing. Him leaving like that tipped her over the edge, and she's pretty close to it at the best of times.'

She stops, gives me an apologetic look, as if she's been talking too much. 'You from England? You've got a really cute accent.'

'I'm a mongrel,' I reply. 'I grew up there and my mum still lives in a town called Guildford, but my dad's American, so my brother and I have dual nationality. I spend a lot of time at my uncle's place in New York – he's in Texas for months with his job, so I house-sit his cats.'

I stop, wondering why I'm telling this woman all this. It's not as if she cares.

'Your uncle in oil?'

'Shale gas.' I grimace. 'Yeah, I know, not very PC.'

'You gotta do what you gotta do.' She shrugs again, then nods at my lip piercing. 'Is there a name for that?'

'An Ashley.'

Naomi grins. 'You don't look like an Ashley, to be honest. More a . . .' she cocks her head to the side as she studies me '. . . you remind me of Emma Stone, actually. Only punkier.'

'Who's Emma Stone?'

'The actress. You know, *La La Land, Cruella*. She was in that really dark Netflix drama, *Maniac*.'

Maniac? Is she taking the piss? Her expression says otherwise. She's studying me thoughtfully, as if trying to work me out. It's not unlike the therapist, Sonoya, but less intrusive somehow.

'Did it hurt?' Naomi nods again at my lip piercing.

'A lot,' I admit. 'I wouldn't recommend it.'

'It's pretty though. Suits you.'

'So where are you from?' I ask, making an effort. There's something about Naomi's easy kindness I'm loath to offend.

'Chicago, River North. Though I grew up in rural Wisconsin.'

'Cool,' I say, unable to think of a better response. Nice people make me nervous, and I've always been crap at small talk. 'I've never been to Chicago but I hear it's great.'

'It is,' she agrees. 'You should visit some day. You travelled much outside New York?'

'My dad lives in Palm Springs, but I've only been there a couple of times. Not really my scene. I've spent a few months on the West Coast, including LA and San Francisco, and I've been to Boston and Philly, Seattle, New Orleans, Las Vegas, places like that. Plus loads of other cities, all over Europe and Australia. Canada too. But my best mates are in New York, so if I'm in the States, I tend to spend most of my time there.'

'I don't blame you, it's a great city.' Naomi glances at the time on her fitness band. 'Anyway, Rory sent me to bring you to dinner. Come and eat. Meet everyone.'

'I'd rather—'

'We made paella especially,' she adds. 'To celebrate your arrival. It's my mother's recipe – you'll love it.'

'You're Spanish?' I heave myself off the bed, searching for the flip-flops.

Naomi's smile widens, exposing a set of perfectly aligned teeth. 'I'm a mongrel too. Part Cuban, part German, part African-American. There was even some Navajo thrown in a couple of generations back.'

'It's certainly worked out well for you,' I say, trying to muster up the energy for dinner.

To my surprise, Naomi envelops me in a hug. 'You seem shell-shocked, Zoey,' she says, her expression full of sympathy. 'Don't worry, you'll be fine. The first few days in rehab are always the worst.'

'I don't need rehab,' I retort. 'There's nothing wrong with me, apart from this bitch of a headache.'

'Sure,' says Naomi, leading the way. 'But you know what I mean.'

I don't though, and I'm nervous as she leads me through the atrium and into a large dining hall that I somehow missed in my frantic search this morning. I take in the massive dark wood table that straddles the room, the enormous wrought-iron chandelier suspended from one of the exposed ceiling beams – what appear to be several dozen candles are flickering away, but they must be fake because you'd need a stepladder and a whole box of matches to light them.

Directly below the chandelier, the centrepiece on the table is a huge shallow bowl filled with tiny succulents and miniature rocks and cacti.

Rocco would love this, I think with a pang. Whoever designed the decor here totally nailed the whole rustic luxe vibe. The attention to detail is spectacular. The artwork, the lighting, the plants, the heavy wooden furniture – so much money and effort has gone into creating this place that for the first time in my life I'm actually envious that rich people get to live like this.

Naomi disappears, leaving me to sit in one of the empty chairs. Mike, seated at the other end of the table, gives me a brief nod before taking out his hankie and mopping his brow. Sonoya, next to him, offers me a smile that makes me feel like a five-year-old who's just been awarded a gold star for good behaviour.

I gaze around at the other faces, some I recognise from earlier in the tent. Most of them seem subdued, more like guests at a funeral than people enjoying the lap of luxury, and I thank my lucky stars I won't have to put up with them for long.

Naomi returns with a stocky Latina I'm guessing is Elena, each carrying a dish of steaming paella. 'One for the meat eaters and one for the vegetarians,' Naomi says, setting hers down on the table. She goes off again to collect several large salads, while Elena loads each plate with food. 'Everything in the salads is from our own garden,' she says to me in heavily accented English, 'so are the olives in the paella.'

'Delicious.' Mike gives an appreciative nod before turning his attention to me. 'You must be starving, Zoey.'

The moment he says it, I realise it's true. My nausea has receded, and the smell of paella makes my mouth water. I tuck in, avoiding eye contact with anyone – what's the point of making an effort? Mike's right though, the paella is fabulous, the rice perfectly cooked – soft on the outside and firmer inside – and mixed with fresh vegetables, beans and large succulent prawns.

'How about we all introduce ourselves?' Rory says in the hearty tone of someone trying to lift the mood in the room.

'Perhaps we could each tell Zoey who we are, where we're from, and how long we've been here.' He nods at Naomi as she takes a seat next to me. 'Why don't you kick things off?'

'We've already met.' Naomi gives my hand a squeeze. 'But I've been here exactly six weeks today. I'm a resident, in case you hadn't guessed.'

It would be an easy mistake to make. If it weren't for the jewellery and the wealthy glow, Naomi looks too happy and healthy to need lifestyle readjustment or whatever nonsense Rory was on about earlier.

She glances at the rather overweight man sitting next to her. 'Max Becker,' he says in an East Coast accent. Early forties, I reckon. Clean shaven, with the same perfect white teeth as Sonoya and Naomi. Like her, this guy looks about as far as you can get from the ravaged husks of addicts that sleep rough on the subway. 'I live in Israel and NYC. Been here just over seven weeks.'

Max turns to the man next to him – the bloke in the beanie. 'Axel,' he says gruffly. 'Portland. Four weeks.' He gives me a quick once-over, then returns his attention to his food. Despite not wanting to be here, I feel pissed off – the guy couldn't make it clearer he doesn't give a shit.

And why is he wearing that bloody hat to dinner?

'I'm Tamara,' says a plump, pleasant-looking woman beside him. 'Tamara Perez-Powell. I'm the occupational therapist here at the Sanctuary, which is a short way of saying I manage all the therapeutic activities, like craft and yoga and meditation, as well as offering aromatherapy and other treatments – anything you require on your journey of healing. Apart from the ceremonies – Rory handles those.'

I frown, puzzled. *What ceremonies?*

Before I can ask, the next person is addressing me. The surly guy I met in the atrium. 'Finley Cooper,' he says, his gaze boring into mine. 'Though most people call me Finn. I'm from, well, various places, mainly New York and California. Been here four weeks so far.'

He looks at the girl beside him. Her I recognise: Riley the screamer. She's in her early twenties, I reckon, and wearing a black jumper – despite the heat – with the sleeves pulled right down over her hands. She scowls at me and turns away.

'Riley?' Sonoya prompts.

'New England,' she mumbles without looking up. 'Five weeks, three days and counting.'

'Come on,' Rory says in a cajoling voice. 'No need to make it sound like a prison sentence, Riley.'

The girl lifts her gaze and gives him a death stare, but Rory continues, unperturbed. 'Sonoya, you've already met,' he says, and the diminutive therapist nods at me. 'Mike too. Alejandro's not with us tonight, so that's it. Welcome to the Sanctuary, Zoey.'

There's a muted chorus of greeting, then everyone goes back to their food.

'Has Alejandro fixed the air con?' Naomi asks Rory, clearly trying to break the silence.

'Yep, it's back up and running.'

'You could have fooled me,' I grumble. 'My room's like an oven.'

Rory looks embarrassed. 'Actually, I'm not sure there is air conditioning in that part of the house. I'll bring you a portable fan after supper.'

'No need,' I tell him – after all, I'm not planning on hanging around.

'So where is Alejandro then?' Riley demands from Rory. 'He always eats supper with us, so why isn't he here?'

Rory glances at Mike and Sonoya.

'He wanted to leave, didn't he? With Ed,' Riley continues, her food untouched. 'I heard them talking about it outside my room. Ed was trying to get Alejandro to go with him.'

Sonoya cuts in. 'Riley, I suggest you focus on your own issues, and stop making a drama where none is required.'

Riley ignores her. 'So how about you tell us why Ed left like that, Rory? He must have said something, given a reason. I get if it was a family emergency or whatever, but why wouldn't he at least say goodbye? Why skulk off in the dead of night?'

Nobody speaks. There's a palpable tension in the room as Riley scans the other faces around the table. 'No one else here want some answers?'

Silence. I glance at Mike, whose face is redder than ever. He's glaring at Riley with an expression a shade away from fury.

'Riley, this isn't appropriate,' Sonoya says firmly. 'We can discuss this tomorrow in—'

Her words are cut short by the sound of Riley's chair scraping against the floor. She gives the therapist a furious look before exiting the room, slamming the door behind her.

'And there she goes,' mutters Max through a mouthful of paella.

'Good fucking riddance,' Axel says. 'I'm sick of her and her *ish-oos*.' He stretches the final syllables in a sarcastic drawl.

'Likewise, Axel,' Finn grunts. 'I think we're all pretty sick of yours.'

Sonoya, Rory and Mike fall into a conversation about the air conditioning. I tune out, focusing instead on Naomi's paella. When did I last have a decent home-cooked meal? In New York I live on take-out and snacks grabbed on the run, barely ever using Dan's tiny kitchen for anything beyond reheating leftovers.

'Gotta say that was pretty impressive, your arrival in the Top this morning,' Max says to me with a grin. 'You looked ready to murder someone.'

'I thought someone *was* being murdered,' I reply, feeling foolish now. 'I didn't know what on earth was going on.'

'This your first time in Mexico?'

I nod.

'So what's your poison?' he asks.

'How do you mean?'

'He means why are you here?' Naomi explains.

I shrug. 'I've no idea. I can't even remember agreeing to come, though apparently I did.' I gaze down at my food. 'To be honest it's all been a bit of a head fuck.'

Max narrows his eyes at me. 'You . . . what . . . don't remember anything at all? Were you high?'

I clearly look offended because Naomi lays a well-manicured hand on my arm. 'Hey, he's not accusing you of anything, Zoey. We've all been there – most of us, anyway.'

'Yeah, I was probably drunk,' I admit. 'I mean, we'd been out celebrating a friend's birthday. But I don't usually get wasted to the point where I forget everything.' I remember what Sonoya said earlier, about my being arrested.

Could that possibly be true?

Max glances down the table, as if making sure no one is listening to our conversation. 'You came in with escorts, right?' He leans in, keeping his voice low.

'Apparently.' I flash back to those two guys in Dan's apartment. It still feels surreal. Unreal.

'They probably slipped you something,' Max murmurs. 'Flunitrazepam most likely.'

I frown. 'What's that?'

'Rohypnol. You know, a roofie.'

Naomi and I both stare at him, aghast. 'Do they actually do that?' Naomi asks.

'So I've heard,' Max confirms. 'If someone's kicking off. Usually it's a pretty small dose, just enough to chill them out, but they don't always get it right. Or maybe you just really pissed them off.'

He raises his eyebrows in an ironic way, then tucks into a second serving of paella. I push rice around my plate, my appetite suddenly exhausted. Had I been kicking off? Did I need calming down? Let's face it, it wouldn't be the first time, would it?

But why? What the hell happened last night?

Out of nowhere another memory breaks through. A young girl with spiky blonde hair and a nose stud, sobbing in one of the toilet cubicles at Unravel. Make-up streaking down her face. Bruises looming on her neck.

Who was that?

'Are they really allowed to do that?' Naomi asks Max. 'Is it even legal to drug someone against their will?'

He shrugs. 'Who says it was against her will?'

'You should complain,' Naomi says to me, ignoring him. 'You could sue.'

'Like they'll ever admit it.' Max laughs. 'Anyway, these escorts know how to cover their asses – they'll magic up a consent form if they need one.'

'I have to get out of here,' I mutter, pushing my plate away. 'How far is it to the nearest town? Can I walk?' I look at Max and then Naomi.

Max laughs again, harder this time, his belly quivering with amusement. 'Over twenty miles, sweetie, most of it across open desert. The USP of this place is that it's completely cut off from civilisation – you have to be flown in and out. I wouldn't recommend you attempt that on foot, even after sundown.'

I gaze at him, open-mouthed. 'Seriously?'

'Yeah, the only way in and out of here is by air. Much of the terrain is too rocky for vehicles.'

'You're shitting me. So you're saying we're *stuck* here?'

'Why do you want to leave, Zoey?' Naomi asks before Max can answer, her head cocked with concern. 'I get you're pissed about the escorts, but this place has an excellent reputation. They've got a long waiting list and it's all built on word of mouth.'

'I want to leave because there's nothing wrong with me!' I say, a little too loudly. Sonoya and Tamara glance down the table. I wait for them to return to their conversation. 'I'm not traumatised and I don't have any addictions,' I hiss at Naomi. 'Sure, I like to party now and then, have a good time, but no more than other people.'

I think of Rocco, whose idea of purgatory is a night in. How would he survive a place like this?

'It's not like I drink every day,' I sniff. 'And I don't do drugs, apart from the odd spliff.'

'Gambling?' Max asks.

I roll my eyes. 'Well, I do sometimes buy a scratchcard with my Camels.' As soon as I say the word, I'm seized by another longing for a cigarette. 'Does anyone around here have any fags?'

Naomi shakes her head. 'No drugs allowed. Not even nicotine.'

'Vape pen?' I ask hopefully.

'Nope. The Sanctuary programme is pretty hardcore, but it works.'

'Seriously, Zoey, you should stay.' Max sits back and sips his mineral water. 'Doesn't matter why you ended up here, you can still get a lot out of it.' He studies me. 'And let's face it, people who have their life together don't accidentally land up in a place like this, do they?'

Heat rises to my cheeks. 'That's not—'

'Who's paying for you?' Naomi cuts in, heading off an argument. 'I mean, if you don't know why you're here, then I guess you aren't footing the bill.'

'I've no idea,' I admit. 'It's a mystery. Another one.'

Naomi's eyebrows lift in surprise. 'This place is far from cheap. It might not be the most luxurious retreat available, but like I said, it has an excellent reputation.'

'How much does it cost?' I ask, curiosity getting the better of me.

'You mean you don't know?' Axel frowns at me – clearly he's been listening in on our conversation.

I shake my head. 'Not a clue.'

'$50k,' Max says.

My eyes widen with shock. '$50,000? What, for the whole programme?' Jesus. That's some serious cash.

'For a month,' Max corrects, and down the table Axel smirks at my stunned expression. 'That's not bad,' says another voice. Finn or Finley or whatever his name is. 'When my dad went into rehab, it cost that for a single fucking week.'

Naomi rolls her eyes but he ignores her. 'Mind you, that was one-to-one, dedicated therapist, private butler and chef. The works. Nothing but the best for dear old Dad.' His expression is sour; clearly his father's therapy didn't lead to the sort of 'authenticity' Sonoya described earlier.

I gaze at my plate, forcing my exhausted brain to do the maths. Sonoya said I was obliged to stay for at least ten weeks, so that's a minimum of . . . $125k.

Fuck. No one I know has that kind of money.

Except Marcus, perhaps, given he's now a partner in his law firm. But since I haven't spoken to my twin brother in over a dozen years, I can safely rule him out.

'I don't get why it's so expensive though,' I murmer, checking first that none of the staff are listening. 'Okay, it's nice here, but over twelve grand a week? That's insane.'

'You're paying for the isolation, and quality input from the team,' Naomi explains. 'They keep the numbers low – six people max. It's one of the reasons this place is so expensive, given the facilities are pretty limited. That, and the ceremonies, of course.'

'The ceremonies?' My frown deepens.

Naomi cocks her head again. 'Don't you know about them?'

'Not a clue. Mike and Rory didn't mention them earlier.'

But Rory's voice cuts in before Naomi can explain. 'Zoey, just to let you know I've put you down on the meal rota for Friday – with Riley.'

'What meal rota?'

'We all take turns to help Elena with the evening meal, or one of the other staff if it's her weekend off, like this next one,' Rory explains. 'Don't worry, you'll never have to do it alone.'

'You're kidding,' I blurt, astounded. 'You can't afford more kitchen staff? Given what this place charges?'

Mike and Sonoya eye me warily. I notice Finn is pressing his lips together in a conspicuous effort not to laugh.

'We don't need more staff,' Rory continues. 'Our therapeutic model stipulates that residents contribute to the running of the Sanctuary. Many people who come here have never had to do any sort of ordinary domestic work, so our view is that it's part of learning to take personal responsibility.'

I consider this. Fine. Everyone should learn how to do basic chores. One season cleaning chalets in Zermatt showed me rich peeps could do with a serious lesson on clearing up after themselves – though, to be fair, I'm hardly one to talk.

But you'd think $50k a month should let you off cooking your own meals.

'We regard domestic work to be beneficial,' Rory continues. 'It helps build a sense of accomplishment and routine.'

Axel rolls his eyes. 'Gotta remember to stick cleaning toilets on my resumé.'

'Who knew smashing things up required a resumé?' Finn mutters. 'I thought having a trust fund was Antifa's only membership requirement.'

'Go fuck yourself, asshole,' Axel snaps back. 'Like Daddy ever asked you for any qualifications or experience.' He turns to me before Finn can say another word, his eyes flicking to my piercings and the skull-and-mohican tattoo on my arm. 'So what do you do for cash then, Zoey? Don't get me wrong, it's good to see someone over thirty still rocking that pop punk aesthetic, but presumably you do something to earn your keep. Did you marry up, like our Naomi here? Do a bit of charity work perhaps? Raising money for the Avril Lavigne fan club?'

I give him a withering look. 'I'm not married actually, and I certainly don't scrounge money off my parents. Not that it's any of your business.'

Axel raises his hands in the air and widens his eyes in mock alarm. 'Only trying to make conversation.'

'Don't bother.'

Out of the corner of my eye, I sense Finn silently assessing me. I turn to face him, but he lifts his gaze to the ceiling, feigning interest in the chandelier. I sit there, stomach churning with irritation. No way I'm staying in this mad house with a bunch of fucked-up rich dudes.

My headache pulses in time with my heartbeat. I push back my chair and get up to leave, but Naomi puts a hand out to stop me. 'Please stay. I could do with somebody pleasant to talk to, and I made cheesecake for dessert, using strawberries from the garden.'

I sit down reluctantly.

'Zoey, can I say something?'

'Okay.'

Naomi eyes me, her expression gentle. 'Listen, I can see you're not exactly overjoyed to be here, but honestly, I reckon you should give the Sanctuary a go. You have . . .' she stops, biting her bottom lip and appearing to think better of whatever she'd been about to say.

'What?' I prompt, surprised to find I actually want to know.

Naomi sighs. 'Granted, I've only just met you, Zoey, but if you don't mind me saying, you have a kind of messed-up vibe.'

'*A messed-up vibe?*' I snort. 'Is that an official diagnosis? Do you all get to share the therapy as well as the chores?'

She ignores the snark in my tone. 'I've been around the block a few times. The more you get into this therapy stuff, the more you understand what's driving all of us.'

'And what's that?' I try to keep the cynicism from my voice. Naomi seems kind, and genuine, and I can tell she means well; it's not her fault I'm in no mood to hear it.

'The search for meaning in our lives,' she replies. 'And self-acceptance.'

I don't comment. It sounds like the sort of psychobabble Sonoya came out with earlier. Or Mum, when she's trying to have one of our 'serious talks'.

'So why are you here?' I ask, deflecting the focus from me.

'Oh, the usual. Alcohol, uppers, downers, you name it,' Naomi reels off, seemingly unembarrassed by the admission.

'My husband went off with my best friend, and I kinda spiralled down from there.'

'I'm sorry to hear that,' I say, meaning it. 'That's a shitty thing for him to do.'

'Yeah,' she sighs. 'But on the upside, his guilty conscience is paying for me to be here, so there's always that.' She picks up a lettuce leaf and chews it thoughtfully. 'So do you really have no idea who's paying for your stay?'

'Nope. Me and my dad aren't in touch, and anyway, he doesn't have that amount of spare cash knocking around. Nor my mum. The only person I can think of is my brother, but I don't . . .' I stop.

'Don't what?'

'We've been estranged since our late teens. I know he's doing well, financially speaking, but I'm pretty certain he wouldn't give me the change in his pocket.'

'Maybe someone else borrowed the money,' Naomi suggests. 'If they're concerned about you.'

I contemplate this. Would Mum do that for me? But even if she could raise that much, the idea she'd spring it on me out of the blue doesn't make sense.

'Whoever did this clearly cares about you.' Naomi reaches out and squeezes my hand again. 'Why not see what you can get from this place? If you want to move forward, you've got to take yourself out of your normal environment, away from all the noise and drama, away from the safety of your usual routines, whether that's shooting up or opening a bottle of wine or flicking through Instagram. People think they can rely on willpower to break bad habits, but that's bullshit – it's like trying to stick to a diet while working in a cake shop.'

I nod, more to be polite than anything else.

'If you're like me, like most people around here, you have a problem not simply with your distractions of choice, but with a certain way of . . .' Naomi picks her words carefully '. . . a certain way of interacting with the world.'

'Such as?'

'Okay . . . well, I've really started to see that much of my more destructive behaviour is driven by impulsiveness.'

I squint at her. 'How so?'

'Some people believe addiction is actually an impulse control disorder,' chips in Rory, who's clearly been eavesdropping.

'A what?' I ask.

'An inability to resist doing things that will ultimately harm you. Never giving yourself the space to think through the consequences. You know, like a friend drops round and wants to go out, and the next moment you're sitting in a bar, knocking back the Bacardi, even though you've promised yourself a thousand times you'll tidy the house or cook yourself a healthy meal.'

His eyes linger on me and I feel my face flush. How many times have I done exactly that in the last few months alone? Broken promises to myself. Resolutions to clean up Dan's apartment, search for a decent job, ring Mum for a proper chat – all flying out the window the moment a message from Rocco or Franny pings on my phone.

My head throbs, and suddenly I feel sick again. Not simply nauseous but on the verge of throwing up. 'I have to go and lie down,' I mumble, getting up and leaving before anyone can stop me.

7

I throw up in the toilet in the shower room, thankful there's no one else in this wing of the house to hear me. Then strip off, stomach raw, and lie spreadeagled on the bed to avoid any part of my skin touching. I doze off for a few hours, then wake again, the pain in my head now a dull throb, my thoughts heavy and gloomy.

Did Mum really borrow so much money to send me here? After all, every time I go home to the Victorian terrace house in Guildford, I face the same monotonous questions. What are you going to do with your life, Zoey? Why not look for a proper job? Don't you want to settle down and have a family?

My equally monotonous answers: I don't know. I don't want to. I'm not ready.

You're thirty-two now, says my mother's voice in my head. How much longer do you need?

And she's right. Since turning thirty, it's getting hard to justify my habitual sofa-surfing, backpacking from city to city, finding cheap places to stay, a bit of casual work to get me by. Hanging out with my friends in New York whenever Dan's in Texas.

But still, why would Mum send me all the way out here? Pay for a bloody *helicopter*, for God's sake. It doesn't make sense.

The air in the room seems to close in on me. I lie there, craving a cigarette. All of a sudden I have another flash of that spiky-haired girl in Unravel. Sitting on the loo seat, sobbing, head leaning against the graffitied cubicle wall.

Those finger-tip bruises on her neck, growing darker by the minute.

Who was she?

What had happened to her?

I grasp around but the memory has gone. *Did I do that to her?* Is she the person Sonoya claimed I assaulted?

Here, in the dead of night, I'm less certain this is something the therapist made up to keep me here, and I can't get it out of my mind. The idea that I attacked someone. That I got arrested.

I've done some stupid shit in my time, but I've never gone that far. Never actually hurt anybody.

Agitation makes me restless and fidgety. I get off the bed and peer out of the window. A half moon casts long shadows through the cacti and scrubby bushes, tinting the distant hills with silver.

How far did that Max guy say it was to the nearest town? Twenty miles?

That's walkable, isn't it? And perhaps I'll come across a road at some point, can hitch a lift. I hesitate, gazing out into the night. I'm desperate for a cigarette now, and maybe a couple of tequilas . . . It's my first time in Mexico, after all – it'd be rude not to.

Fuck it. I can't stand another minute of this. I dress in the gear I washed earlier and retrieve my leather jacket and Doc Martens from the wardrobe and pull them on. I gaze at the hat and sunglasses, wondering whether to take them with me.

Would Sweaty Mike consider it stealing?

I decide to leave them – I'd rather walk out of here in the clothes I came in, my pride and conscience intact.

Slipping into the dark corridor, I pass into the atrium and beyond. Luckily, a few lamps have been left on, giving enough light to see. As I reach the store cupboard I discovered earlier, I open the door and peer into the gloom. Bingo! I take a torch from the top shelf, then find the kitchen. It's exactly where Naomi described it last night – at the rear of the main house, right next to the laundry room.

I refrain from turning on the lights, reluctant to alert anyone. I shine the torch around instead, going straight to the double-door fridge, looking for something I can take with me. There's no bottled water, but I spy a container with a carry handle of what appears to be a gallon of lemonade. I take it, along with a half packet of biscuits left on the counter.

Meowwww.

The cat startles me, and I almost drop everything. 'Shhhh!' I hiss, as Simpkins starts purring so loudly I'm afraid it'll wake someone. But he doesn't take the hint, letting out a tirade of determined mewling, padding up to a stainless steel bowl on the floor and staring at it pointedly.

I glance about. Spotting a fresh bag of cat kibble on the far end of the counter, I rip it open and fill the bowl, then make my escape. I head for the reception area, hoping I won't bump into anyone and have to explain what I'm doing, fully dressed, carrying stolen lemonade. I go directly to the office, praying it's not locked.

No such luck.

Hell. How will I get back to New York without my passport? I'll have to contact the US consulate, I guess. Pretend I've lost it. Or get in touch with Mike and insist he send it to me – once I'm gone, he'll have no reason to keep it. Ditto my phone.

As I approach the heavy double doors at the front entrance, I'm seized again by the conviction that they'll be locked. But the left door opens soundlessly, and I step outside, punching the air with relief. Here, beyond the thick walls of the house, it's much chillier than I anticipated. I'd forgotten deserts can get pretty cold at night.

I shiver in my leather jacket, considering whether to go back inside and find something warmer. But I don't want to risk being apprehended; besides, walking will keep my body temperature up.

Switching the torch beam to low, I creep around the side of the building and head towards the gates in the boundary wall. As I pass the jeep in the carport, I wonder why they bother keeping a vehicle if there's nowhere to drive.

Most likely it's a story they tell people, to discourage them from hiking to the nearest bar. To preserve the mystique of being so remote. Chances are we're not as far from civilisation as they make out.

Taking a deep breath, I open the iron gates and set off in what I hope is the right direction, scanning the ground with the torch for tyre marks. Though I always think of deserts as sandy, this is more a reddish-brown dust, and there's no sign of any tracks.

Damn.

I spin around, getting my bearings. I should head away from the hills, I reckon, across the flat plain to the rear of the Sanctuary – after all, if there is a road nearby, it'd make sense to build it on level terrain. I squint into the night, and sure enough, I think I can see a faint halo of light in the distance.

I set off, keeping the beam on low to preserve the battery, trying to take a direct line between all the plants and rocks towards the glimmer on the horizon. Some of the cacti are huge – taller than me, taller than a man – looming out of the darkness like giants. I examine one with the torch. Its spikes are fearsome, as long as my little finger and as sharp as a needle.

I walk for an hour or so, the lemonade container growing heavier and heavier. I swap it from one hand to the other, but it's only a matter of minutes before my arm grows tired again. I gulp down as much as I can manage, then turn to study the surrounding landscape.

Am I still going in the right direction?

I switch off the torch, searching for that dull glow in the distance. But it seems to have disappeared – drowned out, perhaps, by the thousands upon thousands of stars, scattered across the night sky like glitter. There are so many, brighter than I've ever seen before, the gauzy haze of the Milky Way in the background. I gaze up at them in awe, and a kind of fear – I'm filled with a sudden overwhelming sense of how small I am, how insignificant.

How vulnerable.

I shiver in the cold night air, and turn to look back towards the house. But it's gone. No sign of any lights at all.

A curl of dread unfurls in my stomach. This is beginning to feel like a really bad idea. But there's no going back now, I realise – chances are if I tried to retrace my steps, I'd miss the Sanctuary by miles. Having to skirt around rocks and killer cacti is making it almost impossible to walk in a straight line.

What should I do? Keep going, I decide, pushing my misgivings aside. I'm getting out of here, even if it kills me.

I stride out purposefully, but within yards I trip on a stone and fall to the ground, narrowly missing one of the meaner-looking cacti. I pick myself up again, and it's only now I realise I'm not alone. What I mistook for silence while walking reveals itself as a whole soundscape of chirrups and squeaks. I swing the torch around, and a dark shape scuttles away.

What lives in the desert? Small mammals maybe. Hard to

imagine anything thriving in this environment. Chipmunks? Mice? Rats?

I haven't a clue.

I fish out the packet of biscuits from my jacket pocket and chew on one as I walk. My stomach feels raw and empty after throwing up all that paella. I should have brought something more substantial to eat, but it's hard enough lugging the lemonade mile after mile. I wish I'd thought to hunt down some kind of backpack – it would have made this whole expedition a lot easier.

I reach for another biscuit. But as my hand finds the packet, I hear something louder – and much more unsettling – than the small squawking noises around me. A series of sharp staccato barks, followed by a strange, strangled howl.

I freeze, ears straining in the desert night. *What the holy hell was that?* If this place is as remote as they say, then it can't be a dog.

For the first time a chill of real fear descends on me. If it's not a dog, then what is it?

A wolf?

A coyote?

My skin breaks out in goosebumps. Are coyotes dangerous? They attack people sometimes, I think, remembering that night we got drunk in Central Park and Rocco told me about a young folk singer who was killed by a pack of them in Canada. Sure, Rocco was trying to spook me, but I'm pretty certain he didn't make it up. I recall how, shortly afterwards, we both passed out on the grass in Sheep Meadow, only to wake a few hours later to find someone had stolen our money and credit cards.

That's one thing I don't need to worry about at least – fat chance I'll be mugged out here.

I screw up my courage and carry on, for what feels like mile after mile. As long as I'm walking, I'm not churning over how I got here. Who paid for it. How on earth I'll pay them back.

But the longer I walk, the less progress I make. My boots are beginning to rub. Doc Martens aren't designed for serious hikes, I'm discovering, especially not across terrain as rough as this. Even with barely half left, the lemonade feels ridiculously heavy. And I'm desperately tired, though at least that damn headache has gone.

After what seems to be hours, I take another break, sitting on a flat rock, desperate to rest my aching feet. Right at the edge of the torch beam, a nearby stick suddenly twitches and slithers away.

A snake.

A fucking snake!

I leap up with a squeal, whimpering with fear and exhaustion, urging myself on, trying to ignore that the torchlight is growing incrementally fainter with each passing minute. Keep going, I tell myself. You'll reach a road soon.

You have to.

A moment later the beam flickers, then goes out. I stand in the darkness, pressing on the switch, banging the base with the heel of my hand. But the batteries are completely dead. All I have now is the pale moonlight, rapidly sinking towards the horizon.

I gaze around me, the shapes of the taller cacti, hostile somehow, their bulk full of menace. *I'm going to die in this place*, I think, finally admitting to myself I'm completely lost. I snivel from terror and a desperate fury at my own stupidity.

So much of our destructive behaviour is driven by impulsiveness.

Naomi's words in my head now. A warning, a judgement.

I close my eyes, remembering the time I blew my last $200 on the dragonfly tattoo on my shoulder, simply because Franny was getting one too. Or when I bought a cheap one-way ticket to Reykjavik, figuring I'd pick up a bit of bar work and hang out for a few months, only to find it was so ridiculously expensive Mum had to lend me the fare home.

Or just waking up in the bed of some random guy I'd only met the night before. Slipping out before there could be any complications or awkwardness.

Naomi's right, I realise, my stomach gnawing with hunger. Why don't I ever stop and *think*? I mean, who treks across the wilderness with only half a packet of biscuits and a bottle of fucking lemonade?

I start crying in earnest. Loud, jagged breaths overtake me and I sink to the ground, wishing it would swallow me whole and this would be finally over. I feel lost and alone, and I'm missing my friends so much it hurts.

Are they missing me too, I wonder? Or are they getting on with their lives, barely giving me a thought?

Ever since I met the pair of them, during a stint working in a bar in East Village five years ago, Franny, Rocco and I bonded like long-lost siblings. Rocco is more of a brother to me now than Marcus, my actual twin. He and Franny are most of the reason I go to New York as often as I do – not simply because Dan needs someone to mind his cats. Franny and Rocco are my substitute family. My gang. My partners in crime. They're the people I rely on to have my back whatever mess I might get myself into.

Only they're not here.

I'm utterly and completely alone.

I sit there, sobbing, until a radiance appears on the horizon. Only it's not light from a nearby town, I realise; the sun is rising.

Instead of relief, my anxiety intensifies as I recall yesterday's impossible heat. But there's nothing I can do now except watch the dawn break over the desert, at first no more than a pale glow, gradually transforming into a deep fiery orange as the sun edges into view. The long shadows grow ever shorter as that fierce ball of fire lifts into the deep blue sky, flooding the wilderness with golden light and heat.

I'm truly in the middle of absolutely nowhere, I realise, as soon as I can see about me properly. Plus it's growing hotter by the minute, scorching my pale city skin. I want to scream at myself in frustration.

Why didn't you bring that hat and sunglasses, Zoey?

What the fuck were you trying to prove?

Taking off my jacket, I drape it over my head to shield my face. I unlace my Doc Martens and pull them off, letting the warm air dry the tender skin on my feet, rubbed into blisters in several places. I pick up the lemonade, drink half of what's left, and eat the remaining biscuits. Then lace up my boots again, and get going.

I don't think about what might happen if I can't find a road. I won't let myself. If there's one thing I'm good at, it's pushing away things I'd rather not confront.

God knows, I've had enough practice.

I'm reaching a clutch of shallow hills, wondering whether to climb over them or skirt around the side, when I hear a faint buzz. I turn and scan the landscape, but see nothing beyond endless dirt and cacti.

Did I imagine it?

I stand there, listening, spinning slowly to look in every direction. Then finally, ecstatically, spot a small patch of dust in the distance.

A car!

I drop my jacket and the lemonade and start jumping up and down, waving my arms, shouting at the top of my voice. I don't care who's in that vehicle. Bandits, drug gangs, the police. I just don't want to be stuck out here alone any longer.

It's the jeep, I see as it gets closer, relieved when it heads straight for me. It comes to a halt a few yards away. Rory climbs out, followed by a Hispanic guy in his thirties I'm guessing is Alejandro.

'Thank God,' Rory mutters, approaching me. I'm so grateful they're here I'm tempted to hug him, but I'm way too stubborn to show it. 'We've been searching for you for hours,' he says, in a voice etched with relief as well as irritation.

'Fancied a hike, did you?' Alejandro's face crinkles into a grin, and he gives me a conspiratorial wink.

'Just a stroll before breakfast.'

Rory scowls at the pair of us. 'You can forget breakfast,' he says darkly. 'That'll be well and truly over by the time we get back.' He glances behind him. 'Let's go. I don't like the look of that sky.'

I follow his gaze, surprised to see what I least expected: dark clouds looming out of nowhere.

8

We set off at a right angle to the direction I'd been walking – so much for staying on track. The jeep bumps and jolts over stones and lumps of dried earth, the jerrycans of fuel and water in the boot clanking away like a drunk percussionist. Rory frowns through the windscreen, his attention focused on not careening into any of the larger cacti – those bastards would play hell with the jeep's paintwork.

'*Tormenta*,' Alejandro says in Spanish, studying the horizon to his left. I've no idea what that is, but his expression suggests it's not good. I peer outside, but can't see anything except a wall of cloud in the distance.

'You should pull over,' he advises Rory. 'No point trying to outrun it.'

Rory ignores him. We drive for ten minutes or so, the sun high in the sky now, the light blinding. Even on its maximum setting, the fan in the jeep is struggling to keep us cool.

Alejandro casts worried glances out of his side window. 'I really don't like the look of this,' he mutters.

I crane around again. A huge orangey-yellow cloud is obscuring the point where the sky meets the desert. 'Jesus,' I gasp. 'What is it?'

'Dust storm,' Rory says ominously. 'Coming our way.'

'Are they dangerous?' I watch it draw closer by the second.

Neither of the men replies. Alejandro is busy ensuring the windows are closed, then clicks off the ventilation system; within moments, the heat builds to a stifling level.

'*Mierda*,' he mumbles, as seconds later the cloud engulfs us. Another moment or two after that there's a loud thump, and the jeep lurches to the left. I hear a flapping noise before Rory jams on the brakes.

'What was that?' I ask, as we come to an abrupt halt.

'We ran over something sharp.' Alejandro glares at Rory. 'Probably a stone.' He pulls his shirt over his nose and mouth and gets out of the jeep. I can just make him out as he moves around the vehicle, checking the tyres.

A second later he's back inside. 'Yeah, we've got a flat.'

'What are we going to do?' My apprehension is building again; perhaps I'll die out here after all. 'How long do these storms last?'

Alejandro shrugs. 'Anything from a few minutes to an hour.'

We sit in the jeep, silent, staring outside, listening to the gathering wind. The sun has almost disappeared, reduced to a vague patch of brightness in the gloom. A minute later, I start coughing. I can't stop. I'm choking and spluttering and gasping for air.

'Dust in your throat,' Rory says. 'Drink something.'

I slug down the last of the lemonade, and sure enough the coughing subsides.

'Nothing to do but wait it out.' Alejandro reaches into his side pocket and hands out muesli bars. We wait it out in the infernal heat, chewing and sweating and peering into the gloom all around. No sign of the storm abating – if anything the dust cloud seems to be getting thicker, the wind stronger.

'Will someone come and get us?' I ask eventually. 'You can call for help, can't you?' I nod at the mobile phone charging in the front of the jeep.

Rory laughs. 'What are they going to do? Send out a helicopter?'

'But what if we can't fix the tyre, or we break down?'

'You should have thought of that before you pulled a stunt like this, Zoey.' Rory turns to me. 'It's not simply your own life you've endangered.'

He looks annoyed, and I can hardly blame him. My cheeks flush with shame. I didn't even consider who'd be sent to rescue me from my own stupidity.

'What about the tyre?' I ask. 'Can we still drive with a puncture?'

Alejandro shakes his head. 'It'll buckle the wheel arch, maybe even damage the suspension. At best, we could only drive at a few miles an hour – it'd be quicker to walk.'

'We'll change it when the storm has passed,' Rory adds. 'Meanwhile you might as well get some sleep.'

The instant he suggests it, I realise how exhausted I am. Using my jacket as a pillow, I stretch out on the back seat and close my eyes, falling into a jumble of confused dreams. When I surface, I'm alone in the jeep. A thick layer of dust obscures the view through the windows, but outside I hear voices, tense and low.

'What did he say to Mike?' Alejandro sounds angry. 'Ed must have given a reason why he upped and left like that.'

'Keep it down,' Rory murmurs. 'You'll wake her up. Didn't he tell you?'

'No. He refused to say. Just asked me if I wanted to go with him.'

'And did you? Riley said she overheard the two of you discussing it. She seems to think you wanted to leave.'

Alejandro sighs. 'Then Riley clearly misheard because I'm still here, aren't I? Do you know what Ed said to Mike and Sonoya?'

'Apparently it was a business emergency.'

'So why was Ed so pissed off?' Alejandro persists. 'Why

didn't he say goodbye to everyone before he left? Why did he try to persuade me to go with him?'

Silence.

'Rory, I'm not stupid, I know something's going on. We've shed, what, five support staff in the last year? And don't give me that bull about guests needing to learn domestic skills. I can barely cope with what needs doing, and Elena works every waking hour. Do you have any idea how long it takes to keep everything watered and those damn chickens fed? How much Elena has on her plate, what with the meals and the cleaning? Neither of us has had a break in six months. Mike said he'd get replacements when Miguel and Conchita left, but that was over two months ago – we can't manage this way any longer.'

'Okay,' Rory says sheepishly. 'I'll speak to Mike about it.'

'So you keep saying,' Alejandro replies, his tone bitter. 'Anyway, we'd better change this wheel and get back before anyone else takes off.'

A moment later I hear the boot being opened. I sit up and rub my eyes, pretending I've just woken, then climb out of the jeep.

'Good snooze?' Alejandro is heaving the spare wheel from the boot, his dark curly hair matted with dust and sweat.

I nod, gazing around. The air smells clean and the sky has returned to its usual shade of deep turquoise, but dust has covered the desert like snow, settling on every cactus and stone, piled in soft drifts on the ground, turning the jeep from black to a dull orange-brown. The sun is directly overhead now, our shadows short.

I watch as Alejandro carries the wheel around to the punctured rear tyre, then returns to the boot, emerging with a small black tool kit. Opening it up, he selects a wrench, then crouches in front of the busted tyre.

'You done this before?' Rory asks, an edge to his voice.

'You want to take over?' Alejandro narrows his eyes at him. 'Be my guest.'

Rory shakes his head and turns away. I watch Alejandro use the wrench to loosen the bolts that attach the wheel, then glance back at Rory. He's got a pair of binoculars in his hands, checking out the surrounding landscape. What is he hoping to see? Some rare bird? Or a breakdown vehicle coming to our rescue?

'Pass me the jack somebody!'

I glance down. Alejandro is flat on his back underneath the jeep. Rory strides over and hands him the jack, watching as Alejandro places it carefully around the rear of the tyre then eases himself from under the vehicle. Attaching some kind of ratchet to the other end, he cranks the jack and the wheel slowly lifts from the ground. Rory pulls it off and puts it in the boot.

I watch for a minute, then gaze about me, drinking in the strangeness of our surroundings as a breeze picks up little flurries of dust and blows them across the desert. There's a raw, empty quality to this place. No signs of human life as far as the eye can see.

Though plenty of other kinds of life, I think, remembering last night. The howl in the dark. The stick that morphed into a snake.

'Just got to screw the lug nuts on tight,' Alejandro says as he lowers the jack so the new wheel sits on the ground. 'We don't want that darn thing coming off.' He gets up and admires his handiwork. 'It should do.'

'Let's go.' As Rory steps forward, there's a sharp crack. We peer down at the sat phone under his foot.

'Shit!' He picks it up. The phone's stubby little antenna has snapped off. Alejandro takes it from him and checks the screen.

'*Coño!*' he swears to himself in Spanish. 'No signal.'

'You sure?'

Alejandro nods. 'It's fucked.'

'You should have left it in the jeep!' Rory rubs his manicured beard.

'Does it matter?' I interject, sensing they're both on the brink.

Rory grits his teeth, clearly trying to get a grip on himself. I glance at Alejandro. He looks pissed off too – and worried. 'We're in trouble,' he admits. 'We need the sat phone to guide our way home.'

'Isn't there a spare?'

Alejandro shakes his head again. 'Not with us.'

I swallow, gazing at him in horror. 'You mean . . . what . . . we're properly lost?'

Rory's expression is grim. 'Normally we could simply follow our tracks back to the ranch, but with this storm . . .' He waves his hand to illustrate the obvious – any tyre prints are now covered in an inch of dust.

Despite the heat, a chill runs through me. *What the fuck are we going to do now?*

'There's not a radio in the jeep?' I ask hopefully. 'Some other way we could call for help?' But the answer is written on their faces, and I feel another sharp lurch of guilt: it's my fault they're out here in the first place.

'Well, this might be an excellent opportunity for Rory here to show off his wilderness survival skills.' Alejandro doesn't bother to hide his sarcasm.

'At least I thought to bring an extra gallon of water.'

'Just not another sat phone,' Alejandro snaps back.

I walk a few yards, peering at the ground. Finally I spot what appears to be a vehicle rut. Crouching, I brush the dust away with my hand to reveal the imprint of a tyre.

'Here.' I beckon them over. 'If one of us walks ahead of the jeep, we can check we're on the right track. Literally.'

It may take ages, but eventually we should get back safely.

'Can't see we've got another choice,' Alejandro agrees. 'What's the alternative? We sit here for days hoping Mike coughs up for a chopper to search for us. Or we die of heat and thirst.'

Rory nods. 'I'll walk ahead and make sure we're going in the right direction. You two can follow in the jeep.'

'I'll come with you,' I insist.

'You're not exactly dressed for a hike, are you?' Rory glances at my Doc Martens, covered in dirt now, the royal blue leather scuffed and scratched.

'Take my hat,' Alejandro removes his and puts it on my head. 'Last thing we need is a case of heatstroke.'

I accept it gratefully, and catch up with Rory while Alejandro cleans the jeep's windscreen. Walking side by side, Rory and I set off, bending to check for tyre prints every twenty yards or so. Eventually I find a shrub that isn't covered in prickles; snapping off a branch, I use the leaves to sweep the dust away.

Even so, our progress is agonisingly slow. Alejandro takes to switching off the engine, catching us up once we're almost out of sight.

'I'm sorry,' I say to Rory, after half an hour of dogged silence. 'I know this is my fault.'

'You were upset,' he shrugs. 'And we should have made a better job of warning you of the dangers.'

'So nobody has done this before?'

He stops and looks at me. 'No, Zoey. No one has run off before. Why would they?'

I swallow, squatting to check the dirt, then straighten up. 'Why is everyone so upset about this guy Ed?'

Rory stiffens, but doesn't comment.

'I don't know this place,' I continue. 'I've never been in any rehab or wellness retreat or whatever you call it. But the atmosphere seems a bit tense. I prefer to know what I'm getting myself into.'

'A mess,' Rory admits, glancing back at the jeep.

What does he mean? Generally? Or the mess we're in right at the moment? Something in his tone warns me not to pursue it, so I hobble ahead, ignoring the pain in my feet, and check we're taking the right line through the cacti and brushwood.

We carry on in silence for another thirty minutes or so. Less than a mile an hour, by my reckoning. Even with the hat, I'm dizzy with heat, and despite my earlier nap, so tired I could curl up in the dirt and sleep.

'Go and get some rest,' Rory says finally, when I can no longer hide my fatigue. 'I've got this.'

I don't argue. I wait for Alejandro to catch up, then climb into the front seat, taking a long drink from one of the water bottles. 'How far have we gone?' I ask him.

'About three miles. By my calculation we have ten to go.'

I groan. Then remember we're only in this situation because of me. 'I'm sorry,' I say to Alejandro. 'As I said to Rory, this is my fault.'

His smile is easy-going. 'Why did you run away?'

'I don't know.' I lean my head against my arm. 'I couldn't stay there, going over and over everything in my head. It was . . . too much.'

'I get that.'

I clear my throat. 'Sonoya told me yesterday that I'd assaulted someone, back in New York. That I'd been arrested for it, but somebody intervened and got me sent here instead.'

Alejandro raises an eyebrow, but doesn't comment – clearly

this is news to him. But what about Rory? Does he know why I'm here?

'Thing is, I can't remember anything about the whole evening – it's pretty much a blank,' I continue. 'So I thought maybe Sonoya was making it up, to stop me leaving.'

Alejandro chews the side of his cheek, thinking. 'I doubt it, Zoey,' he says finally. 'I barely know you, sure, and I don't generally know any of the details about why people are here – that's down to Mike and Sonoya – but I can't imagine they'd make that up.'

My stomach sinks. I've a horrible feeling he's right, that it's true I attacked that girl in the toilet for some reason. I feel sick with guilt and shame.

Why? Why on earth would I do that?

I've never hit anyone in my life, if you don't count the odd scuffle with Marcus when we were little. Like that time he secretly drew penises all over my primary school homework and I got told off by the teacher. By Mum too, when I gave him a nosebleed.

'Why don't you talk to Sonoya about it when we get back?' Alejandro suggests. 'She and Mike worked hard to fit you in – that's why you're stuck in one of the old staff rooms. They haven't been used since we built the new annex.'

I frown at him.

'We're at full capacity,' he explains. 'There's another guest due in a couple of days, otherwise you could have had Ed's suite.'

'So the Sanctuary's full?'

Alejandro nods. 'I was surprised Mike made an exception. Somebody must have pulled a lot of strings to get you in.'

I digest this as we edge forward again, the question gnawing at me. Who did this for me and why?

Especially if I'd done something so awful.

'You okay?' Alejandro asks, as we wait for Rory to check the way ahead.

I shrug, turning my head away. The sympathy in his eyes is too much.

'You really can't remember what led to you coming here?'

I swallow. 'Nothing. Only a few flashbacks to the evening before.' I glance at him. 'That guy Max said the couriers might have given me Rohypnol.'

Alejandro doesn't speak for a minute or so. 'It's possible,' he says eventually. 'I've heard they sometimes offer people medication if they're distressed.' He sighs. Turns to me. 'Listen, if I were you, I'd forget about it. Apologise to Mike when we get back, then make the most of your stay.'

'I don't really fit in,' I say. 'I'm not rich or anything. I have zero in common with the people there.'

'Hey,' Alejandro gives my arm a consoling squeeze, 'you gotta look past that. *El hábito no hace al monje* – the habit doesn't make the monk.'

I can't help but smile. 'What the hell does that mean?'

'Everyone's the same underneath their clothes. They're all human, and they all have their own issues. Just because somebody is rich, it doesn't make them a bad person, any more than being poor makes you a good one.'

I mull this over. He's right. Naomi is clearly wallowing in money, but she seems genuinely nice. And I've known plenty of broke arseholes – myself included.

'That said,' Alejandro continues, 'someone having money doesn't make them better than you either, whatever they might think. Don't forget that, and don't take shit from anybody. But keep your temper – never let people have the satisfaction of knowing they've got under your skin.'

I give Alejandro an admiring look. He's a proud man, I can see that. Kind and thoughtful too.

'Don't you get sick of it?' I ask. 'Being here all the time?'

Alejandro shrugs. 'Sometimes.'

'What about your family? They must miss you.'

'I don't have any.' He rubs the stubble on his cheeks. 'My parents died a few years ago. I've got a sister, but she moved out to Puerto Rico with her husband. We're not in touch.'

I know how that feels at least. I think about Marcus, living his life in Sacramento. Never giving me a second thought.

'I suggest you get some more sleep,' Alejandro says, studying me. 'You still look beat.'

I do as he says, scrambling into the back and stretching across the seat again. Within seconds, I'm out cold.

9

'Hey, Zoey.'

Alejandro is gently shaking my shoulder. I sit up, rubbing my eyes. Outside, Rory approaches the jeep, his face dusty and tired.

My stomach sinks. *What's wrong now?*

Then I see it. In the distance, about a quarter of a mile away, the unmistakable outline of the Sanctuary and its outbuildings. Relief floods through me, followed by a chaser of apprehension; I'm not looking forward to the inevitable showdown with Sweaty Mike.

'You ready?' Alejandro turns to me. 'You could be in for a rough ride.'

He's not referring to the terrain – that much is obvious. Rory climbs in and we drive the remaining distance at a steady pace, pulling in through the gates and parking under the carport. I get out of the back, limbs achy and stiff.

How long was I asleep? One hour? Two? I still feel as ropey as hell. Perhaps I can have a rest in my room before facing the music.

I'm out of luck. As we approach the building, a reception committee awaits: Max, Riley, Axel, Mike, Naomi – pretty much everyone bar Sonoya and Finn.

Riley shoots a glance from Rory to Alejandro, her gaze finally resting on me. 'Where the fuck have you been?' she asks in an accusatory tone.

I'm too tired for this crap. I wave her words away and turn to go inside. But Mike's voice stops me dead.

'Zoey. My office, if you please.'

I turn around, anger rising. Who the hell does he think he is, speaking to me like that? I'm not ten years old. This isn't fucking *school*.

Out of the corner of my eye, I catch Alejandro's slight shake of the head and remember his words in the jeep: *Keep your temper.*

Don't let people know they've got under your skin.

I walk indoors, noticing the Sanctuary has escaped the worst of the dust storm – only a thin layer visible on the veranda. Sonoya is waiting in the office, standing by the window – she's clearly been watching our arrival. As I slump into the chair opposite Mike's desk, she gives me a long, questioning look. There's something in it I can't fathom. A curious sense of . . . disappointment, as if I've let her down.

Or let myself down. I can see in her eyes how ungrateful I must appear, trashing this opportunity to turn my life around.

More than a hundred grand's worth of opportunity at that.

Mike arrives, sits opposite. Despite the air conditioning, he's perspiring profusely, his face puce and shiny. He leans back, folding his arms across his chest.

I say nothing. Simply wait for him to crack.

He clears his throat. 'Sonoya and I were just discussing whether to inform the local police of your absence.'

I raise an eyebrow. 'It's not a crime, is it? To leave the Sanctuary.' I don't meet Sonoya's gaze, immediately regretting my choice of words – after all, according to her, I *did* commit a crime, back in that club.

'No, Miss Baxter,' Mike says evenly. 'It's not a crime to leave the Sanctuary, but it'd be remiss, wouldn't it, not to report your absence? What would you prefer, that we let you die out there in the desert?'

'So why didn't you?' I retort. 'Report it, I mean? I've been gone for hours.'

Mike hesitates, but Sonoya cuts in. 'Rory and Alejandro volunteered to search for you. The local police would have to call on the department to send out a helicopter – it was far quicker to look for you ourselves.'

'Well,' I say, 'as you can see, I'm perfectly fine.'

Mike reaches into his desk and pulls out a map. He unfolds it in front of me and draws a circle with his forefinger. 'All this,' he says, 'is desert. And here . . .' he points to an X in the middle '. . . is where we are right now. And this . . .' he moves his finger to a small clump of squares and rectangles some distance away '. . . is the nearest town. The fact that Rory and Alejandro managed to find you is practically a miracle. As it was, you were heading in totally the wrong direction – assuming you intended to get out of there alive.'

I swallow. Staring at this map, now I can see – graphically – what a stupid thing I did. 'I'm sorry,' I say, squirming under Sonoya's scrutiny. I can't bring myself to look at her.

'What were you hoping to achieve, Zoey?' she asks.

I shrug. 'Nothing. I simply wanted to get out of here.'

'Why?'

I lift my gaze to hers, surprised by the directness of her question. 'I'm not sure. Maybe because of the shock of landing up here, unable to remember anything about it. And . . . I clearly don't fit in.'

Mike snorts. I clench my fists in an effort not to snap at him.

'Zoey, you are perfectly entitled to be here,' Sonoya says firmly. 'As entitled as anyone else.'

'So why am I in one of the old staff rooms?' I ask petulantly, though of course I know the answer. 'I feel like bloody Cinderella. You'll have me cleaning out the grates next.'

Sonoya's cheeks tinge pink, but Mike isn't rising to the bait. 'We juggled things around to fit you in, Zoey. We have a long waiting list, and we're completely at capacity. We were asked to do this as a personal favour.'

I chew the inside of my lip, feeling sulky even though I'm perfectly aware I'm being unreasonable.

'Please don't see the accommodation as a judgement on you,' Sonoya's voice is conciliatory. 'It was purely a matter of logistics.'

'We seem to have wandered from the point.' Mike's small round eyes fix on mine. 'I'd like to remind you that you signed an agreement not to leave the centre without permission.'

'Oh, for God's sake, this isn't primary school,' I say, exasperated. 'I'm an adult. I don't need anyone's permission to go anywhere.'

'You do, Zoey,' Sonoya replies, 'if you wish to stay on the programme.'

'And if I don't?'

'Then you can leave,' Mike chips in. 'But I would remind you that you'll be liable for the cost of removing you from the Sanctuary, and I will also have to inform your benefactor, who I assume will be obliged to tell the police that you've defaulted from your commitment.'

My benefactor? I bristle at the phrase. This isn't a fucking Dickens novel. 'How much?' I ask. 'Exactly. To return to New York.'

Mike checks something on his laptop screen. 'Three thousand dollars for the helicopter and at least another thousand for a commercial flight from Hermosillo. Plus, as I mentioned, the cost of bringing you out here. Let's say around ten thousand dollars, given we had to put you on a private plane from La Guardia.'

Ten thousand dollars? My mouth drops open and Mike gives me a tight little smile. I sense he's enjoying this.

He's about to go in for the kill when Rory walks into the office. 'Alejandro needs you urgently,' he says, glancing in my direction. 'There's another issue with the air con.'

Mike gets to his feet. 'Have a long hard think,' he says to me. 'Let me know tomorrow what you decide.'

I get up and walk out, Sonoya on my heels. 'Zoey, please reconsider your decision to leave. I had to argue your case very strongly, to let you stay.'

'Why would you do that?' I frown at her. 'Why would you give a shit?'

The therapist gives a tiny, almost imperceptible shrug. 'We can help you. And I think you need it, despite what you believe.' She sighs, looks at her watch. 'I suggest you have a shower and ask Elena to make you some food, then perhaps we could have a talk this afternoon?'

I nod, too tired to argue, and she walks away. I'm about to slink off to my stuffy little room when something occurs to me. I glance back at the office – the door is still ajar. Without thinking, I slip inside and close it behind me. Moving to the desk, I spin the laptop around, praying I'm not too late.

Bingo!

The screen is still active – Mike didn't bother to shut it down before he left. I navigate to the web browser, and open a new window. I'm logging into my email account, when I get another idea – if I want to discover who's behind my stay at the Sanctuary, I'm better off looking in Mike's inbox than mine.

I hover the cursor over his email icon, hesitating. I might not be overburdened with scruples, but I baulk at snooping in someone's private messages.

But how else will I get to the bottom of this?

I click on the icon, scrolling the list of subject lines. Many appear to be from banks and financial institutions – I reckon I can safely ignore those – and I try one instead from a Tomas Bauer and quickly scan the contents. Just an inquiry from a prospective client. I scroll down further until I spot a name I recognise: Ed Temple.

Is that *the Ed?* The one who flounced off under cover of darkness?

I open the email. The text is short, a couple of lines that make me blink with surprise.

Mike, if you ever threaten me again, in any manner whatsoever, I will destroy you. You, Sonoya, the Sanctuary, and both your reputations.

Fuuuuuck.

I scroll to the end, hoping to find the preceding message, curious to discover what on earth Mike said to make Ed this angry.

But there's nothing.

Outside, through the open window, I hear voices. Over by the outbuildings. Mike, I realise, talking to Alejandro.

Get a move on, I urge myself, marking Ed's email as unread and signing into my own account. I'm unsure what I'll find – most people message me on social media, after all – but I want to contact Mum and ask if she knows what's going on.

A whole raft of messages is waiting in my inbox. Two from Mum, several from Fran and Rocco, one from Uncle Dan, and – I blink again – even one from my dad. It gives me a jolt of anxiety. What does he want? Last time we spoke, three years ago, Dad made it clear he wouldn't engage with me unless I apologised to Marsha.

And there's no way on God's earth I'll ever do that.

I click on the first message from Mum, sent yesterday morning.

> Zoey, what's going on? I can't get hold of Dan and your phone isn't responding. What's this about needing bail? Please call and tell me what's happening. Mum x

I frown at the screen. *Bail?* I open her next email.

> I've managed to speak to your friend Franny and she told me the police have dropped the charges. But she said you have to go to some sort of private recovery centre, and that you're not allowed to contact people while you're away. How much is that going to cost???
>
> I hope you're all right. I don't know what's going on, but please, Zoey, use this as a chance to turn your life around. Mum xx
>
> PS. Fran is looking after your uncle's cats until he gets back next week.

I stare at the words on the screen, trying to process what I just read. One thing is obvious – Mum had nothing to do with me being here.

What the fuck is going on?

I click on the message from Fran.

Zoey, I hope you're okay. I'm so relieved you're not—

I don't get any further. I reflexively slam the laptop shut as the door swings open, bracing myself for Mike's furious indignation. But that chirpy occupational therapist stands in the doorway, dressed in a lurid pink and purple kaftan, taking in my furtive demeanour. I grope for her name – and an excuse.

But honestly, what could possibly justify what I'm doing?

'I'm sorry,' I stammer. 'I needed to let my mum know I'm okay.' I take in her expression. Oddly, she looks more curious than angry.

'So you weren't . . . what . . . snooping or anything?'

My cheeks start to burn. 'Honestly, Tamara,' I say, finally remembering her name. 'I only wanted to read my emails. I couldn't think of any other way, given I don't have my phone.'

'It wouldn't work here anyway,' Tamara says evenly. 'Not unless it's signed into the satellite internet network.'

I get up and edge towards the door. 'I'm really sorry,' I repeat. 'Could you do me a favour and not mention this to Mike?'

She studies me, her face impassive. 'Okay, Zoey,' she replies, after a moment or two. 'As long as you promise not to do it again.'

'I promise,' I say hurriedly, wondering why I feel so relieved. Does that mean I've decided to stay?

Tamara's face breaks into a smile, and to my astonishment she wraps me in a hug. 'It'll be our secret.'

10

'Sorry I'm late.' Sonoya takes the other chair in the consult room. She looks flustered – two pink spots in her cheeks, her forehead creased into an anxious frown.

My chest tightens with apprehension. Did Tamara rat on me after all? Or did Mike work out I'd been on his laptop? Maybe my email tab stayed open when he powered it back up.

But no. If Mike had realised I'd been snooping on his computer, he'd have kicked me out immediately. Perhaps Sonoya's upset about that email from Ed? I've been pondering what he wrote while chilling in my room. How exactly had Mike threatened him?

But right now I have more burning questions. 'Who is paying for my stay at the Sanctuary?' I ask the therapist as she lines up her phone and file on the table and picks up her notebook. 'I'm pretty certain it's no one from my family.'

Sonoya sits back, giving me her full attention. Her straight black hair is pulled neatly into a clasp at the nape of her neck, and she's wearing a light, floral perfume. I'm struck once again how delicate she is – at least to look at.

'The money was paid via a holding company,' she says.

'A what?'

'A company that owns stock in other businesses.'

'So what was it called, this holding company?'

'I can't disclose that,' she replies, her expression giving nothing away.

'You can't or you won't? Wouldn't you consider I have a right to know?'

Sonoya doesn't answer.

'Are they covering everything?' I ask. 'I mean, if I stay, I won't find myself landed with a bloody great bill, will I? Because I seriously do not have a bean.'

The therapist shakes her head. 'All costs associated with your time here are covered. There'll be nothing for you to pay.'

'Unless I insist on leaving before the end of the programme.'

'That's correct.'

We both sit in silence for a moment or two. I take a deep breath and force myself onward. 'What you told me, about being involved with the police – was that true?'

'Why would you think it wasn't?' Sonoya frowns again.

'I dunno. I thought perhaps you made it up to keep me here.'

She gazes at me. 'No, Zoey. We didn't make it up.'

I exhale slowly. There goes my last vestige of hope. 'Can you tell me what happened?' I ask quietly. 'Do you know?'

'Only the basics. You were arrested at the club for assaulting a man with a beer bottle.'

'*A man?*' My eyes widen. 'So it wasn't that girl in the toilets?' I feel a rush of relief as I remember that broken look on her face. The fear and anguish in her eyes. I couldn't bear to think I'd done something so awful.

Though God knows, attacking some random guy with a bottle is hardly any better. 'Is he okay?' I ask. 'The man?'

Sonoya keeps her gaze fixed on mine. 'Are you sure you can't recall any of this, Zoey?'

I close my eyes for a moment. An image of the girl, crying in the loo. The way she kept rubbing at her neck, the bruises already beginning to show. 'There was a girl at the club, very distressed. But I can't remember anything else.' I glance at Sonoya. 'Was it to do with her?'

Sonoya leans forward and takes the file from the coffee table and checks inside. 'The police report doesn't say. It only records that you assaulted a Mr Bradley Havell, and were taken to Midtown Precinct North. But after negotiation with your lawyer, charges were dropped on condition you attend a recovery centre for at least ten weeks.'

'But I don't have a lawyer,' I reply, bewildered. 'Who was that? One of those free ones you get?'

'Nicola Salerno comes from a top New York firm, I'm told.'

Oh shit. How much does that cost? 'I'm . . . I'm not going to have to pay her bill, am I?' I ask nervously.

Sonoya smiles. 'No, I understand she was given a substantial retainer to act on your behalf.'

I stare at the therapist, winded with surprise. 'By the same person who paid for me to come here?'

'I believe so. I'm afraid I can't help you more than that. We were simply asked to arrange an escort and offer you the full programme of treatment,' Sonoya continues. 'That's all.'

'And I agreed?'

'Yes. It was explained to you what your options were, and you signed the waiver Mike showed you.'

'Was I happy about it?'

Sonoya smiles again. 'That I don't know. I'm guessing not particularly.'

I try to piece this together. 'So, they what, these escorts . . . just rocked up at my uncle's apartment?'

'They accompanied you there from the police station. We had to collect your passport and a few of your belongings. And make sure the apartment was left secured, and the cats were cared for.'

'Did your escorts say anything? About how I was – in myself.'

'Simply that you seemed very lethargic – apparently you slept right through both flights.'

I chew this over for a minute or so. 'Are you certain these escorts didn't give me something?'

She checks in the file. 'It says you were offered a small dose of Ambien.'

Like hell, I think. Whatever they gave me, it was a lot stronger than that. But if that's the case, there's no point quizzing Sonoya about it; I won't get anything else out of her – assuming she even knows.

But I'm desperate to discover more about what happened in the club, and who bailed me out – literally, it appears – from this mess. 'So I attacked – allegedly – this Brad guy, and some random person decides to hire me a top lawyer and get me off the hook,' I recap, making sure I understand. 'But you can't tell me who that is or how they were involved.'

Sonoya inhales. 'That's about the sum of it, yes.'

'Because they've hidden their identity behind this holding company?'

She nods.

'Yet Mike said earlier you were asked to fit me in as a personal favour.'

Sonoya's cheeks tinge a darker shade of pink. Gotcha.

'I said *the money* was paid via a holding company,' she counters.

'So you're aware who it is, the person who asked if I could join the programme?'

Sonoya nods again. 'But they expressly requested not to be identified, Zoey. So I am sorry, I can't tell you any more.'

They requested not to be identified. I take this in. Surely that means it's someone I know? I clench my teeth in frustration.

Who the hell is it?

'Zoey, I want to use today's session to get the lie of the land, so to speak. So if you've no more questions, let's move on.' Sonoya settles back in her chair. 'Tell me about your family. You said you're certain none of them paid for you to be here. Why did you assume that?'

'Because they're not loaded like everyone else in this place. Because they haven't got the odd $100k to splash around on therapy.' Or even if they did, there's no chance Dad or Marcus would ever shell it out on me.

'You sound rather bitter about this, Zoey. Does it upset you that your family isn't wealthy?'

'I didn't say that. My brother's doing well, apparently.'

'Is this your twin, Marcus?'

I narrow my eyes at Sonoya. 'How do you know about him?'

She checks back in her file. 'As I said before, you gave us permission to request your medical notes – at least those that are online. That includes your birth details.'

Did I? I can't remember. I could have agreed to donate my organs for all I know.

'Yes,' I sigh. 'Marcus was my twin brother.'

'*Was?*' Sonoya frowns. 'He's not dead, is he?'

I breathe in slowly, letting my gaze drift to the window with the view towards the gardens. I can just make out Riley, bending over, still wearing those baggy black clothes. 'I haven't spoken to my brother in years.'

'How long exactly?'

I do the maths. 'Twelve years and five months. Since we were both at university.'

Sonoya blinks. 'That's a long time, Zoey. Do you want to talk about that?'

'Not really.' Truth is I try not to think about Marcus at all.

'It might be helpful for both of us,' she persists.

'I really don't want to go into it.'

I sense the therapist weighing up whether to push me further. Watch her decide against it.

'How about we talk about your mother and father then? How are things with them?'

I sigh, wishing we could skip this stuff. It feels so clichéd. Tedious. 'Mum's fine. We get on okay, at least most of the time. I haven't seen much of my dad recently. He lives in Palm Springs.'

'You don't get along?'

'Not since I refused to apologise to Marsha.'

'Marsha?'

'Wife number three.'

Sonoya makes a note on her pad, takes a quick glance at the clock on the wall. 'I want to go into this in more detail in our next session, Zoey, but it seems to me you've had a difficult time with your family. I'm interested to discover how this relates to your current situation.'

'My current situation?' I echo.

'Being arrested for assault. Your lifestyle. Your medical notes were quite revealing, Zoey. Several episodes of depression. Your overdose at your mother's house.'

'I told you that was an accident. I wasn't trying to kill myself. I'd never do that.'

'Talk to me about your life then. I'd like to hear about your work, romantic relationships, that sort of thing.'

I groan. 'There's not much to say.'

'You're thirty-two – there must be a fair bit. You're single, right? Tell me a little about your relationship history.'

'I don't have one, and I don't particularly want one.'

'Do you like men . . . women?'

'Men. But that's the problem. I'm not sure I really *like* them that much, if you see what I mean.'

Sonoya frowns again. 'Actually I don't think I do.'

'I've simply never met anyone I want to spend my life with.' Except perhaps Rocco – but then he's gay, so there's never been anything sexual between us.

'Why do you feel that way?' the therapist asks.

'I dunno. I suppose I haven't seen it work out well for most women I know. It's always the same story. They cheat on you, or knock you around, or simply laze about expecting you to take care of them.'

'Woah!' Sonoya widens her eyes in mock surprise. 'Some huge generalisations there, Zoey.'

'Right?' I cock an eyebrow at her. 'And how's that going for you, Sonoya? I mean, you're here most of the time, so I guess you're single too.'

Her lips twitch, but she doesn't comment.

'After all, I've only been here five minutes, and already I know that Naomi's husband left her for her best friend, and Riley's completely fucked up by some incident with a guy when she was fifteen.'

'I can't comment on other people's histories.' Sonoya sighs. 'So have you ever had a serious boyfriend?'

'Not really. There was one bloke in Melbourne, an artist. But that was never going anywhere because he didn't want to live in the UK and I couldn't stay in Australia – it's almost impossible to get a permanent visa now.'

'Anyone else?' the therapist asks.

'There were other guys, casual things,' I say, a little too defensively.

'So you've never been in love?'

The question startles me. 'I guess not,' I mumble, realising it's true. 'I've had crushes, yes. But I've never actually fallen in love with anybody. To be honest, I don't really believe in it.'

'This is definitely something to explore further,' Sonoya says, making another note. 'Now, why don't you tell me about your career.'

'I don't have one of those either,' I say flatly. 'As I'm sure you're aware.'

'Why not?'

I shrug again. 'I've never worked out what I want to do. Most things need qualifications, and I dropped out of university before finishing my degree.'

'What were you studying?'

'Law.'

'So you wanted to be an attorney?'

'A barrister. I liked the idea of defending people in court. At least the ones who were innocent.'

Sonoya studies me for a second or two, then makes yet another note. I try not to let it annoy me – the woman's simply doing her job after all.

'So what do you do for money?' she asks.

'Anything, within reason. Bar work, waitressing, delivery driver, cleaning, dog-walking.'

Sonoya twirls her pen in her fingers, considering. 'What would you say they have in common, Zoey?'

'Shit pay?'

That earns me another smile. 'Plus they require very little commitment from you. No proper employment contract, no career progression. And if you don't mind me saying, all rather beneath you.'

'Beneath me?'

'You're clever,' Sonoya explains. 'Sharp. You'd have made an excellent lawyer. Before you dropped out, I'm willing to bet you were doing well in your law degree.'

I run my tongue around my teeth, uncomfortable with the compliment. If indeed it was a compliment.

'So why did you choose this kind of life?' she asks.

'What kind of life?'

'Rather . . .' she searches for the word '. . . aimless.'

'I wanted to travel, see the world, try living in different places, so casual work is pretty much all you can get. And half the time you shouldn't even be doing that.'

She frowns again.

'If you haven't got a visa – it has to be cash in hand.'

'But you spend most of your time between New York and the UK, am I right?'

I nod.

'Why not settle in one or the other?'

I jiggle the back of my lip piercing with my tongue, giving this some proper thought. 'Best of both worlds, I guess. Plus I can't remotely afford my own place in New York. And I don't want to leave Mum alone in the UK.'

Sonoya glances at the clock. 'Okay, I reckon that's enough for this session. Let's chat again in a couple of days.'

I nod.

'Does that mean you've decided to stay?' she asks as she gets to her feet.

'I'm not sure,' I say obstinately, unwilling to capitulate so easily. 'I'll think about it.'

'Meanwhile, will you at least promise me you won't run off again?'

'Yes. You have my word on that.'

'Right then.' Sonoya picks up her phone and other bits, and throws me a parting smile. 'I'd be very pleased to work together, Zoey. I know you believe you've no reason to be here, but I'm confident you'll get far more out of your stay at the Sanctuary than you can possibly imagine.'

11

Despite the heat in my room, I doze off before supper and sleep like the dead till the next morning. By the time I wake, the sun is rising over the hills, flooding the desert with light. I grab a quick shower, root in my wardrobe for some clean clothes – there's not much in my style, but beggars can't be choosers so I put on a pair of beige leggings and a baggy white Kenzo T-shirt with a tiny stain on the hem, then make my way to the kitchen in search of caffeine.

Viewed in broad daylight, the kitchen reveals itself to be as spacious and elegantly designed as the rest of the house. Dark wood cabinets cover three walls, and all the worktops are marble, including the central island. As well as a massive double-doored fridge, there's a large range cooker and every kind of food processor and cookery gadget you could think of.

I find ground coffee in one of the cupboards, and try to work out how to use the Lavazza machine. Sadly none of my dead-end jobs had me trained as a barista, and I'm still struggling with the hot water fill when Rory appears.

'You're up early,' he says in a cheerful tone that suggests I'm forgiven for that whole desert rescue thing. 'Did you sleep okay?'

'Like the proverbial log.'

'I'm not surprised – that was quite a hike yesterday.' Rory takes the mug from my hand and sets off the coffee machine, while I use the opportunity to study him properly. He reminds me of a celebrity contestant in one of those survival shows, in his jungle-chic shorts and polo shirt, and tightly-clipped beard. Who cuts their hair out here, I wonder?

'I'm really sorry about yesterday,' I say again.

Rory hands me a mug of fresh coffee, then crosses to a tall cupboard and opens the door to reveal a large freezer. 'Let's forget it and move on. It's Elena's day off, so we're fending for ourselves.'

'What exactly does she do on her day off?' I ask, curious, as he removes a bag of frozen croissants. 'It's not as if she can go home or do a bit of shopping.'

'She likes listening to the radio and doing puzzles in her room. Elena reads a lot too – we've plenty of Spanish novels in the library.'

'But when does she get a proper vacation away from here? When do you, or Alejandro, or anyone?'

'We book them in so it coincides with a guest arriving or leaving – that way we get a lift into Hermosillo.' He looks at me. 'Why do you ask?'

'No reason,' I shrug. 'Simply wondering how this place works.' I indicate the croissants Rory's loading onto baking trays. 'So how do you get all this food?'

'We grow a lot ourselves, plus Mike arranges a supply plane a couple of times a year – we've got a bank of large chest freezers in the supplies shed. Sometimes the choppers bring stuff in if we're running short.'

'There's a runway?'

'There's a strip just to the east of the house – Alejandro keeps it clear.'

'Jesus,' I mutter. 'When does that guy ever sleep?'

'What do you mean?' Rory frowns.

'I mean there's only a few of you running this whole place,' I say, remembering Alejandro's outburst outside the jeep. 'I'm surprised you haven't got more staff, that's all.'

Rory's gaze lingers a moment, then he picks up the tray and loads it into the oven. 'We manage. But yes, Mike is looking for extra staff – it's not easy to find people who are willing or able to stay out here for such large chunks of time.'

I guess he's right – God knows, it wouldn't be my cup of tea. 'Naomi mentioned some kind of ceremony last night,' I say, changing the subject.

'Twice a month we hold an ayahuasca ceremony.' Rory wipes his greasy fingers on a tea towel. 'It's one of our principal thera-peutic modalities.'

I stare at him, incredulous. '*Ayahuasca*? You mean the psychedelic?'

'I prefer to think of it as a medicine,' he says, 'given I'm a trained shaman.'

I try not to smirk at the word 'shaman', but evidently make a piss-poor job of it because Rory stiffens and turns away. 'I'm sorry,' I explain, 'it's simply that I'm not even allowed to have a cigarette, or an aspirin for a headache, and you've just said we're given *actual drugs*. I get the meditation and yoga stuff, but *psychedelics?*'

'Actually, there's a lot of research at the moment for their use in treating addictive and other entrenched behaviour patterns,' Rory says, his tone defensive. 'Particularly for those who've tried and failed with mainstream treatments. We've had very promising results.'

'Okay.' I sip my coffee and watch the croissants beginning to rise and brown in the oven. I'm starving, I realise. I could eat all of them.

'Seriously,' Rory continues. 'Ayahuasca is extremely effective in setting people on the road to authentic healing. I've seen lives turn around overnight.'

The road to authentic healing. Therapeutic modalities. I have to stop myself rolling my eyes. 'And you, what, oversee the whole thing?'

'Me, Tamara, Sonoya and Alejandro. Don't worry, we monitor everyone carefully for adverse effects.'

I ponder this. 'So that's why people choose to come here?'

'One of the main reasons, yes. I met Mike on an ayahuasca retreat in Peru. We were so impressed by what we experienced there, we decided to open a centre offering alternative addiction therapies. We have a long list of very satisfied clients.'

'You met Mike on a *retreat in Peru?*' I laugh. That's the last thing I could ever imagine Sweaty Mike doing.

'He lost his wife and kid in a car accident. When his business folded as well, he turned to the ceremonies to help process his grief.'

'Oh God.' I put my mug down. 'Poor bloke. I had no idea.'

'You shouldn't judge others by appearances,' Rory says. 'I'm guessing you don't much like it when people do it to you.' He stares at my piercings, making his point.

I blush a little, feeling chastised. He's right. I don't like it. I'm sick of people judging me, assuming because I'm small and slight and look young for my age that I'm some punky kid they don't have to take seriously; practically every time I go out in New York, I have to show ID to prove I'm old enough to drink.

'If I stay, will I have to participate?' I ask, watching Rory remove the croissants from the oven. 'In the ceremonies, I mean.' I must admit, the thought scares me a little; despite my appearance, I've always steered away from hard drugs, scared they'll make me freak out or something.

'It's entirely up to you, but most people do. Occasionally we don't consider someone is stable enough, so they sit it out.'

'I'll think it over.' I refill my coffee, grab a couple of hot croissants and make to leave.

'Scheduled activity this morning is basket weaving with Tamara, out on the terrace,' Rory adds before I go.

I give him another incredulous look. *Basket weaving?* He has to be kidding.

'Group this afternoon after lunch,' he continues, unperturbed. 'Then Tamara's leading a yoga and mindfulness meditation before supper.'

'Thanks,' I say. 'I'll bear it in mind.'

'Don't forget group is every weekday,' Rory reminds me in a school prefect tone, 'and attendance is compulsory.'

Or what? I wonder as I make my escape. *We're sent to our room without supper? Set extra homework?*

I eat my croissants on one of the wicker sofas on the terrace, relishing the cooler air in the courtyard and trying to ignore my nicotine craving. This place is gorgeous, I decide, watching the goldfish dart in and out of the lilies in the pond – there are dozens of them, some tiny, barely longer than my little finger.

Do they have babies, I wonder? Or are they another thing flown in on a regular basis?

I spot Simpkins, stretched out on the lawn in the shade under the tree. I make a *psst-psst* sound and click my fingers to call him, but he just twitches his tail and ignores me.

'Hey, I thought I might find you out here.' Naomi sits on the opposite sofa, setting a mug of black tea on the table between us. She looks radiant in her floral sundress, her hair scooped into a loose plait that keeps it off her shoulders. Around her neck is a chain of tiny grey pearls that match the studs in her ears. 'I can never decide if this is my favourite spot, or the vegetable garden.'

'Is it nice there?' I ask, admiring the palms and tropical flowers in the borders surrounding us and thinking how much work it must be to keep them so lush and healthy.

'I'll take you later if you like,' Naomi offers. 'We grow most of our own fruit and vegetables, along with cut flowers for the house. I often help out with the watering.'

'Where do you get the water?'

'Most of it is recycled. Plus there's a huge tank, under the sheds – it's filled with rainwater.'

'Does it ever rain?' I frown. 'I thought this was a desert.'

Naomi laughs. 'It does rain in deserts, you know – only not that often. Apparently the monsoon thunderstorms can be pretty spectacular at this time of year.'

I sigh, trying to take this all in. 'This place does my head in. Who built it? And why stick it in the middle of nowhere?'

'Some billionaire drug baron had it built as his secret hideout,' Naomi explains. 'Hence the location – well out of the reach of the police. Sonoya, Rory and Mike bought it after he got killed in a turf war with a rival gang.'

'Blimey. How do you know that? I can't imagine it's something they advertise on the website.'

'Alejandro told me. He knows everything about this place.'

'Well, it's certainly remote – I can vouch for that.'

Naomi grins, taking a sip of her tea. 'Yeah, I heard about your little excursion.' She drops her gaze to my flip-flops. 'I see you got some nice blisters as a souvenir. Next time borrow a pair of walking boots – there's all sizes in the supplies shed.'

'All sizes? Really?'

'You should ask Alejandro to give you a tour. They've got everything in there: food, soft drinks, clothes, pool and gardening supplies, cleaning materials, tools, duplicates of almost every piece of equipment. Alejandro reckons if the world ended, we could easily survive here for a year or more.'

'That's a comforting thought,' I quip. 'I'll sleep better at night knowing I'm safe from the zombie apocalypse.'

Naomi grins again, and I polish off the last of my croissant, licking my finger and using it to pick up the buttery crumbs. 'Seriously, how do the staff cope being out here so much? Are they all single?'

'Mike's been single since his family died, and Alejandro was married, but they split before they had kids,' Naomi replies. 'Not sure about Rory, though I heard he and Tamara had a thing going once – they're both wedded to the Sanctuary anyhow. Elena's a widow, and her children have grown up, and I've no idea about Sonoya.'

I chew this over. God knows, I'm not much for relationships either, but I'm certain I couldn't live like a nun my whole life.

'I better go deal with my laundry.' Naomi gets to her feet. 'See you at Tamara's basketwork session?'

I pull a face. 'I can't honestly say I'm tempted.'

'Come on,' she urges. 'It'll be fun. Starts at ten, out on the veranda.'

I go back to my room, grab the hat and sunglasses, and venture outside for a good look around the property. Walking the perimeter, I study the scenery. Two days in, my ears have attuned to the softer sounds of the desert. The breeze rustling the leaves of the twisted little shrubs. The gentle buzz of insects hanging in the hot air. The occasional *squeee-squeee* of a hawk hovering high overhead.

I'm starting to appreciate, too, the stark beauty of this place, the subtle changes in the landscape as the sun arcs across the sky, a constantly shifting kaleidoscope of light and shadow. In daylight, the larger cacti seem more majestic; proud, prickly sentinels against the backdrop of the distant hills – some a single fat spike, others more complex, like lopsided candelabra.

How old are they, I wonder. Five years? Ten? A thousand?

I walk around the back of the outbuildings, the heat increasing with each passing minute; already I'm sweating profusely into my fresh clothes. But the temperature seems to drop as I reach the kitchen garden, the presence of so much growth and greenery transforming the hot air into something more muted, more bearable.

Naomi's right, it's a wonderful spot, nearly as luscious as the courtyard. Rows of tomato vines hanging with fruit, some huge, some small, some red, some yellow, even black ones. Lettuce and salad leaves of all descriptions. Every type of pepper imaginable, and lots of squat little bushes covered in chillies. I recognise courgettes and beans and corn, and another bed full of herbs like mint and thyme, chives, rosemary and oregano.

Over in the corner, free range chickens scratch about in a large pen, clucking and chirping to themselves as they peck at the dirt. To the left of them are several raised beds packed with the brightly coloured flowers used to decorate the house. Beyond the gardens, there's a sizeable orchard filled with trees studded with fruit. I wander through it, trying to identify them: oranges and lemons – their flowers giving off a sweet, heady scent – along with peaches, nectarines, plums, cherries and figs. There are even kiwis and passion fruit, their leafy vines trailing across an intricate network of poles and wires.

Wow, this place really is an oasis. Dan would absolutely love it here. Whenever we're both in New York, he takes me to the local farmers market, buys a ton of fresh ingredients, and treats me to a homemade Tex Mex feast.

As I skirt back to the veranda, I catch sight of Finn doing laps in the pool, his dark hair bobbing in and out of the water. Just around the corner, I bump into Tamara and Alejandro, both carrying large punnets of dried grass.

'You joining us, Zoey?' Tamara's wearing a turquoise, gold and peacock-blue tent dress, and her tone is jolly – no hint of any weirdness after catching me in Mike's office. 'It'd be wonderful to have you.'

'You'll love it.' Alejandro gives me a conspiratorial wink from under the rim of his hat. 'How are you feeling today?'

'Better,' I admit. 'I slept really well last night.' I nod at the dried grass. 'Are we seriously supposed to make baskets out of that?'

Alejandro laughs. 'Tamara's a witch. She can transform anything into something beautiful.'

I refrain from pointing out that witches usually turn people into frogs, and sit next to Naomi, who nudges me, nodding at Alejandro as he heads back to the sheds. 'Don't you think he looks like Michael Peña?' she whispers.

'Who?'

'You know, the actor. Been in lots of films. *The Martian. Crash.* And that series *Narcos*, about the Colombian cocaine baron.'

'Never heard of him. But yeah, Alejandro's attractive.'

'I've got a bit of a thing for Latino men,' Naomi admits, sorting through a pile of colourful string. Moments later, we're joined by Max and Riley.

'Good to see you're still with us, Zoey,' Max says, 'I was wondering if you'd gone for another stroll.'

I smile, flipping him the finger, and Max grins back at me. Like all the guests here, his teeth are white and perfect: clearly these people can afford first-class dentistry.

Riley sits at the other end of the table, as far away as she can get, avoiding eye contact. What's her problem with me, I wonder? You'd think I'd stormed into that tent to murder rather than rescue her.

'Okay.' Tamara lifts a punnet onto the table. 'Let's kick off with a simple bowl.' Grabbing a handful of stalks and a length of red twine, she rolls the grass into a long thin sausage, deftly winding the twine around it; I watch, fascinated, as she coils the bound grass like a snake.

Looks easy enough.

I pick up some grass and try to emulate her movements, but the stalks are prickly and difficult to handle, and my coil keeps springing apart before I'm able to tie it in place.

'Here, use this.' Naomi takes a long blunt needle and threads it onto the end of my twine. 'You can catch the string in the round below.'

'It helps if you twist the grass as you go.' Tamara demonstrates on her own project. In the time it's taken me to form one coil, she's finished the bottom of what appears to be a sizeable bowl.

I take a breather, pouring myself a glass of juice from the jug on the table. 'Oh man, that's good,' I gasp.

'Isn't it?' Naomi grins. 'Squeezed fresh from the orchard this morning.'

I have a second, larger sip. It's probably the most delicious thing I've ever drunk – a perfect blend of sweet and sharp, and the most intense orange flavour – it's all I can do not to gulp it down in one go. I force myself to drink slowly, checking out Riley as she wrestles with her grass. She's wearing another baggy black sweatshirt, sleeves pulled right to the tips of her fingers; I'm willing to bet my life that if she pulled them back I'd see razor-thin silver welts in her skin – everything about her radiates self-hatred.

I try to catch her eye, give a friendly smile as a peace offering, but she studiously avoids looking in my direction.

'How are you getting on?' Tamara asks me.

I show her my sorry excuse for a basket. It's lumpy and misshapen, listing to the side like a drunk, bits of grass poking out everywhere. 'This isn't my thing, to be honest.'

I glance at the others. Max has nearly finished some kind of wide-necked urn. It's pretty impressive work, as neat as Tamara's. Naomi's is a little wonky, as is Riley's, but at least theirs don't resemble scarecrows.

'Not bad for a first go,' Tamara reassures me. 'It's simply practice. Want to try another?'

I shake my head, holding up my chafed fingers as an excuse. As she goes off to fill the water jug, Finn appears, his wet trunks dripping across the veranda. 'Hi,' I say as he passes, but he strolls on without a word.

'Take no notice,' Naomi murmurs when he's out of earshot. 'He hardly speaks to anyone.'

I grimace, and have another sip of my juice. 'Can I ask you something?'

'Sure?'

'That guy Ed – do you happen to know his surname?'

'Ed Temple. Shame you didn't meet him,' she says, looking a little subdued. 'He was really cool.'

'What was he like?'

Naomi considers. 'He's one of those rare people who gets along with everybody, you know what I mean? A totally genuine guy. Even Axel liked him – or at least he never gave Ed a hard time.'

'So what was his story? Why was he here?'

'For the ceremonies mainly.' Naomi picks up my bowl, using a pair of scissors to give it a haircut. 'But he liked to get away from his usual routines, the distractions of the internet and so on. Ed was totally into it all – the therapy, the hikes, the wilderness stuff. He was even talking about setting up his own foundation.'

'*His own foundation?*'

'Ed's ridiculously wealthy,' Max chips in, checking over his handiwork. 'He sold his tech company for over six billion. He's looking for the next thing to do with his life, wants to find a cure for all trauma and addiction.'

Naomi sighs. 'That's why it's so odd, him leaving that way. Really out of character.'

'Anyway, he's gone now,' Riley mutters. 'Screw him.'

She sounds aggrieved, and when I glance up there's a tear running down her cheek. Suddenly she thumps her basket on the table and storms off. I rise from my seat to go after her, but Naomi puts a hand on my arm.

'Leave it, Zoey,' she says. 'It's best to give Riley plenty of space.'

12

'Group in five.'

I glance up from my book to see Sonoya staring down at me as I'm sprawled on my bed, Simpkins a dead weight across my left leg. 'I'm not really—'

'Group therapy isn't optional, Zoey.' She turns to go.

'Why are there no locks on the guest bedrooms?' I call after her, making a point.

'Suicide risk,' Sonoya says simply, and walks away.

I extract myself from under the cat, slip on my flip-flops, and trudge towards the Top. I have to admit it's aptly named – right down to the little red flag flying from the centre pole.

Rory and Tamara are already there. I sit in a chair opposite and watch as the others troop in: Max and Naomi, deep in conversation, Axel ignoring everyone, still wearing that infernal beanie; Tommy Hilfiger, I notice on a leather tab on the brim. Finn files in a few seconds later, with Riley bringing up the rear – the second she spots me, her face breaks into a scowl.

'Problem?' I ask, raising an eyebrow.

'You're in my seat.'

This shit is getting old, so I stay put. Riley hovers for a moment, then chooses another chair across from me, shooting me a look of pure malice, then hunches over and stares at the tarpaulin covering the floor.

Naomi shifts up next to me. 'You got any idea what's going on?' she whispers, leaning in. 'I just saw Mike in his office, looking as if he's about to have a heart attack. Elena has been rushing around making up the presidential suite.'

'*The presidential suite?*' My eyes widen. 'You don't mean—'

Naomi laughs. 'Of course not, silly. It's simply a nickname for the annex on the other side of the house – Ed was in there before.'

'Right, let's start.' Sonoya claps to get our attention. 'I thought this afternoon we could examine the issue of avoidance and cross addiction. Those of you who've been here for a while are aware we focus on addictive patterns, rather than any particular substance or behaviour. But it can still be useful to acknowledge the issues we have with those substances or pleasure-inducing activities, and that cross addiction is common.'

She gazes around the circle, eyes resting briefly on each of us. 'So I thought we could kick off today's session by volunteering which particular issues, substances or behaviours you struggle with, then perhaps we'll consider how they relate to each other. Who would like to start?'

Axel yawns, loudly, making a performance of his boredom. Why is he here if he hates it all so much? I wonder – then realise he might well ask the same of me.

To my surprise, Riley raises her hand. 'My main issues are food, and cutting. I used to have a problem with sex, too, but that doesn't seem to be the case any longer.'

'You've actually *had* regular sex?' Axel smirks.

'Fuck off, dude,' Riley retorts, not even looking at him.

'Is cutting an addiction?' Naomi asks tentatively. 'Surely that's a coping mechanism?'

'Anything that has an element of compulsion about it counts as an addiction,' Sonoya says, staring Axel down with a deadpan expression. 'Would you like to share something?' she asks him.

He sits up in his seat. 'Yeah, I'm addicted to sarcasm, and I'm super delighted to be here.'

'You forgot coke and porn,' Finn mutters. 'And being a massive dick. You're super addicted to that too.'

Axel throws him a malevolent look, and I feel a twinge of apprehension that things are about to kick off – judging from what I saw the day before yesterday, group can get a bit volatile.

'Anyone else want to contribute?' Sonoya asks, glancing around. She seems unperturbed by how the session is going – terribly, in my opinion – but for all I know this is normal.

'Gambling,' Max says with a shrug. 'Plus weed and coke.'

'Alcohol, sleeping pills, shopping,' Naomi volunteers, as Sonoya's gaze settles in our direction. 'I once maxxed out three credit cards in one day. I have times when I can't stop buying stuff, then every now and then I have to clear out my house and donate it to charity.'

I gawp at her, struggling to believe Naomi does any of those things. She exudes a cheerful normality, a girl-next-door wholesomeness – if you lived next door to people who were absolutely loaded.

Sonoya swings her gaze to Finn, who looks straight back at her, his features expressionless. 'Coke, Adderall, occasionally meth. Ritalin, Xanax. And booze, of course.' He too makes these admissions in a matter-of-fact tone, as if he were reeling off a shopping list.

'Jesus,' snorts Axel. 'No wonder Daddy's company shares nosedived. Did you leave him anything left to sell?'

Finn gives Axel a deadpan stare, but doesn't rise to the bait. There's something in his manner that's almost . . . I search for the word. Detached? No, more . . . disconnected. Apart from his obvious contempt for Axel, he seems devoid of any emotion at all.

'Zoey?' Sonoya turns to me. 'How about you? Would you like to share some of the things you struggle with?'

'I don't really have any addictions besides nicotine,' I shrug. 'I can go days without drinking. I smoke the occasional bit of weed. I've never had a problem with food, and I'm not sure the odd lottery card counts as a gambling habit.'

'What do you do?' Max leans forward, scratching one of the large hairy legs emerging from his cargo shorts.

I frown at him. 'What do you mean?'

'Hey, I'm not getting at you,' he says. 'I'm simply asking what you do. You know, with your life.'

'I . . .' I stop and stare at Sonoya, my better mood evaporating. Has she told people what I said to her yesterday? But she insisted everything in those therapy sessions is confidential.

Suddenly the urge for a cigarette is so strong I can barely hold in the agitation. To hell with this, I decide, getting to my feet, but Sonoya fixes me with a firm look. 'Please stick with this, Zoey. We ask people to sit with their discomfort, rather than run from it.'

I lower myself back onto the chair, reluctant to make a scene. 'I do plenty,' I growl at Max, who merely returns my glare with interest. 'I travel. I see the world. I've done lots of things. Not everyone has to have an exciting career, or run a company, or earn loads of money. Life is about more than that, isn't it?'

Finn raises an eyebrow, while Sonoya and Rory regard me steadily. I shift in my chair, feeling curiously exposed. What kind of bullshit is this? Why should I have to explain myself to a bunch of total strangers?

'I still want to know why Ed left like that,' Riley says out of nowhere, her voice tight with emotion. 'It's the elephant in the room. Why aren't we talking about it?'

Something flashes across Sonoya's face, a ripple in that implacably calm, cool exterior. 'As you're aware, Riley, we cannot disclose a client's reasons for leaving. We have to respect his privacy.'

'I *do* respect it,' Riley insists. 'I don't understand why he didn't even say goodbye, that's all. I simply want to know what happened. Was he called away? Was there . . . what . . . a family emergency? I keep thinking about it. What would make you slink off without a word?' She pulls her sleeve over her hand and uses it to swipe away another tear.

I study the floor, remembering Ed's email, wishing there were some way I could bring it up without revealing I'd been snooping on Mike's computer. Impossible though. I lift my gaze and find Tamara watching me, as if reading my mind.

'Let's move on,' Sonoya says briskly, but I notice Rory chewing his lip thoughtfully. I get the distinct impression he too would have liked her to answer Riley's questions.

'Does social media count as an addiction?' Naomi asks. 'How about the internet in general? Sometimes I find it impossible to put down my phone and get on with the stuff I need to do. I catch myself checking emails and messages and social media, over and over, going around in circles.'

Sonoya nods. 'We engage in addictive patterns as a way to numb or push down emotions – so anything can be used compulsively, including work or food or social media, to ward off feelings of shame or sadness. It's part of the task of recovery and healing to identify the areas in which you are vulnerable, as well as develop habits and strategies to sever their control over your life.'

'I struggled with food,' Tamara admits. 'After I got off the meth and cleaned up, I began compulsively eating. So I started running every day to keep the weight off, and pretty soon I was struggling with that too. In the end I got a knee injury, from overdoing it.'

I frown at Tamara, confused. *Got off the meth?* I thought she was a therapist, not a guest.

'Most rehab facilities have staff who have personally battled addiction – myself included,' Rory says, reading my expression. 'We may be on the other side of it now, but it means we can relate to what you're going through.'

'What were you addicted to?' I ask him.

'Alcohol, mainly. Coke as well, but I'd started dabbling with other stuff.' Rory, too, doesn't appear remotely embarrassed by his admission. 'It was deeper than that though. I was addicted to my work, to chasing success. It made me behave in ways I'm not proud of.' He looks directly at Finn as he says this, who stares back with a tight expression that's impossible to interpret.

Christ on a bike – this really is the blind leading the blind.

I'm beginning to feel like the most normal person in the room as Sonoya starts outlining strategies for how to tackle cross addiction.

I tune out.

'You all right?' Naomi asks as we brave the fierce heat outside the Top. 'It can be a bit overwhelming, your first time in group – especially when everyone else knows each other.'

'I'm fine,' I assure her. 'But none of it felt particularly relevant – not to me, anyway.'

Naomi tilts her head. 'Are you sure, Zoey? I know that's what you told me, and I don't disbelieve you, but I keep wondering why you're here then. Why would anyone go to all that trouble and expense, if there's nothing wrong with you?'

'That's what I don't understand either,' I reply, wishing I'd remembered the hat. Even in the short walk back to the house, I feel the sun burning my face. 'I'm going to talk to Sonoya again, to get to the bottom of it.'

'Okay,' Naomi replies, but her expression remains doubtful.

We walk in silence, heading into the building. I try not to feel annoyed with Naomi. She's simply being nice, I tell myself. And why wouldn't she be sceptical about me being here?

I would, in her shoes.

'What's the deal with Finn anyhow?' I glance behind us to make sure he's not within earshot. 'He seems kind of . . . weird.'

'What?' She laughs. 'Weirder than the rest of us?'

'Yeah, actually. Weirder than the rest of you. As in . . . absent. Aloof.'

Naomi tips her head to the ceiling, considering what to say. 'You know who he is, right?'

I shake my head. 'Only that his name's Finn. And that he's in dire need of a personality overhaul.'

'You mean you haven't heard of Finley Cooper?' She pauses at the foot of the atrium stairs. 'The son of the pharma billionaire, Geoff Cooper? He owns the LiveWell group.'

I shake my head again. 'I don't think so.'

'You must have,' Naomi insists. 'Finn's the guy who sued his own father when he got addicted to Tranqwell, LiveWell's flagship anxiety med.'

'Oh, hang on.' I search my memory. 'Was there some big drama about his sister? Didn't she date some famous actor?'

'She did, before she died.' Naomi's expression is pained. 'She OD'd in Finn's apartment during a party – he was so high he didn't find her till midday the next day.'

'Shit . . . *that* guy. He's married to that model, isn't he? The one who does the make-up ads on TV.'

'Verity O'Donoghue. Yeah, but I don't think it's going well.'

Jesus. I feel a pang of pity for Finn. He may be an arsehole, but that's one shitty hand he's been dealt. 'Has he talked about any of it?'

'Not much in group,' Naomi says. 'He's pretty tight-lipped about it all, understandably. Paranoid about stuff getting out in the press – not that any of us would do something like that.'

'Wasn't he prosecuted for his sister's death?' I rack my brains, trying to remember the details. I'm not one for social media or gossip magazines, but the story was everywhere for months – even in the UK. I recall shots of him walking, stony-faced, hand in hand with his beautiful wife.

Naomi shakes her head. 'Police were trying to press charges for manslaughter. They claimed he provided the drugs. Then they dropped the case – probably his dad intervened.'

'They dropped the case because there was no evidence against me, Naomi.'

We both spin around, wide-eyed with shock. Finn is standing right behind us, well within earshot. A flush of guilt makes my face burn.

Fuck. How much did he hear?

He eyeballs the pair of us, his expression impenetrable, then turns on his heels and walks across the atrium, back the way he came.

'Shit,' I murmur, when he's gone. 'So . . . what . . . Did his dad force him to come to the Sanctuary? He doesn't exactly seem pleased to be here.'

Naomi arches an eyebrow at me. 'Are you?'

'That's not the same,' I snap back.

'Hey, I was kidding.' She puts an arm around my shoulder. 'I know what it's like, your first time. It all seems strange and scary.'

'You've done this before?'

She nods. 'Yep, though previously it was more conventional rehab. This is my third stab at turning my life around, and hopefully my last. This time I'm determined to make it stick.'

13

I hear it before I see it. A buzz in the distance you might easily dismiss as a fly trapped inside the room – God knows, there are plenty in mine.

But as the buzzing gets louder, I shove on my flip-flops and hurry to the veranda. Naomi, Riley and Max are already there. Finn appears a moment later with Axel, closely followed by Tamara, Rory and Mike. We all gaze upwards, but there's nothing to see but sun-drenched sky.

We twist around, trying to locate the source of the sound.

'There!' Naomi points out a speck on the horizon that could be a bird, but quickly resolves into the outline of a helicopter. We watch, hands shielding our eyes, as it approaches the Sanctuary, pausing to hover eighty yards or so to the side of the Top. Slowly it descends, the roar from the rotor blades gradually subsiding to a whine.

Two men get out and open a door. A woman emerges, dressed in a flowing white top and a short pale-blue skirt with high-heeled wedge sandals, hanging on to her hat as she walks under the blades. She's tall, I notice, almost as tall as the men beside her. I watch her speaking to one of them, as Mike, Rory and Sonoya set off to meet them.

Handshakes, greetings, then some discussion – the woman gesticulating at Mike. She walks away for a moment, and stands, hands on hips, staring at the ground, until Mike approaches and talks to her.

'What's that about?' Max asks.

'No clue,' Naomi replies. 'Do you know who she is?' She looks at Finn.

'I've got a good idea.'

'Don't be a tease. Tell us.'

Too late. The party is already approaching the house, the two men carrying several large suitcases apiece. I study the woman as she comes into view. Her huge sunglasses obscure half her face, but she exudes an airy elegance that speaks of wealth and beauty.

A few yards short of the entrance, the woman turns to the man beside her. I don't catch what she says, but by the way he hovers by her side I'm guessing this is her bodyguard. He nods, then ushers her indoors, passing us without so much as a smile or gesture of acknowledgement.

'Fuck me,' says Naomi quietly.

'Yeah, this is gonna be fun,' Finn agrees.

I squint at both of them. 'How do you mean?'

'Don't you recognise her?' Naomi asks.

'Nope.'

'Don't worry,' she grins. 'You will.'

She follows the others, and I trail them all into the lounge. The woman is reclining on one of the sofas, long tanned legs stretched out before her. She's beaming up at Rory, and as I watch, she removes her sunglasses.

A stomach punch of surprise takes my breath away. My mouth actually drops open with shock.

Maia French.

Maia fucking French!

The face that's graced a dozen films and a thousand magazines, filled endless gossip columns, fuelled countless social media and blog posts, is sitting right in front of me. It's surreal.

I can't take my eyes off her. She exudes a cool sense of poise, of always being the centre of attention.

'Perhaps we could all introduce ourselves.' Rory sweeps a hand around the room. 'Max, why don't you start?'

One by one we say our names. 'Zoey Baxter,' I mumble when it's my turn, unused to greeting someone famous.

Her eyes glide over me, revealing nothing. I'm craving a cigarette again, completely out of my depth. It's one thing hobnobbing with CEOs and the offspring of billionaires, but this is something else entirely.

Maia French!

I can't get my head around the fact she's just a few feet away. If only Franny and Rocco were here, I think. Rocco would have kittens. He'd probably ask for her autograph. Or a selfie.

'Supper is in an hour, but would you like anything in the meantime? Perhaps a drink?' Sonoya, at least, seems unfazed by the arrival of a cultural icon into our midst.

'Maybe a chilled sparkling water?' Maia lilts, in her West Coast accent and trademark lisp. 'I'll take supper in my room, actually. I'm a little tired.'

Without another word she gets to her feet. Rory leads the way to the annex, Sonoya and Mike right behind them.

'Imagine wanting your fucking bodyguard to accompany you to rehab,' Max sighs. He glances at Finn. 'Kudos you didn't bother to bring yours.'

'Is that what the row was about when the helicopter landed?' Naomi asks.

Max nods.

'How do you know?'

'Alejandro just told me. Apparently Mike's had to put him in charge of her security instead – as if he hasn't got enough to do.'

'They should have let him stay,' Finn says wryly. 'I bet that bodyguard needs all the therapy he can get – by all accounts she's a total nightmare and as shallow as a puddle.'

Naomi rounds on him. 'Christ, Finn, that's harsh. You of all people should know better than to believe the nonsense they print in the newspapers.'

Finn reddens. 'You're right,' he mumbles. 'I apologise.'

'Let's at least give her a chance,' Naomi continues. 'She's a human being, like the rest of us.'

'Didn't she recently split up from her fourth husband?' Riley asks. 'You know, that celebrity dog groomer.'

'Christ knows.' Max flops onto the sofa in the space Maia French vacated. 'I guess we'll find out. Wonder if they'll make us sign an NDA.'

'A what?' I ask.

'Non-disclosure agreement,' Naomi explains.

'Sucks not having the fucking internet,' Axel grumbles. 'Or a phone to take photographs. Imagine how much those would be worth.'

Finn's expression darkens. He glares at Axel, then walks away.

'Fucksake, Axel, why do you always have to be such a prick?' Naomi sounds as exasperated as I've ever heard her. 'You know what happened to his sister.'

Axel shrugs. 'Not my fault that's the way the world works.'

'God, you're a creep,' Riley snaps at him. 'Seriously, dude. Underneath all that activist crap you spout, you're just a basic arsehole.'

I head off before this gets any worse. In lieu of a cigarette or a nice cold beer, I go to the linen cupboard and pick a swimming costume in my size, pulling it on in my room. I take a towel, put on the sunhat and go out to the pool.

Damn. Finn has beaten me to it, doing lengths in his measured crawl. I turn back, but he calls after me.

'You not coming in?'

I spin around. He's standing in the shallow end, water dripping from his hair and face. 'I might have a paddle in a minute. When you're done.'

Finn tilts his head. 'A paddle?'

'I can't swim. I don't like getting out of my depth.'

'You can't *swim?*' He gives an incredulous laugh. 'You're kidding!'

'Why would I joke about it?'

'Sorry.' Finn shrugs. 'Why would you? It's simply that you don't meet many adults who can't swim. It's like not being able to read or something.'

'I can read fine,' I retort, glaring at him. 'I just can't swim.' Or drive, I think, but no way I'm admitting that to Finn.

He strolls up to me, rubbing a towel through his wet hair. He's pretty fit, I notice; his physique screams self-discipline, tight and gym-toned. 'Your parents never taught you? Never gave you lessons or anything?'

'Some of us haven't got a pool in our back yard,' I snark.

'What about school?'

'I was excused swimming classes. I had to have grommets for my ears; I wasn't allowed to get my head under water.'

He sniggers. 'Grommets? What on earth are they?'

'Never mind.' I scowl. 'You finished here or do you want to hang around being an arsehole?'

'Be my guest.' He waves his hand at the empty pool and heads back to the house. I wait till he's gone, feeling strangely uncomfortable. What is it with that guy? He certainly has a knack for getting under people's skin.

* * *

I'm sitting on the top step of the pool, cooling my feet in the water, when the entourage arrives. Maia French, in a stunning white bikini, flanked by Alejandro and Mike.

I stifle a groan. I was enjoying the peace and quiet after all the drama of group and Maia's arrival. Mike eyeballs me. I get the strong sense he wants me to bugger off, so I stay resolutely put – if Ms French wants the pool to herself, she'll have to wait until I'm done.

Instead of getting into the water, she drapes a towel across the lounger with the best view of the desert. 'You guys can leave me to it,' she says, dismissively, to Mike and Alejandro. 'I'll be fine.'

Alejandro takes the hint, but Mike hesitates. 'Let me know if there's anything else you need.'

'Thank you, Michael,' Maia says with sweet finality. 'I'll catch up with you soon.'

Mike disappears. Silence descends, except for the occasional slap of water against the edge of the pool. I dangle my legs deeper, making an effort to relax, appear casual, as if I hang out with celebrities every day of my life. But try as I might, I can't ignore that I'm sharing this space with one of the most famous women in the world.

I study Maia surreptitiously as she reclines on the sunlounger. She's wearing another pair of enormous blingy sunglasses, the top of the frames encrusted with what I suspect are real diamonds. I can just make out the name on the side – Bulgari.

Vulgari, more like.

There's a little diamond bracelet on her ankle, and not-so-little diamond studs in her ears. Jesus. I could probably buy a small house with the value of her jewellery alone.

But there's no denying she's as beautiful in person as on camera – all long bronzed limbs and honed physique. That classic jawline and rosebud mouth. Her hair – at least what's visible under her white crochet sunhat – is immaculately high-lighted and as glossy as morning dew.

'You been here long?' she asks out of the blue.

I clear my throat. 'Three days.'

'And what do you think?'

'About this place? It's okay.'

Is this actually happening? screams part of my brain. *Am I really having a casual conversation with Maia French?*

Wait till Franny and Rocco hear about this. They're never ever going to believe me.

'What's your name?' she asks after another minute or two of silence. 'I'm sorry, I forgot.'

'Zoey.' I reply. 'What's yours?'

I don't know why I say it. Just to annoy her perhaps, to see her reaction.

Maia obliges by removing her sunglasses and turning to give me her whole attention. I'm surprised to see she's smiling. 'I can't remember the last time someone asked me that.'

'I know your name really,' I admit. 'I'm simply fucking with you.'

To my astonishment, she laughs. 'I can't remember the last time somebody did that either.'

I find myself grinning in return. 'It must get on your nerves. People grovelling all the time.'

'Every last one, sweetie,' she sighs. 'Every last one.'

Her eyes linger on my face, and I wish I had some make-up with me. Hers is perfect, her skin so flawless it looks like CGI. 'Was that painful?' she nods at my lip piercing.

'Hurt like hell. And took an age to heal.'

'Cute though.' With that she lies back and closes her eyes. I take it I'm dismissed. I grab my towel and return to my room, dripping.

If I had any lingering doubts about staying, this has rid me of them all. My curiosity is well and truly piqued and as I walk into my room, I realise I'm actually excited to see how this will all play out.

14

'See you in ten?' Tamara calls as I head out of the library. 'Don't bother showering first – you'll need one afterwards to wash off the aromatherapy oil.'

I have a shower anyway, reluctant to arrive all sweaty. I make my way to the therapy room, a little apprehensive – I've never actually had a massage before. Who knew it involved so many candles? The place resembles a Catholic church at Christmas, tealights and pillar candles scattered on every available surface. With the lights dimmed, it emanates a warm, cosy glow.

Though not as warm as my room, thank God.

'I'm off to fetch some iced water,' Tamara says. 'Wrap up in a towel and make yourself comfortable.'

'Do you want me to . . . err . . . take off all my clothes?' I ask. 'Sorry, I've never done this before.'

Tamara gives my shoulder a reassuring squeeze. 'Keep your panties on, Zoey. But remove everything else.'

I strip off in the candlelight, feeling weird. Not embarrassed exactly – goodness knows, I'm no stranger to getting naked. It's more I feel . . . exposed, somehow. Vulnerable. I'm reminded of what Sonoya said a week ago, when I first arrived, about using clothes and possessions as something to hide behind, a kind of armour.

Surely, though, they're also a way of expressing ourselves, of declaring to the world who we are? In my case poor, grungy, and hung up on the 1980s.

Tamara returns, placing a large glass of water on the sideboard. 'Shall we do your back first?' she suggests, turning away while I climb on the table and lie on my stomach. 'Nice tattoos,' she says as she rolls down the towel, pouring lavender-scented oil into her hands and starting to knead my shoulders. 'When did you have those done?'

'I got the dragonfly on a trip to Fire Island with my friend Franny. The skull and roses was a birthday present from my other friend Rocco – his brother Louie is a tattoo artist in Brooklyn.'

'Cool friends.' Tamara presses her fingers deep into the ridges along my spine. 'They look great.'

'My mother doesn't think so,' I say, making an effort to relax, to let go of my self-consciousness and enjoy the experience; after all, this is considerably less painful than getting inked.

'She's not keen on tattoos?'

'Mum thinks they're ugly and a waste of money.'

'What about your dad?' Tamara asks. 'Does he approve?'

'No idea – he's never seen them.'

A few moments of silence as Tamara takes this in. 'So you're out of touch with your father then?'

'Uh-huh.'

'Any particular reason?'

'I was rude to his wife. He wanted me to apologise. I refused.'

'Okay.' Tamara presses the heels of her hands into my shoulder blades and drags them down my arms. I feel like a lump of dough, but in a good way. 'That's hard. And you must miss your brother too.'

I frown into the face hole in the table. The only person I've told about my rift with Marcus is Sonoya. 'How do you know about that?'

Tamara pauses for a second, then resumes the pressure on my upper arms. 'Lucky guess, I suppose.'

I twist my head to look at her. 'How do you mean?'

'Could you roll over so I can work on your front?' Tamara turns away again as I shuffle onto my back, covering myself with the towel. 'When you've been doing this for a while,' she says, pouring more oil, and working on my left leg, 'you learn to read people. We reveal ourselves in so many ways. Not simply in words – often what we don't say is more important than what we do – but in our gestures and facial expressions too. We give off tiny signals all the time.'

'Tells, you mean? As in poker?'

'Exactly. You learn to read them, especially in a place like this.'

I guess that's true, but it's hard to see how she could read that I'm estranged from my twin. Does it show somehow? Like an absence? A missing limb?

'So how long have you been here?' I ask, keen to take the focus off me.

Tamara's smile widens. 'Right from the beginning, so nearly a decade now. Happiest ten years of my life.'

'Wow,' I say. 'That's amazing.' I pause, wondering whether it's okay to ask. 'So you mentioned in group a few days ago . . . about being an addict once?'

'Crystal meth.' Her tone is matter-of-fact, as if it were the most normal thing in the world.

'Was it bad? Coming off it?' I examine Tamara's healthy skin and full cheeks. Like everyone else here, she has perfect teeth. She doesn't look at all like I imagine a meth addict.

Tamara starts massaging my foot, managing somehow not to make it ticklish. 'To be truthful, Zoey, it's the hardest thing I ever did. But when my son was placed in my sister's care, I knew I had to leave my husband and get straight. My brother lent me the money to go into rehab.'

'So your husband was an addict too?'

She nods. 'Still is, the last I heard.'

'Where's your son now?'

'Oh, he's doing great,' Tamara beams. 'He trained as a mechanic at college and is working in a garage in Albuquerque. He's recently been promoted to team supervisor.'

'You must miss him,' I say, as she picks up my other foot, digging her thumb into the ball of my big toe.

'All the time. But Aaron's got his own life now. Recovery saved my life, so I vowed to devote mine to helping other people. I trained in various healing modalities while Aaron was at college, and when he left home, I sold my house and car and everything and came to live and work here.'

'Blimey.' I'm genuinely impressed. 'That's a brave thing to do.'

Tamara pauses, her eyes fixing on mine. 'I did it because I believed in this place, Zoey, in what we are doing, with all my heart. The Sanctuary is everything to me.'

I can see she's sincere, and recall what I overheard Alejandro saying about the staffing problems. That email from Ed. Does Tamara know about that?

'Is everything okay here?' I venture. 'With the Sanctuary, I mean.'

Tamara places my foot down and frowns. 'Why do you ask?'

'It's just that . . .' I hesitate, wondering if this is wise '. . . people seem upset about this Ed guy leaving so suddenly. Alejandro in particular.'

'Did he say anything to you?' Her gaze never leaves my face.

'Not exactly. I overheard him and Rory arguing, out in the desert. Alejandro seemed pissed off about stuff, that's all.'

'What stuff?'

'I'm not sure,' I demur, wishing I hadn't started this. 'I got the impression he isn't happy, and that perhaps there were staff issues. Like I said, he was upset about Ed leaving too – though everyone seems upset about that. I'm starting to think the man was some kind of saint.'

Tamara laughs. 'Ed was no saint, but he and Alejandro did spend a lot of time together. Too much, really.'

'What do you mean?'

'Alejandro is on payroll, so he should be careful not to overstep the mark with our guests – you know, not cross the boundaries between therapist and client. And he definitely shouldn't be stirring things up with other staff.'

'But he's not a therapist,' I point out. 'Alejandro does all the practical work, doesn't he?'

'Still applies.' Tamara wipes her hands with a towel; when she's finished she turns back to me. 'Can I give you some advice, Zoey?'

'All right,' I say reluctantly. In my experience whenever someone wants to give you advice, you're not about to hear anything good.

'Use your time here wisely. Don't get involved with other people, or their dramas – focus on your own healing. Do you understand what I'm saying?'

I nod, sitting up and drinking the water she hands to me. 'Thanks for the reminder. And the massage – it was great.'

Tamara's face sheds its serious expression and breaks into her trademark smile. 'You're most welcome, Zoey. I'm very pleased you enjoyed it.'

I have another shower, then grab my hat and sunglasses and head outside. I'm kicking myself now for mentioning anything to Tamara. She's so nice, and has put her heart and soul into this place. What was the point of worrying her?

Curiosity killed the cat, Zoey.

My mother's voice in my head again. She often says I'm too nosy, always wanting to get to the bottom of things – even when they're none of my business.

Tamara's right, I decide, walking around the perimeter. I should focus on my own stuff, not other people's. After all, Ed might have owed money to the Sanctuary – perhaps Mike threatened him with action if he didn't settle his bills. There could be any number of reasons why someone would write an email like that.

I reach what is becoming my favourite spot, a terraced rockery studded with flowering shrubs and spiky yucca. I sit on a low wall, enjoying the physical afterglow from the massage, but I can't quite shake off what Tamara said about Marcus. I thought I'd come to terms with it, our . . . I search for the right word . . . *estrangement*. It's been so long it feels almost as if he's dead. Mum hardly mentions Marcus now – not to me anyway – though I know she calls him every few weeks. In the face of my implacable refusal to discuss anything to do with my brother, she's given up trying to heal our rift.

For the first time I wonder what that has cost her. After all, like most twins, Marcus and I were inseparable when we were young. Mum loved all of it: our devotion to each other, our secret words for things, our refusal to ever be parted for more than a few minutes – a phase that lasted right up to secondary school. Even then, we hung out with each other more than with our friends, and no one was surprised when we decided to study the same subject at the same university, and share a house together.

Ugh. I kick at a stone, sending it skittering over the dry earth, finally admitting something to myself. I miss my brother. Even now.

No, you miss the child he *was*, I remind myself; not the adult he became.

I can't forgive what he did – nor what he made me do.

I get up and move on. As I round the corner I stumble across Alejandro mending a section of wall, removing loose stones and cementing them back in.

'You not on Maia duty?' I say to him.

He chucks his trowel into the bucket and gets to his feet. 'I'm taking a break,' he sighs, pulling off his gloves. 'Anyway, I think Ms French has realised nobody here presents a threat to her security.'

I gaze at his handiwork, and how much more he has to do. Several sections along this stretch are crumbling, loose stones heaped at the base. 'Why is there a wall here anyway?' I ask. 'Why bother with one?'

'Guy who built this place wanted to mark his boundary – and keep out the coyotes of course.' Alejandro smirks at my horrified expression.

'So there's really coyotes out here? Shit, I think I heard them – you know, when I . . .' I leave my sentence unfinished – Alejandro is aware what I'm referring to. 'Are they dangerous?'

'Not generally, but they're sometimes attracted by human settlements, drawn in by the smell of food and garden waste. They can become a bit of a nuisance.'

I gaze around uneasily. 'Is there anything else I should be scared of?' I shudder, remembering the snake that came to life in my torch beam. I hate creepy-crawlies; it's one reason I prefer cities.

'You should chat to Rory, he's the expert on local wildlife. He'll tell you there's nothing to be afraid of. You just have to be careful when you're out and about. Cautious.'

I survey the section of wall he's mending, how much he has to go. 'This place is lucky to have you, Alejandro.'

'Yeah, it sure is,' he mumbles, taking off his hat and wiping sweat from his forehead with the back of his hand. I take in his dark eyes and curly hair. Naomi's right. Alejandro's a pretty attractive guy. Doesn't he get lonely, I wonder, stuck out here with no one to share his bed?

'Do you have to do all of this alone?' I ask instead. 'All the groundwork and stuff?'

He nods. 'We had a gardener, but he couldn't hack it – the isolation, I mean.'

'Can you?'

'You get used to it.' Alejandro sighs. 'Eventually. I guess you become kinda wedded to the place.'

'Have you spoken to Ed since he left?' I try to make the question sound casual.

'Ed?' Alejandro narrows his eyes at me. 'What makes you ask that?'

'I had the impression the two of you were pretty close.'

Alejandro runs his tongue over his teeth and stares out to the horizon. 'We hit it off, sure. I liked Ed, one of the best guys I've ever met. He treated everyone the same, whatever their position.'

I study him, wondering what makes me trust this bloke. 'Can I tell you something?' I say quickly, before I think better of it. 'Only you must promise not to say a thing to anyone.'

Alejandro squints at me from under his ranger hat. 'Sure.'

I take a deep breath, throw caution to the wind. 'After Mike gave me a dressing-down in his office, I did something I shouldn't.'

I pause. Clear my throat, dredging up the courage to continue.

'What is it, Zoey?' Alejandro prompts. 'Just tell me. I won't judge you for it.'

'Okay . . . well, Mike left his laptop open and I sort of . . . decided to check my emails. I really needed to find out who paid for me to be here. And then . . .' I feel my face burning, 'and then I realised I'd be more likely to get an idea if I looked in Mike's inbox.'

Alejandro's expression is unreadable. 'And did you find what you were looking for?'

I shake my head. 'But I did see a message from Ed Temple.'

'Did you read it?' His eyes narrow.

'Yes,' I admit. 'It was very short. It simply told Mike never to threaten him again. That if Mike did, he'd destroy him, and Sonoya. All of this place.'

Alejandro looks stunned, his face rigid with shock. For a moment I think he's about to have a go at me for snooping at Mike's emails. 'Are you sure?' he asks instead. 'Are you absolutely certain that's what it said?'

I nod. 'It was short, and to the point.' I study his expression, trying to guess what he's thinking – but if Tamara can read tells, I can't. 'I don't suppose you have any idea what it was about?'

'No,' mutters Alejandro, stuffing his gloves into his pocket. 'But I'm sure as hell going to find out.'

I grab his arm. 'Please, you promised you wouldn't tell anyone what I did.'

'No need to worry.' He pats my hand. 'I won't involve you.'

All the same, as I watch him hurrying back to the house, I'm filled with foreboding. What was Tamara's advice, barely half an hour ago?

Don't get involved with other people, or their dramas.

Way to go, Zoey.

Way to go.

15

It must be over a hundred degrees in the Top – at least it feels like it. I shift in my seat, sticky and irritable. Naomi may love this old tent, but as far as I'm concerned, the new building destined to replace it can't arrive a moment too soon.

'Most people experience trauma in some form during their lives.' Sonoya is dressed in a loose blouse and cut-off cotton trousers, looking as cool and composed as ever as she scans each of us, careful to measure out her attention evenly. Her gaze settles briefly on Axel, who is about as horizontal as you can get on a high-back chair, legs spreadeagled in front of him, head tipped backwards, eyes conspicuously closed. And still wearing that stupid beanie.

'Hey, Axel,' Rory says, in a cajoling tone. 'We're not that dull, are we?'

'Fuck off, dude,' Axel replies.

'If we don't process traumatic incidents,' Sonoya continues, unperturbed, 'we often turn to addictive patterns as a kind of self-medication, to stop ourselves feeling pain and shame. So I thought today, perhaps we could talk about an event in our lives that we perceive as a core trauma.'

Axel groans. Max scowls and throws him a filthy look. I don't blame him. Axel's belligerent teenager routine is getting pretty stale, and his animosity towards Rory seems to be worsening by the day.

Jealousy, Naomi reckons. After all, Rory is everything Axel isn't – sincere, hard-working, accomplished. Okay, Rory's a bit too uptight for my liking, but he's still an all-round solid guy.

'Who would like to go first?' Sonoya asks.

'Plenty of trauma in my history,' Max ventures, fanning his face with his hat, the air wafting the curls in his hair. 'Half my family died in the concentration camps. How do you process that?'

Sonoya nods. 'That is indeed a very heavy burden, Max.'

'I often wonder if that's why I gamble,' he says.

'How do you mean?' Naomi frowns at him

'I've spent a lot of time thinking about it.' Max shifts his weight in his seat, trying to get comfortable. 'You're in the wrong place, at the wrong time, and you end up in a gas chamber along with everyone in your village. Gambling is about playing the odds – in a strange way, it's chasing the illusion of control in a random universe.'

Sonoya nods again, and I experience a rush of empathy for Max. What's the shit in my life compared with what he and his family have had to endure?

'Anyone else want to share something?' Sonoya glances around the group. We all sit there in silence. No one, I suppose, wanting to diminish what Max has just said. All except Maia, who raises her hand.

'Go on,' Sonoya says encouragingly.

It's the first group Maia has attended in the week since she arrived – the rules, it seems, don't apply to Ms French, who's kept herself confined to her room, with the odd excursion to the pool. She hasn't even joined us for supper yet.

I take the opportunity to study her. She's immaculately made up, wearing a short flowy summer dress and high strappy sandals, a blue denim Chanel handbag at her feet. She looks as if she's off to some A-lister beach party rather than slumming it in group with the rest of us.

'My dog died,' she says flatly, 'Tonto. My favourite Pekinese.'

Everyone stares at Maia in astonishment. Is she taking the piss? Axel makes a stifled noise. He's covered his face with his hands, laughing so hard his shoulders are shaking – for once, I don't blame him.

I mean, I remember how upset Marcus and I were when our dog Juno died when we were seven. But surely that isn't the most traumatic thing Maia has ever experienced in her life? What about all those bloody marriages? The divorces can't have been a picnic in the park.

'Could you elaborate?' Sonoya prompts her, ignoring Axel. 'How did that make you feel?'

'Horrible, obviously.' Maia's expression is faintly puzzled, as if the therapist should be able to intuit her inner world. I find myself feeling sorry for Sonoya – her one-to-one sessions with Maia must be torturous. Despite that flash of humour the other day at the pool, the woman seems to be utterly vacuous. Beautiful to look at, sure, but all surface – everything appears to bounce off her, including the light.

'When I was six I found my father in bed with the maid,' Riley butts in, clearly bored with this exchange. 'I couldn't understand why they were both naked.'

Axel snorts, then sits up and opens his eyes. 'Care to tell us more, Riley? What, exactly, were they doing?'

I stare at Riley, bemused. To be honest, I can't get past the idea that people actually have maids.

'What did you do?' Maia asks, and Riley blinks under her scrutiny – before this point, she's barely even noticed Riley exists.

'Nothing,' she shrugs. 'I simply closed the door.'

I study her, making a mental note to ask Naomi what happened with that guy who fucked up Riley's life. She's never spoken about it in group – at least not in the ten days since I arrived.

'I imagine that was quite distressing,' Sonoya says. She looks tired, and this session can't be helping.

'I was pretty pissed off,' Riley admits. 'I liked her. She was kind. She used to play patience with me, with a little deck of cards she kept in her pocket.'

'Patience is a solo game,' Axel points out in a snarky tone.

'So you were angry with her?' Rory asks.

'No.' Riley's face reddens under his gaze. She pulls her sleeves over her hands, then tucks them beneath her legs. 'I was upset that she was going to leave. My father always made them leave afterwards.'

Axel snorts again, and the colour in Riley's cheeks grows deeper. Rory's expression hardens – I get the impression that right now he'd happily murder Axel. Along with most of us, I suspect. Indeed Naomi told me the other day that Alejandro got pretty close to punching Axel, a week or so before I arrived.

'I had something happen,' I say quickly, wanting to draw attention away from Riley's distress. 'At university.'

Sonoya's gaze swings to my face, her expression openly curious. 'Go on, Zoey.'

My pulse quickens and my stomach is heavy with dread. Am I really going to do this? 'There was this girl in my year. Laura. We weren't friends exactly, but she was on my course. Laura was nice, kinda shy. Kept to herself. We were in the same tutorial group so I saw her around quite a lot.'

I stop. Trying to gather my thoughts. Why the hell am I doing this? I glance at Naomi, who gives me an encouraging smile.

'This thing happened to her, Laura, and she left, very suddenly. And a few days later we heard that she'd killed herself.'

I look around. Everyone's attention is focused on me.

'That's it, really.'

Naomi frowns. 'I get why you might be upset about it, Zoey, but I don't understand why that was traumatic for you personally.'

Sonoya nods in agreement. There's a silence while everybody waits for me to explain.

'She . . .' I hesitate. My mind flashes back to that seminar, waiting for the lecturer to arrive. A group of boys are watching something on a laptop; then they look at Laura, one nudging the other, smirking.

'We'd had this Halloween party for the law students, though loads of other people crashed it when we ended up in the student bar. Everyone got really drunk, including Laura.'

I remember it was nice, seeing her enjoying herself, letting loose. And when Marcus turned up, I even introduced him to her.

Didn't think twice about it.

'Afterwards someone posted the video in the chatroom for our course.' I clear my throat. 'A girl giving one of the guys oral sex. And you could see it was Laura, she had this deep red hair, so it was obvious.'

I glance up. Riley is staring at me, her forehead creased into a frown. 'Does this story have a point?'

'The next day, she wasn't in our tutorial,' I continue. 'So I went round to her house to check she was okay. I knew she was upset about the video. Laura was a really private person, and I don't reckon she had much experience . . . you know, with guys.'

I pause, swallow, wondering again why I'm doing this. I absolutely do not want to get into this shit at all.

'Go on, Zoey,' Sonoya encourages me. 'Tell us what happened.'

Taking a deep breath, I force myself on. 'When she came to the door it was clear she'd been crying . . .' I stop. Bite my lip. 'I tried to help her, talk to her, but she shut the door in my face. The next day I heard she'd gone home. And then a few days after that, somebody told me she was dead.'

There's a pause while everyone takes this in. Max frowns at me. 'I'm confused. I don't mean to belittle this in any way, but like Naomi said, I don't understand why you found this personally traumatising.'

'I . . .' I swallow. 'I should have tried harder,' I stammer. 'To help her. I should have done something sooner.'

'Done what?' Naomi asks, her expression perplexed. 'What could you possibly have done?'

'I . . . I . . .' I burst into tears.

'Oh fuck you, Zoey,' Riley glares at me, her voice hard. '*Fuck you*. You don't get to be sorry for yourself here. This wasn't your ordeal, was it? It was hers – and it killed her.'

'No . . . you don't understand.' I shake my head. 'I . . .'

A hot tight sensation builds in my chest, and suddenly I can't breathe. This is too much. I leap up and run out of the tent, heading away from the house, deeper into the desert, into the heat, no longer caring about getting lost or sunburned. But I don't get far before Rory catches up. He's panting, sweat marks across his T-shirt.

'Go away,' I shout, tears streaming down my face. 'Leave me alone.'

He shakes his head. 'Can't do that, Zoey, sorry. I have to make sure you come back safely to the Top.'

'Just leave me be,' I sob. 'Please give me some time on my own.'

Behind him I spot Finn approaching. Oh God. I clench my fists in frustration. That's all I need. Then I see he's carrying my hat and sunglasses.

'I'll talk to her,' he says to Rory, in a tone that sounds oddly more a command than a request.

Rory hovers, uncertain. 'It's my job to escort her—'

'I'll do it,' Finn says firmly, and to my astonishment Rory nods and walks away.

Finn places the hat on my head. I take the sunglasses and cover my eyes.

'You okay?' he asks. 'What do you need?'

'A stiff drink,' I quip, not entirely joking. 'Actually, make that three.'

Why on earth did I just do that in the Top, I wonder? Blurt out a confession. What was I hoping for . . . absolution? Forgiveness?

'C'mon,' Finn murmurs. 'It's as hot as hell out here. Let's sit by the pool.'

'Shouldn't you go back to group?'

'I'm sure they'll manage without me.'

We walk to the house, then skirt around the veranda to the pool. Finn kicks off his black Armani sandals and dangles his legs into the water. I follow suit.

'You want to talk about it?' he asks.

I shake my head.

'Fair enough.' Finn lifts his legs out of the water and lets them drip onto the side of the pool. 'I'm guessing you don't know about Riley,' he says. 'About what happened to her?'

I shake my head again.

'Her brother was at Harvard when Riley was fifteen. One weekend he brings a friend home. The guy assaulted her. Crept into her room at night. Told her that if she said anything, he'd convince her parents she invited him, and that she'd be the one who got into trouble.'

'Jesus . . . that's awful.' I stare at him, aghast. 'What did she do?'

'Riley kept her mouth shut. This guy, he was a star student, top of his year. She knew it would be his word against hers. But in the end she had to say something anyway.'

'Why?'

'She got pregnant.'

I pull my gaze from his, stunned. 'Jesus. What did she do?'

'Her parents made her have a termination.'

'And that bloke, the one who raped her? What happened to him?'

Finn shrugs. 'She told her family. Her brother confronted his friend, who insisted it was consensual. They believed him, not her, and refused to go to the police, even though she was underage.'

'Oh God, poor Riley.' No wonder she was so upset about what I said.

'The whole episode really messed her up,' Finn explains. 'She started truanting from school. Cutting and anorexia. Her parents even had her kidnapped and taken to one of those teen boot camps, followed by a residential boarding school. Since then, various psychiatric institutions. She only agreed to come here because her father threatened to cut off her allowance.'

'How do you know all this?'

Finn shrugs again. 'Group. And talking to her.'

I mull this over. I can't make Finn out. One moment he's moody and stand-offish, the next he's like this, thoughtful and kind. Is it a rich guy thing?

'Naomi seems to think you hardly talk to anybody,' I say. 'At least that's what she told me when I arrived.'

'I talk to Riley, especially since Ed left. Only I'm discreet about it. She's a very private person.'

I swish my feet in the water, watching the light play on the ripples as they radiate across the pool.

'Does she remind you of your sister?' I ask on impulse.

Finn thinks about this. 'Huh,' he says. 'You might be right. Maybe she does remind me of Maddy.'

'What happened with her?' I ask. 'Your sister.'

Finn glances at me, then looks away. 'You don't know?'

'I know she died, but I don't pay much attention to all the stuff in the papers. Sorry.'

'Don't apologise,' he laughs. 'It reflects well on you. Most of what they write is pure garbage.'

'It must be horrible, living with that kind of attention.'

'It was worse for my sister. Fucking paps wherever she went, taking pictures after she broke up with Neo Hallinger. She couldn't set a foot outside the front door without some asshole shoving a camera in her face.'

Neo Hallinger, the actor. Even I've heard of him. There's barely a film released in the last five years without his name in the credits.

'Then the inevitable smear piece followed,' Finn continues. 'The comments about Maddy's appearance, what she was wearing, the speculation on how she was coping. It was relentless.' He removes his hat and runs his hands through his hair, not quite meeting my gaze. 'Like you say, it does something to you, that level of attention. Screws with your head.'

I feel a twinge of sympathy for Maia, how much she must have to put up with. No wonder she seems so closed off, so shut down.

Finn reaches into his pocket and pulls something out. I almost gasp with surprise. A packet of Marlboro. 'Where the hell did you get those?'

'Ah, that would be telling.' Finn winks. 'Let's just say somebody owes me a few favours.' He holds out the packet. 'Want one? I figured I owe you an apology.'

'What for?'

'I was a dick to you the other day. Mocking you for not being able to swim.'

'Doesn't matter.' I give in and take a cigarette, handing back the packet. 'Everyone thinks you're a dick anyway.'

Finn raises his eyebrows, but doesn't seem particularly offended. 'Is that what *you* think?' He produces a lighter and ignites my cigarette.

'You come across as stand-offish.' I take a long deep drag that makes my head spin, the neurotransmitters in my brain firing up in sheer delight. 'And arrogant.'

Finn draws on his own cigarette, considering this. 'That's fair, I guess. I've been pretty wrapped up in myself since I got here. Plus dealing with the detox and cravings doesn't exactly improve your mood.'

'Isn't this cheating?' I hold up my cigarette. 'I mean, you've paid all this money to come here – what's the point if you're not going to do it properly?'

Finn shrugs. 'It's all about self-control, I reckon. It took me a while to figure that out. What's the difference between someone who enjoys alcohol and an alcoholic? Self-control. You can have nice stuff – but you have to be able to keep it within limits.'

I chew this over. 'Sure. But isn't that why we're all here? Because we have a problem staying within limits?'

'Or maybe we never recognised the need for them, if you see what I mean.'

'Perhaps.' I lean back, savouring the nicotine buzz in my head. 'So what went on with your sister?' I ask. 'You don't have to tell me if you don't want to.'

'It was my fault.' Finn stares into the shimmering blue water. 'My marriage was on the rocks, I'd had another huge fall-out with my dad. I was either drunk or coked up to the eyeballs

– frequently both. I didn't realise how low Maddy had become. Anyhow, I threw this party . . .'

He pauses, squints into the sun. 'Hell, I was always having parties. People would turn up and we'd get high and it would go on from there. More people. More drugs and booze. Rinse and repeat.' Finn closes his eyes for a moment, gathering himself. 'Long story short, my sister overdosed. The worst of it was nobody noticed until the next day. We thought Maddy was . . . was simply sleeping it off. I didn't realise she . . .'

His voice breaks, and I resist the urge to reach over and touch him. 'I didn't notice. That was the worst thing. I saw her, lying on a bed in one of the spare rooms, and I assumed she was sleeping.' He swallows. 'She'd found my stash and taken a huge overdose, and I was too fucked up to notice.'

'I'm sorry,' I say. 'I didn't mean to stir this all up. You don't need to talk about it.'

Finn gazes at me, his jaw tight, his expression oddly stiff. 'I do though. That's what we're here for, isn't it? I've spent a lifetime not talking about stuff.'

Me too, I realise. And I also understand how much braver Finn and Riley are than me. Prepared to look things full in the face, to work through them.

'So what happened? Afterwards?'

'After that I was a total mess,' he continues. 'Everything spiralled out of control. Verity moved out. Dad kicked me out of the company and I started the lawsuit. I was in and out of rehab, but nothing worked.'

'So why are you here then?' I ask, genuinely curious. 'If it hasn't worked before.'

Finn sniffs. 'A last resort, I guess. I heard about this place, the ceremonies. Plus I needed to get the hell out of New York. Out of the world too. Get completely offline.'

He glances at me. I avert my eyes, bemused by this sudden change in Finn. I assumed he couldn't stand me – or anyone else here. As we sit in silence I wonder what prompted this reversal.

'So how about you?' he asks after a while. 'You got any more skeletons in your closet you want to share?'

I consider telling him about that guy in the club. Getting arrested. But it all feels so sordid, and I'm loath to put Finn off just as I'm getting to know him.

Suddenly, without warning, he takes off his ridiculous watch and places it on a sunlounger, then pulls off his shirt and slides into the water, swimming around in his shorts. 'Come on in,' he beckons.

I shake my head. 'I told you, I can't swim.'

Finn wades to the side, resting his chin on his arms. 'We gotta fix that. Let me teach you.'

'No way.'

'Why not?'

'I don't know . . . I just can't. I had lessons when I was older, but I couldn't do it.' I remember Marcus teasing me, taking any opportunity to show off how much he loved the water. I remember too how that made me feel.

Stupid. Inadequate.

'What's your worst fear, Zoey? About swimming, that is. The absolute worst thing you imagine might happen.'

I think about it. 'Sinking, I suppose. Not being able to reach the surface, the air.'

'You mean like this?' Finn puts his head in the water and spreads out his arms and legs and floats, then stands again. 'See? You can't sink – the water pushes you back up. It's actually quite difficult to reach the bottom of the pool, you have to work at it; the moment you stop propelling yourself down, you float up again. Watch.'

He swims to the deep end, then shows me, kicking his legs and pulling with his hands and arms to reach the bottom; the instant he stops, he drifts straight back up to the surface.

'Let me teach you,' he says, returning to the shallow end of the pool.

I shake my head. 'Thank you, Finn, but I really don't want to.'

'Well, then do it for me. As they're always reminding us, we're supposed to help each other while we're here. Let me tick that box. I promise I won't let anything bad happen to you – just sit on the step with me.'

I sigh, relenting. Slipping off my shorts, I join him on the middle step. The water is right up to my chest and I feel insanely nervous.

'All I want you to do is put your head in, face first, and count up to ten.'

I swallow. 'I don't think I can.'

'Simply hold your breath and put your head into the water. You can hold your breath for ten seconds, can't you?'

I inhale, then lower my face, pulse thumping in my ears as I count. Six . . . seven . . . eight . . . nine . . . ten. I pull my head up immediately, heart racing, water dripping from my hair.

Finn is smiling at me, and without his sunglasses on I notice how intensely blue his eyes are. 'Well done. Now do it with your eyes open.'

'Why? How's this going to help?'

'It's how my dad taught me,' he says. 'He had me swimming in an hour. First of all you get used to having your face under-water and holding your breath, then you move on to actual swimming. So go on, try again, this time with your eyes open.'

I do as he says. I draw a deep breath and put my face in the water, staring at the bottom of the pool while I count.

'Not bad.' Finn looks pleased as I sit back up, pushing the wet hair from my eyes. 'Next time around, we'll try floating.'

'Next time?' I lift an eyebrow into a question mark.

'Not gonna let you leave this place before you can do ten laps minimum.'

'Why the change in heart?' I ask, curious. 'I got the impression you didn't like me much.'

Finn pulls a face. 'Likewise. You did call me an asshole.'

'So what changed?'

He sighs. 'Well, now I think about it, maybe you remind me a little of my sister too. And she'd have agreed with you – I am an asshole, and it's time I started working on that.'

16

'How are you feeling after yesterday's group, Zoey?' Sonoya regards me steadily. No matter how long I maintain eye contact, I'm always the first to look away – I swear the woman never blinks.

'Not great,' I admit. Supper was a nightmare after Elena and I finished in the kitchen and sat down to eat. Riley refused to speak or even glance in my direction – you could feel the animosity coming off her in waves. I tried to find her afterwards, to see if we could sort it out, but she wasn't in her room or anywhere else I looked. I gave up, went to bed and got an early night, hoping she'd cool off enough for us to talk in the morning.

'That was a delicious lasagne you made,' Sonoya says. 'Did you find it a positive experience?'

I roll my eyes. 'You're forgetting I don't have my own personal chef, Sonoya – I have to cook for myself all the time.' I don't admit I rarely bother, that in New York I live off takeaway, while Mum does most of the cooking at home.

Sonoya seems undaunted. 'Would your life be better if you had your own chef?'

'Show me the woman who wouldn't have an easier life if she didn't need to cook for herself,' I laugh. 'Or for anyone else, for that matter.'

'So you think life is easier if you're wealthy?'

'Don't you?' I counter.

'You'd be surprised,' the therapist says. 'I've seen many who've been given too much, too young – except the stuff they really need, such as unconditional love or quality time with busy parents. We get a lot of bored, restless people here with no purpose in life, and enough cash to fill that void with drugs and alcohol.'

'Plenty of broke people have no purpose in life either,' I point out. 'Like me.'

Sonoya sighs. 'Wouldn't you say, Zoey, that in many respects that's your decision?'

'How do you mean?'

'I mean you described the kind of employment you've had since dropping out of university.' She glances at her notes. 'Bar work, waitressing, delivery driver, cleaner, dog-walking. I'm not saying those are necessarily dead-end jobs, but you haven't stuck at any long enough to develop a career, or a stable income.'

'I'm lazy,' I shrug, 'and lack commitment. We've already established that.'

Sonoya fixes me with her unblinking gaze. She reminds me of an owl, I decide, her expression so studiedly neutral it's impossible to guess what she's thinking.

'The incident in the club,' she says, changing tack. 'Is that the first time you've been in trouble with the police, Zoey?'

My tongue fidgets with my piercing as I wonder exactly what information she could access with that waiver.

'Zoey?'

'Nope.'

'Can you expand on that?'

I sigh. 'Okay, I got a caution once, back in the UK.'

'What for?'

'Keying a guy's car.'

'Keying?' Sonoya's expression is puzzled.

'Using a key to scratch the paintwork.'

She makes a note, then puts down her pen. 'Why on earth did you do that?'

I sigh again, louder this time. 'He was pestering a friend of mine in the pub. Wouldn't leave her alone, though it was clear she wasn't interested. It pissed me off. So I went out into the car park and keyed his car – only I didn't factor in the security camera.'

The therapist ponders for a moment. 'So, let me sum up. You've been in trouble with the police twice now. You drop out of your degree, perhaps as a result of what you told us in group yesterday, but as you insisted before, you don't want to go into that. You move around, never staying in one place for more than a few months. You've never had a serious boyfriend or a proper job. And your relationship with your father and twin brother has completely broken down. And you're thirty-two, Zoey. Nearly thirty-three.'

'What can I say?' I shrug again. 'Time flies.'

Sonoya leans forward, resting her elbows on her knees. 'All of this occurred after the incident with this girl Laura, and it seems to me your life was on track until that point. I think that derailed you in some essential way, and we should definitely talk about it.'

I chew the inside of my cheek, playing mute.

'Did you do something to hurt Laura, Zoey?'

My head jerks up. Sonoya is studying me so intently it makes the skin on my face prickle. 'What do you mean?'

'I'm wondering, given what you told us in group yesterday, if you feel guilty in some way.'

I don't respond.

'Talk to me, Zoey. Help me understand.'

'Understand what?'

'Why this incident holds such significance for you. We were

discussing trauma. I imagine this was distressing, of course, but like Max and Naomi, I don't exactly see why you experienced it as traumatic.'

My chest tightens. 'As I told you, she killed herself. Laura. She went home and swallowed a whole bottle of her father's pills. They found her dead in the morning.'

There's a momentary lapse in Sonoya's carefully curated neutrality. A slight tension in her cheek, in her jaw. 'That's very sad,' she says finally. 'Upsetting for everyone.'

'You could say that.'

'But Zoey, I still don't understand why this carries such a burden for you.' She sits back in her chair, her fingers caressing her pen in that way she does when she's concentrating. 'It seems you did try to help, so I'm not sure I'm getting the full picture. Can you walk me through it?'

I inhale. Gaze out of the window, wondering whether to confess how I am connected to what happened to Laura. But I can't face it. I don't even want to think about it.

What's done is done.

Laura is dead. Dragging all that back up serves no one.

'I don't know. I guess the whole thing was just . . . when I heard Laura had died. Nothing felt the same after that.'

'Is that why you dropped out of university? It was only a week later, wasn't it?'

I look up at her sharply. How does she know that?

'Your medical records, Zoey. You were prescribed antidepressants back in your home town, rather than by the university health service. So you returned to your mother's house?'

I nod.

'And you went on medication. Let's leave aside the incident where you took too many sleeping pills. I'd like to know what it is you're hiding, Zoey.'

I stare at her, wide-eyed. What the hell? Are therapists always this pushy? Why is she so desperate to get inside my head?

'Fuck off, Sonoya.'

She puts her pen down and looks at me. 'Are you going to fight me all the way? This is clearly a major episode in your life – after all, a few weeks later you ended up in hospital having your stomach pumped.'

'No,' I bluster. 'I just . . . I mean, I didn't sign up for this kind of interrogation.'

'Is that what you think this is?'

'It feels like one. I wasn't expecting therapy to be so . . . intrusive.'

Sonoya's cheek twitches. She seems to be considering her response carefully. 'Listen, Zoey, we're not only here to help our residents get over substance abuse and other addictive patterns, we're here to support them in dealing with their issues and getting back on track, to find real meaning and purpose in their lives. And that requires dealing with past trauma – as we say, pain is—'

'—the price of freedom. Yeah, I know.'

She pauses, waiting for me to go on, but I remain stubbornly silent.

'You might not be a full-blown alcoholic, Zoey. You may or may not have a problem with marijuana addiction, or a dysfunctional relationship with sleeping pills, but clearly you've been medicating your unhappiness in your own way, with cigarettes, with your lifestyle, with your refusal to take stock and deal with the trauma in your past. I'm here to support you in getting to the root of that unhappiness.'

'But I'm *not* unhappy,' I insist. 'Okay, I might not have my life exactly together, but I have a good time – apart from the occasional hangover.'

'Let's recap again,' Sonoya says, counting off on her fingers. 'No career, no lasting romantic relationships. No home of your own. No children. Are you telling me you don't want any of those things?'

'No . . .' I pause. 'Of course I want them. They simply . . . haven't happened yet.'

'And I doubt they will unless we get to the source of your depression and anxiety, Zoey. That's my point.'

I don't answer.

Sonoya sighs again, when it's clear I've nothing more to add to the conversation. 'Did you make a decision about whether you want to participate in the ayahuasca ceremony on Saturday?'

'Sure,' I say. 'Why not? It's pretty much all anyone's been talking about, and I have terrible fomo.'

'Fomo?'

'Fear of missing out. You should spend more time on the internet, Sonoya.'

'Well, I need to be certain you're in a stable enough condition. It can be hard on the body, and the psyche.'

'I'm surprised you're in favour of it at all – given ayahuasca isn't a licensed medicine.'

Sonoya smiles. 'I admit it's a little unconventional, but I have been persuaded of the benefits. And I've seen the results since working here. They're impressive. In fact, there's increasing evidence backing the therapeutic profile of psychedelics in addiction, as well as a range of other mental health issues.'

I give her a sceptical look. I didn't have Sonoya down as the type to support something so far outside the mainstream.

But then she's here, I suppose.

'We know ayahuasca is not addictive,' she reassures me. 'There's little risk of abuse, but you'd need to talk to Rory for a better understanding of how it works. He's the expert, not me.

He'll give you chapter and verse on its use as a healing agent, but basically it appears to help people gain insight into the underlying causes of their problems.'

I squint at her, still unconvinced. 'So you honestly believe it works?'

'I've seen people transformed by it, literally overnight. In terms of therapy it can bring about a major breakthrough, particularly for those who find it difficult to express their emotions verbally, for whom talking cures are of limited benefit.'

'Well, then.' I inhale. 'I guess I'd be stupid not to give it a go.'

'I'll let Rory know,' she says, getting to her feet. 'He'll walk you through what to expect.' She looks at me. 'I think you'll find it a fascinating experience.'

'Have you tried it?'

Sonoya blinks. 'Actually, no.'

'Why not?'

'That's an interesting question,' the therapist muses as she follows me out of the consult room. 'I suppose I've never really felt the need.'

17

'Hey, can we talk?'

Riley's face peeks out from behind a thicket of tomato leaves, her expression apprehensive. 'What about?'

'About what happened in group yesterday,' I say. 'I'm sorry what I said upset you so much. I didn't mean it to.'

She scowls and disappears. I glance around the vegetable garden. There's such a glut of tomatoes I can't see how we could possibly eat them all. Strings of cherry-sized fruit hang from every plant, most of them ripe. I pluck a couple off the nearest and pop them in my mouth, savouring the burst of acid sweetness.

'Riley?' I prompt, when I get no reply.

A loud sigh from behind the greenery. 'There's nothing to say, Zoey. I don't want to get into it again with you.'

'Okay, but can we at least call a truce? We're here to help each other, after all. You don't have to hide away.'

'I'm not hiding from you,' Riley says defensively.

'You're literally doing that right now.' I peer through the greenery.

'Chrissake,' she grumbles. She puts down her secateurs and walks round to where I'm standing. 'I'm not hiding from *you* actually . . . I'm hiding from everyone. Nothing's been the same here since Ed left. Everyone's so . . . tense, so angry. It's doing my head in.'

'I get that. You want to talk about it?'

'You going to the ayahuasca ceremony tomorrow?' Riley asks instead.

I nod. 'You?'

She shakes her head. 'Sonoya says I'm not in the right place at the moment.'

Sonoya might have a point, I think, but have the sense not to say it out loud. 'That's too bad.'

'I'm not that bothered.' Riley sniffs and lowers her long sleeves over her forearms. 'I did the ceremony last month, before you arrived.'

'How was it?'

'Well, I vomited a lot, saw a load of weird psychedelic patterns. To be honest, I can't remember much after that.' She pulls a face. 'Apparently I freaked out. Again.'

'Is it that bad?' I feel a twinge of apprehension. 'The ayahuasca, I mean.'

'Not always. Not for everyone. Ed said it transformed his whole world view in one session. He met this female plant spirit who showed him exactly how he should move forward with his life.' She swallows, looks away.

'You're still missing him, huh?'

A spasm of pain crosses her delicate features, and all of a sudden she seems much younger than her twenty-three years. 'Yeah. But fuck him, leaving like that.'

'Have you found out anything more about why he did?' I ask, anxious to keep the conversation going and get our relationship on a better footing.

'Nope, but I'm going to keep on at Sonoya until she tells me. I reckon she pissed him off.'

I frown. 'Pissed him off how?'

'She's really . . . I dunno.' Riley chews her lip as she searches for the right word. 'Pushy, I suppose. I've had a lot of therapists, but none like her – it's as if she's really trying to get inside your head, discover all your secrets.'

I gaze at her, remembering my earlier session with Sonoya. Pushy – that's exactly how it felt.

'So I'm wondering if she said anything to upset Ed,' Riley continues, 'or . . .' She pauses.

'Or what?'

Riley sighs. 'You'll think I'm stupid. I don't know. It's just a feeling that something isn't right—'

She's interrupted by a volley of angry-sounding Spanish. We both glance towards the nearest outbuilding, in time to see Alejandro squaring up to Mike. Alejandro has him pinned against the shed, clearly on the verge of punching him, when Sonoya appears out of nowhere. We watch her grab Mike and pull him towards the house; when I look back, Alejandro has gone.

'What on earth was that about?' Riley frowns at me.

'No idea,' I say, but I'm not sure that's true. I've a horrible feeling that what we just witnessed is linked to what I told Alejandro a few days ago, about Ed's email. 'I don't suppose you speak Spanish?' I ask Riley. 'Did you understand any of it?'

She shakes her head again. 'Spanish wasn't exactly my thing at school – actually school wasn't exactly my thing either. But I picked up one phrase.'

'What?'

'Alejandro said something about the police.'

I frown. 'You sure?'

'*Policía Federal.* It's not hard to translate.'

'What did Mike say?'

'No idea.' She turns away.

I stare at Riley's back, unsettled by the whole incident. 'I'll leave you to it,' I say, desperate to get out of the relentless heat.

I walk up to the house, going in through the main entrance. As I pass the office, the door opens and Mike storms out, his face redder than the tomatoes in the garden. He strides past without so much as a glance in my direction; a second later Sonoya emerges, pale and anxious. She gives me a curt nod then disappears towards the clinic.

Enough, I decide. I can't deal with this right now.

Going to my room, I change into my swimming costume and grab a towel, making my way to the pool. I practise what I did yesterday with Finn, putting my face under the water, holding my breath and counting to ten. It's still scary, but each time I make myself do it, it feels a little more natural, a little less intimidating. Already I'm more relaxed in the water, able to enjoy how it laps around me, cooling my skin.

'Hey, glad to have found you.' Rory appears, clutching a clipboard. 'I'd like to have a chat about the ceremony tomorrow evening. Ten minutes, in the consult room?'

I study him, wondering if he's aware of what just happened with Alejandro and Mike. If he is, he doesn't seem bothered.

'Sure.' I get dressed, hanging my costume and towel to dry on the veranda. By the time I reach the consult room Rory is already there.

'Good swim?' he asks.

'I don't swim exactly, but I'm learning. Finn's teaching me.'

'Really?' Rory raises an eyebrow.

'Really,' I confirm. 'I think he's turning over a new leaf.'

'That's cool,' Rory replies. 'Like we say, we're all here to help each other. Okay, so I wanted to run you through what will happen tomorrow; if you're happy, you can sign the consent form.'

'Right.'

Ayahuasca is a blend of two plants, he explains to me: the ayahuasca vine – Banisteriopsis caapi – and a shrub called chacruna – Psychotria viridis. The mixture is brewed into a tea, which contains a powerful hallucinogen called dimethyl-tryptamine or DMT.

'Do you know what that is?' Rory asks.

'I haven't tried it, but I've heard people discussing it. The weird beings they met "on the other side", that sort of stuff.'

Rory nods. 'Was that with straight DMT?'

'I think so.'

'Well, ayahuasca is more of a medicinal and spiritual experience, but there are often some unpleasant physical side effects – nausea, vomiting, diarrhoea. And it'll last four to six hours. I'll be there the whole time to guide you through. Sonoya, Tamara and Alejandro too.'

'Have Tamara or Alejandro tried it?' I ask. 'Sonoya said she hadn't.'

'Tamara did once, some time ago.' He looks oddly awkward, and I wonder if it was during their rumoured affair. 'It's very important before we start the ceremony, that you consider what you want from the experience,' he continues. 'Establishing a clear intention beforehand is essential.'

'Why?'

'Ayahuasca is a profoundly sacred experience,' Rory intones, looking so earnest I suppress an urge to giggle. 'That's why we call it a ceremony. It's crucial you treat it with reverence. Those who don't, those who go into it for the wrong reasons can end up with a deeply unpleasant episode.'

'A bad trip?'

'Basically.'

'Sounds scary.'

Rory gives me a reassuring smile. 'You'll be fine, Zoey. I can usually tell who will have a more difficult time, and even then, it may be a necessary part of their personal growth. It might not be pleasant, but the spirits know how best to effect change. There are no wrong answers.'

'Do you seriously believe that stuff?' I ask, curious. 'About spirits, I mean.'

'Absolutely.' Rory's expression is deadpan. 'They showed me exactly what I was doing wrong in my life and how I had to turn it around.'

'During your trip to Peru?'

'Yes. It was in an ayahuasca ceremony while I was there that I realised I needed to completely change tack.'

'From what. What were you doing before?'

'I was a photographer.' A cloud passes across Rory's face. I laugh. 'That doesn't sound so bad.'

He shifts in his seat, clearly uncomfortable. 'It wasn't a good path,' he says.

I wait for him to explain, but evidently Rory's unwilling to say more. Instead he hands me the clipboard and I scan the one-page disclaimer. Standard stuff about having been informed of the risks and side effects, and the Sanctuary not being liable for any adverse consequences.

I sign my name at the bottom, then hand it back. 'Is everything okay here by the way?'

'What do you mean?' he frowns.

'I heard Alejandro arguing with Mike earlier. They both seemed pretty upset.'

Rory's frown deepens. 'I've no idea,' he says, tucking my form into his clipboard. 'But I can't imagine it was anything serious.'

18

'You gonna join us, Zoey?' Naomi finds me curled up in an armchair in the library, reading a book about indigenous Mexican tribes. 'Max has lit the firepit and we're playing poker. Riley and I have prepped snacks, and lots of different mocktails.'

I abandon the book and follow her outside, down to one of the lower terraces behind the pool, a small area of crazy paving with rustic wood-and-stone seating encircling a firepit. Finn, Max, Axel and Riley are sitting at a wicker table, Max shuffling a pack of cards. To my surprise, Maia appears, dressed in a strappy top and wide-leg silk trousers, her face immaculately made up, her long blonde hair tumbling loose around her shoulders.

'May I join in?' she says in her lilting voice.

'To what do we owe the honour?' Axel snipes. 'You sure you want to slum it with us commoners?'

She flips him the finger, and I like her a little more; whatever else you can say about Maia, she has chutzpah.

'What's the game?' she asks, sitting next to Finn.

'Poker,' Max says. 'Texas Holdem. You gonna join us?'

Maia nods, grabbing a stack of coloured counters that I recognise from one of the board games in the lounge.

'Zoey, you in?' Max asks, and I have to admit I don't know how to play.

'You're kidding.' Finn frowns at me. 'You've never played poker?'

'Never.'

'I'll teach you.' Naomi sits and pats the space next to her. 'You can help me with my hand.'

I watch as Max shuffles the pack and deals two cards to each player. None for himself, I notice. 'You okay doing this?' I ask, worrying about his gambling habit; Naomi filled me in on how Max lost his wife and kids, and nearly a seat on the board of his own company.

'As long as I stick to dealing not playing,' he replies. 'If I change my mind, lock me in a store shed. Preferably the one with all the food.'

Naomi shows me her cards, angling them so nobody else can see. 'We place our first bet now. What do you reckon?'

I stare at her hand. A jack of spades and an ace of hearts. 'Haven't a clue.'

She ponders, then places three counters on the table. Max raises an eyebrow. 'You feeling flush, Rivera?'

Naomi laughs. 'My ex agreed to cover any expenses while I'm here. So, you know, if I lose, I win.' She winks at me.

'You mean you're playing for real money?'

'IOUs,' Max says. 'To be honoured when we leave.'

'So how much are these worth?' I nod at all the chips.

'Yellow $100, red $500, black $1000.' Axel sniggers at my shocked expression. Finn and Maia must have $10,000 apiece; Axel, Riley and Naomi's piles are smaller, but probably more than I'd earn in several months waiting tables.

'This is the blind,' Naomi explains, as I try to follow the action. 'First we have the flop, then the turn, then the river.'

'That's about as clear as quantum physics.'

'Try playing your own hand,' Max suggests.

'You can have some of my chips,' Finn offers. 'Max is right. Playing is the easiest way to learn.'

'And lose,' I say. 'Thanks, but count me out. This is one bad habit I definitely can't afford.'

'Bad habits?' Maia gives me an inscrutable smile. 'You said you didn't have any.'

'I don't,' I reply defensively. 'Not really.'

She adds a couple of black chips to her bet. 'I hear someone paid for you to be here, sweetie – clearly somebody believes you have a problem.'

I glare at her. Who told Maia that? Rory? Finn?

'My worst night I lost nearly half a million dollars,' Max confesses, deflecting the conversation.

Naomi's eyes widen. '*Seriously?*'

'I was young,' he shrugs. 'Reckless. The older I got, the less I lost.'

Apart from your family, I think sadly, but don't say it.

'I bet $50k on one hand once when I was blackout drunk,' Axel boasts. 'And won. Man, that was a great night.'

'No war horsing,' Riley growls, her expression disapproving. 'You know the rules.'

I look at her. 'What does that mean?'

'Dwelling on your glory days,' Max explains. 'Romanticising the highs and lows of your addiction. Engaging in pissing contests with other addicts. Point taken, Riley – thanks for the reminder.'

I consider this, remembering the times Franny, Rocco and I would meet up for brunch after a particularly heavy night out, picking it to pieces. Who did or said the most outrageous thing. Quite often me, I realise with a squirm of discomfort. Egged on by Rocco, sure, but I was always up for it. Like that time he bet me $100 to dance on the bar in Sunny's. Or when I stuck a picture of my bare arse on social media and half my friends deleted me.

Not to mention assaulting that guy in the club with a beer bottle. Why the hell did I do that if I wasn't completely off my skull?

For the first time since I arrived here, I'm wondering if I might genuinely have a problem. Not a full-blown addiction, perhaps, but can I honestly claim I'm in control of my life?

'Fuck yeah!' Axel cheers, throwing down his cards in triumph.

'That's me out.' Naomi gets up from the table and goes to sit on the terrace wall. I join her, and we watch the sun sink into the horizon, bathing the desert in liquid gold. For ten minutes or so I'm perfectly content, listening to the chatter in the background, the crack and spit of the logs on the fire, the sound of the cicadas singing in the trees around us.

'For most people truth is a fucking inconvenience.' Axel's voice snaps me out of my reverie; his luck must have run out, because he's sounding increasingly belligerent. 'Everything is fractured. All we can do is tear it down, and that's work, man, whatever you believe.'

'So smashing things up is work now?' Max counters, clearly exasperated. 'Give me a break. It's fucking child's play. Stick the worst possible interpretation on anything your opponents say, and always argue in bad faith. If someone disagrees with you, call it a dog whistle. Frame yourself as the ennobled victim and insist every single thing you think or do is normal and acceptable.'

'Better than the status quo.' Axel kicks at a loose stone in the paving. 'You just gotta commit to doing it right. Organise protests and riots—'

'Oh yeah, sure, dude.' Finn's voice drips with sarcasm. 'Disrupt and dismantle, deconstruct and subvert. Burn it all down. And what are you gonna put in its place, huh? Some fucking Marxist utopia? Have you actually read *any* history, Axel?'

'Hey, guys,' Naomi calls over. 'Let's keep it civil, okay?' She turns back and rolls her eyes at me.

'Why does Axel always wear that hat?' I whisper. 'His head must be baking.'

She laughs. 'Because his hair is receding – that's why you never see him in the pool. Plus he thinks it looks rad and edgy.'

'Is he some kind of anarchist?' I ask, tuning out of the argument.

'He likes to think so.' Naomi sighs. 'As my dad says, there's no one more ruthless than an idealist.' She glances back at the group gathered around the card table. 'Axel's showing off for Maia. He's got the hots for her, though it's obvious she's not interested in him – I reckon she's set her sights on someone else.'

'Who?' I feel a stir of unease. '*Finn?*'

'I'm not saying.' Naomi grins, tapping the side of her nose. 'It's just a hunch – though I'd bet my last bottle of vodka on it.'

'But isn't hooking up against the rules?'

Naomi rolls her eyes again. 'Of course, but that doesn't mean it never happens. Except in Riley's case,' she whispers. 'She has a huge crush on Rory, but it's definitely not reciprocated.'

'Has she?' I blink. Clearly I've been oblivious to all this – but then I always am. I never have any inkling when someone is interested in me, not until they make it obvious.

'Yeah, it's one reason she's so super sensitive around him.'

'Jesus, I can't keep up. I thought this place was about recovering, not hooking up with people.'

Naomi flashes me another amused smile. 'You know, sometimes you come across as much younger than thirty-two, Zoey.'

She leans back, studying the stars appearing overhead. 'It happens, but everyone knows rehab relationships are ephemeral; the first taste of the real world and they evaporate.'

'I'm out,' I hear Finn declare. I peer round at his pile of chips and see it has dwindled to one yellow. Shit. That's a lot of money to lose. I study his face as he gets to his feet – he doesn't seem bothered.

'Come on, Finley, man,' Axel moans. 'Get some more chips. It's not like Daddy can't afford it.'

Finn ignores him. He chucks another couple of logs on the fire, then sits beside us, studying a particularly large saguaro a few yards beyond the boundary wall. 'You two nervous about the ceremony tomorrow?' he asks. 'It's a first for both of you, isn't it?'

'Yeah,' Naomi replies. 'Actually I haven't decided whether to do it.'

'You have to!' I protest. 'Or I'll lose my nerve too.'

'You'll be fine,' Finn reassures her. 'Just relax and go with it.'

'How many ceremonies have you done?' I ask him.

'Only one.'

'What was it like?' Maia joins us, placing herself next to Finn. I allow myself a frisson of envy, careful not to let it show on my face. She looks so beautiful, sitting there, like a perfect china doll. I always assumed those social media pictures she posts were heavily photoshopped, but now I'm not so sure.

'Hard to explain,' Finn replies. 'I think ayahuasca is different for everybody.'

'Everyone keeps saying that.' Maia sighs, picking up a strand of her hair and examining the end. 'Whoever you ask, it's the only answer you get.'

Why is she here? I wonder, not for the first time. A week on from her arrival, I'm still not clear what's brought Maia to the Sanctuary – or what she hopes to get out of it.

'Ed said it was the most transformative thing that ever happened to him,' Naomi says. 'He told me that in his first ceremony he and this guy Luke, who was here at the same time, actually met up in their visions.'

Maia frowns. 'What do you mean?'

'Apparently they both shared the same hallucination,' she explains. 'A spirit revealed that they were soul twins or something, that together they could transform the world.'

'Sounds like some wishful thinking right there.' Finn examines a large ant that's crawling up his leg. 'Ed's a great guy, but he can be a bit grandiose.'

'Someone called me that once,' Maia pouts.

'I'm not sure it's possible for you to be grandiose.' Naomi gives her a hug. 'You've pretty much got it all.'

'Except love,' she sighs, 'and happiness.' She gazes at us. 'What makes you happy?'

I shrug. 'Having a good time . . .'

'All the time?' Finn raises an eyebrow at me.

'*Spinal Tap!*' I grin, giving him a high five.

'Spinal what?' Maia frowns, confused.

'It's a film from the eighties,' Naomi tells her. 'About a spoof rock band.'

'A rockumentary,' I quip, and Finn and I start giggling.

Maia frowns at the pair of us. 'Screw you,' she says, stomping off.

'Oh God,' I groan, once I've recovered. 'She thinks we're taking the piss out of her.'

'She'll get over it.' Finn stands, still grinning. 'I'm going for a swim. Fancy a dip?' He looks at both of us.

'I'm gonna get an early night,' Naomi says. 'Big day tomorrow.'

'You ducking out the game?' Axel jeers as we pass him. 'What's the problem, Finley? Daddy got you on a tight leash?'

Beside me, Finn's hand reflexively closes into a fist.

'Leave it,' I say quietly. 'He's not worth it.'

'You okay?' I ask Finn, once we're out of earshot.

He shakes his head. 'Fuck that guy. He's something else.'

'Axel's a walking personality disorder. He'll get himself killed one of these days.'

'That day can't come soon enough,' Finn mutters, taking off his clothes to reveal he's already wearing swimming trunks. 'He gets right up my nose. I can't stand those fucking trust fund kids with a saviour complex. He's fuelled by resentment because his dad called his bluff.'

'How do you mean?'

'Basically his father gave him a choice – give up the activism or his inheritance, the latter contingent on him coming here and getting his shit together. Guess which one he chose?'

I smile. 'Don't let him get to you, Finn.'

'Oh, I can handle Axel.' He sighs. 'It's the people who appear fine on the surface but are full of suppressed rage – those are the ones you need to watch out for.' He looks at me standing there. 'You not coming in?'

'Forgot my costume,' I say. 'I'll watch you.'

'Good heavens, Zoey, swim in your underwear. I don't care.'

I grimace, then strip to my T-shirt and knickers, while Finn executes a perfect dive into the deep end. In a few strokes he surfaces, resting his arms on the edge of the pool and grinning up at me.

'Very fetching, Baxter.'

I do a little curtsey to hide my embarrassment and get in the water.

'Right. Stand in the shallow end here, and place your hands on the side.' Finn demonstrates. 'Then simply lift and straighten out. I'll support you.'

I do as he says, stupidly conscious of his hand pressing against my stomach as I float.

'Lie flat on the surface and kick your legs a little to stop them drifting down. Can you feel how the water pushes you upwards?'

I nod. 'But you're holding me up too.'

'Am I?' Finn lifts both arms, and I realise I'm floating on my own. There's a second or two of panic, then I relax into it.

'Try what we did before. Put your head in the water and count to ten.'

Lowering my face, arms outstretched, I make myself do it.

'You see?' Finn grins as I come up for air. 'Easy, right?'

I give him a dubious smile.

'Now do it again. Hold your breath with your head under, only this time kick your legs like this' – Finn scissors his legs in the water – 'and pull yourself with your arms.' He mimics a breast stroke in the air. 'Remember, you're in the shallow end, so you can stand up whenever. Reckon you can give it a try?'

I chew my lip. Hesitating.

'I just lost ten grand to a total asshole, Zoey.' Finn gazes at me. 'I need you to help me redeem the rest of this evening.'

I pull the wet hair away from my face, curiously touched; if this is a ploy to get me to comply, it's working. I walk to the side of the pool and summon up my willpower.

'Take a breath, head down, push off from the edge,' Finn encourages me. 'You'll be across in a few strokes.'

I don't think, I just do it. A moment later I'm moving through the water, counting off the seconds, five . . . six . . . seven. At eight, my hand touches the opposite side of the pool and I surface, gasping.

'I did it!' I squeal. 'I swam right across!'

Finn is grinning from ear to ear. 'You certainly did, Baxter. Well done.'

I punch the air, genuinely elated.

'Let's call it a day.' He gets out of the pool. 'All you have to do now is practise swimming in the shallow end until you're more confident, then you can do lengths.'

He retrieves a couple of towels, handing one to me. We wrap ourselves up and stretch out on the loungers, studying the stars now crowding the darkening sky. Below us, Riley and Axel bicker as the game continues.

'I hope to God Riley is winning,' Finn murmurs.

I turn to look at him. 'Is it true you sued your dad?'

'Tried to.'

'Why?'

''Cause his drug is as addictive as hell and it's ruining people's lives.' There's a tension, an anger in Finn's voice that tells me this runs deep. 'And instead of dealing with that, he spends obscene amounts of money trying to cover it up and smear any negative research.'

'So what happened?'

'He kicked me out of the company, obviously. I called off the lawsuit after my sister died – the family had enough to deal with.'

'Have you both made up?' I ask.

Finn does a bark of a laugh. 'Dad doesn't make up with anyone, Zoey. Piss him off, and you're dead to him. Finished. You no longer have any value.'

'He sounds . . .' I search for a tactful word, 'difficult.'

Finn tilts his head towards me and smiles. 'You could say that.' His gaze lingers. 'How about your dad?'

'Alive and well and courting melanoma in Palm Springs, along with his third wife.'

'Ahh, the infamous third wife.' Finn grimaces. 'Also difficult.'

'Yep. Which is why neither of us have spoken to each other in years.'

'You didn't get on?'

I sigh. 'I objected rather vocally to her constant criticism of everything I said and did. Dad took her side. Told me not to contact him again unless I was willing to apologise.'

'And you're not?'

'Not yet. Though I'll concede I was a bit of an arsehole towards her. But it was a two-way street, she said plenty of stuff too, and Dad refused to ever see it.'

'That's rough.' Finn pauses, turning his gaze to the desert. It's getting hard to see the cacti now, as twilight descends into night. 'So no other significant male presence in your life?'

The question prompts a lift of emotion that I instantly suppress. How should I answer that? Am I going to tell him about Marcus?

'Only my Uncle Dan, and my friend Rocco,' I say. 'But he's gay.'

Finn looks back at me. 'So who are you closest to?'

'Mum, I guess. And Dan.'

'What's your type then – romantically, I mean? When it comes to guys – or girls.' He holds his hands up. 'Not making any assumptions here.'

I give this some thought. 'Male, alternative, artistic, termi-nally self-absorbed. Going on past record, anyway.'

'That sucks,' says Finn. 'So nothing serious then?'

'It appears I am deeply commitment-phobic in many areas of my life, not simply in relationships – as Sonoya pointed out at length this morning.'

'Why is that, Zoey, do you think?' Finn turns on his lounger, facing me. Giving me all his attention.

'I don't know.' I shrug. 'I'm only starting to figure it out.' I squint at him. 'How about you? Are you hoping to get back with your wife? Or will you get a new model?'

As soon as the words are out of my mouth, I realise I've gone one pun too far. Finn turns away. 'I don't know either,' he says after a prolonged silence. 'Verity's given me many chances, and I blew them all – I'm not convinced she'll ever trust me again.'

'But you still love her?' I ask, finding I'm dreading the answer.

Finn tips his head back and looks upwards, checking out the crescent moon. 'To be honest, Zoey, I'm starting to wonder if I even know what that is.'

I gaze at him. 'What a pair of fuck-ups we are, eh?'

'We're all misfits here.' Finn sighs. 'Including the staff, I reckon. Going by the argument this morning anyway.'

'You heard it too?'

He nods. 'Something has really got under Alejandro's skin. I thought perhaps it was simply Ed leaving, but I reckon it's more than that.'

'You don't know?'

Finn shakes his head again. Now would be an excellent opportunity to tell him about Ed's email, I realise. Only I don't want to. I don't want to spoil the mood.

But he gets up and grabs his clothes. 'I'm gonna take a leaf out of Naomi's book and hit the sack. Long day tomorrow, what with the ceremony and everything.' He studies me. 'You nervous?'

I nod.

'You'll be okay.' He squeezes my shoulder and walks away. I watch him leave, pushing down my disappointment. Talking to

Finn is starting to feel like confiding in a friend. In someone I can trust.

Then I remember what Naomi said earlier, about rehab relationships being ephemeral. *The first taste of the real world and they evaporate.*

Take note, Zoey. No point indulging this crush.

Besides, Finn's so far out of your league it's ridiculous.

19

Ceremony time.

Me, Naomi, Finn, Axel, Maia and Max, sitting in a semicircle in the Top, each with a padded mat and pillow, plus a couple of thick wool blankets woven with an Aztec design. Beside each of our makeshift beds, a plastic bucket, several rolls of loo paper, and a large bottle of water.

I'm praying I won't need the bucket. The thought of throwing up in front of other people revolts me – even after a skinful, I've always made it to the loo in time.

Do you really want to do this? asks a persistent voice in my head.

Are you sure it's a good idea?

I glance at Naomi, who looks fidgety and nervous. Finn and Max, who've done this before, seem more relaxed, even excited. Maia's expression is obscured by the huge sunglasses she insists on wearing, even indoors. Axel is lying on his mat with his eyes closed – impossible to tell what's going through his mind.

I'm scared, I admit to myself, giving Naomi a thumbs-up of solidarity. I can't say I'm looking forward to an encounter with my inner demons – I doubt they're entities I want to hang out with.

Finn catches my eye and winks at me, a half-smile playing on his lips, and I wish I'd chosen a space closer to him. I could use the reassurance, I think, remembering his kindness yesterday in teaching me how to swim.

You can do this, I tell myself, focusing on what Rory said this morning. Whatever you fear or experience, try to welcome it. Don't run or fight it. Everything ayahuasca shows you is there to teach you something.

Be prepared for it to get intense. Very intense, he'd stressed, gazing at each of us, one by one. View the purging and crying as a gateway, an essential first step to eliminate negativity, toxicity and harmful energy.

A minute later Rory arrives, Tamara, Sonoya and Alejandro on his heels. Alejandro is carrying a tray of lit candles which he places at intervals behind us; Sonoya sets up the CD player and fills the tent with soft Native American music.

The effect is curiously like sitting in the centre of a magic circle, and the atmosphere shifts from nerves to anticipation. Using one of the candles, Tamara lights what appears to be a bundle of dried sticks, and proceeds to walk around the back of the tent, waving the smoke in the air. Sage, I recall from Rory's rundown this morning – to ritually cleanse the room of negative energy.

I glance at Naomi again, and catch the hint of an eye roll. Clearly she's thinking exactly the same thing – *What the fuck have we got ourselves into?*

Sonoya, Rory, Tamara and Alejandro take their places in the circle, and for the next half-hour Rory leads us in breathing exercises, much like the ones we do with Tamara in yoga. Breathe into your lower diaphragm and out through your head chakra or something.

Eventually Alejandro disappears for a few minutes, returning with a large plastic bottle filled with thick brownish liquid. Rory starts intoning some sort of prayer, then takes the bottle from Alejandro and blows into it, as if dispersing evil spirits. Max is watching him intently, but Axel is openly smirking.

'Don't forget, everyone's experience of the vine is different and unique,' Rory says, his expression so solemn I too get an urge to giggle. 'Remember the objective you set this morning. And don't fight it. Open yourself up to whatever it has to teach you.'

'Amen,' says Axel sarcastically.

Rory ignores him, calling us up one at a time to the front of the circle, starting with Naomi. 'Set your intention,' he says gravely as Tamara pours the thick brown liquid into a shot glass and hands it to her. Naomi hesitates, then downs it in one, pulling a face that says everything about the flavour.

Finn goes next, then Axel, sauntering up to Rory as if ordering a pint from a bar. After Max, it's my turn.

'Set your intention,' Rory repeats as Tamara passes me the glass. *Show me who I've become*, I say in my head. It's what I decided on this morning, after Rory made various suggestions – though now I'm not so sure it's actually what I want.

I peer at the syrupy brown sludge in the little glass, hoping they've added sugar or flavouring to make it more palatable. Down the hatch, I decide, and throw the viscous mixture into my throat so fast I start gagging and coughing. It's vile. Like engine oil might taste if mixed with vinegar, the flavour both rancid and bittersweet.

When Maia's had her dose, lingering to whisper something to Rory while Tamara's back is turned, we all return to our mats, sitting or lying facing the centre of the room, as instructed. Without warning, Tamara blows out all the candles, leaving us in pitch darkness. I pull the blanket closer around me.

In the background Rory begins a sing-song chant in a language I don't recognise. I succumb to a surge of fear. *You're fine*, I reassure myself, steadying my breathing. Nothing can go wrong. Rory, Tamara, Sonoya and Alejandro are all here to watch over us – they've done this dozens of times before. They know what they're doing.

I try to relax. *You're safe*, I repeat to myself. *Nothing bad is going to happen.*

Remember to breathe, like Rory said. Just breathe.

And welcome what comes.

The minutes tick past. The darkness, the sheer weirdness of the situation warps my sense of time. How long have I been here? Half an hour? More? A weird buzzing starts in my head. Despite the chill in the tent after sundown, all at once my body is filled with heat. My heart begins to race in my chest.

What's happening? I throw off the blankets and wriggle out of my jumper, then lie back down, closing my eyes again.

Beside me, the sound of somebody retching. One of the guys. Max? Finn? A faint rippling starts in my body. I feel . . . strange. Dislocated.

In the blackness behind my eyelids, shapes and shifting shadows appear. Then all of a sudden the medicine grabs me and drags me into another reality. My vision explodes into fractals of infinite complexity, an impossible, ever-fluctuating kaleidoscope of crazy geometry, a spiralling, swirling, surging synaesthesia of energy and vibrant colour.

It's stupefying, crazily beautiful, and totally incomprehensible. Time stretches and elongates, each moment sliding seamlessly into the next as the ayahuasca vine winds itself around my perceptions, its grip tightening with every second.

'What the fuck?' I hear myself gasp, before I'm assaulted by a surge of dizziness and nausea.

I open my eyes, terrified. Some of the candles have been relit, and as I gaze around, the space surrounding me starts to bend and fold. A throbbing sound grows inside my head. When I move my hands they shimmer and sparkle, leaving a trail in the air.

'Oh God.' I turn to see Naomi curled up in a ball, moaning. Sonoya by her side, rubbing her back.

I am safe, I mutter to myself, remembering what Rory said – *The medicine will only give you as much as you can handle.*

And exactly what you need.

No going back now, Zoey, a soft feminine voice whispers in my head. *Nothing to do but surrender.*

So I do. I lie down and close my eyes again, and watch the parade of plants and serpents, birds and animals, bounding, soaring, twisting and racing at lightning speed through my inner world, as though exploring a new habitat. At first, they ignore me, but after a while, a fantastical cougar-like animal stops and peers into my eyes, having a closer look before darting away. Over and over, the creatures visit me. Curious, yet somehow indifferent to my presence among them.

Rory starts singing again. An *icaros*, I remember he called it – a sacred song. Naomi whimpers, and there's a sound of vomiting from several directions. As if on cue, I'm immediately racked by the worst nausea I've ever experienced, rising up into my throat like a huge ball of bad energy that Rory's song seems to command my body to expel.

A loud groan that I realise is coming from me. I sit, grab my plastic bucket and bring up the contents of my stomach, retching and heaving, barely able to breathe between convulsions. I stare down at the tangle of luminous neon snakes writhing around in my bucket, spilling over the sides and disappearing into the near-darkness.

I recoil in horror.

Oh God. *What the fuck have I done to myself?*

A hand on my back. Tamara's voice in my ear. 'It's okay,' she whispers. 'You're expelling all the darkness from within you – the fear, the anxieties, the stress, the regrets, the hatred and self-loathing.'

Again and again it happens, wave after relentless wave. My throat, my stomach, my muscles ache from being sick, my heart pounding and thudding with every spasm.

I sense Alejandro moving around the circle, offering a second dose. To my surprise I straighten up and accept it without hesitation. Throw it down again.

It's thicker this time, richer and stronger. I'm leaving the shallows and diving into the deep end now – the vine of the soul, as Rory calls it, opening every door so I can explore all the contents, all the things I'd locked away.

'I don't love myself,' I hear myself sob. 'I've abandoned myself.'

A voice answers. A voice in my head, a whisper from the desert.

Don't be afraid, Zoey.

But I am afraid. I'm terrified because suddenly I know what's coming. I know what's coming and I can't face it.

I get up and sprint out of the tent, running in bare feet across the stony ground, ignoring the pain. My awareness shrinks to nothing but my body and the moment. My head and racing heart. The jagged, laboured sound of my breathing. I run and run then collapse onto the earth, and from deep inside recall my intention:

Show me to myself.

Suddenly I shoot from my body straight up into the heavens. My consciousness fragments into billions of tiny points of light and energy. I'm everywhere, all at once. And nowhere at all. I've gone, and yet am still here. Dreaming, but conscious.

I'm not afraid any more. I feel completely . . . at one with everything. Myself, the earth, the skies, the infinite stars, the universe.

You have to stop running, Zoey, says a voice.

Turn and face yourself.

An instant later, I'm consumed with memories from the past. All the pain and disappointment I've ever experienced fill every corner of my mind. My whole life appears before me. I see visions of myself and Marcus as children. I overhear my parents arguing, see my mother crying in the kitchen after my father left. I watch all of us growing older, our skin thickening and our hair turning coarser, right before my eyes.

Back in the tent Rory sings a haunting melody. I'm sorry now, ashamed for ever doubting him, for mocking his sincerity, and I cry and cry like I've never cried before.

On and on it goes, all the times I argued and misunderstood. All the times I hardened my heart and refused forgiveness. All the times I ran from real connection, real intimacy. I see every moment I resisted, shrank away. Every fear and doubt and insecurity. I'm shown all my wrong-headed ideas and pretensions and stupid, thoughtless impulses. All the lost opportunities, all the time I wasted, all the help I rejected, the disappointment on other people's faces.

Somewhere in the distance, Axel is howling and screaming like an animal in pain. Beneath, beyond, Rory's voice rises and falls as he chants and sings, and I sense his awareness everywhere around me as I relive each moment, my entire life unfolding all over again, this time showing me what I should have done or said, this time experiencing exactly how much love I withheld. I see my mother's loneliness and disappointment, my father's attempts to reach through my anger and judgement. Dan's patience, refraining from expressing his disquiet about the mess I'm making of my life. I see Marcus, desperate for forgiveness, for understanding. I see everything that happened since I abandoned my place at university, all the way to that night in the club in New York.

And in that moment I'm there again. Music pulsing through me as I leave the spiky-haired girl in the toilet. I'm angry. Really angry, as I search out the man who left those marks on her neck. Who reduced her to a sobbing, broken wreck.

I find him by the bar, all tattoos and attitude. A walking cliché, right down to the sneer on his face as I approach, rage surging through me.

'Why?' I scream against the loud thump of the music. '*Why did you fucking do that to her?*'

Still screaming, still shouting, as the bouncers haul me from the club and shut me in the back office until the police arrive.

How did I let everything end up like this?

I've been so difficult, so lost, so wild. I have to love myself, I realise. I'm always running away. Running around the world. Running from home to New York and back again whenever things get tough. Running from purpose, responsibility, embracing any distraction to avoid dealing with myself. Always making excuses. Dulling my senses with alcohol and cigarettes.

Running, always, from love.

'Zoey.'

Slowly I become aware I'm not alone.

'Breathe, Zoey,' Sonoya's voice reminds me. 'Breathe in and out and open yourself to whatever comes up. Remember what Rory said – there are no wrong answers, and if you feel like you're dying, die and see what comes after.'

I have everything I need, I finally understand. Right here, inside.

I had it all along.

Sonoya's hand on my shoulder as I start crying again. 'Don't fight it,' she whispers. 'Embrace it. Tell me what happened, Zoey. Tell me what you've been too afraid to confront.'

So I do.

20

'Okay, let's get started.'

Rory gazes around the Top. The paraphernalia from last night has been cleared away, the wooden chairs returned to a circle. 'I hope all of you are feeling rested. Group today is focused on helping you process what you learned last night during the ceremony.'

He slides his gaze across each of us, and I do the same. Riley isn't here. Max and Finn seem to be in a stupor of exhaustion, their eyes glazed with lack of sleep. Naomi is sitting with a quiet smile on her face, her wavy brown hair clipped back and her skin as fresh and dewy as ever. Maia is hunched over, staring at the ground.

It's Axel who really snags my attention. It takes a moment to realise what's so different about him – he's not wearing that stupid beanie. His hair, sparse at the temples, is short and mussy with sweat; without his hat, his whole face looks oddly naked.

'So who'd like to relate their experience of the medicine?' Rory continues. 'Only what you're willing to share. I appreciate some of it might be very private, and that's fine.'

Max raises his hand. Rory straightens up in his seat, focusing his attention as Max takes a deep breath, and makes eye contact with each of us in turn. 'Man, it was fucked.' He closes his eyes briefly as if trying to recall precisely what he'd felt and seen. 'I mean, I've done it before, but the previous time was more . . .

disjointed. Just the geometry stuff, you know, so I wasn't prepared for what happened.' He stops, fades off into his thoughts.

'Did it help?' Tamara asks. She's wearing a vibrant gold and emerald green sundress I've not seen before, that reminds me of the kaleidoscope of colours in my visions last night. She appears fresh and bright, despite how little sleep she probably got.

In contrast, Rory looks particularly rough, pale and haggard, as if he hasn't slept at all, and Sonoya is missing entirely.

'Shit, I don't know.' Max clears his throat. 'I suppose so. It was all so much to take in. I did what Rory suggested, wrote a lot of it down before I went to sleep, and more this morning. Everything I can recall.'

'So what was it like?' Axel asks, his expression curious. No hint of irony in his tone.

'Gruelling. Almost unbearable, but in a good way – or at least, I think it will be good.' Max sighs, scratching the stubble on his cheek, and the chair creaks as he shifts his weight. 'To tell the truth, I don't know how to describe it. It was like . . . like I was shown the gap . . . no, the gulf, *the chasm*, between who I believed I was and who I actually am. It was . . .' he grasps for the word, 'intensely *painful*. A shortcut to a higher way of viewing reality. Like being stripped of the ego, but at the same time revealing what a shitshow you end up with when you let it run your life.'

'That's why ayahuasca is considered sacred.' Rory massages his forehead, clearly struggling to appear brighter than he feels. 'It's not a recreational drug. It's not fun and it's not easy. It can drag things up deep in your subconscious. It can be terrifying.'

'Yeah,' Max nods his head. 'It was like staring into the world's most truthful mirror, one that could see right into your soul. It was . . . humbling. But also like a horror show, and you can't turn away.'

He gazes at us. Not in that normal way people look at each other, but his eyes locking first on mine, then on Finn's, then around the circle, as if he expects all of us to understand.

And I do. That's the weird thing. I know *exactly* what Max means.

I close my eyes, flashing back to those visions while I lay on the ground in the desert. The life review that played out in my head. The sense that I was being shown the very essence of myself, and precisely how I had fucked up my life, in every excruciating, agonising detail – including that terrible night in the club.

You have to stop running, Zoey.

'It was the same for me, man,' Axel's voice pulls me back. 'The medicine totally kicked my butt.'

I snap my eyes open and stare at him. I can't get over how different he seems, and it's not simply the missing beanie. It's his whole demeanour that's so odd.

Earnest, even excited.

'The problem is with thinking,' he continues, his gaze locking with Max, who frowns at him, probably as freaked out by this change in Axel as I am. 'Thinking is our core addiction. I don't just mean us, here, but everyone – or at least most people on the planet. I realised last night, when I turned into a coyote, that our essential problem is we're addicted to our thoughts.'

Rory studies him, but doesn't appear particularly surprised. Tamara simply regards him with her usual beatific smile. I glance at Finn, and our eyes meet; his widen imperceptibly, a *what-the-fuck?* look.

'Our mind drip feeds thoughts to us like a drug to keep us in the story,' Axel continues, his hands dancing as he speaks, as if re-enacting some inner drama. 'Hell is living in that made-up world, reacting to our emotions, to the things we perceive as outside ourselves.'

'The story?' Finn frowns. 'How do you mean?'

'This.' Axel gestures around the Top. 'Everything, what we believe is real, our lives, the world. It's completely constructed by our thoughts, our reactions, the stories we tell ourselves. Last night I saw what the world would be like if we stepped away from that and experienced reality as it really *is*. You know, like, *raw*. The medicine, it sort of explodes your ego, and you get to see what's left . . . which is all that there is.'

'The world is constructed by our own thoughts?' Naomi's brow furrows in confusion. 'You mean like a video game?'

'Or *The Matrix*?' Tamara suggests. 'Like an alternate reality?'

'Yeah, a colleague of mine said ayahuasca is a kind of Oracle, a mirror to the soul,' Max says. 'You can plug in any question you have and get the answer – only you might not like it.'

'Sort of . . . I guess,' Axel agrees. 'I haven't entirely worked it all out yet. I'm going to, but there's a lot of garbage I need to clean up within myself first. I'm writing it all down. Every single thing I remember. And there was so much of it. When I was outside the Top, when Tamara was with me, I became a coyote, then an eagle, then another time I was a Native American warrior, and I killed some guy, then I turned into a snake—'

Finn snorts, his expression sceptical. Clearly he thinks Axel's winding us up.

Axel merely blinks, but stops talking.

'Finn,' Rory asks, 'do you have anything you'd like to share?'

Finn shakes his head. 'I'll pass.'

Rory turns to Maia. She's still hunched over, still staring at the ground.

'Maia?' he prompts, and she raises her head wearily. My eyes widen in surprise. She's not wearing her sunglasses, nor any make-up, and the effect is disconcerting. Gone is that hard, unreachable icon; in her place is someone far younger – and far more vulnerable.

'I don't want to talk about it,' she mumbles, dropping her head again.

What happened, I wonder? Did she have a bad trip? She looks exhausted. Broken.

Rory's gaze lingers for a moment, then moves on. 'Naomi, how was it for you?'

Naomi shrugs. 'It was . . . fascinating. I didn't have any amazing breakthroughs, not like some people here.' She glances at Axel, who smiles back at her without a hint of mockery. 'I just saw lots of colours and patterns and stuff.'

'Perhaps next time you'll go deeper,' Tamara reassures her. 'That's often how it works, I've found.'

'Maybe,' Naomi nods. 'To be honest, it sounds rather scary. I'm not sure I want to be confronted with all that.'

'I don't blame you,' Max says. 'Bits of it were harrowing. No sugar-coating, no excuses, no rationalisations. Simply the stark reality of who you are. It wasn't entirely pleasant.'

'Yes, that's exactly right,' Rory agrees. 'And it takes a great deal of courage to face it.' He turns to me. 'How about you, Zoey?'

I sigh, considering what to say. 'I don't think I can put it all into words. There was so much.' Out of the corner of my eye I see Finn studying me. 'I saw all the patterns, the colours, all that stuff. It was magnificent, and sort of terrifying too.'

'Yeah,' Max agrees. 'How could all that just be in your mind?'

'Maybe it's not,' Tamara suggests. 'I can only speak for myself, but I believe the ceremonies take you out of your mind, which acts as a filter to block most of what we deem reality. What you saw is some of what's out there, but your brain normally prevents you from seeing it.'

'Like dead bodies?' Maia says suddenly. She lifts her head and gives Rory a curiously accusing look, then gets up and leaves the tent.

Rory glances at his watch, clearly disquieted. 'Perhaps we'll call it a day.'

At that moment, Mike appears, looking more hassled and sweaty than ever. 'We have to clear the site this afternoon,' he says, hovering behind Rory. 'I'm afraid we have a problem with the electrics again and we need to turn the power off for a few hours while we fix it. We've organised a barbecue up at Tolteca Rocks, leaving at four.'

'No way,' Naomi moans. 'I'll stay in my room and catch up on some sleep.'

'Not an option,' Mike says. 'Sorry. The only people remaining on site will be Sonoya and me.'

Max frowns. 'What about Alejandro and Elena?'

'Yes, of course.' Mike's face flushes, as if he's blundered somehow. 'They'll remain here, but Rory and Tamara will accompany you.'

With that he disappears. I glance at Finn, who looks as puzzled as I feel. Why schedule this at such late notice? And right after the ceremony, when everyone's energy levels are depleted?

I turn to Rory, who's frowning at the floor. He doesn't appear too happy about it either. Only Tamara seems energised by the prospect, but then she's never fazed by anything.

'I'll go help Elena prepare the food,' she says, bouncing to her feet. 'See you all later.'

21

'Good thing Fariha isn't here – she'd totally freak out over these kebabs.'

Naomi hands one to me, squatting on a nearby rock. She pulls a chunk of meat from her bamboo skewer and groans with pleasure. 'These are delicious. It must be the wood smoke.' She gives a thumbs-up to Rory, who's manning the barbecue, a metal grill suspended over an open fire.

'Who's Fariha?' I ask, taking a bite. Naomi's right. The kebabs are fabulous, cooked with thyme like a Greek souflaki. I wash mine down with a slug of orange juice. It tastes different, I notice; sharper, even more intense. Ever since I woke this morning, my senses seem heightened, as if I'm experiencing a hyper-real version of the normal world.

Probably a hangover from the ayahuasca – Rory warned us it would take a while to clear our systems.

'Fariha left a few weeks before you arrived,' Naomi explains. 'In fact she was kicked out. But she was incredibly picky about food – wouldn't touch anything that hadn't been practically sterilised first.'

'Is that why she had to leave?'

'God, no. She smuggled in a consignment of coke and marijuana.'

Riley actually laughs, and takes a break from eye-balling Rory. 'That was some party. She was wild, a real Kuwaiti princess, expelled from every boarding and finishing school she was sent to.'

'Where is she now?' I ask.

'Back in Kuwait, I think,' Naomi replies. 'I felt for her – she seemed genuinely scared when she left. Women who don't behave aren't well tolerated there.'

'Or anywhere,' Riley mutters darkly.

I give her an enquiring look, but she ignores me, returning her attention to Rory. He's talking to Maia, who I notice has changed into a pair of high-cut khaki shorts and a pretty lemon-yellow blouse – even without make-up she's the epitome of wilderness chic.

'You look tired,' Naomi says to me.

'I'm knackered,' I confess. It was only an hour's hike to the rocky outcrop where we're having the barbecue, but after the drama of last night's ceremony, and group earlier, I'm ready to drop. 'I may not leave this place any the wiser, but at least I'll be fitter. Who knew the road to healing is so physically arduous?'

'Pain is the price of freedom,' Naomi intones in a passable imitation of Sonoya's deadpan delivery. 'The previous rehab I went to was practically a spa; this one feels more like a boot camp – with psychedelics thrown in for light relief.' She swallows the rest of her kebab and wipes her fingers on a tissue. 'What wouldn't I give though for a couple of beers to wash this down.'

'There's Mexican root beer.' I nod at the stash of food and drink on the ground behind Rory.

Naomi pulls a face. 'That stuff's loaded with sugar – it'll kill you quicker than alcohol. You want another kebab?'

'No thanks, I'm stuffed. But don't let me stop you.'

While Naomi goes off to reload her plate, I lean back and take in the scene. As the sun sinks towards the horizon, the heat is abating, the air almost comfortable. The barbecue site is a lovely spot, surrounded by large boulders and a few trees, which cast welcome shade. Tamara is sitting a few yards away, talking to Max and Axel, who's now wearing a leather ranger's hat in place of his beanie.

I look around for Finn, but there's no sign of him. We've barely spoken since the ceremony last night. He disappeared to his room right after Mike's announcement, only re-emerging when we set off this afternoon. But something in his manner, a return to his old aloofness, warned me off talking to him – all the way here, he trailed a hundred yards or so behind everybody, making it clear he wanted to be left alone.

All at once, I'm so sleepy I have to close my eyes. I rest against the rock, using the sweater I brought with me to cushion my head, tipping my broad-brimmed hat to shade my face. Within seconds, I'm lost in a confusion of dreams that echo the visions from last night. I'm hearing those songs again, the ones Rory sang, and I'm rising up into the sun-drenched sky, and it's like floating in the water. I'm weightless and free, and I wonder how I could ever have forgotten how easy it is to surrender and let yourself be lifted ever upwards.

A shout pulls me back. I sit up, assuming it was Riley, but it's Maia who woke me. She's standing about thirty feet away, gesticulating at Rory, while Tamara hurries towards them both.

'It wasn't a hallucination,' she cries, her voice brittle with emotion, then covers her face with both hands.

'Maia, calm down!' Rory's tone is edged with desperation, more pleading than reassuring.

'I told you. I saw somebody in—'

Rory cuts in. 'I explained that during the ceremony you may experience visions—'

'I DID NOT FUCKING IMAGINE THIS!' Maia yells over him. 'I wasn't hallucinating or seeing things. It was *real*.'

'Maia, please.' Tamara's voice is steady and soothing. 'Let's go for a walk. We'll talk about this together.'

I don't catch Maia's response, but a few seconds later she runs off, Tamara and Rory rushing after her. Everyone stares in their wake, their expressions shocked. It's clear what we're all thinking – what the fuck was that about?

'Sounds as if she had a bad trip last night.' Naomi grimaces as she sits back beside me. 'It can get very scary.'

I frown. 'You have any idea what she saw? Or thinks she saw?'

'Nope. She's been in her room most of the time. I'm surprised she came here with us.'

'She's a fucking diva,' Riley mutters, her eyes fixed on the figures in the distance. 'I wish she'd clear off.'

'That's a bit mean, Riley,' Naomi says. 'After all, your first ceremony didn't go so well, did it?'

Riley glowers at us and turns away.

'Do you think Maia's okay?' I whisper to Naomi. 'She seems really . . . volatile.'

'She'll be fine, but I doubt they'll let her do another ceremony.'

'Were yours scary? Your visions?'

'A bit, yes.' Naomi relaxes back against the rock. 'At one point, I got freaked out by all the crazy stuff I was seeing and thought I was going to die. I had a kind of panic attack, and Rory came over and did that shaman thing and blew a load of smoke over me.'

'Did it work?'

'Yeah, it did.' She laughs. 'Snapped me right out of it. It was really weird.'

'Would you do it again? The ceremony, I mean.'

'I'm not sure. Would you?'

'Not sure either,' I muse. 'It was pretty intense.'

Naomi yawns. 'I ate too much. I'm gonna take a leaf out of your book and have a doze.'

'Here, you can use my jumper as a pillow.' I get up and leave her to it. I go for a wander in the wilderness surrounding our barbecue spot, drinking in the sounds, the smells, the sensation of warm sun on my skin. As I walk, I try to identify what's around me. I've been reading the nature books in the library, plus Rory seems familiar with every inch of the arid landscape and everything that lives in it: saguaro, barrel and hedgehog cacti, ocotillo, buckhorn and cholla make up most of the plants in this area, along with mesquite and palo verde.

But it's the things that move that interest me more: bobcats, cottontail and jack rabbits, coyotes and wolves, desert tortoises. More alarmingly, a number of species of snake, scorpion and tarantula, and something called a gila monster, which according to Rory is a venomous lizard. So far I haven't seen much though, only hawks, a few iguanas, and a brief glimpse of a weird-looking pig called a javelina.

I take a deep breath of clean desert air, relishing the solitude, wondering for the thousandth time who paid for me to be here. I want to know now, more than ever. I want to tell them how grateful I am, how this place might just change my life. I want to say thank you, and let them know that so far, it's been money well spent.

'Penny for them?'

I start with surprise. Turn to see Finn squatting on a rock several yards away, half hidden by a large saguaro.

'Nothing interesting,' I lie. 'I was simply thinking about how refreshing it is to be outside in all this nature. I'm starting not to miss the city so much.'

'You're not going all Thoreau on me, are you?' Finn squints at me. He looks pale and haggard, as if he hasn't slept at all.

'Who?'

'Henry Thoreau, the writer and naturalist.'

'Never heard of him. What's he famous for?'

'Spending a lot of time outdoors.'

I laugh. 'Is that all?'

'An awful lot of time.' Finn grins. 'He was all about true value residing in nature, not in money or any of the other things society values. He hated the whole concept of capitalism, consumerism and luxury, advocating that people should live simply. So basically the polar opposite of my father.'

I gaze at him. Finn seems troubled, but trying to put a cheerful front on it. 'You okay?' I ask. 'You've been a bit quiet since the ceremony.'

He takes a deep breath, releasing it slowly. 'It was a strange night.'

'Yeah. It's hit Maia hard.'

'I know, right? That was odd, her outburst. I wonder what she thought she saw.'

'What did you see?' I sit on a nearby rock, careful to keep my distance. 'You didn't say anything in group.'

Finn sighs. 'It was fucked up. I didn't want to get into it there, in front of everyone.'

I recall what I told Sonoya last night. How she'd hugged me, and thanked me for being so honest with her. She seemed pleased about my 'breakthrough', as she called it.

No way I could talk about that in group – even without Riley there.

'It was like a revelation,' Finn says out of nowhere, gazing at the horizon. 'Though more . . . disjointed. Confusing, but also . . . I don't know how to describe it.'

'You don't have to,' I say quickly.

He glances at me. 'I do think I need to, Zoey. I probably should tell someone.'

'In that case, I'm happy to listen.'

Finn swallows. 'I saw my sister. She came and spoke to me. It was the freakiest thing I've ever experienced,' he whispers, and his eyes well up. I want to go over and hug him, but something holds me back.

'Maddy told me how sorry she was, leaving me like that. How I had to forgive her, and myself.' He swallows again. 'Then she said this really weird thing, but it was so clear.'

I gaze at him. 'What was it?'

'She said . . .' He inhales. Hesitates, then presses on. 'She said "love is all there is; everything else is a distraction".'

I don't speak. There's nothing to say. We let those words hang in the warm air surrounding us, until that moment fades into the next. I watch a bird hover in the sky, wings fluttering. Some kind of raptor, I reckon, a kestrel maybe.

'Can I ask you something?'

'Okay,' Finn replies, but his voice sounds wary.

'What would make someone spend a very large amount of money on somebody else without letting them know that they'd done it?'

'An anonymous benefactor, you mean?'

'I guess so.'

Finn scratches his nose. 'Has this got anything to do with you being here, Zoey? Because if you don't mind me saying, you don't strike me as the type.'

'The type of what?' I fire back, slightly offended.

'The type of person who's used to having whatever they want.'

I squint back at him. Is that a compliment – or a subtle insult?

'Like Maia, you mean?'

Finn snorts. 'Yeah, you could say she represents the extreme end of the spectrum.'

'You don't like her?' I feel an emotion close to relief.

'What's to like?' He sighs, leaning forwards. 'Maia's a human onion. You could peel her back, layer after layer, and every time you think you've got to the core of something authentic, all you'd find under it is more layers of bullshit.'

'That's pretty harsh,' I object, remembering her wry humour by the pool, the distress on her face earlier as she shouted at Rory. 'I don't think she has everything. It must be hard to have a decent relationship if you believe people are with you because of your fame or money.'

Finn shrugs, then turns to me. 'Anyway, you didn't answer my question – are you saying someone has paid for you to be here and you don't know who? Probably a relative of yours.'

'I've no idea who it was.'

There's another lengthy silence. I study the setting sun, the way it sinks towards the horizon, gradually, yet almost perceptible to the eye. How long has it been since I simply sat and observed the world around me? This place is getting under my skin, I realise. Slowing me down, giving me the space to breathe.

'Does it matter?' Finn asks, after a minute or so. 'I can see why you might want to know who paid, but I don't think it's crucial, not to you being here. If anything, it makes it more . . .' he stops.

'More what?'

'More important. An opportunity you should make the most of.'

I consider this. Maybe he's right, maybe not knowing is better.

'For once in my life I'm glad I haven't got my phone,' Finn says after a pause. 'I didn't realise until last night what a drain it is, always checking the news, emails, text messages, social media. How so much of that is negative and depleting.'

He sighs, and his shoulders slump. 'I reckon that's what my sister was trying to tell me. That I need to focus on what's important – all the rest is noise. That I should stop over-analysing, stop blaming myself for everything. Axel's right, thinking is our core addiction, the one underneath all the others. Only we're not aware of it – at least, not most of the time.'

Finn's expression is so forlorn that I throw caution to the wind and reach out to squeeze his hand. To my dismay, he flinches and draws away.

'Sorry,' I mumble, mortified. 'We should go back to the others,' I add, getting to my feet. 'Rory wants to pack up before sunset.'

But Finn keeps his eyes fixed on the distant hills, lost in some world of his own.

I leave him to it.

22

I fall asleep the moment we get back to the Sanctuary, waking as the sun rises the next morning. On impulse, I grab my costume and make my way to the pool, grateful to find it empty. I stand, mesmerised, as a breeze ripples the surface into thousands of tiny sparkling points of light.

How come I never noticed how beautiful it was before?

I gaze out across the desert, to the mountains in the far distance, and what once seemed dry and barren now seems impossibly alive. As if the very hills themselves, the soil, the air, the sky are full of life and energy.

Leaving my towel on a lounger, I step into the water, the delicious coolness sending shivers of pleasure up my spine. Without thinking, without allowing myself to question what I'm about to do, I gently tip backwards, lifting my legs from the bottom and letting my head rest in the water.

I'm floating.

I'm actually floating!

In place of my usual anxiety, I feel a deep trust in the water to hold me up, as if it too is alive, and here to support me. I close my eyes, savouring the sensation of it against my scalp, the way my hair flows out around me.

All this time, it was so easy.

I float for minutes, eyes shut tightly against the glare of the sun. Fragments of the ceremony drift back. The colours. The visions. The extraordinary sense of wonder. There's a lightness in my mind, lingering still, after the gruelling ordeal of that life review.

Why have I been making everything so difficult for myself?

'Zoey.'

I drop my legs and stand. Finn is gazing down at me, and I experience a flash of sadness, of humiliation, remembering how he shied away from me yesterday.

'Mike wants to speak to us all,' he says, acting as if that awkward moment between us never happened. 'In the lounge before breakfast.'

By the time I've changed into my clothes, I'm the last to arrive. All the seats on the sofas and chairs are taken, so I sit on the edge of the coffee table.

Only two people missing, I notice – Maia, and Rory. I've barely seen Maia since her outburst at the barbecue. When she finally reappeared as we were packing up, flanked by Tamara and Rory, she was silent and subdued, the brim of her oversized sunhat pulled low over her face. She ignored everyone on the hike back to the Sanctuary, striding ahead as if hurrying to the safety of her room.

Mike clears his throat. 'Thanks for coming, everybody. There's something difficult that I . . . we need to tell you.' His tone is so hesitant, weary and somehow so un-Mike-like that a sense of foreboding grows in my empty stomach.

'There's no easy way to put this,' he continues, voice falter-ing. 'I'm afraid there was an accident and Alejandro was found in the pool. It appears he hit his head as he fell in, and drowned.'

'You mean *he's dead?*' Naomi gasps, her features rigid with shock. 'What . . . I don't understand. When did you find him?'

'Right after the ceremony.'

'And you're only telling us now?' Finn frowns. 'What the—'

'We didn't want to alarm everyone,' Sonoya cuts in, her expression inscrutable.

'So where is he?' Max demands. 'Alejandro's body. Where is it?'

My attention is caught by Rory. His demeanour is so stiff and tense it's as if hearing this is causing him physical pain.

'The police flew in yesterday, while you were having your barbecue.' Mike swallows again, clearly agitated. 'They took his body with them.'

'So you what . . . invented that crap about the electrics to get us off the premises?' Max looks furious. His cheeks are flushed and he's biting down on his bottom lip, as if to prevent himself saying anything worse.

'I apologise for the subterfuge.' Mike removes a tissue from his trouser pocket and wipes the sweat from his brow. 'We didn't want to cause a stir until the police had been.'

'So they what . . . simply picked him up and flew him out of here?' Finn asks. I glance over, noting his baffled expression.

'Well, not exactly,' Mike blusters, his cheeks flushing crimson. 'They checked around the place, examined the pool and so on. You could see where he struck his head as he fell in.'

Could you? I didn't notice anything amiss this morning.

Did they clean it up already?

'I don't understand.' Naomi seems stunned – and confused. 'Wouldn't there have to be an investigation or something?'

'They'll be carrying out an autopsy, of course,' Sonoya says. 'But the evidence was conclusive. There was a contusion on his right temple where he caught his head as he fell.'

I shudder, remembering my swim only minutes ago. All the while I was floating in the pool, enjoying the sensation of the water on my skin, I had no idea that someone – *Alejandro* – had died there so recently.

On the tail of my bewilderment, a pang of sadness and grief. I really liked Alejandro. I might not have known him for long, but he seemed a genuinely good person.

And now he's gone.

Impossible somehow. Unfathomable.

A wail from the sofa. Riley is crying, her head in her hands, rocking back and forth. Tamara sits next to her and cradles Riley in her arms – to my surprise, Riley lets her.

'We understand this is a huge shock for everyone,' Sonoya continues. 'Alejandro was an integral part of the Sanctuary community, and he will be deeply missed, by all of us. While Mike works on getting someone to replac—' She stops herself, choosing better, more tactful words. 'While Mike finds somebody to take over Alejandro's duties, we want to stress that the Sanctuary will continue to operate normally, and we'll make every effort to ensure this does not interfere with your therapeutic journey.'

Max gives a derisive snort. 'You're fucking kidding, aren't you?' He stares at Sonoya wide-eyed. 'What . . . we're supposed to carry on as usual?'

'If anybody feels they no longer want to complete the programme, we will of course arrange flights and a transfer to the airport,' she replies evenly.

I study her face. To look at her you'd think Sonoya was merely announcing a change to the schedule. She seems completely detached from the bombshell that's been dropped on all of us.

'All activities will proceed as normal,' she carries on, 'but we can discuss this in group later. In the meantime Tamara and I will be available if any of you would like an individual counselling session.'

Max stares at her in disbelief, then gets to his feet without comment and walks out of the lounge.

'Sorry, I have to go too,' Mike says, in a rushed, apologetic tone. 'As you can imagine, I have a great deal to do.'

'Fuck,' says Naomi, trailing me to my room. 'Poor Alejandro. His family must be devastated.'

'I don't think he had any.' I stand at my window while Naomi sits on the bed. 'At least that's what he told me.'

Outside, Rory is hurrying into the nearest storage shed. Did he know about Alejandro when we were at the barbecue? Did Tamara?

I assume so, given the whole thing was set up to get us all out of the way.

Naomi reads my mind. 'Isn't it rather odd they didn't tell us yesterday? I suppose they couldn't have people freaking out while the police were here,' she continues, answering her own question. 'Imagine if Riley had gone into one of her meltdowns.'

I nod, my head a confusion of thoughts. 'Do you think that's what Maia was upset about at the barbecue? She seemed certain she'd seen something, that she wasn't imagining it.'

Naomi's eyes widen as the penny drops. 'What? *You think Maia saw Alejandro's body in the pool?*' She mulls it over. 'I guess it's possible. Though Rory seemed convinced it was down to the ayahuasca, and I don't believe he's the type to lie.'

I ponder this. Naomi has a point. Would Rory try to convince Maia she was hallucinating if what she saw was actually real? It would be a pretty shitty thing to do, and I too have a hard time believing Rory would do that.

'You going to stay here?' Naomi asks, cutting into my thoughts.

'I don't know,' I reply. 'Are you?'

'I guess so.' She sighs. 'Jesus Christ, what I wouldn't give right now for a bottle of wine.'

'Before breakfast?'

Naomi flashes me a rueful smile as she gets up and leaves. 'Trust me, Zoey, it wouldn't be a first.'

Only two of us show up for Tamara's morning yoga session. One of them is Maia. She barely glances in my direction as I grab a mat from the pile and pick a spot on the veranda.

'You okay?' I ask, surprised to see her here after her melt-down yesterday. Is she aware what happened to Alejandro, I wonder? Has anyone told her yet?

I get a wan smile in lieu of a response as she unrolls her Burberry yoga mat – Maia, it seems, brought all her own equipment to the Sanctuary – then returns her gaze to the desert view. Tamara arrives a minute later, her demeanour as cheerful as usual. I study her in amazement. Does anything ever ruffle her feathers? For all you'd know looking at Tamara, nothing out of the ordinary has happened at all.

'Just the pair of you?' She beams at us both.

'Apparently,' I say.

Tamara positions her mat and slowly, assuredly, takes us through the Salute to the Sun yoga sequence that's becoming familiar to me now, and for the first time I find I'm working through it with an intense, almost laser-like concentration. Despite my sadness at the news about Alejandro, it feels good to be here, watching the sun climb above the hills, breathing the sweet desert air, enjoying the warm stretch of my muscles as I push myself into the warrior pose.

'Focus on your breathing,' Tamara reminds us in her soft, soothing voice. 'Picture your first breath, the moment you're born, and all those we take right up until our last. The inhale and the exhale are the metronome of our lives. Whenever you turn your attention to your breath, let it bring you home to yourself. Feel the rhythm in your chest, how it expands and contracts—'

'Ow!' Maia yelps, massaging her leg.

Tamara's forehead furrows with concern. 'You okay?'

'Cramp in my calf. It's fine now.'

I watch Maia out of the corner of my eye as she pulls her long limbs back into the asana. It's only as she bends to roll her mat at the end of the session that I see her face properly. She's been crying. Her skin is bare, her eyes puffy and tired.

I guess she does know about Alejandro.

'Are you all right?' I ask, once Tamara has disappeared.

'Fine,' Maia replies in a clipped, leave-me-alone tone. She puts on her sunglasses, picks up her water bottle, and turns to go.

Something inside me snaps. 'How do you stand it?' I ask, replacing my mat on the pile in the corner of the veranda.

'Stand what?' Maia pauses. Actually looks at me.

'Being so cut off from everyone. Being so aloof. So . . .' I struggle for the right words, 'so *above* everybody. Don't you get lonely? Do you enjoy living like that?'

For a second or two nothing happens. Then Maia's cheek twitches. 'I . . .' She stops. Swallows. I wait for her to continue, but she doesn't. Nor does she leave.

She simply stands there, looking dazed.

'Why not tell me what's going on?' I say, more gently. 'Why were you so upset yesterday? At the barbecue.'

Maia closes her eyes for a moment, seems to come to a decision. 'Let's go to my room.'

She walks away, and I follow, obediently, like one of her little lap dogs. She leads me to the far end of the house, and into another small annex I haven't noticed before. A second later I'm standing in a suite of rooms. There's a spacious lounge, with a vase of fresh flowers on the coffee table between a pair of matching sofas. A leather-topped desk offers a gorgeous view out over the courtyard, and two more doors lead to what I assume are a bedroom and bathroom.

Jesus, how much does this place cost? It's as big as Dan's apartment.

'Have a seat.' Maia gestures to a sofa. 'You want anything to drink?'

'That would be lovely.'

'What would you like?'

'You choose,' I say. 'I'm easy.'

Maia smiles. 'Of course you are.'

She disappears through a door. Again I'm struck by a sharpness in this woman, an intelligence too easily ignored. It occurs to me how difficult it is to have brains as well as beauty. To have to deal with people who can never see past the perfect features, the porcelain skin and large baby-blue eyes. That ineffable aura of wealth and fame.

What must it be like to have nobody see the person you are inside?

Maia returns with two bottles of fruit-infused water, handing one to me. It's cold, straight out of the fridge – she must have her own kitchenette in there.

'If I tell you,' Maia says, settling onto the sofa opposite, folding her legs into an effortless lotus pose, 'will you promise to believe me?'

I nod.

She presses her lips together, considering where to begin. 'During the ceremony, I didn't have a lot of the ayahuasca – only the first dose, and I asked Rory beforehand to make sure it was small. I had a bad trip once, on LSD, and didn't want to go too deep too soon. So not much happened. I saw a few fireworks for a minute or two, then decided to call it a night.'

'Okay.'

'Anyway, as I was walking back, it occurred to me the pool would be empty and I might have a dip. I always do that at home in Pasadena, have a swim before I go to sleep. Only there it's more . . . private. And I was slightly high from the ayahuasca, I guess, and everything was kind of . . . sparkly, so I thought it might be a fun thing to do.'

I nod again, trying not to be irritated by Maia's blithe assumption that it's normal to have your own private pool at home.

'There was nobody around, everyone was busy with the ceremony. I prefer to swim . . . you know . . . naked.'

'Skinny dip?'

'Yes.' She takes a long slug of her drink, and I notice her hand is trembling. 'I took off my clothes and was about to get in . . . and that's when I saw it.' She pauses, bites her bottom lip. Her eyes leave mine and drift towards the ceiling as she blinks away tears.

'What?' I ask, trying not to sound impatient. 'What did you see?'

'A body in the pool.'

I gasp. '*You saw Alejandro?*' So I was right. That was what she was shouting about at the barbecue yesterday.

Poor Maia.

'He was face down, floating in the water. I got dressed as fast as I could and ran into the house and shouted for help, and Mike came out of the office. I told him what I'd seen and he made me stay in my room while he went off to check.'

'That must have been horrible,' I say, with genuine sympathy.

Maia studies me carefully, with an assessing, almost challenging gaze, as if making her mind up about something. 'That wasn't all,' she adds, taking a sip of her drink. 'I noticed a movement in the bushes behind the pool. It was a person, hurrying away.'

I stare at her in horror. '*You're saying there was someone else there?*'

Maia nods. 'I told Mike, and Sonoya. Rory too. They all blamed the ayahuasca. Mike said I was hallucinating, but I know what I saw. After all, they lied to me, Sonoya and Mike. They pretended at first the body in the pool wasn't real, only of course it was, wasn't it?'

I think about this. She's right. Clearly they didn't tell her the truth, not initially. But even though she saw Alejandro's body, it doesn't mean the other bit was real – after all, the ayahuasca made me see all sorts of crazy stuff.

But what if Mike and the others are wrong? What if Maia really did spot someone else by the pool? That would mean somebody was there, when Alejandro was drowning – and instead of raising the alarm, they slipped back into the night.

Why would you do that?

I can't think of a single, non-damning reason.

'I guess you haven't any idea who it was?' I ask Maia. 'The person in the bushes.'

She shakes her head. 'The main pool lights were off and it was pretty dark. I only saw their outline as they disappeared.'

'So you couldn't tell if it was a man or a woman?'

She shakes her head again.

'You didn't go after them?'

Maia gives me a scornful look. 'I went to get help, Zoey. For all I knew, Alejandro was still alive.'

In that case, I'm tempted to ask, *why didn't you try to save him yourself?* But if you spend your whole life with people waiting on you hand and foot, I suppose that might be your first reaction.

'Maia, don't you think Mike has a point?' I say gently. 'I mean, how can you be sure it wasn't just the ayahu—'

'You promised,' she snaps, lips tight with anger. 'You promised to believe me. Besides, he lied to all of us, didn't he? Mike made up that bullshit excuse to get rid of us while they brought the police in.'

I hold up my hands to appease her. 'I am not saying I disbelieve you, I'm simply wondering how you can be so sure. We were all pretty fucked up. I saw all sorts of shit, and none of it was real. As in the sense of it actually happening in the world.'

Maia hugs her knees, chewing the inside of her lip. She looks like a sulky teenager, I think, then berate myself – hallucination or not, the woman has had a nasty shock. 'There's something strange going on here,' she says quietly. 'I can feel it.'

'Feel it?' I frown at her. 'How?'

'The vibe here, the bad energy. So many people are lying in this place. Can't you sense it too?'

I shake my head. 'Nope.'

'That's why I came here,' she sighs. 'To tune into that side of myself, to detox from all the bullshit. My life is so . . . superficial. I wanted space to dive deeper, to feel more. I was hoping that's what the ceremonies would give me.'

I offer a sympathetic smile. I guess she was disappointed then.

'You're probably aware my mother was a psychic,' Maia adds, as if it were common knowledge. For all I know, it could be.

'Err . . . no. Sorry.'

'She was pretty cool,' Maia continues undaunted. 'She could see auras around people, sense their energy. She was also clairvoyant. My mother could take someone's hand and see things that had happened to them, and sometimes events in their future too. I inherited some of it from her. I'm very sensitive to people, to their auras.'

'Okay.' I try to keep the scepticism from my face.

'Like yours,' she says, gazing at me. 'Lots of blue and indigo, but tinged with grey.'

'Is that bad?'

Maia narrows her eyes at me. 'I know you're not being honest about what happened with that girl Laura. It's there, in your aura, even after the ayahuasca, even after all the purging. And it's not going away until you face it.'

I sit there, mouth open, stunned into silence. Then get up and leave.

23

I find Finn sitting on the bench at the top of the veg patch, staring out over the desert. There's a late-afternoon haze hanging in the air, the hills in the distance barely visible. As I approach, I catch a whiff of cigarette smoke.

'Want one?' He holds out the Marlboros.

I shake my head. 'You know what? I figure the least I can do here is kick the habit.'

Finn shrugs. Returns the packet to his pocket.

'How are you getting hold of these anyway?' I ask. 'You got people making a clandestine drone drop or something?'

'Nothing that glamorous. Let's just say someone here owes me a few favours, and I'm mercenary enough to flex that particular situation.'

I'm tempted to find out more, but resist. *None of your business, Zoey.*

'You going to stay at the Sanctuary?' Finn asks.

I think about this. I suppose I haven't much choice – I can't imagine Mike rescinding his threat to make me pay the costs of bailing out of the programme. 'I guess so,' I say. 'Are you?'

'I'm not sure.'

Despite myself, despite his rejection yesterday evening, I experience a frisson of panic at the prospect of Finn leaving. I push it down, pulling my thoughts together.

'I talked to Maia this morning,' I say. 'She told me she left the ceremony early and saw Alejandro in the pool.'

'Jesus!' Finn exhales a small cloud of smoke. 'No wonder she was in such a state at the barbecue.'

'But that's not all. She also said she saw someone else, over in the bushes, moving away from the body.'

Finn turns to me. 'Seriously?'

'That's what she said. And she swears it wasn't the ayahuasca.'

A silence as he takes this in. 'Is that why she didn't come to group this afternoon?'

'Probably.' Though she wasn't the only one who broke the rules and skipped it. Max didn't come either, nor Rory, so Finn, Naomi, Riley and I spent an awkward hour raking through our feelings about Alejandro's death with Tamara and Sonoya. It was only afterwards, once we trooped back to the house, that I realised underneath my shock and sadness lurked a deeper sense of unease.

'Do you believe them?' I ask Finn. 'About the police being here.'

He takes another long drag on his cigarette, considering my question.

'I mean, wouldn't we have heard a helicopter coming in and leaving?' I say, frowning to myself. 'The barbecue spot was, what . . . two, three miles away. Would we hear a chopper from there?'

'I'm not sure,' Finn says. 'I wondered that too.'

'We were only gone for four hours. It just seems very conven-ient that the police flew in, agreed it was an accident, then immediately left again, taking Alejandro with them.' I chew the inside of my cheek. 'But then what do I know about how the police operate in Mexico?'

'So what are you suggesting?' Finn frowns at me. 'That they're covering up his death?'

'I'm not sure,' I admit. 'It feels odd, that's all.' I try to meet his eyes but can't quite manage it. I pretend to study the vegetables instead. Some of the tomatoes are rotting on the vine, and the lettuce are growing tall and bitter.

'Thing is, they lied to Maia,' I continue. 'They pretended the body in the pool was a figment of her imagination. And then openly admitted they'd made up the reason why we had to go to the barbecue yesterday.'

Finn stubs out his cigarette, then turns to me. There's something unsettling in his expression.

'What?' I prompt, feeling uncomfortably warm under his scrutiny.

'This is your first time in rehab.' Finn's tone is cold, almost hostile. 'Or whatever you prefer to call it.'

'You know it is.'

'Well, let me give you some advice, Zoey. Don't shit stir. Don't create drama or get involved in anyone else's. Stick to your own stuff and mind your own business.'

Tears of humiliation spring to my eyes. Jesus. Where on earth did that come from? All I did was tell him what Maia said this morning. I thought he'd be interested, would want to know. I assumed Finn had misgivings of his own, given his earlier reaction to Mike's announcement.

What made me imagine Finn was someone I could confide in? I experience another hot flush of humiliation as I recall again how he recoiled from me last night.

'I wasn't,' I say, indignant. 'I . . .' My voice trails off. Didn't Tamara say much the same thing? And what am I doing, if not creating drama? 'I'm sorry,' I mumble, getting to my feet. 'I'll leave you to it.'

I walk off, swiping tears from my cheek, half hoping to hear Finn call me back. But there's no sound except for the birds and cicadas, and a faint rustle as a few dry mesquite leaves blow aimlessly in the desert wind.

I've had enough. I skip supper and decide on an early night. I take a long shower, change into one of the pyjama sets supplied from the store, and pick a crime novel from the library. Something pacy to take my mind off everything. I climb into bed, pull the sheet over me and settle to read.

It's hopeless. My eyes skim the words, but my mind keeps churning over that conversation with Finn.

Don't create drama, Zoey.

I feel chastised. Judged. Recalling it makes my cheeks flare with shame, and I realise how much I care about his opinion.

Far more than I should.

It's then I feel a strange prickle on my leg. I ignore it at first, assuming it's an insect bite I shouldn't scratch, but a moment later it turns into a definite tickle along the side of my calf.

Something is under the sheet with me.

I shoot out of bed so fast I bang my elbow on the wall, dropping my book on the floor. Pulling back the sheet, I let out a terrified scream.

A few seconds later, a knock on my door. 'You okay, Zoey?'

'No!' I wail, breaking into violent sobs.

Rory comes in, Mike and Tamara on his heels. 'Whatever is the matter?' Mike frowns at me bewildered.

I point at the bed, my hand shaking. There on the stark white sheets is an enormous black-and-yellow spider.

'Oh my God,' mumbles Mike. 'How the hell did that get in here?'

'Aphonopelma chalcodes.' Rory's beleaguered expression lifts a little. He approaches the bed for a closer look. 'Probably a male.'

I back away, pressing myself against the wall. 'What the fuck is it?'

'Western desert tarantula,' Tamara explains.

'Jesus Christ,' Mike murmurs. 'That's all we need.'

'How on earth did it get in?' Rory muses, gazing around the room. 'Do you keep your window open?'

'Sometimes,' I stammer. 'Do you think there's any more in here?'

'Highly unlikely.' He returns his attention to the spider.

'It was in my bed . . . *under the sheet* with me. I felt it . . .' I shudder, my teeth beginning to chatter from shock. 'I felt it brush against my leg.'

'Actually *in* your bed?' Rory frowns. 'Are you sure?'

'Of course I'm fucking sure,' I snap back. 'Otherwise I'd have seen it, wouldn't I?' I stare at the giant spider in horror. It's starting to move again, plodding slowly, almost drowsily towards my pillow.

I squeal, retreating to the doorway. Mike picks up my book and approaches the bed gingerly.

'Hey no, don't kill it,' Tamara cuts in. She walks over and scoops the spider into one hand, using the other to form a little cage.

'Be careful,' Rory warns her. 'They're venomous, and have urticating hairs.'

'I've dealt with worse.' She laughs. 'Though usually with two legs rather than eight.'

I shrink back as Tamara passes, heading out the door and along the corridor to the rear entrance.

'Make sure you take it right off the property,' Mike calls as he trails after her.

Rory gazes at me. 'You okay?' he asks, though I'm trembling so hard it's a pretty dumb question.

'Let's say I could really use a drink right now.'

'I can offer you a root beer or a soda?' He lifts the corners of his mouth into a half-hearted smile. He looks exhausted. Defeated almost. Clearly he's taking Alejandro's death hard, despite their differences.

I shake my head. 'What was that spider doing in here?' I stammer.

'They sometimes wander into houses, especially during mating season. But we've never seen any inside before.'

'Just my luck I end up with one in bed with me.' I shiver with disgust, recalling the sensation of it crawling against my leg.

Rory gazes at the bed, clearly flummoxed. 'Was the sheet heaped up or anything? Was it trailing on the ground?'

I shake my head again. 'I made my bed this morning. Tucked it all in.' Being more tidy and organised is another of my post-ceremony life resolutions.

'Go and sit in the lounge while I make you a chamomile tea,' Rory suggests. 'It'll help soothe your nerves. And then I'll check every inch of your room to put your mind at rest.'

I nod, grateful, feeling even more so when I find the lounge empty – I'm too freaked out for casual conversation. I slump on the sofa, remembering that night a large house spider streaked across the floor of the childhood bedroom I shared with Marcus. Mum and Dad were downstairs, arguing, so Marcus got out of bed and trapped it under a glass – even though he hated spiders as much as I do – then released it into the back garden.

I don't think I ever loved my brother more than in that moment.

'Here you go.' Rory appears, handing me a mug. I'm not usually a fan of herbal teas, but it's warm and soothing so I drink it anyway.

'I searched your room,' he says. 'All clear – apart from the usual flies. I'll ask Elena to give it a hoover in the morning, but in the meantime I've changed your sheets, in case your visitor left any souvenirs.'

'Such as?'

'Tarantula hairs have little barbs – if you get them embedded in your skin, they can be irritating and difficult to remove.'

I'm overtaken by another shiver of revulsion. 'Do they bite?'

'Yes, if they're scared,' Rory says. 'But it's not particularly dangerous – about the same as a bee sting. Unlikely to do you any harm at all.'

I clear my throat, gathering the courage in this moment alone to broach what has bothered me since Mike's bombshell announcement. 'Did you know about Alejandro?' I venture. 'I mean, before we went to the barbecue? Were you aware that Maia had actually seen a body in the pool?'

Rory stares at me. Clearly he knows exactly what I'm getting at.

His features tighten as he decides how to respond. 'No, Zoey, I didn't. Mike said in the morning that Alejandro was in his room recovering from a migraine. He got them, now and then. And we were all pretty tired, after the ceremony.'

'And later?'

'I thought, as most of us did, that we were vacating the Sanctuary so that Mike and Alejandro could deal with the electrics.'

'So when did you find out he was dead?'

Rory swallows. 'When I got back. I wanted to speak to Alejandro about a supplies issue, and that's when Mike told me.'

I gaze at him, surprised he's being so open about this, yet wondering if he's telling the truth. I want to think so. I desperately need to believe Rory's being sincere. Because if he's not, if he's lying, it means he's a charlatan, and that everything he's claimed about ayahuasca, about truth and revelation, is pure bullshit.

I don't know much about shamanism, for sure. But I'm pretty certain positive integrity is a prerequisite, and that gaslighting a vulnerable woman who saw something as shocking as a dead body floating in a pool is nothing any decent healer would embrace.

I return to my room after finishing the tea, nerves still jangling. Despite Rory's assurances, I examine every nook and cranny, pulling back the fresh sheet to check the bed again before climbing in.

As I'm trying to relax enough for sleep, there's a knock at the door and Tamara appears, her smile warm. 'Just coming to see if you're okay – that must have been a hell of a shock. Anyway, I wanted to tell you that our little friend has been safely escorted off the premises.'

'Thank you.' I give her a grateful look. 'I really appreciate you doing that.'

'No trouble at all. Encounters with critters happen from time to time, but it's particularly hard if you're phobic.'

'I thought Rory said there'd never been a tarantula in here before.'

'No,' Tamara muses. 'But we've had our fair share of snakes and lizards, even the odd scorpion.'

I shut my eyes, suppressing another shudder.

'You've had a rough day, haven't you?' she says gently, perching on the corner of my bed.

'You could say that – but then it's hardly been a picnic for anyone, has it?' I consider asking Tamara the same question I just asked Rory – was she aware at the barbecue that Alejandro was dead? That the body Maia saw in the pool was actually real?

But I'm too tired. And too shaken up by the whole massive-spider-from-hell episode.

'I guess you aren't really cut out for this, are you?' Tamara's voice is sympathetic. 'Being a city girl and all. Especially if you're scared of creepy-crawlies.'

I grimace. 'Yeah, well that one was pretty super-sized.'

'Have you heard that Max is leaving tomorrow?' she asks, cocking her head to the side.

I nod. 'He told me before supper.' I was gutted to hear it. I haven't known Max long, but I like him, his intelligence, his gruff kindness. I'm going to miss him.

'I kind of assumed you'd do the same. Jump at the chance for a free lift out of here.'

I frown at Tamara. 'So Mike wouldn't make me pay the cost of leaving if I go with Max?'

'Not under the circumstances.'

I hug my knees under the sheet, trying to take this in; despite everything, it hadn't occurred to me I could actually go.

'Anyway, I'll let you get some sleep.' Tamara pats my leg as she stands. 'Think it over. You've got till tomorrow afternoon to change your mind.'

24

'What time does your chopper arrive?'

'About three,' Max replies, tucking into his sandwich. I gaze around the dining room. We seem to be the only two people who've turned up for lunch.

'You think you'll be okay?' I ask him. 'In yourself, I mean.' *You won't go back to gambling, will you?* I want to say, but it doesn't seem tactful.

Max runs a hand through his hair. 'I'll be fine, Zoey. I was due to leave in a week anyway.'

So why not wait? I want to ask. Why go to all the trouble and expense to leave early? Is he upset about Alejandro, about the accident? Or is he pissed off that Mike and Sonoya covered it up until the police had left?

But Max seems preoccupied, and Finn's words echo in my head. *Don't shit stir. Stick to your own stuff and mind your own business.*

I help myself to bean salad from the buffet, topping it with greens from the garden, wondering who will prepare all this now. The news that Elena is leaving with Max on the helicopter – for an extended break, according to Mike – made for a sombre mood at breakfast this morning, despite Mike's assurance it would be only a few days before he found cover. Naomi was particularly quiet, barely talking as she ate her muesli, skipping Tamara's life drawing class entirely.

I take my food and sit by the pond in the courtyard. Simpkins joins me, purring and kneading, and together we watch the fish idling beneath the lily pads while I eat. At the same time I try to pin down why I feel so unsettled. Is it lingering shock from finding that monster spider in my bed? Despite the heat, I shiver again as I recall the sheer horror of seeing its huge body outlined against my crisp white sheet.

But that doesn't quite explain why I'm so jittery. I stick the tips of my fingers in the water, trying to gather my thoughts. They boil down to a single question – one I've wrestled with on and off all night.

Should I leave too?

Maybe Tamara's right. Maybe I'm simply not cut out for this.

I still have time to grab the few belongings I arrived with and join Max on that chopper. Granted, I don't have a plane ticket onwards from Hermosillo, but if I ring Dan and ask him to bail me out, he'd Paypal the money into my account – enough to get me back to the UK at least. Then I'd have to stay at Mum's and work to pay for the legal advice I need to clear up this issue with the police.

After all, how would the NYPD know I hadn't completed the Sanctuary programme? Would they even care? The more I think about it, the more I suspect it was just a face-saving exercise – one conjured up by my fancy lawyer as an easy way for Bradley Havell to back down. Perhaps he didn't want to press charges. Or perhaps his girlfriend threatened to press charges of her own, and he decided to drop the whole thing.

Who knows? But I'm confident I'd be able to sort it out.

I stroke the cat, gazing up into another sunny, cloudless sky – no sign of the famous monsoon rains you get at this time of year. Is it raining back in the UK, I wonder? Whenever I stay at Mum's I always seem to hit the worst weather, endless grey drizzly days that require a coat and brolly to set foot outside.

Is that what's keeping me here? The sunshine? After all, it was only a few weeks ago that I was desperate to leave. What changed?

Me, I realise.

Those visions during the ceremony, the sessions with Sonoya, talking to Finn and Naomi, and seeing how bravely other guests are squaring up to their problems – all of it has forced me to face what I've spent so many years avoiding. Sonoya's right. I am afraid of commitment. I might not be a heroin addict or full-blown alcoholic, but I've found my own ways of numbing my emotions – the travelling, the partying, the refusal to settle to anything at all.

The feeling I had at the barbecue has solidified into certainty – this place is my best chance to turn all that around. If I go home now, I'll slide back into old habits. It'll start with meeting friends for a casual drink, and end up with the kind of dedicated partying that leaves little room – or cash – for anything else.

Or I'll get itchy feet after a couple of weeks in Mum's spare room, and start browsing for cheap flights to Calcutta or Katmandu.

Most likely, I'll simply rock up again at Dan's, and one text from Franny and Rocco will trash my good intentions.

If I'm ever going to break free, I need to stay here and finish the programme, however flawed the Sanctuary may be, whatever problems it might face. I need to use my time with Sonoya and the others more wisely, and begin making proper, grown-up plans for what I intend to do with the rest of my life.

'One sec!'

Naomi takes a minute or so to answer her door. When she arrives, I can see why. The open suitcase on her bed is already stuffed with neatly folded clothes. The ornate carved wardrobe is empty. On the dresser, a clutch of make-up and toiletries wait to be packed into a Chanel vanity case.

I gaze around, then look at Naomi, taking in her shifty, apologetic expression.

'I decided before lunch,' she says sheepishly. 'I was about to come and tell you, but I barely had time to pack.'

'Okay,' I reply, though it isn't. I feel sucker-punched with emotion. 'Why are you leaving?' I try not to show how upset I am – Naomi owes me nothing, after all. 'You've still got a few weeks to go.'

Naomi swallows, looks away. Going to her dresser, she bundles her toiletries into their case and zips it up. I watch, wondering how I'll manage without her. I'd been counting on having Naomi around as a comrade in arms; her warmth and friendship are one of the things that's got me this far.

'I'm sorry, Zoey.' She sits on the bed and faces me properly. 'I just feel . . . I don't know . . . that I've got as much out of being here as I can.'

I sit beside her. 'So this isn't because of Alejandro?'

'Not in the way you imagine. I suppose his death made me realise that life is short, and none of us knows how long we have left, do we? And I want to make the most of mine.' She lifts her eyes to the ceiling, blinking back tears. 'This is the fourth time I've done rehab or whatever you call this, and I can see now I'm using it as a crutch. It's too easy, isn't it, not drinking in a place where you can't drink at all? I need to face life out in the real world.'

'Are you sure you're ready?'

Naomi sighs. 'As ready as I'll ever be. When I get home, I'm going to start applying for jobs; I might not need the money, but I sure as hell need to do something more positive than drinking and shopping and scrolling through social media.

And I'm determined to attend AA meetings and work through the steps.'

I nod. I can't argue – what Naomi's saying makes sense.

She puts her arm around me, squeezing my shoulders. 'Don't worry about me, Zoey. I'll be okay. I might have only done one ceremony, but I really think it's shifted something in me.'

'I'm going to miss you,' I say – and it feels like the most honest thing I've told anyone in years.

'I'm going to miss you too.' She releases me, holding my gaze. 'But I honestly believe you should stay here and make the most of it. I've seen a change in you already.' She gets up, closes her suitcase and heaves it off the bed, then smiles at my forlorn expression. 'You still have Finn. He really likes you, you know.'

I grimace. *Not as much as all that.*

'Seriously,' Naomi insists. 'You two are good for each other. He's come out of himself since you arrived. I only hope . . .' her voice trails off and the sadness returns to her face.

'You hope what?'

'I don't know . . . I hope that what's happened with Alejandro doesn't mess things up for either of you.' She glances out of the window, her eyes lingering on the view outside.

I frown at her. 'What do you mean?'

'I'm not sure. I know Mike and everyone are doing their best to ensure everything carries on as normal, but it all feels . . . a bit strained.'

Before I can formulate a response she comes over and folds me in another hug. 'Forget what I just said, I'm in an odd mood. Look after yourself, and make me a promise, will you? Actually two. Promise me you'll use every moment here wisely. It's a good place, despite what's happened – it can turn people's lives around.'

'I promise. What's the second?'

Naomi grabs a gold filigree pen from her handbag and a piece of the Sanctuary headed note paper, and jots down an email address and phone number, pressing it into my hand.

'Promise me you'll stay in touch when you get out. And any time you need help, Zoey, or someone to talk to, you know where to find me.'

25

Sonoya looks exhausted. More than usually pale, with shadows under her eyes that make-up can't hide. She's putting a brave face on it though, her expression giving nothing away.

'So, how are you doing today?'

'I dunno.' I shrug, glancing out of the consult-room window. Simpkins is under the shade of an olive tree, eyeing the chickens down in the kitchen garden. 'It's all been a bit weird, since the ceremony. What happened to Alejandro. Max and Naomi leaving yesterday. It feels as if everything has changed.'

'Yet you chose to stay, Zoey,' Sonoya comments. 'Why was that?'

I take a deep breath. 'Maybe it was the ceremony. It opened up something in my head, made me see . . . I don't know . . . it's all been overshadowed by what's happened since. But I think you're right, about me being afraid of commitment. I've spent the last twelve years either running away or distracting myself, and it's time I dealt with that. And I knew if I left now, it would be so much harder, that I'd slide back into familiar patterns.'

'I'm very pleased to hear it,' Sonoya says, but her smile is forced. Beneath her calm exterior, I sense she's struggling to keep up appearances.

'Why haven't you tried it?' I ask her again. 'Ayahuasca?'

The therapist inhales, considering how to respond. 'Like I said before, I haven't felt it necessary. Besides, it's not safe, not while our clients are under the influence themselves. We need to have people around who are . . . grounded in reality.'

'But you must be tempted, surely? Aren't you curious?'

'Not really.' Sonoya gives a little shrug. 'I do, however, accept it has real therapeutic value – I've seen the positive results it can bring in terms of breaking old patterns. As I said before, I'm not a sceptic.'

'Okay.'

'It's like being a medical practitioner – you wouldn't expect your oncologist, for instance, to have had cancer themselves, would you?'

'Fair point.'

'So you told me some things, during the ceremony, that I'm curious about, Zoey. Why don't we go through them in more detail?'

I gaze through the window again. I very much would like not to do that, but remember my promise to Naomi.

Make sure you use every moment you're here.

'It's hard to talk about,' I say.

'Pain is the price of freedom, Zoey,' Sonoya intones. 'I think you understand that now.'

She's right. Not thinking about something is the same as running away – only in your head. And I can't keep doing that.

'Why don't you walk me through it again from the beginning,' Sonoya suggests. 'Talk to me about that evening, when that girl . . .' she glances at the notes on her lap '. . . Laura, wasn't it? Tell me when you found out about the video.'

'Yes, her name was Laura. The shy girl on my course. Someone posted a video of her giving a guy oral sex. Loads of people saw it. She got really upset, then she left. Then . . . well, you know the rest.'

'Let's back up a bit, Zoey. Tell me more about Laura.'

I sigh. 'I really didn't know her that well. She was very quiet . . . introverted. Nice, though – she lent me her tort notes once when I had a bad cold and missed a tutorial. I was always encouraging her to get out more, have a drink and let her hair down a bit. She wasn't even going to go to the law students' Halloween bash – I was the one who persuaded her.'

'So what exactly happened there?'

I inhale, my chest tightens and my heart beats faster as I force myself back to that night. 'The party was fancy dress, and Laura came as Jessica Rabbit, in a tight red dress that was pretty cool with her red hair. She looked amazing, actually, and she hung out with our crowd, drinking and chatting to some of the guys. Later in the evening I went to the loo, and when I returned she'd disappeared. I assumed she'd got tired and gone home . . .' I pause, steadying my breathing.

'Go on,' Sonoya prompts.

'And then on the Monday, at the seminar on contract law, I was sitting with Laura – I arrived late so hadn't had a chance to ask her where she got to that night – and people kept looking over at us. You know, giggling and stuff. So I asked this guy what the fuck was going on and he handed over his laptop . . . he'd actually downloaded the video, from the chat room.'

I pause again, swallow. Close my eyes for a moment, and there it is, playing in my head. Soft focus, a little wobbly. He must have been holding the phone in his left hand, because his right hand was caressing Laura's hair as she . . .

I open my eyes, wiping the image from my mind.

'Tell me what you saw, Zoey.'

'It was on his left thigh. A birthmark.'

I'd have known it anywhere. How many times had I seen it before? Ten thousand? A million? How many times had I seen my twin naked in the years we grew up together?

'So that was the moment you realised it was your brother Marcus.'

I nod.

'How did that make you feel?'

'Angry. Disgusted. I'm not sure what was worse, that he filmed her doing that to him or that he shared it with half the university. I went straight back to our house, the one we'd moved into together after our first year in halls, along with two other girls. Marcus wasn't there. I tracked him down eventually to the gym on campus.'

'You,' I hissed at him as we stood outside in the autumn drizzle. 'It was you in the video with Laura.'

My brother did something I never expected. He smiled. Like it was funny, like this was . . . something to be proud of.

For the first time in my life I felt tempted to hurt him. Really hurt him, not like those scuffles we had as kids, the shoves and the pinches. I wanted to pick up a heavy object and smash him with it. I wanted to punch him in the face, grab his head and bang it against the brick wall behind us.

She'd always had a crush on him, he said. She'd been up for it. Said he'd meant to keep the video private, but a mate got hold of his phone and . . . I tuned out. It was lies, excuses. It was as if I didn't even know him. Had never known him. Here he was, my own brother, the person I'd spent nine months closer to than any human being spends with another, and yet he was a stranger to me.

'How could you do that to her?' I yelled at him, as he pulled me round to the rear of the gym, afraid someone would overhear. 'How could you, Marcus? Laura's in pieces. You've utterly humiliated her.'

Silence, his eyes veering from mine.

'You know that's sexual harassment, don't you? If she reports it to student welfare – or somebody else does – you could be kicked out.'

'You're not going to tell anyone,' Marcus said. It was more a statement than a question. As if he never doubted I'd be on his side.

'So what did you do, Zoey?' Sonoya's voice pulls me back into the room. My fists are clenched and my stomach is tight with anger, even after all these years.

'I went round to Laura's house on Barrow Street. I wanted to talk to her, to apologise, to explain, but she shut the door in my face. So I resolved to try again the next day, but by then she'd gone home to her parents. I spent the rest of the week dithering, wondering what to do. I couldn't even look at Marcus. I waited until I heard him leave before I got up. I was late for my morning lectures, and missed one tutorial completely, because I couldn't bear to lay eyes on him.'

I inhale, trying to slow my breathing in the face of what's coming.

You can't keep running for ever, Zoey.

'So when did you discover what Laura had done?' Sonoya asks gently.

'In one of my lectures. Another friend told me.'

I can remember Lexi's whisper as if it were yesterday: 'Did you hear about Laura?' she said as I sat down and opened my notebook. 'She killed herself.' There was excitement in her voice, as if this were some drama she'd seen on TV.

And the whole world collapsed in on me.

'I walked right out of the lecture,' I tell Sonoya. 'Returned to my house, packed my stuff and left. I've never set eyes on my brother since.'

'So you didn't mention to anyone what happened?'

I shake my head, cheeks flushing with shame. 'No, I never told the university what Marcus had done, and I didn't tell my mother either. I concocted some bullshit about hating my course, and made myself scarce whenever he came home.'

I glance up to see Sonoya studying me. And there's such sympathy in her expression it makes me want to howl with anguish.

'You protected your brother from himself,' she says.

I swallow. 'I just couldn't do it. Couldn't face being the person who dumped him in it. Who got him chucked out, who ruined his life.'

'So you ruined your own instead.'

Those six words pierce me through. Sonoya's right.

That's exactly what I've done.

'I . . . I felt so guilty,' I say, the words tumbling out of me now. 'I kept thinking, if I'd acted immediately, if I'd reported Marcus straight away and made certain Laura received proper support, then she might not have . . . you know. I was so angry with Marcus, but also with myself. I felt culpable . . . pathetic.' I gaze at Sonoya. 'Have you never done anything like that? I mean, failed to do the right thing? Something you're deeply ashamed of?'

An expression flits across her face, a kind of reflexive pain. She closes her eyes for a couple of seconds. 'I . . .' she starts, then falls silent. We sit like that for a minute or two, until I'm so uncomfortable I barely know what to do with myself.

'Sonoya . . . are you okay?'

The therapist opens her eyes. Clears her throat. 'Actually, Zoey, I'm not feeling terribly well. Do you mind if we leave it here?'

'Sure.' I nod, and she's out of the door before I've even got to my feet, her notes clamped tightly against her chest.

26

'Good to see you at meditation this morning,' Rory says once the session is over and Tamara and Axel have left. 'This your first time?'

'Decided I'd give it a go, though I'm not much good at it, to be honest.' I couldn't get comfortable sitting on the cushion. My legs ached and then my nose itched and it was all I could do not to fidget and scratch.

Rory looks sympathetic. 'It's hard when you begin. Or rather, it's difficult to get your head around what you're supposed to be doing – which is basically nothing.'

'You'd imagine doing nothing would be something I'd excel at.' I laugh. 'Shows how wrong you can be.'

'It's not about stopping your thoughts, Zoey – that's almost impossible for all but the most experienced meditators. Regard it more as learning to observe them. You're aiming to create a gap, between you, the thinker, and the thoughts themselves.'

'I see,' I say, though I'm not sure I do.

'I really recommend a daily practice.' Rory picks up his cushion from the floor. 'It's easier to experience it than explain, if you get what I mean.'

'Do you meditate every day?'

Rory nods. 'Half an hour in the morning and half an hour at night. It keeps me steady.'

'Trouble is, I have zero willpower and even less motivation.' I sigh. 'Much as I'd love to be someone like Sonoya, all calm and poise, I'm not sure I'll ever get there.'

'Sonoya has plenty of issues of her own,' Rory says, then stops, his expression awkward. As if he's already said too much.

I raise an eyebrow in surprise. But then, what do I know? What can you really tell about a person? Look at Maia, her hidden psychic depths – not such a shallow puddle after all.

'Actually I wanted to check you're ready for the hike this weekend,' Rory says. 'How are those boots I found for you? Do they fit okay?'

I nod, though I can't say I'm looking forward to wearing them. The big hike into the hills involves fifteen miles each way in blazing sunshine and two nights camping in the wild, and sounds about as much fun as getting my teeth scaled. But next to the ceremonies, it's the major event of the programme, and I know Rory is keen for it to go ahead as usual.

'I'll wear them beforehand,' I say, 'break them in.' I glance at him, wondering whether to bring it up. I decide it can't do any harm. 'Rory, do you mind if I ask you something?'

'Of course.' He sits on the wooden steps of the veranda, and I hover beside him.

'I spoke to Maia a few days ago. She seemed pretty upset about what she saw during the ceremony.' I pause, waiting to see if Rory will speak, but he just gazes at the desert, spread out in front of us. 'She said she spotted someone disappearing into the bushes, when she found Alejandro's body in the pool. She believes it was real.'

Rory looks down at his hands. 'I'll talk to her. Thanks for mentioning it.'

'So you're not worried? It sounds pretty weird. Could ayahuasca make you see anything like that?'

'People have many kinds of visions with ayahuasca. They all have a role in helping us grow.' He gets up to put his cushion in the cupboard. 'Think of it this way, we each inhabit a reality created by our own minds, from our subconscious fears and our longings. So, as with dreams, what we experience during the ceremonies is there to communicate something. Anyway,' he glances at his watch, 'I have to run. I'll catch up with you later.'

I pick up my hat and sunglasses and take the veranda route to my room. Just around the corner, I find Riley sitting on the swing seat with a view out towards the pool. She gives me an ironic smile that suggests she's heard every word of my conversation with Rory.

I stop. 'Were you listening to us?'

'Not purposefully.'

I swallow down my irritation. Stupid of me to tackle Rory without checking first we were completely alone. 'You okay?' I ask Riley, wondering why she's sitting out here on her own. She's been quiet in the two days since Naomi and Max left, even more withdrawn than usual.

She sniffs. 'Do you care?'

I sit on the little wooden table opposite. 'Yeah, I do actually.'

It's true, I realise. I gaze at Riley, and in my head I see Laura. I might not be able to discern people's auras, but I'm perceptive enough to recognise that underneath all that snark and animosity is someone longing for emotional connection. I can't make up for what I did to Laura, but I could at least take the time to get to know this girl right in front of me.

As if on cue, Riley finds a tissue and wipes her nose. For a second the sleeve of her black T-shirt slips down enough to reveal the criss-cross of silver scars beneath.

'Why do you do that?' I nod at her arm.

Her cheeks redden as she tugs her sleeves back over her hands. 'Did,' she corrects. 'I've pretty much stopped now.'

'Pretty much? Have you done it here?'

Riley shakes her head. 'I promised Ed I wouldn't.'

'So why did you do it? Before.'

She juts out her chin, eyes narrow with suspicion. 'What's it to you?'

'I'm curious, that's all.'

'Why I do it?' Riley shrugs. 'Because I'm angry or upset. Because I'm not angry or upset and just need to feel something. Because I'm bored or depressed or anxious. Because I'm happy but can't let myself ever be happy, because it's a lie. Because I'm lonely but can't stand being around other people.'

'Don't you have friends back home? People you can talk to?' I feel another pang of pity for this girl – I can't imagine how I'd survive without Rocco and Fran in my life.

'Not really.' She sighs. 'To be honest, I don't often meet anybody I'd even want to be friends with.'

'How do you mean?'

'Nobody seems interested in anyone but themselves.' Riley picks at a mark on her trousers. 'You can spend hours with them and all they ever talk about is what they're doing or did or going to do. They don't ask a single question in return. After a while, you start wondering, what's the point?'

'Not everyone's like that,' I say. 'Some people are nice, you know.'

Riley nods in a way that suggests she doesn't agree, then changes the subject. 'Is Maia planning to leave?'

'I don't know. I don't think so.'

Riley raises an eyebrow. 'That's odd. You'd imagine she would, given what she says she saw. You have to wonder what's keeping her here.'

I ponder this. Riley's right. Given the trauma Maia claims to have experienced, you'd think she'd leave the first chance she got. 'Did you notice anything?' I ask, remembering that Riley remained in the house during the ceremony.

She shakes her head again. 'I went to bed early and slept through the whole thing. Besides, my room is at the back, looking over the courtyard. I wouldn't hear a thing over on the pool side.'

'Okay.'

'But I did see something in the morning,' she adds, as I get to my feet.

I turn around. 'What?'

'I woke up early, just after dawn, and went to the garden to water the seedlings before it got hot. I heard the jeep returning.'

'The jeep?' I frown. 'Returning from where?'

'No idea. But Mike and Sonoya got out of it.'

I squint at her. 'You sure?'

'You doubting me, Zoey?' Riley's expression darkens.

'Dawn is about five, yes? So where had they been?'

'How the fuck should I know?' She shrugs again. 'Nowhere to go around here, is there? Apart from rescuing runaways.' With that, she gets up and goes off without so much as a backward glance.

I leave her to it, noticing the pool is empty. I change into my costume and float in the cool blue water for a while, then swim several laps, lengthways now, right up into the deep end. Since the ceremony, my fear of sinking seems to have disappeared.

As if it were never there.

I climb out and towel myself down, stretching out on a lounger. Just ten minutes, I decide – not long enough to burn. I'm developing a light tan, and it suits me. I look fitter and healthier – the decent food is doing wonders for my skin.

Lying back, eyes closed behind my sunglasses, I try to practise what I learned with Rory this morning. Just observe your
thoughts, his voice repeats in my head. Don't judge them. Don't
engage with them, simply let each one glide past like a cloud
drifting across the sky.

But it's hopeless. My mind insists on chewing over my conversation with Riley. What were Mike and Sonoya doing in that
jeep so early?

Where on earth could they have been?

Are they having some kind of secret affair?

Or maybe they needed to talk in private, without fear of
being overheard. Though who would be up to hear them at that
time? Something niggles at the edge of my thoughts. A conclusion I don't want to face.

I try again to clear my mind, to focus on the present moment,
the sensation of heat on my skin. The sound of the hens chit-
tering to themselves as they scratch about in their compound.
The quiet hum of bees in the flowers surrounding the pool.

But my thoughts drift inevitably to Finn. We've barely spoken
since he accused me of creating drama a few days ago. I've seen
him at group and at meals – with Elena gone, we're all taking
turns to help Rory and Tamara prepare our food – but the rest
of the time he's been hiding in his room, reverting to his old
reclusive self.

I roll onto my front and close my eyes, but a high trilling
sound snags my attention. I turn back over, and spot a small
bird hovering by a bushy shrub with bright crimson flowers. It's
gorgeous, a glorious iridescent blend of pink and emerald. A
hummingbird, I realise, watching, fascinated, as it darts from
flower to flower in a constant flash of colour.

A second later it flies away, and as I drop my gaze something
else catches my eye. A patch of turquoise, right beneath the

bush, obscured by the canopy of leaves. Not a bird or a flower, but something metallic, glinting in the sun.

I get up and reach under the bush, feeling a rush of confusion as my fingers close on the hard, flat object.

A phone.

I gawp at it, astonished. An actual mobile phone.

I glance about to make certain I'm alone, then quickly hide it in the folds of my towel and hurry to my room. Closing the door, I sit on the bed and study the smartphone in my hands. Covered in a gel sleeve with bright geometric patterns, it's an old model, the screen scratched, the glass cracked in the corner.

Whose is it?

It can only belong to one of the staff, surely, unless a guest sneaked in a phone to use on the quiet. But how would that work? You'd have to be signed into the Sanctuary network. Plus this doesn't strike me as the kind of mobile any of the guests would have – even my own model is more up-to-date.

But if this belongs to any of the staff, they'd have missed it by now.

There's only one explanation – this belonged to Alejandro. He must have dropped it when he fell into the pool, and nobody noticed.

Not even the police?

But then, why would they be looking, given his death was an accident?

I gaze at it, at the same time sad and slightly weirded-out. It doesn't seem right, somehow, that his phone is here and Alejandro has gone. I remember when our dog Juno died, staring at his collar and lead, his squeaky toys, his favourite bouncy ball, unable to process how he could be gone and yet his things remained. It felt so wrong. Impossible to comprehend.

On impulse, I press the start button and to my surprise the screen springs to life – I'd assumed that after five days the battery would be dead. I swipe it with my forefinger, hoping Alejandro might not have bothered with a security lock.

Nine dots appear.

Damn. I have to draw the right pattern to unlock the phone. Before I can even attempt to guess which he might have used, it starts vibrating in my hands, and a name flashes up on the screen.

Ed Temple.

I almost drop the phone in shock, then instinctively swipe to accept the call. But the instant it connects, the screen goes blank.

I press the restart button, but nothing happens. Damn. The battery has finally died.

Behind me, there's a knock at the door. I quickly stuff the phone under my pillow.

'Come in,' I call, and Finn appears. 'Fancy some lunch?' he asks.

I try to arrange my face into a less furtive expression. 'Why not.'

'Jesus, it's hot in here,' he says, gazing around. 'Come up to my room. I'll make us something to eat.'

'It's a date,' I reply, immediately regretting my choice of words. 'I mean, yeah, fine.'

He grins. 'See you in ten.'

'Hang on,' I call after Finn. 'Where is it?'

'Up the stairs, turn right, last door at the end of the corridor.'

27

I sort through the clothes I've been lent and find a yellow sundress. Apart from a tiny hole on the skirt, it's in excellent condition and will tide me over until I get some laundry done.

I go up to Finn's room, the one where I stood on the balcony that first morning I was here, trying to work out where the hell I was.

It feels more like three years ago than three weeks.

'Hope this is okay.' Finn indicates the two plates of salad on the coffee table, each with a fresh baked roll. 'I'm helping Tamara with supper tonight, so I grabbed what I could.'

'This'll be fine.' I sit in the armchair and take a sip of orange juice.

'Anyway, I wanted to say I'm sorry,' he says, his expression sheepish.

'What for?'

'For how I reacted when you tried to talk to me the other day. Telling you to mind your own business.'

'Did you?' I demur. 'I really don't remember.'

Finn studies me, weighing something up.

'What is it?' I ask, swallowing a mouthful of salad.

'Thing is, Zoey,' Finn lowers his voice to avoid being over-heard by anyone in the corridor, 'I checked, and you're right. The local police have no record of a death out here five days ago.'

I frown at him. 'What do you mean you checked? *How?*'

'It doesn't matter,' he says, his tone defensive. 'The point is no police report has been filed.'

'So . . . you're saying, what . . . they were never here?'

'Yup. Mike and Sonoya lied.'

I put my plate down, my appetite gone. 'How do you know, Finn?' I repeat. 'How did you find this out?'

'There's really only two possibilities, aren't there?' Finn continues, ignoring my question. 'Mike and Sonoya are covering up the accident for some reason, or . . .' he stops, hesitates.

'Or it wasn't an accident at all.'

The moment the words leave my mouth I realise this is what has hovered at the edge of my mind ever since Maia told me about the person in the bushes – at the very least, someone watched Alejandro drown without making a move to help him.

'But that doesn't add up,' Finn says. 'We were all at the ceremony, bar Riley, and I really don't think she's the murdering type, for all her hysterical drama. And I can't believe Mike or Sonoya would hurt Alejandro.'

'They did have that argument,' I remind him. 'Alejandro and Mike. So clearly there was something going on.'

'But Alejandro was practically holding the Sanctuary together single-handed,' Finn retorts. 'As we've discovered, this place is pretty fucked without him. It simply doesn't make sense that they'd hurt him.' He stares down gloomily into his food, then pushes his plate away.

'Actually, Riley said earlier she saw Mike and Sonoya returning in the jeep at dawn,' I tell Finn. 'After the ceremony.'

He jerks his head up to look at me. 'Really? So are you thinking what I'm thinking?'

'I reckon they buried him in the desert and sent us off on that barbecue so they could pretend the police had come and taken his body away.'

237

Finn's hand drifts to the packet of Marlboro just visible inside the pocket of his shorts. Clearly he's itching for a cigarette, but it's too risky to smoke in his room. 'But why would they go to all that effort to cover it up?' he asks, thinking out loud.

'To protect the reputation of the Sanctuary, I suppose. I heard Rory and Alejandro arguing, out in the desert, when they thought I was asleep in the jeep. The Sanctuary already has financial problems. Alejandro was complaining about how many staff they'd dropped, how the whole place was subsisting on a shoestring.'

Finn nods. 'So if they reported the accident to the police, they'd face a full investigation and have to close for the dura-tion. Plus the guests – *all of us* – would have to be interviewed. I think you're right. Easier to pretend the police already knew, then dispose of the body.'

He stops, thinking some more. 'But what about Alejandro's family? Wouldn't they want to know exactly what happened? And surely they'd want to bury his body?'

'He told me in the desert that he doesn't have anyone really, only a sister in Puerto Rico, and they lost touch some time ago. Chances are, she's not even aware he's dead.' I'm hit by a wave of sadness that Alejandro died leaving no one around to miss him.

Finn rises and walks to his desk, pulling a sheaf of papers from the drawer. 'I also asked somebody to do a bit of digging into the Sanctuary itself – they got hold of the company report with the names of the directors and shareholders. Unfortunately, businesses in Mexico aren't required to file accounts, so I couldn't get any info on the financial status.'

'So who are the directors?'

'Mike, Sonoya and Rory. They're all shareholders too – along with Tamara.'

Tamara? I didn't realise she'd actually invested money in this place. When she said she'd given up her whole life to come here, I thought she meant selling her house and leaving her son behind.

'How did you get all this?' I gesture at the papers in his hands. 'Seriously, Finn, you can't just conjure this stuff up and not tell me how you came by it. How did you contact whoever's been looking into this for you? You don't have a phone or access to the internet, do you?'

Finn sits back on the sofa. He inhales, seems to come to a decision. 'You remember what I told you about my sister?'

I nod.

'I told you how she . . . well, all of us, but particularly Maddy as she was so young and pretty . . . we came in for a lot of press attention. You know, the paparazzi, always after stories and gossip. And they fixated on my sister when she broke up with Neo.'

He pauses, gathering the strength to continue. 'She was really cut up about it. Heartbroken. And the paps kept trailing her around, taking pictures wherever she went, printing shit about her. She came to stay with me in New York to try to get away from it, but of course they soon found out she was there. Kept door-stopping us. Maddy was so freaked by it she took security with her wherever she went, then pretty much stopped going out at all.'

His eyes glisten and he gets to his feet, going to stand by the balcony doors. 'Like I said before, she got really down, and I didn't notice. Or rather, I wasn't paying enough attention. I was tied up with my own stuff – the lawsuit with Dad, him kicking me out of the company, my marriage on the rocks. And then I had that party, and Maddy . . .' His voice breaks.

'Finn, I don't understand,' I say gently. 'What does this have to do with how you got hold of this information?'

He twists to face me. 'I'm telling you. Rory was the pap who broke the story on her bust-up with Neo Hallinger. That was his job, before he had his so-called epiphany and trained to be a fucking *shaman*. He made my sister's life a misery.'

The bitterness and anger in Finn's tone is unmistakable. I stare at him in shock. 'Rory? *Rory was a press photographer?*' I shake my head, trying to take this in. 'How do you know this?' I ask after a minute or so.

Finn narrows his eyes at me. 'They print the name next to the photographs, Zoey. It's called a credit.'

'Of course. Sorry,' I blunder, attempting to marshall all the questions in my mind. 'So were you . . . um . . . were you aware of this before you arrived at the Sanctuary? Did you know who Rory was?'

'Yes.'

I don't bother to hide the shock on my face. '*Is that why you came here?*'

Finn breaks eye contact, rolling his tongue around his teeth in that way he does when gathering his thoughts. 'Yes, and no. I needed to go away, get my act together. I was a mess. *I'm still a mess*. But, yeah, I was keeping tabs on Rory and a few other people who screwed over my sister. And that was how I came to hear about the Sanctuary and its psychedelics programme. But I was genuinely interested, Zoey – it wasn't all about Rory.'

'But it was a bit about him,' I say, wondering exactly what Finn had planned.

'Yeah.' He nods. 'You're right. I guess I couldn't resist the opportunity to fuck with him. My being here at all was enough to do that.'

'So Rory knows who you are?'

'Obviously.'

'And that's why he does things for you?'

'Pretty much, yes.'

'Including letting you have access to cigarettes and his phone, and those documents?'

Finn nods again.

'So, you're what, *blackmailing him*?'

'I'm not blackmailing anyone, Zoey.' Finn looks annoyed, his dark brows furrowing. 'Though, yeah, he's scared I'll say something to Mike and Sonoya – I imagine they'd take a dim view of his past, don't you?'

I blink at him. I imagine they would. 'And you're . . . what . . . enjoying this?' I blurt, my voice rising. What is it with guys? Why is it always the same messed-up shit? 'I thought you came here to get clean, to sort your bloody life out, but in reality it was to torment Rory.'

Finn frowns then looks away again. 'Well, you're not exactly squeaky clean yourself, are you?' he says finally. There's a hardness in his tone that makes this hot day feel cold.

'What the hell does that mean?' Did he see me hiding that phone earlier? Am I going to tell him about it?

'Those background checks, Zoey. I ran one on you too.'

What the fuck?

I leap to my feet, chest tight with indignation. '*You ran a background check on me?* What right do you have to do that? And why?' I explode, resisting the urge to kick him. I'm wearing flip-flops and I'd probably hurt myself more than Finn.

I pace the room, trying not to clench my fists. 'So what did it say?' I ask finally. 'Your report on me.'

'Not much.' Finn shrugs. 'To be honest, it's surprising how little you've done with your life.'

I stop and stare at him. 'Gee, thanks.'

'You're still basically living at home, Zoey. Apart from never having a proper job.' He looks at me, but I don't rise to the bait; it's nothing I haven't heard from Sonoya, after all.

'So were you ever going to tell me that you were about to be charged with assault before you came here?' Finn asks.

I gape at him. 'I . . . I . . .' No words come.

'I can see why you might want to play it down, sure, but I thought we were all about being honest here, Zoey. I shared that stuff about my sister after all.'

Finn's cheeks are red, and I realise he's as pissed off with me as I am with him. He looks hurt, as well as angry. I feel my own anger, my indignation that he's been poking around in my life, drain away.

He's right. I haven't been upfront with him, have I?

'If it's any consolation, Zoey, the guy you bottled in that club is doing fine. But what I'd like to know, is why you did it? Was he an ex? Or is this something you do routinely when you're wasted?'

I spin around. Walk up to the balcony doors and back again, breathing hard. 'No, Finn, I don't go about bottling people when I'm drunk.'

I close my eyes and he's here, the memory surfacing again. The sneering look on that man's face as I approached him across the dance floor. Tattoos right up his neck and over his left cheek – exactly as that girl, the one crying in the loo, had described.

'I saw what you did to your girlfriend,' I yell above the thump of the music.

He inclines his head towards me. I can smell his aftershave as he spits in my ear. 'Get lost, bitch. Or I'll do the fucking same to you.'

'I snapped,' I confess to Finn, putting a hand on the wall to steady myself. The air in the room seems to have thickened and

I can hardly breathe. 'He beat up his girlfriend. She had bruises all round her neck and was too scared to go to the police – she was convinced he'd kill her if she did.'

Finn's eyes widen, but he doesn't speak.

'I lost it,' I say, cheeks flaring with heat and shame. 'Something broke inside me and I picked up the bottle and hit him with it. A couple of bouncers grabbed me and they held me till the cops came. That's about all I remember.'

'Jesus!' Finn whistles, shaking his head.

'I'm not exactly proud of it, okay? And I could be in a whole heap of trouble when I return to New York.'

'That's not what I meant.' Finn walks over to me. 'He could have really hurt you, Zoey. Don't you get that? You're fortunate the worst that happened was the police threatening to charge you.'

He gazes down at my face, his expression as serious as I've ever seen it. A hint too, unless I'm imagining it, of something like tenderness.

'Don't you see, Zoey? You're lucky you got out of that place alive.'

28

I wake early and lie in my narrow bed, skin sticky with sweat, mind churning over yesterday's conversations with Riley and Finn.

Is it really possible that Mike and Sonoya buried Alejandro's body in the desert? The idea is so gruesome, so fantastical, I'm struggling to believe it. But what other logical explanation could there be? They didn't report his death to the police. And for the life of me I can't think where else they could have been going in the jeep in this isolated wilderness so early in the morning.

Why did Mike and Sonoya cover up Alejandro's death? I keep asking myself. Was it simply to avoid the disruption, the bad publicity? Or is there another, more sinister reason?

Did someone want Alejandro dead?

But why? What could he have done that would give someone a motive to kill? I think back to our conversation in the jeep, his open manner and friendly concern. Alejandro was a decent guy, he seemed to get along with pretty much everyone, bar Rory.

And Mike, I think, my stomach tightening with dread as I recall again that argument Riley and I witnessed just before the ceremony. Could Finn be wrong about Mike being reluctant to hurt Alejandro? Even worse, could it have something to do with what I told Alejandro about Ed's email?

Policía Federal. Alejandro had threatened Mike with the police.

Oh God. *Did I unwittingly give Mike a reason to kill him?*

I peer into the darkness, the pressure building in my head as question piles upon question. What are Finn and I going to do? Do we challenge Mike and Sonoya, demand an explanation for their fairy story about the police? Do we tell the others what we've discovered?

Perhaps we should leave, and go to the Mexican authorities ourselves.

I'll talk to Finn again today, I decide – see what he reckons we should do. Perhaps I'm overthinking things, in that way we're all prone to do when we can't sleep.

As dawn breaks, I resolve on an early swim to clear my head. But as I reach the veranda, I find Axel performing sun salutations on one of the yoga mats.

I pause, transfixed. Of all the people on the programme, Axel is the last I'd expect to see doing a downward-facing dog. Up until he took the ayahuasca, he treated all the centre activities with undisguised contempt, rarely bothering to attend. He made it abundantly clear with everything he said and did, that he was only at the Sanctuary under duress.

I carry on past, but Axel calls out my name.

'How are you?' he asks, as I turn to face him.

There's something peculiar about his expression, and it takes me a moment to work out what it is. He's smiling at me. No trace of his trademark sneer.

'I'm fine,' I say. 'You?'

'Never better.' His eyes fix on mine with a curious intensity. 'It's such a beautiful morning. I never noticed that before, how amazing it is that each day unfolds in its own perfect way.'

I blink at him in astonishment. Who is this person? What the hell happened to him during the ceremony?

Sure, many of us experienced profound insights, but no one else has been quite so radically transformed as Axel. His bitterness, his acerbic cynicism, his unending sarcasm, seem to have completely disappeared. He even looks . . . fresher. Younger, somehow, as if this were a top-end health spa rather than a radical alternative to rehab.

It's disconcerting, almost creepy. Like some kind of reverse demonic possession.

'It is lovely,' I agree, glancing out across the desert to where the sun floats on the horizon.

Axel continues his persistent scrutiny. 'You seem . . . troubled, Zoey. Is anything wrong?'

'Not enough sleep,' I reply, with a dismissive wave of the hand.

'No,' he says emphatically. 'There's something heavy on your mind.'

I stare back at him. 'What makes you say that?'

Axel shrugs. 'Intuition.'

Intuition? Wasn't that what Maia said too? Christ, can Axel see my bloody aura as well, or am I really easy to read?

'Have you spoken to Maia?' I ask, ignoring my better judgement. 'About what happened to her during the ceremony?'

Axel's sunny demeanour is suddenly eclipsed. 'It's not true,' he murmers. 'It was just visions.'

I frown, confused. 'Yours or hers?'

'Rory explained it to me.' He closes his eyes. 'Those things aren't real, they're simply possible realities, things you're really afraid of, things you need to face.' He gazes up at me, his expression bordering on pleading. As if he wants reassurance.

'I'm sure you're right,' I lie, wanting to escape. I almost prefer the old Axel to this weird, body-snatched version. 'I'll leave you to it.'

I hurry off to the pool before he can say anything to deter me. Dropping my towel on the lounger, I walk to the deep end and stand on the smooth flagstones, peering into the clear blue depths below me. Then I do something I would never have believed possible a few weeks ago.

I dive right in.

A delicious coolness embraces me as I slice through the water, hand touching the bottom of the pool before I surface and swim to the other side.

I'm towelling my hair, back in my room, when I remember the smartphone. If I can get into it, I reason, it might shed light on what happened to Alejandro. I take the mobile from its hiding place under my pillow and try turning it on again.

The screen remains stubbornly black.

Where's Alejandro's charger? I wonder. *For that matter, where are all his things?*

Chances are, nobody has got around to clearing out his stuff yet – Mike and Sonoya have been too focused on keeping the Sanctuary running smoothly until Alejandro's replacement arrives and Elena returns from her break. If I pick the right moment, when everyone's busy, I might be able to get into his room.

As luck would have it, I bump into Mike on the way to breakfast. 'You seen Tamara?' he asks. 'We're supposed to be having a staff meeting.'

'I'm here,' she huffs behind him. 'Sorry, I was cleaning up in the kitchen.'

They disappear into the office; as they close the door I catch sight of Sonoya and Rory, already sitting around Mike's desk.

Perfect timing, I decide, diverting into the staff annex, the separate building I explored when I first arrived, the one with the locked doors. I head down the corridor, trying to think up an excuse should I bump into anyone.

But that's unlikely. Elena's gone, and everyone else is in the office.

As before, the first couple of doors I try are locked. But the next is open, and as I glance inside it's obvious this is Tamara's room – it's crammed with souvenirs from her craft sessions, every surface covered in grass baskets holding a variety of bangles and other gaudy bits of home-made jewellery, along with various macramé pot holders, overflowing with lanky spider plants. There's a huge crochet blanket on her bed; behind it hangs a large embroidered tapestry depicting a giant saguaro, desert hills in the background.

I shut the door and move on. I find Alejandro's room at the end of the corridor – at least I'm guessing it was his bedroom because it's completely empty. Everything has been removed, bar a white T-shirt I spot screwed up under the vacant wardrobe.

Where have they put the rest of his things? I think of the jeep returning from the desert, and it occurs to me Mike and Sonoya weren't doing anything so sinister as burying Alejandro's body. Perhaps they simply dumped his belongings somewhere, though for the life of me I can't imagine why they'd do that.

Bending down, I retrieve the T-shirt. The front is printed with a sun logo, the word 'cerveza' underneath. Some brand of local beer, I'm guessing. I lift the fabric to my nose, catch the unmistakable scent of Alejandro's aftershave. The smell fills me with another rush of sadness, and behind it, a rising sense of anger. He might have no family to miss him, but there's something callous about disposing of his body without a ceremony.

In that moment I know I can't just leave the Sanctuary – not until I've got to the bottom of whatever is going on. I owe it to

Alejandro; he was a good man, and didn't deserve to be treated like this.

Reluctantly, I screw up the T-shirt and replace it under the wardrobe. Glancing around one final time, I shut the door, wondering if anyone noticed his phone was missing when they cleared the room out. Have Mike or Sonoya actually looked for it?

I'm retracing my steps when a thought occurs to me. On impulse I open Tamara's door again and step inside, scanning the floors. Sure enough, there's a charger dangling from the socket by her bed. I check the lead – it would definitely fit Alejandro's phone.

I stand there, hesitating. How much time have I got?

Five minutes? Ten?

Get on with it, Zoey. I remove the charger and hurry back to my room. Plugging it into the socket by my cupboard, I connect the phone and press the power button.

A few seconds later, the screen lights up, displaying the nine-dot security pattern. I'm tempted to try to break the code, but it'll charge more quickly if I'm not draining any power.

How long have they been in Mike's office now? Fifteen minutes, perhaps?

I return to the reception area and dawdle by the entrance, pretending to study the huge oil painting on the opposite wall. I can hear the murmur of voices in the office. Sonoya speaking, then Rory's response, in a definite tone of protest.

Followed by the sound of a chair scraping on the floor.

I run to my room and pull out the charger, stuffing the phone back under my pillow, then race around the rear of the house to reach the annex. I knock gently on Tamara's door. No reply. I quickly slip inside and replace the charger by her bed, then creep out again.

'Zoey?'

I swing and find myself face-to-face with Maia, standing in the doorway of one of the locked rooms. My eyes widen in surprise, mind whirring as I finally put two and two together.

Maia's cheeks flush, then her expression settles into defiance. 'What are you doing here?'

'I could equally ask you the same,' I say, though the answer is obvious; Maia has spent the night in Rory's bed.

She stares at me, assessing. Did she hear me earlier, trying the doors? I wonder if my aura is giving me away. What might be the colour of guilt, of subterfuge?

Without a word, she locks Rory's door, pockets the key, and walks away. I follow her out of the annex, relieved when I reach the safety of my room. I have a feeling Maia won't dob me in. Clearly her curiosity is limited, or she decided it's not in her interests to press me further.

How long has this thing with Rory been going on? I wonder. *Was last night a one-off, or have they been at it for a while?*

Will she tell Rory she saw me?

But what could he do? After all, if he informs Mike or Sonoya that Maia caught me leaving Tamara's room, then he'll give away his own secret – that he's having an affair with a guest.

And like his history with Finn's sister, I can't imagine that'll go down well with Mike and Sonoya.

I reckon I can safely assume that Rory will keep schtum.

29

Group that afternoon is a slog. Without Max and Naomi, the energy in the Top feels depleted. Riley is even more introverted than usual, squatting on her chair chewing her nails, while Axel sits there absorbing all of it with that strange, beatific smile he's worn since the ceremony. He doesn't even take the piss when Maia tells a long anecdote about her film agent, which seems to hinge on her refusal to work with a woman younger than her.

I study Rory surreptitiously throughout, wondering if Maia's told him about seeing me in the staff annex, but his gaze, when it falls on me, is no different to usual. At one point I'm sure Tamara clocks me watching him, flashing me a discreet smile.

Oh God, that's all I need. She probably thinks I fancy Rory too.

I glance over at Finn, but he's sitting forward in his chair, elbows resting on his legs, eyes downcast. I tried looking for him earlier, but there was no sign of him in his room, or anywhere else.

Does he regret telling me about his connection to Rory?

Or is he more shocked by what I did to that man in the club than he's letting on? Perhaps Finn's decided he's better off steering clear of me altogether.

I'll tackle him later, I decide; after all, we have to discuss what to do about Alejandro. And I should tell him about the phone; with Elena away, it was my turn to help Tamara hoover and dust this morning, so I haven't had a chance to try bypassing the screen lock yet.

Maybe Finn will know some clever hack. Or know where to find out.

By the time group is over, I'm so hot and sweaty I decide on a shower before catching up with Finn. I go straight back to my room, grab my toiletries and lock myself in the little bathroom. Turning on the shower, I step inside, reaching for my shampoo; in that instant, the water suddenly switches from pleasantly cool to scalding.

I yelp in pain. As I grasp for the lever to turn it off, I slip and hit my head on the control valve.

Fat drops of blood drip onto the shower tray, turning the water pink. I climb out of the cubicle carefully, wipe steam from the mirror and examine my head. There's a gash in my scalp above my left eye. I grab a towel and press it down on the wound while I check the scalded skin on my shoulders, already smarting and sore.

I sit on the loo seat, feeling woozy and shaken, flashing back to that time Marcus tripped on a paving stone in the garden and cracked his head open. There was so much blood I started screaming, and it took Mum as long to console me as it did my brother. Even now, I can remember his pale, scared face as Dad drove us to the doctor's surgery; when the nurse announced he needed stitches, Marcus started wailing; I grabbed his hand and held on to it tightly, refusing to let go until it was all over.

All of a sudden, I'm missing my brother so much I feel I'll keel over from the force of it. How did we get from there to here, where we haven't exchanged a single word in years? I'm overwhelmed by grief, by a sense of loss.

What a fucking waste.

Focus, Zoey, I urge myself. Keeping the towel pressed to my head, I scoop up my clothes and scoot into my room. Somehow I manage to get dressed in shorts and a loose shirt without getting blood on them, then make my way to Sonoya's clinic, praying she's there.

'Zoey.' She frowns as she opens the door. 'Are you okay?'

'I think so. I banged my head in the shower. The water came out boiling – there must be something wrong with the thermostat.'

Sonoya winces when I slide down the shoulder of my T-shirt to reveal my reddened skin. 'Goodness, that's almost a scald. How on earth did it happen?'

'No idea. One second the water was a normal temperature, then it suddenly switched.'

She gets up and removes the towel. 'It's only a small gash,' she says, parting the hair gently to get a good look. 'Scalp wounds always bleed heavily. If we keep applying pressure, it should stop on its own.'

'So I don't need stitches?'

'Not sure. Let me check your shoulders first.'

I slip off my top and sit while she inspects my skin. 'That water must have been very hot,' she murmurs, sounding concerned. 'You'll be fine though. The skin hasn't blistered, but you will have to keep it out of the sun for a while.'

Going to the medicine cabinet, Sonoya removes a sterile dressing pad and presses it to the wound on my head. She pulls up a screen on her computer, taps in some notes, then turns back to me. 'You stay here for a few minutes, Zoey – I'll ask Mike or Rory to take a look at that shower immediately. You may have to use another bathroom for a while if they can't fix it.'

She shuts the lid to her laptop and gets to her feet. 'Do you feel okay otherwise? No wooziness? Headache?'

'Nope. I'm all right. A bit shaken up.'

'Continue applying pressure to the wound. I'll be back shortly.'

I sit there, holding the pad to my head, thinking about that shower. Why would the temperature suddenly change like that? Don't they have safety things in them to stop that happening?

Who knows? I understand as much about plumbing as I do poker.

I glance around the little clinic. Strange to think it's only three weeks since I found myself in here, terrified and bewildered.

So much seems to have happened – and so much has changed.

A moment later it occurs to me that Sonoya might have a spare charger lurking in here; I don't know how much juice the phone got earlier, but it can't hurt to give it some more. I get up and check outside the clinic door to make certain the coast is clear, then cross to Sonoya's desk, trying the drawers. Locked. Pressing the pad against my head, trying not to put any strain on the wound, I bend under the desk and scope out the plug points.

Damn. No sign of a charger.

But as I straighten up, I notice something else, barely visible in the laptop's USB port. I give it a gentle tug, and out slides one of those tiny phone memory cards, embedded in a reader. On impulse, I pull out the card and tuck it in my bra, replacing the reader into the port. If I can get into Alejandro's phone, I might be able to access it before Sonoya realises it's gone.

An instant later, the door opens. 'How are you doing?' Sonoya says, just as I'm sitting back in the chair.

'It seems to have stopped.' I remove the pad and she examines the wound.

'Yes, it has. That's good. Be careful not to do anything too energetic before it heals over. No swimming, I'm afraid.'

'Can I still go on the hike tomorrow?'

'You should be okay. Keep it well covered and stay in the shade where you can.' Sonoya glances at her little silver watch. 'Sorry, I have to go. I've got therapy sessions scheduled with Maia and Finn,' she says, unlocking her drawer and withdrawing her notebook. 'But if you feel unwell in any way, any symptoms of dizziness or confusion, come right in and get me.'

I follow her outside, my stomach sinking as she locks the door of the clinic behind her.

Damn. How will I replace that memory card now?

I need to do it before the hike, after all. Mike is remaining at the Sanctuary; the last thing I want is him discovering it's missing, and raising hell on our return.

30

I bump into Rory as he emerges from the shower room, a box of tools in his hand. 'Sonoya told me what happened. Said the water was scalding?'

I nod. 'It was ferociously hot.'

'Seems to be working fine now.'

'Really?' I blink at him. 'It was almost boiling.' I pull up the sleeve of my T-shirt so he can see my red skin.

'I can't see how that happened.' Rory frowns. 'Those things have safety devices in them. You'd have to manually override it.'

'Are you saying somebody *did it deliberately*?' I stare at him.

'No,' Rory says quickly. 'Of course not. Only Alej—' He stops. 'I checked it, but I don't honestly know what I'm looking for. It could be faulty, I guess. I suggest you avoid that bathroom from now on – you can use the one in the staff annex if you like.'

'Okay,' I agree. After all, it gives me a good excuse to be there. Perhaps I could borrow Tamara's charger again.

'You reckon you'll be all right for the hike tomorrow?'

'Sonoya thinks so.'

Rory looks relieved. 'Okay, I'll carry some of your stuff in my pack, to keep the weight off your shoulders. But give me a shout if it gets too much – it won't be the first time I've had to hike with two backpacks rather than one.'

He gives me a smile, and I return it, finding myself hoping that things work out for him and Maia. After all, whatever mistakes Rory's made in the past, he's clearly changed for the better.

She could do a lot worse.

Once Rory's gone, I take Alejandro's mobile, lock myself in the shower room, and fire it up. Only 17 per cent battery. How long will that last?

Not long, probably, given the age of the phone.

I stare at the nine-dot grid. I'm tempted to start swiping at random, then remember I only have five attempts before it locks. I learned this the hard way, having got so drunk at a party once that I forgot my security pattern – Rocco's friend Tony, who works in a telecoms store, had to do a factory reset.

I lost everything, my pictures, messages, the lot.

I recall what Tony told me, when he advised me to come to him if I ever forgot it again: most people's patterns are pretty simple and easy to hack. We're lazy, he said, and don't have time for anything complicated, so most of us start in one of the corners – if you're right-handed, he explained, chances are it's the top left.

Was Alejandro right-handed? I picture him building that wall, changing the tyre on the jeep. I'm pretty sure he was.

I gaze at the screen, hesitating. As it catches the light above the sink, I spot smudge marks from Alejandro's fingers, and experience another sting of sadness, seasoned with anger. Whatever happened to him, he didn't deserve it.

Then something occurs to me. I angle the screen carefully under the light, examining the smudges over the nine-dot grid. It's difficult to be sure, but I can faintly see horizontal lines across each of the three rows of dots – though it's impossible to make out how they're linked.

I get to my feet. Using the edge of the bar of soap, I draw nine dots on the mirror, then link them with three horizontal lines. How many ways can you join them? All I come up with is two Zs, one stacked on the other, or a shape like an S or a 2 with vertical joins.

I work it out – that's four combinations, but if you reverse directions, that makes eight total. Possibly more. Maths was never my strong point, and with the battery running low, time isn't on my side.

I try the most obvious. Beginning from the top left corner, I draw the number 2, ending on the bottom right.

Nothing.

I do the same thing the other way around, making an S.

Still nothing.

I retry the S shape, starting from the bottom, but the phone stays stubbornly locked. Damn. Two more tries remaining.

I study the mirror, forcing myself to work it through logically. Alejandro was a busy, right-handed man – what would be fast, natural and easy to memorise?

A loud knock on the door. 'Zoey, you in there?'

Tamara. What the hell?

'Yes.' I try not to sound too irritated. Is there anywhere in this place you can get some privacy?

'You've been in there a while, that's all. You feeling okay?'

'Fine,' I say. 'I'm . . . err . . . you know.' I flush the toilet for good measure.

'Right. Sorry to disturb you, but Sonoya mentioned you'd hit your head in the shower and said to keep an eye on you. You weren't in your room, so—'

'I'm all right, Tamara. Thank you.'

'Anyway, I was wondering if you would like a healing session. I could do some reiki. Might help calm you after your accident.'

'Thanks,' I repeat. 'Maybe later.'

Silence. My ears strain to hear her footsteps. As soon as I'm certain I'm alone, I study the screen. On impulse, I try doing two Zs, one on top of the other.

No banana. In desperation, I reverse the direction, and to my astonishment, the screen suddenly changes and rows of icons appear.

My heart leaps. I did it! I punch the air with elation, which lasts exactly as long as it takes to check the power icon.

Hell. Only 13 per cent left. The battery seems to be completely fucked. Could it be down to being left outside for several days? Perhaps it got damp – those bushes by the pool are on some kind of automatic watering system. I remember Mum dropped her mobile in the loo once; though she fished it out immediately, it was never the same after that, and she had to charge it twice a day.

Focus, Zoey.

What do you need to do?

I click on the email icon and browse through Alejandro's Gmail account, but pretty much everything is in Spanish. I try to decipher what I'm reading, but there doesn't seem to be much of interest.

What am I looking for anyway? I ask myself. Something from Ed perhaps.

No recent emails from him, so I access the activity log and find Ed's call from yesterday, the one I didn't manage to pick up. My finger hesitates over the reply button – what will I say if Ed answers?

Does he know Alejandro is dead?

How could I explain having his mobile?

Then I recall this phone is routed through the Sanctuary's satellite internet Wi-Fi. Could Mike or Sonoya detect it's being used?

No, ringing Ed is not a good idea. If nothing else, I don't want to use up what little battery there is left stuck in what might be an entirely pointless call.

I check the power icon again. Fuck. Just 9 per cent left.

On impulse, I click the gallery icon and check out Alejandro's pictures. Lots of the glorious desert sunsets. Close-ups of birds and lizards. Some mammal that looks like a cross between a mouse and a squirrel. And . . . *ugh* . . . several shots of what appears to be a nest of baby scorpions.

I scroll back further, and my breath stops in my throat. I pause, enlarging the photograph. Rory and Maia, locked in an embrace at the far end of the orchard.

I swipe to the next. There's a whole series of pictures of the two of them together, slightly grainy, obviously taken at a distance with the zoom function on high. But it's easy to identify Maia, with her strong jawline and trademark white-blonde hair.

I check the date of the photographs. Ten days ago.

Three days before Alejandro died.

I'm assailed by a mix of disappointment and confusion. Was he spying on Rory and Maia? Why on earth would he take these? There's only one reason I can imagine – Alejandro meant to use them in some way. But how? To get Rory in trouble with Mike and Sonoya? Or . . . I recall what Finn told me about Rory, about him hounding his sister when he was a paparazzi.

Was Alejandro intending to *sell* these pictures? I wonder how much a newspaper might pay for them, imagining the headlines: '*Maia French in rehab love clinch*'.

My stomach sinks as another possibility occurs to me. *Could Finn have put Alejandro up to this, to get back at Rory?*

After all, it would be the perfect revenge.

I close my eyes, feeling oddly let down by Alejandro; I didn't know him well, sure, but I expected better than this.

It's then I remember the memory card I removed from Sonoya's laptop. I retrieve it from my bra and check for somewhere to insert it. I'm in luck; while newer models don't have one, this is older, with a little slot on the base of the phone.

I pop it in place and a notification appears on the screen. 'Do you want to reformat this card?' I press no, and dozens of file icons appear. I scroll through them. Each has a pair of letters as a title – initials, I realise. I tap on ZB, but there's nothing in it.

Frowning, I navigate back and choose the file marked ET. Ed Temple. There are two items inside – a text document and a sound file. The document contains only a figure: 500k. What the heck does that mean? I click on the sound file and hold the phone to my ear, making sure the volume is on low.

A man's voice, talking about a woman he works with, how he feels about her. 'I'm perfectly aware it's wrong,' he says. 'I know I should stop, but I can't help myself. I can't get her out of my mind. She's all I think about.'

Then I hear Sonoya. 'Aren't you concerned your wife might discover this affair?'

'She won't find out,' the man insists. 'We've been very careful. But—'

I hit the pause button and stare at the phone, open-mouthed. *What the fuck? Is this what I think it is?*

Has Sonoya been *recording her therapy sessions?*

I picture her mobile phone, always placed neatly on top of her file and notebook. I never gave it a thought. As the implications sink in, I feel as if someone just kicked me in the guts. Sonoya has been secretly recording her sessions with Sanctuary guests, and keeping copies – or at least clips – on this memory card.

But why? Why would she do that?

To back up her notes, perhaps? For reference?

Or . . . I think about Ed leaving so suddenly, without speaking to anyone. I cast my mind back to that email he wrote to Mike:

'If you ever threaten me again, in any manner whatsoever, I will destroy you.'

They tried to blackmail him.

That figure in the text file must be the amount they asked for.

Shit. I return to the list of files and find the one marked FC. Finley Cooper. I open it. A wave of nausea hits me as I see several sound recordings. No text document, though.

Not yet, anyway.

Hands shaking, I press play, and Finn's voice is in my ear. I can't really follow it, but it appears to be something to do with his father's company.

'You mean a hostile takeover?' Sonoya asks.

As Finn starts to reply there's a ping from the phone. A notification pops up: 'You have a new text message'.

I pause the sound file. Open the message.

My heart stops. Another wave of nausea rises into my throat.

Only one line, and barely enough time to read it before the battery finally gives up and the screen goes black.

I know what you're doing.

31

I sit there, blinking at the blank screen of the mobile phone. My heart thumping so hard it almost hurts.

Was that message aimed at me?

Who else could it be for? Alejandro is dead, after all.

I swallow. Somebody knows I'm using his phone. No . . . wait. Whoever sent that knows that *someone* is using Alejandro's phone. They must have access to the back end of the Sanctuary Wi-Fi, saw it was active. But whoever it is can't possibly know it was me.

Or could they?

I think about the tarantula in my bed. The scalding shower. This menacing text. Is somebody trying to scare me? Hurt me even?

After all, no one else uses this bathroom, and pretty much everybody is aware of that – except Maia, perhaps, who seems oblivious to anything that doesn't directly concern her.

But who would want to hurt me?

And why?

Riley is an obvious candidate – she's always had it in for me. Axel might have been on the list before his miraculous conversion – anyway, he doesn't seem to dislike me any more than he dislikes anybody else.

Besides, how would either of them have access to the Sanctuary Wi-Fi log?

One thing is certain. If their aim was to scare me, they succeeded. I feel genuinely spooked, my hands trembling. I really need to talk to somebody. And now Naomi has gone, I can't think of anyone but Finn.

Then I remember those sound files, the one I was just listening to. What was he about to tell Sonoya? What was so bad that she could use it for blackmail?

I don't know, but first things first. I have to return the memory card before Sonoya realises it's missing. I remove it, popping it back in my bra, then return to my room and bury Alejandro's phone in the pile of underwear in my wardrobe.

Heading to the clinic, I knock on the door.

'Come in.'

I take a deep breath, trying to appear calm, and walk right up to Sonoya's desk. 'Have you got anything I can use on my shoulders,' I ask. 'They're really sore.'

'Of course.' Sonoya gets to her feet and goes over to the medicine cabinet. While she's turned away, I reach around the side of the laptop and slip the little memory card back into the USB port.

'Here.' Sonoya holds out a small tube of aqueous cream.

My smile comes out more as a grimace. My heartbeat in my head is so loud, I'm half convinced Sonoya can hear it. 'Thanks,' I say in a strangled voice.

'You all right, Zoey?' Sonoya cocks her head. 'Is there anything more you need?'

I stand there, staring at her. *An explanation*, I think. *I need a fucking explanation for what's going on in this place.*

How could you do that? I want to shout. *How could you abuse people's trust that way?*

I recall all the things I've told her, confessed to her, and my cheeks flush with anger and shame.

'I'm fine,' I mumble, heading for the door.

✳   ✳   ✳

I find Finn in the gym, on the exercise bike. He doesn't see me at first. I watch him pedalling hard, his T-shirt patchy with perspiration, as my mind churns over who sent that message. Somebody with access to the Wi-Fi log and a mobile phone, which limits it to Mike, Sonoya, Rory or Tamara.

And Finn, I realise, remembering his leverage over Rory. Though I guess if Finn has found a way around the rules, maybe others have too.

'Zoey.' Finn spots me and hops off the bike. 'I was looking for you earlier. Where'd you get to?'

'I had an accident in the shower. Banged my head and scalded my shoulders.'

'Ouch!' Finn grabs a towel and wipes the sweat from his face as he approaches me. 'How the hell did that happen? Are you okay?'

I shrug. 'No one seems to know how it happened – Alejandro took care of stuff like that. And yeah, I'm fine. I cut my scalp and it bled for a while, but it's stopped now.'

He puts a hand to my head, gently parting my hair. My skin tingles at his touch.

'Looks nasty,' he says, his fingers lingering. I daren't look up. Don't trust my face not to betray my feelings.

'You sure you're all right?' he asks, releasing me. 'You look kinda shaken up.'

I gaze back at him, wondering if I'm going to tell him what I suspect, that someone is deliberately attempting to frighten me.

Am I going to tell him about the blackmail too?

I've been wondering how, exactly, Sonoya goes about it. Perhaps she casually hints in one of the final therapy sessions that it might be in that person's interest to donate to the Sanctuary. Maybe she doesn't even have to go that far; a simple request for a contribution might be enough – guests can put two and two together, after all.

How many people have complied? Until she did it to Ed –
clearly in his case she miscalculated.

'Can we go for a walk?' I suggest. 'We should find somewhere
private.'

As soon as the words leave my mouth, I know how they
sound. Sure enough Finn starts smirking. 'That's definitely an
offer I can't refuse.'

'I just need to talk to you,' I blurt, cheeks burning.

'No problem, Zoey. Let me jump in the shower and I'll meet
you down in the orchard.'

I return to my room, intending to take Alejandro's phone with
me. I'll show it to Finn, I decide, tell him what I found – and ask
him what we should do.

If I can't trust him, after all, what's the point?

But as I sift through my underwear, I come away empty-
handed. It's gone.

I check through the rest of my wardrobe, then search under
my pillow, the mattress – anywhere else I might have put it in a
moment of distraction – but the phone has completely vanished.

I stand there, pulse racing. How long was I away?

Fifteen minutes? Twenty?

Long enough for someone to come in my room and find
Alejandro's phone. But only, I realise, if they knew I had it.

Which would mean that text was clearly intended for me.

32

'So what's up, Zoey?'

Finn picks a fig from the tree, and breaks it open, sucking the inside. There are dozens more scattered across the ground, I notice – oranges too. With Alejandro gone, no one has had time to harvest the ripe fruit.

I wonder where to start. 'I found Alejandro's phone,' I say eventually.

Finn stops chewing. 'You found his cell phone? *Where?*'

'Under a bush by the pool. I was lying on one of the sunbeds and glanced over, and there it was. It was pretty well hidden.'

'How can you be sure it's Alejandro's?' Finn looks sceptical.

I shrug. 'Who else could it belong to?'

He picks a seed from his teeth as he mulls this over. 'So do you have it with you?'

'That's the thing – I haven't got the phone any more. It vanished from my room – just now, while I was talking to you in the gym.'

A frown creases Finn's forehead. 'I don't understand.'

I sink onto a bench under the shade of a peach tree. 'Nor do I. I reckon somebody is trying to scare me actually – or hurt me.' I flash back to what Rory said about the shower controls: *I can't see how those things could go wrong. Someone would have to adjust it manually.*

Finn laughs. 'You serious?' His expression is incredulous, almost mocking.

I bite my lip to stop it trembling, caught between bursting into tears and exploding in rage. Why the hell did I imagine Finn was someone I could talk to?

I turn and walk away, but Finn strides over, grabbing my arm to stop me.

'Hey, Zoey, calm down. I'm sorry, I shouldn't have reacted like that. Come and tell me everything, right from the beginning.'

I hesitate, still churning with indignation, then let him guide me back to the bench.

'So run me through it again. You said you found this phone under the shrubs by the pool?'

'Yes.'

'When?'

'Day before yesterday.'

'Before I told you about the police report?'

I fiddle with my lip piercing, wondering whether to lie. 'Yes,' I admit.

'Okay.' Finn takes this in. 'So, what did you do with it then?'

'I smuggled it into my room, and while I was looking at it, that guy Ed Temple called. The battery went dead before I could answer. So I found a charger and—'

'Hey, back up.' Finn narrows his eyes at me. 'You found a charger *where exactly?*'

I blink at him. I can see why he would be a formidable business opponent. He never misses a trick.

'Tamara's room. I only borrowed it for fifteen minutes or so. I'm pretty sure she didn't miss it.' I don't mention Maia catching me coming out of Tamara's room – nor the fact that she was in Rory's. I figure whatever's going on is their business, not ours.

Finn doesn't reply, so I continue. 'I charged the phone up a bit, and replaced the charger. Then I had to go to group, and I was so hot afterwards I decided to have that shower.'

'So then what?' he prompts.

'I went to Sonoya and she helped stop the bleeding. Then she left me in the clinic while she spoke to Rory about the shower, and I saw . . .' I swallow. I've already admitted to Finn that I took Tamara's charger. And now this? 'I'm not sure why I did it. I spotted a memory card in her laptop, and—'

'You stole it,' Finn cuts in, his expression unreadable.

'I *borrowed* it,' I insist, but even I'm aware that's a lame excuse.

Finn doesn't comment, so I carry on. 'I managed to get past the lock screen on Alejandro's phone and then . . . and then I put the memory card in,' I say, skipping the bit where I found the pictures of Rory and Maia. 'It has a load of folders in it, labelled with initials. I didn't get a chance to look at all of them, the phone is pretty old and the battery was going down really quickly, but I opened the one for Ed.'

Finn stares at me. 'What did it contain?'

'A voice file, of a therapy session with Sonoya. It was a clip of him telling her something . . . very personal.'

To his credit Finn doesn't ask me what. 'So you're saying . . . that Sonoya has been recording her therapy sessions?' he asks, looking incredulous.

I nod.

'But why would she do that?' He seems baffled.

I clear my throat. 'Actually, there's another thing, something I should have told you before. When I got back to the Sanctuary, after running away, Mike left his laptop open. I wanted to access my emails, but I was also desperate to discover who paid for me to be here. So I had a quick look in Mike's inbox. And . . .'

I feel my cheeks grow hotter. I sound like a snoop or a spy, prying into people's personal lives. 'I saw an email from Ed, and I was curious because everyone seemed so upset about him leaving suddenly—'

'So you had a look.'

'I'm sorry. I know it sounds as if I make a habit of poking about in people's private business, but I don't. Not usually.'

'What did it say, Zoey?'

'It was very short. It said if Mike or Sonoya ever threatened him again, he'd destroy them.'

Finn's features tighten. He looks winded, as if someone punched him. He gets up and walks to the peach tree, leaning on the trunk for support, and gazes over the boundary wall to the wilderness beyond. Neither of us speaks for a minute or so, until he turns back to me.

'Blackmail,' he says simply.

I nod. 'I reckon so. Like I said before, from what I overheard out in the desert, the Sanctuary has had financial issues for some time – it must cost a bomb to keep this place going.'

'Yeah,' Finn agrees. 'It must.'

'There was a figure in a text document in Ed's file, with a number in it: 500k,' I tell him. 'I reckon that's how much she asked him for.'

'So you think Sonoya records her sessions, then keeps the voice clips if people disclose anything confidential.'

I nod. 'Anything they might not want to be made public.'

'Were there any recordings of me?' Finn asks, his eyes fixed on my face, alert for tells. 'Did you listen to them?'

'No,' I say. It's half true, after all; I didn't get the chance to properly listen to any of Finn's voice files.

He rubs his cheek, clearly relieved, and I wonder what he's afraid might be exposed. *What do I actually know about this man?* I ask myself, remembering those clandestine shots of Maia and Rory. Is it really possible Finn put Alejandro up to that?

I wrestle with asking him outright, but let's face it, if Finn did that, he'll never admit it.

And his poker face is far better than mine; he won't give himself away.

'What did you do with this memory card?' he asks, sitting on the bench again.

'Put it back in Sonoya's computer.'

'So you've no proof of any of this?'

I gaze at him. Finn's right. I should have kept that memory card. If I had, we could go to the police and blow this whole thing out of the water; after all, even if we turn up in Hermosillo, saying Alejandro is dead, what do we have? Why would they believe us?

I know what you're doing.

Someone at the Sanctuary is watching me and trying to scare me off. Somebody knew I had Alejandro's phone, and that same person took it from my room. Do they also know I looked at that memory card? That I'm aware of the blackmail?

All of a sudden, I'm properly frightened. Alejandro's death might not have been an accident, after all. And if someone did kill him, it's likely to be the same person messing with me.

What if next time it's not a tarantula in my bed, but something more deadly?

'Christ, Zoey,' Finn groans. 'What a fucking mess. It's all so . . . hard to believe.'

'Do you believe me?' I ask, wishing I'd had a chance to properly listen to his sound clip after all. If I had, I could prove everything I've just said.

But then, if I'd heard it, maybe I wouldn't be sitting out here with him at all. Maybe I'd know better.

I glance about, half hoping to see other people around, but we're alone.

'There's something I should tell you,' Finn says, ignoring my question.

'What?' I ask, assuming he's about to confess what he revealed to Sonoya.

'I wasn't sure whether to tell you or not, but I guess you have a right to know.' He looks at me, as if for confirmation.

'*What?*' I repeat, more insistently.

Finn inhales, rubs his cheek again. 'In that background check I had run on you, I received some information.'

My stomach tightens. This isn't going to be anything I want to hear.

Finn doesn't speak for a moment or two, then seizes my hand, folding it in his. 'Do you want to know, Zoey, who got those charges dropped? Who paid for you to come here? Would you like me to tell you?'

I try to inhale, but it feels impossible to get air into my lungs. '*You mean you've found out?*'

Finn nods. 'But I'll only tell you if you want me to.'

'*Of course* I want you to!' I gasp. 'Who was it? My dad? My uncle? Was Dan simply pretending it wasn't him?'

Finn shakes his head. 'His name is Jacob Harris.'

Jacob Harris?

I feel the blood drain from my face. I stare at Finn open-mouthed, trying to breathe.

'Do you know him?' Finn studies my reaction.

'Yes.'

Jacob Harris is a name I haven't heard in years. Someone I've tried very hard not to think about this last decade or so. I drop my head in my hands, trembling with shock. And suddenly I'm there again, at Laura's funeral. I'd snuck into the rear of the chapel, as the service was starting, hoping nobody would notice me, that I wouldn't have to explain who I was or why I was there.

Not that I could have answered. In truth, I had no idea what had brought me. Guilt, perhaps? Some kind of penance? As I listened to the service, to the audible sobs from Laura's mother in the front pew, I felt more and more like an imposter. The last person who should be witnessing her grief.

I sat it out though. Heard friends and family reading eulogies to Laura, to her hard work and kindness, gazing at the photos projected onto a screen at the front end of the chapel. Laura as a baby, smiling up at her parents. Laura as a toddler, taking her first steps. Laura in her new uniform about to embark on her first day at school. Laura at her eighteenth birthday party. Laura in her prom dress, surrounded by her friends.

It was unbearable. Excruciating. I felt frozen inside, unable to cry. The moment the service was over, after that ghastly velvet curtain slid around the coffin, I made for the exit as quickly as I could without drawing attention to myself.

Too late.

'Are you a friend?' asked a voice behind me as I reached the flower garden that surrounded the crematorium. 'Sorry, I mean were . . . were you a friend of Laura's?'

I turned to the man behind me. Tall, nice-looking. His short red hair the exact shade of his sister's.

'No,' I stuttered. 'Yes . . . sort of. She was on my law course.'

'You're not going, are you?' he said. 'I saw you heading off, but I wanted to invite you to have a drink and some food at my parents' house. Do come along. I think you're the only person here from her university.'

'I can't,' I said quickly, trying to find an excuse, but my mind offered nothing.

'Can I ask your name?'

I swallowed. 'Zoey.'

'Zoey . . .?' He left a blank for me to fill in my surname.

Something collapsed inside me. 'Zoey Baxter,' I admitted, seeing Jacob's expression shift.

'Zoey Baxter . . . you mean . . . you're *Marcus's sister?*'

I nodded, cheeks on fire, tears pricking my eyes.

Jacob Harris stepped towards me. 'What the fuck are you doing?' he growled, grabbing my arm. 'Why are you here, Zoey?'

Why am I here? I asked myself again. *What on earth possessed me to do this?*

'I only wanted to . . .' I burst into tears.

Jacob's grip tightened. 'Don't you dare play the victim here,' he spat at me. 'You knew, didn't you, what your brother did?'

'I'm sorry, I tried—'

'You didn't try particularly hard, though, did you? You didn't report that disgusting video your brother took. Instead, you went round to harass my sister—'

'No!' I protested. 'I didn't. I simply wanted to talk to her. I wanted to see if she was okay. I was worried—'

'Oh fuck off.' Jacob released me, his face twisted with anger and grief. 'I can't believe you had the nerve to turn up here.'

He walked away, shaking his head. I stood, paralysed, watching him return to his parents, watching him speak, their heads swivelling in my direction.

Then I ran. Actually sprinted across the perfectly mown lawn. Ran all the way to the train station. Have been running ever since.

'Hey, *Zoey.*' Finn is kneeling in front of me, holding my hands as they tremble, his thumbs caressing my skin. 'Zoey, you okay?' He pulls a tissue from the pocket of his shorts, studying me as I dab my eyes. 'I take it you know Jake Harris then.'

'Not exactly,' I croak, clearing my throat. 'I only met him once. Briefly.' I sit up and take a deep breath, pulling myself together.

Finn frowns. 'So have you any idea why he'd intervene with your arrest, negotiate with the NYPD, and pay for you to come here?'

'None whatsoever.' I force myself to meet Finn's gaze. 'It doesn't make any sense at all.'

It makes the opposite of sense. Jacob Harris hates me. He pretty much believes I killed his sister.

Finn's expression remains deadpan. 'I mean, he's cool, but it seems a lot to do for somebody you barely know.'

My eyes widen. My pulse is racing and I feel dizzy. 'You mean *you've met him*? When? How?'

'Here,' Finn gestures at the house. 'Jake arrived the same time as Ed – they were friends. Both had recently sold their businesses, they met in some conference in London on emerging technologies. Ed told him about the Sanctuary, so they decided to do the programme together. We only coincided for a few days, but Jake seemed okay. A mess though. Big drinker, lots of party drugs.' He sighs, dropping his gaze. 'But then I'm hardly one to talk.'

Nor me, I admit to myself.

'You okay?' Finn gives my hands a squeeze. 'You seem really . . . shell-shocked. So you never imagined Jake was responsible for you being here?'

'Frankly he's the last person on earth I'd have guessed. Like I said, it doesn't make any sense.'

Finn gazes at me, his face full of concern. 'You wanna talk about it?'

'Actually I might go and lie down for a while.' I get to my feet. 'I need to rest before the hike tomorrow.'

'Are you up to it? What with your head and everything.'

'I'm not sure,' I admit. 'But I'm not keen on staying here alone.'

'Mike'll be here,' Finn says, then reads my mind. 'I guess that's not exactly reassuring – if this blackmail stuff is true.'

'Sorry you don't believe me,' I mutter, turning away.

'Hey, I didn't say that. I simply meant we need proof, Zoey, not speculation. There could be other explanations for those files.'

'There's some innocent reason why Sonoya secretly records her therapy sessions and keeps clips of them?' I throw him a scornful look.

'You should have brought that memory card straight to me,' Finn says. 'But—'

'Fuck you,' I cut in, heading back to the house as fast as I can.

33

I don't go and lie down. I need to find somewhere I know I won't be disturbed, where I can be alone with this mess of thoughts. I climb up to the tower roof, and sit in the lone deck-chair wedged between the satellite dish and the weather vane, a fine vantage point for watching the desert sunset. As the sun sinks towards the horizon, the distant hills are already tinged with gold, and I spot a pair of buzzards circling on the warm updraughts.

Odd that people don't spend more time up here. It's cramped, sure, but the views are stupendous – you can see clearly in every direction.

I drop my gaze to the immediate vicinity of the Sanctuary. Over in the kitchen garden, Riley is watering the tomatoes, and Tamara, half hidden by the trees in the orchard, is picking plums for tonight's dessert. From this height, Maia looks more like a Barbie doll than ever, stretched out on a lounger by the pool, lapping up the last of the sun. Rory keeps dipping in and out of view as he visits the sheds, preparing everything for tomorrow's hike. I can even see into the southern half of the courtyard, where Axel is sitting by the fish pond with his eyes closed.

Asleep or meditating? It's hard to tell the difference.

No sign of Mike and Sonoya. Or Finn.

I think of the bombshell he just dropped on me, closing my eyes as I attempt to calm the rush of my thoughts, the pressure around my heart. Jacob Harris – Jake – intervened with the police and paid for me to be here.

But why? Why on earth would he do that?

He hates me.

I recall the loathing on his face as he turned away from me at the funeral. I cried on the train all the way home to Guildford, and told Mum I wasn't going back to university.

Why did I do that? To punish myself?

Marcus stayed on, of course. Every time he came home in the holidays, I went off travelling somewhere. I didn't ever want to set eyes on him.

Punishing him too, I suppose.

So what is this, my being here, at the Sanctuary? I ask myself. Is this also some sort of punishment? Jake's way of forcing me to face up to the role I played in his sister's death?

It would make a weird kind of sense. He must have calculated that isolating me here, compelling me to participate in therapy and the ceremonies would bring everything to the surface again.

But how did he know what happened in the club? How on earth did he manage to broker a deal with the New York police?

There's only one explanation. All these years Jacob Harris has been keeping tabs on me, one way or another. Waiting for his moment.

Then something else occurs to me. A horrible, truly horrifying thought.

What if Jake has set me up? What if someone here, someone who knows him, is doing those things to frighten me?

What if there's something worse in store for me?

Revenge for his sister.

My mood spirals. If I was afraid when I discovered somebody had taken that phone from my room, I'm terrified now.

You need to get out of this place, says an urgent voice. *No matter what it costs, no matter how much it pisses off Mike.*

You need to get the fuck out of here, now.

I leap up and descend the tower stairs, almost running towards the office. I'll tell Mike I want to leave the moment he can arrange a chopper, that I'll pay him back as soon as I'm able. And when he objects, when he refuses, I'll tell him I know about the little scam he has going with Sonoya, and that the cost of my silence is sending me home.

Somehow I suspect he'll find it cheap at the price.

But as I approach the reception area, Rory emerges from the office, slamming the door behind him and striding past me without a word.

There's an expression on his face that feels all too familiar. The look of someone who's been pushed to their limits. The look of somebody whose whole world has collapsed in on them, like an unstable building in an earthquake.

I creep towards the office, hearing raised voices. Mike . . . Sonoya. Then silence. As if one told the other to keep quiet.

I stand there, hesitating. I need to talk to Mike alone. I can't face taking on the pair of them together.

'Zoey? What's up?'

I spin around to see Tamara ambling towards me. 'You seem a bit lost.' She laughs. 'How are you feeling? You think you're up for the hike tomorrow?'

'I'm not going on the hike tomorrow,' I mutter. 'I'm going home.'

Tamara doesn't react at all. 'Let's go and have a chat in the treatment room,' she suggests. 'I'll fetch us both a cold drink.'

I trail after her and sit on the sofa opposite the treatment couch, while she disappears, returning with a couple of glasses of home-made lemonade. I take a sip, listening for any sign that Sonoya has left the office.

'So, what's happened?' Tamara asks, perching on the couch.

'Nothing, really.' I shrug, playing down the turmoil inside me. 'It's simply time for me to go.'

'Is this about the shower accident earlier? Because Rory says—'

'No,' I interrupt. 'It has nothing to do with that.'

'What's the problem then?' Tamara tilts her head with such an expression of sympathy on her face that for a moment I'm tempted to tell her. All of it. Finding Alejandro's phone. The memory card. Discovering that the person who sent me here is the person on this earth who hates me most.

But Tamara's whole life is wrapped up in this place, and I don't want to be the one who destroys it. I can't tell her about the blackmail, or any of it. Not even what Finn just revealed about why I'm here; Tamara may be a little flaky, but she's not stupid – she'll want to know how I found out about Jake.

All of a sudden, she leans over and hugs me. 'Don't go. You've been doing so well. Making such great progress.'

I frown at her. 'I thought you said I wasn't cut out for this?'

'I've changed my mind,' she replies breezily. 'I like you, Zoey. You have a good heart. And you've got guts too – you didn't take the easy way out when it was offered to you. So I don't want you leaving now, right when you're getting to grips with the issues that brought you here.'

She releases me, waiting until I raise my gaze to hers. 'You know, I see a lot of myself in you, Zoey. I mean, back before I got clean and squared up to my demons. I can see that in you, an inner strength. Kindness too.'

I stare at her, wishing I could be honest about why I need to leave, why I haven't a choice. But I can't tell her – it would break her heart.

All at once, I burst into tears. Tamara sits beside me on the sofa and holds me until I'm all cried out. 'You go and get some rest. Come on the hike tomorrow, it'll do you good. And if you still want to go home when we get back, I'll sort it with Mike, okay?'

I nod and thank her.

Grabbing my towel from my room, I take a cold shower in the staff annex, washing away all the dust and the sweat and the anguish, then nudge Simpkins off my bed and climb in.

Seconds later, everything fades to black.

34

'Zoey?'

A loud rap on the door wakes me. Sonoya sticks her head into my room. 'C'mon, get up.'

I glance at the window, see the orange glow of sunrise. Close my eyes again.

'We're leaving in half an hour,' Sonoya persists. 'You should eat before we go. You can't hike on an empty stomach.'

I glare at her. All I can think about is those files on that memory card in her laptop. How can she carry on as if she's done absolutely nothing wrong?

But Sonoya disappears before I'm tempted to say anything. I force myself upright, dressing in shorts and a T-shirt, and my borrowed walking boots. I just manage to throw down a coffee and an oatmeal muffin, grab my rucksack, then it's time to go – Rory's keen we get in the miles before the heat of the day becomes overwhelming.

As we trail across the desert towards the mountains in the distance, I keep to the rear of the group. Finn is up ahead, talking to Rory and Maia, Riley and Axel in tow, Sonoya and Tamara after them. I walk alone, still processing everything that happened yesterday. The shower. The blackmail. The creepy text – who the hell was behind that?

Again, Riley seems the obvious candidate – she's pretty much despised me from the moment I arrived. It occurs to me she was also here when Jake Harris was at the Sanctuary. Perhaps he told her what happened with his sister; maybe that's why she hates me so much.

But no, that doesn't make sense. Jake couldn't have known then, could he, that he'd get this opportunity to send me here?

I well and truly handed him that on a plate.

Besides, I doubt Riley has access to a phone, let alone any way of knowing I was using Alejandro's.

Who else might have sent that message then? Mike or Sonoya? Could either have realised I'm on to them? But why bother? If they wanted rid of me, they could easily kick me out on some excuse. And I can't for the life of me imagine Rory or Tamara wanting to frighten me away – indeed, Tamara was the one persuading me to stay yesterday.

An uneasy feeling stirs in my stomach as I recall again that Finn has access to Rory's phone. *Could it really be Finn who sent that message?*

Why would he though? Why do that, then pretend to be my friend? It doesn't add up. Perhaps I should just tell him about the threatening text, and those pictures of Maia and Rory on Alejandro's phone. Poker face or not, he'd have to say something.

But then I've got no proof of any of it. He probably won't believe me.

'Penny for them?'

I glance up to see Axel hanging back from the others, waiting for me. 'You look miserable,' he says. 'What's up?'

I hitch my pack higher. Though Rory has taken the weightier stuff – my tarpaulin, sleeping bag, and the bulk of my food – it's still as heavy as hell, stuffed with everything else needed to survive two nights in the desert. The straps rub uncomfortably against the skin of my scalded shoulders, but I'm loath to let Rory take it yet; after all, we've only been hiking an hour.

'Just tired,' I tell Axel. No way am I getting into this with him – even in his new incarnation.

He takes the hint and walks silently beside me. Up ahead, I hear Sonoya's voice, calm and measured. I watch her, wondering again how she can keep it up. The pretence that she's only here for our benefit, to help people. I can't get it out of my head, Ed's voice as he talked to her in that session, pouring out his heart, baring his soul, with no idea how she planned to use it against him.

No wonder he was so angry when he found out. Hardly a surprise he left without speaking to anyone.

'Have you thought what you'll do when you leave?' Axel asks, out of the blue. I narrow my eyes at him, caught in a spiral of paranoia. Why is he asking that? Is he aware I was planning to go as soon as we get back?

'I'll return to the UK probably,' I say, as casually as I can manage. 'Spend some time with my mum.'

'I've been giving it some thought myself,' he says. 'I might go back to college. Retrain as an addiction counsellor.'

'Really?' I squint at him. Is he taking the piss?

'Yeah, I know what you're thinking.' He holds my gaze. 'But I was talking to Tamara about it – it actually helps to have had issues yourself.'

'Rory said that too. I think it's a great idea,' I say, finding I mean it.

'What about you?' he asks, after a few minutes of silence as we pick our way through the boulders. 'You planning a fresh start?'

'Nothing occurs to me,' I shrug. 'But then it never does.'

'If you could wave a magic wand and be anything you want, what would it be?'

I consider this. 'A lawyer,' I admit.

'A lawyer? Why?'

'I like the idea of making things right for people, I suppose. And arguing seems to be my super power.' I glance at Finn and Tamara, who have dropped back and are now walking a few yards ahead of us, but they don't appear to be listening. Indeed, Finn has barely made eye contact since we set off; clearly he's annoyed about what happened yesterday.

'You care about justice,' Axel nods. 'Nothing wrong with that.'

'Anyway, it's out of the question. I'd have to go back to university and complete my law degree. It'd cost a fortune and take years, then there's all the vocational training on top.'

'Not necessarily,' Tamara chips in, stopping to wait for us – clearly she was listening to our conversation after all. 'You could be a paralegal, Zoey – you don't need a degree for that. A friend of mine is an attorney, and from what he tells me, justice doesn't come into it much; paralegal on the other hand – you can do a lot of good with that.'

I give her a smile, unconvinced, then pause to adjust my socks. They keep working their way down inside my boots, and I'm starting to get sore where the leather rubs my ankles.

'Any idea how much further till we take a break?' I ask Tamara. 'I need to find another pair of socks.'

'Not far,' she reassures me. 'It's right up around this bluff.'

I glance around. How on earth would she know? Everywhere in this desert looks exactly like everywhere else.

'How does Rory remember the way?' I ask her, curious. 'What if we get lost? We could be stuck out here for days.'

'Rory's done this dozens of times. Besides, he's brought a sat phone. If we hit trouble he'll simply ring Mike.'

Axel frowns. 'What could he do?'

'Come out with the jeep,' Tamara says. 'Get as close as he can. Or if the worst comes to the worst, he could call in an emergency helicopter.'

Right around this bluff proves to be a lot further than Tamara was letting on. We walk for what feels like miles, dodging the largest cacti, weaving through clumps of rock, constantly changing direction. Everybody is beginning to flag in the relentless heat – only Rory and Maia appear unaffected, Maia striding out as if she does this every day, making the whole thing seem effortless in her slim-cut hiking trousers and long-sleeved shirt.

She's tougher than she looks – I have to give her that.

How long has her affair with Rory been going on? I wonder, as we finally stop for lunch, eating the sandwiches Tamara and Riley made this morning. Is it serious? Or simply a rehab fling? Is Rory the reason Maia stayed on at the Sanctuary, given what she witnessed by the pool the night Alejandro died?

Who knows? I chase down my sandwich with a granola bar, then peel off my boots. Two large blisters already, both on my ankle bones.

'Ouch!' Tamara exclaims, examining them. 'Hang on, I have something that'll help.'

I watch Finn as she roots around in her rucksack. He's sitting alone on a rock ten or so yards away, studying the landscape, seemingly lost in thought. I wonder if I should make an effort to talk to him, to patch things up.

Sod it, I decide. He was the one who said he didn't believe me.

'There you go.' Tamara hands me a couple of sticking plasters – the thick fabric kind with a padded strip in the centre. I place them carefully over the blisters and ease my boots back on, then finish up with a long cool drink. I'm insanely thirsty, and tempted to gulp it down – after all, it would lighten my load. But Rory went out of his way in yesterday morning's orienteering session to stress the importance of conserving our water – the two large bottles we're each carrying in our packs have to last until we reach second camp tomorrow, where there's a natural spring.

We set off walking again. The sun is high in the sky now, and it's so hot I'm almost hallucinating. Everybody falls into silence, focused on putting one foot in front of another. On and on, over and over, chipping away at the miles between us and our destination.

'You okay?' Sonoya asks, pausing to let me catch up.

'Fine,' I say through gritted teeth. I want to tell her how upset, how disappointed I am in her. Scream it at the top of my voice so everybody stops dead in their tracks and hears Sonoya exposed for what she really is.

A blackmailer.

But caution holds me back. I'm acutely aware how vulnerable we are out here. If anything happened, if there was a fight or somebody got hurt, we'd be in serious trouble.

Any confrontation will have to wait until we've returned to the Sanctuary.

It feels like an eternity before Rory comes to a halt and heaves his pack to the ground – twice the size of any of ours – and starts unloading it. I shuffle mine off too, sinking onto a rock.

Big mistake. It's in full sun and the hot stone scorches my legs. I squeal, jump up again and find a shadier place to sit.

We're in some kind of small canyon. As well as the usual cacti, green-leafed trees are growing in the shadow of the tall rocks on either side of us. I'm guessing there must be water somewhere, perhaps an underground spring.

Rory motions us to gather around. 'Axel, how about you demonstrate to those who don't know how to set up their tarpaulin?' he asks. 'Everyone else, find a flat piece of ground, and clear away any rocks – Axel will show you how to string your tarp between two trees.'

'What are we going to sleep on?' Maia asks, still glamorous despite a hard day's walking; like Sonoya, she seems to have mastered the art of never breaking a sweat.

'Grass – the dry stems make a pretty decent mattress.' Rory gives Maia an indulgent smile, and out of the corner of my eye, I see Riley scowl. Has she picked up there's something going on between them?

We set about making our shelters for the night. I watch Axel as he hangs his tarpaulin from a rope strung between a couple of the sturdier trees, then join Tamara as she gathers armfuls of dried grass. She looks hot and tired, but still wearing her cheerful smile; she makes short work of her bedding, then helps me with mine.

'Right,' Rory announces, once everyone has sorted their shelter. 'Let's take a walk around the camp to see if we can find things to eat.'

Oh God, I groan to myself. I just need half an hour's rest with my boots off. My feet are sweating and I have to dry out those blisters.

'C'mon, Zoey. You can sleep when you're dead.' Rory extends a hand and pulls me upright, and we trail after him. He takes us on a guided tour of the canyon, describing the native wildlife and showing us some of the edible plants. He's putting on a good front, I observe, remembering his expression as he stormed out of the office yesterday. You'd never guess he had anything on his mind beyond passing on his love of this remote corner of the earth.

'Prickly pear cactus is an excellent food source.' Rory cuts off one of its fat pads with his hunting knife. 'You'll see it in many Mexican supermarkets.' He drops a dozen pads into a nylon bag then moves to a different cactus, covered in what look like spiky red fruit.

'Sweet and delicious,' Rory declares, showing us how to improvise makeshift tongs from a piece of wood to pluck fruit without getting spikes in our fingers.

'There's more than 250 edible plants in the Sonoran Desert,' he explains, once we've gathered all the fruit we can find. Rory shows us a scrawny tree with a number of green pods hanging from its branches. 'Palo verde.' He plucks one and splits it to reveal a few pale 'peas', which resemble Japanese edamame; popping a couple into his mouth, he encourages us to do the same.

I open mine with trepidation. What if Rory has this wrong, and these things are actually poisonous?

Don't be silly. He's done this loads of times, I remind myself. I put one in my mouth – it tastes like a bland garden pea.

Further afield, up near the head of the canyon, Rory leads us to a group of agave. Choosing a younger plant, he uses a small machete to chop through to its heart, then strips off the layers to expose the centre. He cuts this into pieces for us to try – it's surprisingly tender and sweet.

'Like sugar cane,' Axel comments, his expression thoughtful. 'But woodier.' He spits a clump of fibres onto the ground.

Finn grimaces as he chews. 'Frankly I prefer mine as tequila.'

'I'll drink to that,' says Maia, her face breaking into a rare grin.

Once we've stripped the surrounding area of any available food source, Rory instructs us on how to find water. 'Look for north-facing canyons, areas of green vegetation, and water-loving broad leaf trees,' he explains, but I'm only half listening now. All I want in the world is to get back to the camp and take the weight off my feet. Have a snooze, perhaps, under my tarpaulin.

No such luck. The moment we return to our shelters, Rory sets about teaching us how to light a fire without matches or a lighter. He disappears for a few minutes, returning with a couple of sticks. I sit on the dirt and watch him saw a section from the larger one, stripping off the bark with his machete, then carving a small depression into it. The other, smaller stick he strips and sharpens into a point – or the drill, as Rory calls it.

'Right, hold the drill like this and spin.' He twirls the pointed stick expertly between his palms, making a deeper depression in the bigger chunk of wood, then cuts a notch out of the side.

'What's that for?' Riley asks.

'To collect the embers.' We watch, fascinated, as he slots the drill back into the depression and spins it again, more vigorously this time. Within seconds smoke appears, and a clump of black dust. Rory gathers it up quickly and drops it into a small pile of dried grass, then blows on it.

Axel gives a little cheer as it bursts into flames, and we all clap. 'Got to hand it to ya, Rory, that's fucking impressive,' Finn says.

'Here, you do it.' Rory hands out more sticks and I give it a go. It's a lot more difficult than it looks. Try as hard as I may, I can't make an ember, and the palms of my hands get sore from spinning.

'This is bullshit,' Riley says crossly, kicking her stick away.

'This bullshit might save your life one day,' Tamara replies sharply. 'It takes a while to acquire the knack' – she blows on her little glowing piece of straw – 'but once you know how, it's easy.'

'It'll be handy, next time I need to light my bong and can't find my lighter,' quips Axel with a grin.

Rory ignores him. 'As soon as you've got your grass alight, bring it over here and we'll make one big fire.'

Within minutes, flames are crackling through a wigwam of dry wood. Once the fire's established, Rory takes a prickly pear pad – or 'nopal' as he calls it – and shows us how to skim off the spines with a knife. We spear them with long sticks and cook them until they're black.

'*Ugh.*' Riley pulls a face as she takes a bite. 'I thought it might be better second time around. But nope.'

I have to agree. It's pretty disgusting, sort of sticky and tart at the same time. The fruits are better, after the spiky bits are removed – a cross between watermelon, strawberry and guava.

When we've all had a taste of the wild food, we unload the other supplies from our packs. We tuck into sausages and beans cooked in aluminium pans, and potatoes wrapped in foil and baked on the embers.

'Anyone got a rifle?' Axel asks, as a jack rabbit darts out from behind a rock. 'That thing looks tasty.'

'It is,' Rory confirms, and both Riley and Sonoya grimace.

I lie on my makeshift bed, listening to the fire crackle and spit, watching the sky light up in hues of pink and orange as the sun disappears.

'Who fancies a game of poker?' Axel produces a deck. 'While it's still daylight and we can see our cards?'

Sonoya gives him a disapproving look, but Axel ignores her. Everyone agrees, bar me. Even Tamara and Rory throw professional caution to the wind and opt to play.

'Come on, Zoey. Give it another go,' Axel urges. 'We're playing for prickly pears. The loser has to eat all the pads that are left.'

I smile, shaking my head. 'I'm too tired. I'll watch you though.'

I make a pillow out of my rucksack then huddle in my sleeping bag. The air around us is already cooling, and I'm glad of the warmth coming off the fire. I set aside all my worries and concerns. I'll deal with everything when I get back, I tell myself, focusing instead on the sounds of the desert as darkness slowly descends, the chatter of the others as they place their bets.

Finn has his back to me. I can't see his face, so I don't have to endure him studiously ignoring me, as he's pretty much done for the whole hike so far.

'Christ, what wouldn't I give for a good malt,' Axel murmurs, after the deepening twilight brings the game to a close. He glances around. 'Anyone seen Rory since he threw in his cards?'

'I think he's gone for a walk with Sonoya,' Tamara says. 'I saw them wander off ten minutes ago.'

'Where?' Riley asks. 'It's almost dark. What if they get lost?'

'They won't get lost,' Tamara reassures her. 'Rory knows every inch of this place.'

I fall asleep and wake in the night, gripped by a pressing urge to pee. I try to ignore it, but know I won't get back to sleep unless I go. Scrambling out of my sleeping bag, I fetch the little torch issued with our packs. Slowly, carefully, I pick my way around the hillside until I'm out of earshot.

When I find a suitable spot, I check the ground carefully before pulling down my knickers – the last thing I want is a scorpion stinging my arse. I pee for what seems an age. It's only when I stand again that I see it – a small flare of light a few yards away.

I yank my knickers up fast. 'Is somebody there?' I call out nervously.

'Don't worry, I didn't look,' says a voice. 'Though I have to say you're very loud. How much water have you had today?'

Cheeks glowing, I go over to where Maia is sitting, thankful it's too dark for her to see me properly.

'What are you doing?' I ask.

'Drinking in the peace.' She stubs out what I assume was one of Rory's cigarettes. 'Making the most of the last of it.'

'The last of it?' I echo. 'What do you mean?'

She turns to me. 'I'm leaving when we get back.'

'Why?' I ask in a whisper, though really I know – I'm surprised she's stayed this long.

'As I said, this place has a bad vibe. I should have left with Max and Naomi.'

'Why didn't you?'

She sighs. 'Why do you think, Zoey?'

'Rory?'

Maia nods. I can just make out her face in the dark. Her expression is sad. Haunted.

'Have you told him you're leaving?' I squat on the rock next to her, wondering whether to tell her I'm leaving too.

'Of course.' She stares into the darkness. 'I've been persuading him to come with me.'

'Seriously? You really like him then?'

Maia frowns at me. 'You don't think much of me, do you? Or Rory, for that matter. This place is getting to him too.'

'I saw him yesterday, coming out of the office,' I say. 'He looked furious.'

'He was really moody yesterday,' Maia agrees. 'He wouldn't tell me why, but it's since he spoke to that Ed guy – you know, the one everybody keeps on about. I don't know how Rory's coping today, he barely slept last night – whatever Ed told him on that call, it really upset him.'

I stare at her. So Rory has spoken to Ed. Did Ed tell him about the blackmail? It would explain why Rory stormed out of the office like that, if he'd just had it out with Mike and Sonoya.

Either way, it sounds as if Rory genuinely hadn't a clue what was going on.

I feel oddly relieved. Despite what Finn told me about what Rory did to his sister, I'm glad to know he's not a great deal worse than that. He seems a decent guy now. Someone trying to help others and do the right thing, even if Finn can't see that.

'So has Rory agreed to leave with you?' I ask Maia.

She nods. 'Don't tell anybody, will you? Whatever happened with Mike yesterday, it was the last straw. Rory's going to live with me in LA, but there's stuff he needs to sort out first.'

'Do they know you're going? Mike and Sonoya, I mean?'

'Not yet. Rory wanted to get the hike out the way first. He'll tell them when we return to the Sanctuary.' She smiles at me, and I can see she's happy. I'm pleased for her; I just hope this one lasts longer than her previous relationships.

'Come on,' I say, rising to my feet. 'We should get some sleep.'

35

Something wakes me in the night. I sit bolt upright in my sleeping bag, listening, alert.

What was it? A cry of some sort.

An animal?

Coyote?

I peer out from under my tarpaulin, ears and eyes straining, but can't hear or see anything untoward. I lift my gaze upwards. With no light pollution to obscure it, the night sky is breathtaking. A half-moon, surrounded by a myriad stars, the long cloudy streak of the Milky Way.

For a moment I flash back to the ayahuasca trip. That crazy astral geometry. The night sky alive around me. I feel an ache of regret that I'm leaving without the opportunity to experience that again.

Lying there for ten minutes or so, I listen out for that noise, but there's only the soft sound of somebody snoring. I glance over at the dying embers of the fire, at the huddled shapes under their tarpaulins. No one else appears to be awake.

It was nothing, I tell myself, adjusting my makeshift pillow before closing my eyes.

When I surface again the sun is already visible over the far ridge of hills to the east. Tamara is crouched by the fire, boiling water in an aluminium kettle.

'Fancy some tea?' She smiles at me as I sit up.

'Where's everybody else?' I ask, gazing around. The campsite is empty save for Riley, scribbling in a notebook a few yards away.

'Finn and Axel have gone to see what they can forage for breakfast. Maia and Sonoya are looking for Rory.'

'Why?' I get up to join her by the fire.

'He's off walking somewhere.' Tamara lifts the kettle. 'Grab your mug.'

I retrieve it from my rucksack and hand it over. Tamara pours me a cup of greenish liquid that reminds me of the gloop we drank at the ceremony.

'What is it?' I peer at it dubiously.

'Creosote and sagebrush, full of antioxidants and other good stuff. Proper desert medicine.'

I take a sip. It tastes of nothing much at all. Grabbing another granola bar from my rucksack, I chew on it slowly.

'Did you hear anything during the night?' I ask Tamara, remembering the cry that woke me.

'I was out cold. Slept like a baby.'

A moment later Finn and Axel appear, carrying a nylon bag. 'Hey, sleepy,' Axel says, in an almost affectionate tone. 'You're up. You were out for the count.'

'I was knackered,' I admit.

'Knackered?' Axel tilts his head, frowning. 'That another of your British-isms?'

'It means beat. Exhausted.'

'Want some more prickly fruit?' Finn asks me. There's nothing in his expression. I could be anyone.

'I'll stick to granola bars, thanks.'

We sit in silence, girding ourselves for the hours ahead and the hike to the second camping spot on a further ridge. The sun is rising into another cloudless day, and the heat already

building. This time next week, I realise, I could be home endur-
ing a cold wet British summer. My stomach tightens at the
thought.

'No sign of him?'

I look up. Tamara is talking to Sonoya and Maia, back from
their excursion. Maia seems anxious. She keeps gazing about,
clearly hoping to see Rory making his way through the canyon.

'You okay?' I ask her.

Her brow furrows. 'Rory's missing.'

'He isn't missing, Maia.' Sonoya's tone is a little too sharp.
'He's simply not back yet.'

'How long's he been gone?' Riley asks, putting her notebook
in her rucksack and coming over to join us.

'I was up at six,' Sonoya replies, as she sits by the fire. 'There
was no sign of him then.'

'What's the time now?' Finn dumps the bag of wild food at
her feet as Sonoya glances at her watch.

'Eight thirty.'

'Where did you look?' he asks.

'Right around the canyon,' Maia says disconsolately. 'Pretty
much everywhere.'

'I don't suppose you can call the sat phone from your mobile.'
I gaze at Tamara and Sonoya. 'Can you get a signal out here?'

Sonoya shakes her head. 'We need to be in range of the
booster at the house.'

'I'll go find him.' I pull on my boots and get to my feet. 'He's
bound to be around here somewhere.'

'I'll come with you,' Maia says quickly, and Axel and Finn
offer to accompany us.

Tamara glances at Sonoya. 'I'll go with them too. Can you
and Riley pack up the camp? We'll have to leave as soon as we
find Rory.'

Sonoya nods. 'Stay within view of the trees,' she says. 'The last thing we need is any of you getting lost.'

The five of us set off around the curve of the canyon. *Could Rory be lost?* I ask myself. Tamara said he knows this place like the back of his hand. Probably he's gone somewhere quiet to think things over – from what Maia said last night, he's got plenty on his mind.

'Let's split up,' Tamara suggests. 'Finn and I will check this side of the canyon. If the three of you go in that direction, we should meet roughly halfway. Give a loud whoop if you find him.'

'Haven't you already searched around here?' Finn asks Maia.

'Sure.' She shrugs. 'But this is a big place. I guess you could miss someone.'

Maia and Axel set off through the trees and I trail after them, my blisters already beginning to hurt. When I catch up with Maia, I'm surprised to see silent tears rolling down her cheeks.

'This is my fault.' She rubs her face with the bottom of her shirt.

'How?' Axel asks. 'Anyway, Rory's fine.'

'He's probably gone for a bit of time to himself,' I say, then immediately regret it. That was meant to be reassuring, but sounded rude, as if I'm implying Rory was trying to get away from Maia. 'Most likely he fell asleep,' I add quickly. 'He must be exhausted after carrying all that stuff yesterday.'

Maia shakes her head. 'I don't think so,' she mutters, then strides off. Axel and I let her go ahead. We walk slowly, peering behind rocks, checking between the trees. Any place where a man might be resting or dozing.

Though how anyone could sleep through us crashing about the undergrowth is beyond me. Has he done a runner, I wonder?

Maybe Rory reached breaking point and decided to leave us all to it.

Or maybe this is deliberate, it occurs to me, as I come upon a particularly smooth straight branch I can use as a walking stick. Perhaps it's some sort of test, a wilderness survival lesson, and Tamara and Sonoya are playing along with it.

I'm about to suggest this to Axel when up ahead Maia stops dead by a rocky outcrop. A moment later her hand flies up to her face, as if to catch the scream that echoes around the canyon.

Axel and I break into a run.

'Look!' Maia shrieks, pointing to a patch of ground about twenty yards away. For a few moments, I can't see anything, then I spot it.

My breath stops in my throat.

There, just visible beyond a large rock, is a hiking boot. Lying on its side, at an odd angle.

'It's him,' Maia wails, covering her face with her hands.

I push past her, running up to the rock and peering behind it. My pulse pounds in my head as I discover the boot is attached to a leg, and the leg to a body covered by undergrowth. Deliberately concealed, I realise, with a swoop of dread. Forcing myself forwards, I pull aside the decaying leaves and branches, wincing from all the spikes and prickles.

Rory is lying face down in the dirt. Near his waist the earth is dark brown, already attracting a cloud of flies.

Blood, it dawns on me, with a lurch of horror.

Oh God, he's dead.

For a terrible moment I think I'm about to throw up or lose control of my bladder. Seconds later Finn appears, pressing his fingers to Rory's neck, checking for a pulse. Then he crouches down and heaves him onto his back. The blood has congealed all around Rory's shirt. As Finn pulls it up, I see the wound in his stomach. About an inch long, and narrow.

Rory has been stabbed and left to bleed to death. Then someone took pains to cover up his body.

My brain struggles to catch up, to find the words for what I'm seeing.

Someone killed him.

Rory's been *murdered*.

I turn to see Tamara and Axel standing beside us, their faces pale and shocked. I glance behind them. Maia has collapsed onto the ground, hugging her knees and crying hysterically.

Two questions evident in all our expressions: who killed him, and why?

Axel spins in a slow circle, scanning the surrounding terrain. 'Who the fuck did this?' he mutters. 'You think there's anybody else here?'

I glance about, terrified, but there's absolutely no one to be seen. I force myself back to the awful sight of Rory's body. 'How long do you think he's been dead?' I ask Finn.

'A while,' he says grimly. 'He's cold to the touch.'

'Where's his knife?' Axel turns back to us.

Finn gets to his feet, his expression unreadable. 'Likely somewhere close,' he says in a voice curiously devoid of emotion.

I clutch my stick, glad to turn away for a moment from the dreadful sight of Rory lying there on the ground.

And yet not Rory, I realise. He's gone.

The idea of it is so strange, so incomprehensible, I almost forget what I'm doing, and don't spot the phone until I accidentally kick it with my foot.

I bend to pick it up, my hand shaking. The sat phone. I press what I assume to be the start button, but nothing happens.

'Here, let me try.' Tamara takes it from me.

'We need to call for help,' I stammer, glancing at Finn. He's staring at Rory's body as if in a daze, Maia beside him now, clutching Finn's arm and sobbing.

'It's not working.' Tamara's voice quivers as she fights to stay calm. 'I think Rory must have dropped it.'

'Could it be the battery?' Finn asks.

Tamara shakes her head. 'He charged it before we left, and these things are good for a week.'

'What are we going to do?' Maia wails, hanging on to Finn's arm like a lifeline. 'Rory needs help.'

'He's long past help,' Finn says quietly. 'He's been dead for hours.'

An involuntary noise emerges from her mouth, a sort of bellowy wail. 'Who?' Maia asks, gazing about wildly, as if Rory's killer might be lurking behind a rock. '*Who did this?*'

'No fucking idea.' Axel's expression is sorrowful. 'Poor dude.'

Maia looks petrified. 'Do you think we're alone out here?' she says, coming to the same conclusion as Axel. 'Could there be other hikers?'

I glance at Finn, but he doesn't speak. Is he thinking what I'm thinking? That the chances of there being other people around here is close to zero. Which means . . . my mind shies away from the logical conclusion: *one of us killed Rory.*

My limbs tremble, my thoughts spiralling into fear and suspicion.

'We have to go and tell the others,' Tamara says urgently. 'And get the hell back to the Sanctuary.' She peers around her. 'We need a marker people can look for.'

'No!' Maia yelps, her expression horrified. She drops to the ground by Rory's side. 'We can't leave him here.'

Finn pulls off his red polo shirt, laying it on an open piece of ground near Rory's body, weighing it down with a few large stones. 'If they send a helicopter, they'll be able to see this.'

'Good thinking,' Axel declares.

I gaze at Finn, wondering if he's brought another shirt. Otherwise he's going to burn to a crisp. For the first time he meets my eyes, but it's impossible to tell what's going on in his head.

I turn to Maia. She's kneeling next to Rory's body, sobbing. I walk up and put a hand on her shoulder. 'I'm so sorry,' I whisper, low enough so the others can't hear. Though it must be obvious to everyone by now that her relationship with Rory wasn't strictly professional.

'Who?' she chokes. 'Who could have done this?'

No one responds. 'We have to go,' Tamara repeats. Her face is pale with grief and shock, and I recall what Naomi told me when I arrived, about her and Rory once having a thing. *Oh God*, I think, remembering Riley's crush on him too.

How will she deal with this?

'I'm not leaving him!' Maia's voice is more a screech than a sob. 'We're not fucking going without him.'

Tamara crouches beside her. 'We have to, Maia. We haven't any choice. We must get back to the house and alert the authorities.'

'Then we take him with us,' Maia says fiercely. 'We make a stretcher and carry him.'

Finn bends down, so his face is level with Maia's. 'We can't do that,' he says in a firm voice. 'This is a crime scene. We shouldn't touch anything.'

'Aren't we going to look for Rory's knife?' I ask.

Finn shakes his head. 'Nope. Let's leave that for the police.'

He straightens up, extending his hand, and finally Maia allows herself to be pulled to her feet.

*   *   *

Sonoya stands by the now extinguished fire, gazing at us blankly. She doesn't speak for a full minute, simply stares at us, her expression confused. Riley appears, and hovers by Sonoya, as if siding with her in a feud.

'We found him by an outcrop on the west side of the canyon,' Tamara says.

'So he . . . what . . .' Sonoya stammers. 'He fell over or something?'

Finn shakes his head. 'He was stabbed.'

'*Stabbed*?' Riley's eyes widen into circles. 'You mean somebody *killed* him? But why?' she gasps. 'Why on earth would—'

Her words are cut short by a wild cry. More of a scream. Animal-like, frenzied. 'Why?' Maia's expression is frantic, and furious. 'Why do you think? This place is fucked up. Crazy. There was all sorts of shit going down, and Rory knew it.'

Inexplicably, Axel nods. He appears curiously calm, as if this were something to be taken in his stride, something he'd expected.

'Maia,' Sonoya stretches out a hand to console her, 'listen—'

'What's going on?' Maia yells, stepping back. 'There's something going on here, isn't there?'

Sonoya freezes, her expression terrified. 'I don't know what—' she stammers.

'Fuck you!' Maia spits in her face. 'Fuck you, you lying bi—'

'STOP IT!' Finn inserts himself between the pair of them. 'Calm down. We have to focus. We can't do anything for Rory now. The sat phone isn't working, so we need to get back to the Sanctuary and call the police. Let them deal with it.'

'Isn't there another sat phone?' I ask. 'Why did you only bring one?' I look from Sonoya to Tamara.

'We only have three,' Sonoya says in a resigned tone. 'One got broken when you were rescued, and Mike needs the other, in case there's an issue at the Sanctuary.'

'It's ridiculous,' Finn mutters. 'You should have one each.'

'Mike hasn't had a chance to get any more.' Sonoya replies defensively. 'Plus they're not exactly cheap.'

'It doesn't matter,' Tamara cuts in. 'We don't need a sat phone to get home.' She glances at the sky, assessing the time by the sun. 'We should set off right away or we won't make it back before dark.'

'No.' Maia shakes her head vigorously. 'I'm not going. I'm not leaving Rory to the bears and the wolves.'

'There are no bears or wolves around here,' Axel points out, and Riley flashes him a warning frown.

'Maia, listen to me.' Finn grabs her wrists and forces her to face him. 'You have to come with us. It's not safe to stay here alone.'

'Why?' She looks about her wildly. 'I reckon I'll be a heck of a lot safer on my own.'

'What do you mean?' Riley asks, her voice terrified.

'Don't you see?' Maia says fiercely. 'Don't you fucking understand? *It was one of us.* One of us killed Rory.'

'We don't know that,' Sonoya says quietly.

Everyone turns to her. 'What do you mean?' Finn asks.

The therapist swallows. 'We can't be sure, can we, that we're alone? That there's nobody else out here.'

'You mean, like, other hikers?' Maia glares at her, waving her hands at the vast expanse of nothing. 'Are you actually serious? We haven't seen a single person all the time we've been out here. As you and Mike are so proud of telling everyone, this place is remoter than remote. That's half the fucking point of it, isn't it?'

Sonoya doesn't reply.

'We have to leave now,' Tamara repeats, her voice tense and weary.

'We need to find out who did this first,' Maia insists.

'No. The most important thing right now is for all of us to get back safely.'

'But how can we without Rory?' Riley wails. 'Rory is the one who knows the trails.'

'I can do it.' Tamara is making an effort to keep her voice steady, trying to sound confident. 'I've done this walk plenty of times. I remember the way.'

'You sure?' Sonoya frowns. 'It's a long hike.'

'Well, what other option do we have?' She shrugs.

'We could stay here until Mike realises something's wrong,' I suggest. 'Wait for him to send help.'

Tamara turns to me. 'And how long might that take? He's not expecting us for another two days, and then he'll try the sat phone, then probably wait until some time the next day before raising the alarm. I'm not sure we have enough water for that – you can die of thirst in hours in this heat.'

'We could search for some,' Axel suggests. 'Rory taught us how.'

Tamara sighs. 'That's simply for show. There's not much in the way of water until you reach second camp – not enough for six of us anyway. Our safest bet is to return to the house.'

'How about we vote on it?' Finn suggests. 'Who thinks we should hike back?'

Everybody bar Maia raises their hand. I'm guessing no one else wants to spend another night out here with a dead body for company.

'That's settled then,' Tamara concludes. 'Everyone grab their stuff.'

'What shall we do with Rory's pack?' Axel nods at the huge rucksack propped up against a tree. It looks heavy, and I suspect nobody here fancies carrying it in addition to their own.

'Leave it here,' Sonoya says. 'The police can pick it up when they come for the body. Just remove what we might need, and tuck it over by a rock.'

Finn unloads several bottles of water and the remaining food from the rucksack, then carefully closes it again.

A few minutes later we're on our way.

36

We walk in single file, following Tamara as she leads us out of the canyon and back into open country. No one talks as we snake our way around bluffs and boulders, the sun beating down on us mercilessly. It's obvious though, what's on every-body's mind. Despite what Sonoya might think, it's likely one of us killed Rory.

But who? And why?

I churn over the possibilities. Was it Riley? Did she find out Rory and Maia were sleeping together, and murder him in a fit of jealous rage? Or might Sonoya have done it, in an attempt to stop Rory doing or saying anything to damage the Sanctuary? Perhaps Rory threatened to expose her and Mike, during that argument in the office.

What about Axel? Let's face it, his transformation from surly to serene is bloody weird. Maybe the ayahuasca tipped him into a full blown psychosis that he's been masking beneath his shiny new persona.

I fall further and further behind. My feet are killing me. Despite the plasters, raw skin is rubbing against the side of my boots. I pause in the shadow of a huge saguaro, trying to arrange my socks, but they're twisted and sodden with sweat. I should remove my boots and properly position them, but I don't want to fall too far behind. I do the best I can; as I get up, I see Finn waiting for me.

'Here,' he says, as I catch up. 'Have one of these.' He pulls out a packet of Marlboro and offers it to me. I'm tempted, despite my resolution to give up.

'Go on,' he prompts, pushing them towards me. 'You can get back on the wagon when we're out of this mess.'

I hesitate. 'Sonoya might notice.'

Finn lets out a guffaw. 'And that's your main concern, Zoey? Somebody murdered Rory, and you reckon Sonoya gives a shit we're having a smoke?'

I sigh, and take a cigarette. Finn produces a lighter from his other pocket.

'So you had that all along?' I nod at it. 'You could have saved Rory a lot of trouble spinning those sticks.'

Finn throws me a gallows-humour smile and lights our cigarettes. I inhale deeply. The nicotine makes my head spin, but the chemical distraction is exactly what I need.

'I don't suppose you've a bottle of tequila up your sleeve as well?' I squint at Finn.

'I wish.'

We set off, both lost in thought. My mind is crammed with images I can't shift. The horror of seeing Rory lying there, in a dried-up pool of his own blood.

Those flies.

Why? *Why would anyone do that to him?*

'Can I ask you something?' I say to Finn.

'Go ahead.'

'Did you hate Rory? For what he did to your sister?'

Finn stops in his tracks. 'What kind of question is that, Zoey?'

I don't reply. We both know exactly what kind of question it is – a barely concealed accusation.

'Are you serious?' He stares at me, incredulous. 'Do you really believe I would do that to Rory?'

I open my mouth to answer, then find I can't.

Finn takes a final drag from his cigarette then grinds it into the dirt. He lifts his hat and runs a hand through his hair. It's damp with sweat. There are beads of it on his cheeks too. He must be as hot as hell in that fleece he put on in lieu of his red polo shirt.

'Christ, Zoey,' he mutters. 'I'm stunned you'd even imagine I was capable of something like that.'

'You admitted you came here because of Rory.'

Finn doesn't reply. He looks furious. And disappointed.

'You said you wanted to fuck with him,' I persist, 'I mean, in my shoes, what would you think?'

'Listen, Zoey, you have to trust—'

'You're asking me to trust you, despite knowing that Rory played a part in your sister's depression and suicide.'

Finn sighs, turning away for a second or two. 'Okay, you're right. Well, you're wrong and you're right. As I told you, I needed to get away, to sort myself out, and I knew Rory was working here, so I checked out the Sanctuary. I liked its protocol, its philosophy. But yeah, I couldn't resist the urge to . . . fuck with him a bit.'

'Because that's the fast track to recovery, isn't it?' My voice drips with sarcasm. 'Having a score to settle with one of the therapists?'

Finn forces himself to meet my gaze. 'Sure, when you put it like that, it sounds crazy. But in some weird, desperate way I thought it might . . . help. That perhaps I could . . . I can't explain it.'

'It wasn't Rory's fault, you know, what happened to your sister,' I say. 'He was simply doing his job.'

Finn fiddles with his lighter, glancing ahead to see if anybody is paying us attention. 'Easy for you to say – you've no idea what it's like, constantly having the media on your back. How it corrodes everything, how every single thing you do gets twisted and distorted. You have no clue what that does to a person.'

Anger glints in his eyes, and I find I'm asking myself more seriously: *Is it possible Finn did kill Rory?*

Maybe in a moment like this, in a flash of rage.

I pause, steadying myself against a rock, the ground beneath me seeming to tilt and sway. I so want to believe Finn, but what if he isn't telling the truth? What if I make the wrong call a second time, and somebody else pays the price?

Rory's dead, I remind myself; he's already paid a pretty high price.

Taking a deep breath, I carry on walking, Finn silent beside me, his resentment as palpable as the hot air around us. But I don't care. I'm past worrying about how Finn feels right now.

Up ahead, everyone has come to a halt at a rocky outcrop, taking a break, sitting on the ground or leaning against boulders, using their rucksacks as a buffer. I grit my teeth, hurrying to catch up. I need a rest and a drink so badly I'm on the verge of tears. Pulling my second water bottle from my bag, I go to take a sip, but it's weirdly light – when I put it to my lips nothing comes out.

What the hell? My bottle was full last night.

Where has my water gone?

Before I can formulate an answer, there's a piercing squeal of terror and pain. Everybody leaps up – even from twenty yards away I see the fear on their faces.

Only one person not standing. Maia. Her screams are unearthly, a high-pitched wail of sheer terror. Ignoring the heat and pain in my feet, I break into a run. Moments later I'm by her side, next to Sonoya and Tamara. She's lying in the dirt, clutching her hand.

'What happened?' I gasp.

'S-s-snake,' she stammers. 'It bit me.'

'Are you sure?' Sonoya asks her.

'I put my hand on a rock and felt a sharp, stabbing pain,' Maia sobs. 'I saw it slithering away.'

'What did it look like?' Finn gazes at her. 'The snake, I mean.'

'Hard to tell. Brown, maybe . . . with patterns on it.' Maia's eyes widen with fright as she clasps her hand to her chest. 'But there was this noise, a clicking sound.'

'A rattle?' Finn asks.

Maia nods, her face rigid with horror.

'Rattlesnake,' confirms Tamara. 'Not unusual around here, though they're generally pretty shy.'

'Fuck,' Axel says. 'They're venomous, aren't they?'

'Shut up, Axel,' Finn snaps, as Sonoya takes Maia's hand, gripping it tightly to stop it shaking. There, on the pad between her thumb and forefingers, are two distinct puncture wounds, oozing blood. The skin around them is already beginning to redden and swell.

For a moment I think I'm going to faint. That does not look good.

'Don't you, like, have to suck the venom out?' Axel asks. 'I don't mind having a go.'

'That's a myth,' Sonoya says sharply. The worry in her expression speaks volumes; this is not something she is equipped to deal with.

'Surely you carry antivenom?' Finn's tone is a mix of exasperation and confusion. 'If there's snakes around here, I mean.'

Sonoya closes her eyes. 'No. It's only available in hospitals. Snake bites are very rare.'

'There must be something you can do!' I stare at her. 'Don't you have a first-aid kit?'

'It's in Rory's backpack,' Axel says quietly. 'It's my fault. I didn't think to bring it. We already had a lot to carry with the extra food and water.'

Finn looks at him aghast. 'What? It didn't occur to you we might need that too?'

'I could go back,' Axel offers.

Sonoya shakes her head again. 'It's too far.' She inhales, thinking. 'Besides, it wouldn't be much use, beyond a bandage and some antiseptic cream. There's a good chance the snake didn't pass the venom, but we still have to get Maia to hospital.' Sonoya gazes into her tear-stained, terrified face. 'I'm going to wash the wound, then immobilise your hand, okay?'

Maia nods.

'Could somebody pass my water?' Sonoya asks, and Tamara pulls it out of the side pocket of her rucksack. We all watch as Sonoya removes the lid and carefully pours it over Maia's wound. 'Anyone have a clean shirt or boxers or something? And a penknife.'

Axel roots in his bag and produces a beautiful tie-dyed T-shirt. Doesn't comment when Sonoya hacks it into strips and uses it to bandage Maia's hand.

'How far are we from the Sanctuary, you reckon?' she asks Tamara.

Tamara squints into the distance. 'Six . . . seven miles, maybe?'

Sonoya studies Maia. 'Do you think you can walk?'

Maia nods, but winces as she gets to her feet. Axel picks up her backpack and settles it next to his own.

We set off again. More slowly now, but even so, Maia is struggling to keep up. She looks pale, and for the first time, I see a sheen of sweat on her face. The heat seems to thicken as we make painfully slow progress across open desert. I'm desperately thirsty, and a headache is blossoming in my skull.

After an hour, pausing by a small range of hills, Tamara stops and looks around.

'You sure this is the right way?' Axel peers ahead. 'I don't remember these hills on the hike out.'

I spin about, taking in our surroundings. Axel is right. None of this seems familiar.

Tamara uses the hem of her blouse to wipe sweat from her face; as she takes off her sunglasses to clean them, there's anxiety in her expression.

She doesn't know where we are, I realise.

I scan the horizon again, desperately hoping to spot the Sanctuary shimmering in the heat haze in the distance, but there's nothing except dirt and cacti and scrubby little mesquite trees as far as the eye can see.

'Try your mobile,' Sonoya says to Tamara, while extracting hers from her backpack. They both study their screens, searching for a signal, but their expressions make it clear it's hopeless.

Shit. We're lost.

We're actually fucking lost.

I sink to the ground, fighting a rising panic. The last six hours have taken on the aura of a nightmare. Rory's body covered in sticks and leaves. The dark fetid smell of blood-soaked dirt. The rattlesnake. And now this, lost in the scorching desert with no way to summon help.

'I'm all out of water,' Riley says in a quiet voice. It's the first time I've heard her speak in hours. She's barely uttered a word since the news of Rory's death, her expression shut down and unreadable. 'I drank the last bit ten minutes ago.'

'Me too,' I say. 'Mine has disappeared.'

Finn frowns at me. 'Disappeared? How do you mean?'

'I mean it's all gone. It was full last night, but when I went to take a drink earlier, it was empty.'

We all know the subtext of that: we could die of thirst, out here in this baking hellhole.

'What are we going to do?' Axel asks. His question has an innocence about it, like a child assuming the adults will have a solution. I'm struck again by how much he's changed since the ceremony.

What did that ayahuasca do to him? It's as if it totally rewired his brain.

Finn takes out his cigarettes and offers them around. To my amazement, Sonoya accepts one, along with me, Axel and Riley. Sonoya doesn't even ask where he got them.

'Rory's rule of three,' Finn says, lighting us up.

'His what?' I inhale so deeply I get dizzy.

'There's three things that will kill you out here: starvation, thirst, and lack of shelter.'

'And snakes,' murmurs Axel, and Tamara gives him a stern look.

'Right now food isn't our main concern,' Finn continues. 'Nor shelter, not until tonight anyway. It's water that's the problem. We're in the worst heat of the day, and we're sweating hard – that means we could become dangerously dehydrated in a matter of hours.'

'So we need to find water,' Axel agrees. 'But that's going to be easier said than done.' He gestures around him.

He's right. The vegetation is sparse, and the ground appears as arid as anywhere I've ever seen. We could spend weeks searching and not find a drop.

'We don't want to use up vital resources hunting for non-existent water,' Finn continues. 'Even if we found some, it's unlikely it would be enough for all of us – or fit to drink.'

Riley frowns at Finn. 'Okay, so what should we do?'

'Stay put. Rig up our tarps to provide shade. Wait until sundown.'

'But what about Maia?' Sonoya asks. 'We have to get her to hospital soon.'

We all turn to gaze at her. She's sitting on the dirt, pain etched across her lovely face.

Tamara bends down to her. 'How are you doing?'

'Terrible,' Maia croaks. 'But I can manage.'

'But if we wait till nightfall, how will we see where we're going?' I point out. 'Won't we get more lost?'

Finn doesn't have an answer to this. Nor does anybody else.

'I'm going back,' Axel's voice is decisive. 'I'll retrace our steps and work out where we took a wrong turn. See if I can find some water too, while I'm at it.'

'I'll come with you,' Finn and Riley say in unison.

'One of you should stay here.' Finn eyes them both. 'Riley, you stay. Axel and I will go.'

'Take me,' Tamara insists. 'I think I might know where we went wrong. A couple of miles back, by that huge agave. I reckon we should have gone left, not straight ahead.'

'I should come too.' I struggle to get up, but Finn holds up a hand. 'Nope. Not with your feet in that state. Sort them out, and help Sonoya and Riley keep Maia comfortable. Have something to eat, and string up a few tarps to stay out of the sun.'

*　　*　　*

We set up our tarpaulins as best we can, tying them to the tallest bushes we can find, then crawl underneath. I watch Finn, Axel and Tamara disappear into the shimmering heat, heading back the way we came.

There's a sick hollow sensation in my stomach. What if they get lost again, and can't find their way back to us?

How long will we wait before we take our chances and try to return to the house alone?

Snap out of it, Zoey, I tell myself, crawling out from under the tarp and going to Maia. She's lying on the ground, using her rucksack as a pillow, Sonoya sitting beside her.

'How are you feeling?'

She opens her eyes and squints at me. 'My hand hurts. A lot.'

I glance down. Even with the makeshift bandages covering it, I can see the swelling. And a telltale redness creeping up the inside of her delicate wrist.

Don't snakebites make the flesh rot or something? I shudder at the thought.

'Have you got any painkillers?' I ask Sonoya.

'They're in Rory's backpack,' she says. 'Emergency use only.'

I roll my eyes. 'I think we could safely class this as an emergency, don't you?'

Sonoya grimaces and looks away. I'm consumed with an irrational urge to punch her, a surge of anger so strong I feel almost winded. Why doesn't she take some fucking responsibility for this mess?

Calm down, urges an inner voice. *Cut her some slack.* Sonoya's probably as scared and shocked as the rest of us – her colleague's just been stabbed to death, after all.

'It'll be okay,' I say to Maia, then return to my tarp and pull off my boots and socks, grimacing at the state of my feet.

Tamara's plasters have fallen off, and the blisters on my ankles have burst, the skin red and raw. There are fresh sores on my heels and the balls of my feet.

I hang my sweaty socks to dry in the sun, leaving my feet exposed – hopefully the dry air will help. I pull my sleeping bag out of the rucksack and unroll it over the hard ground, then lie down and shut my eyes.

Even under the shelter of the tarpaulin, the heat is over-whelming, yet somehow I fall into a doze. My dreams are jagged and fitful. In one, I'm back in New York with Fran and Rocco, sitting in a bar where the walls are covered in pictures of the desert, and I'm trying to tell them what happened, but the music is impossibly loud and nobody can hear me.

In another, I'm by a river, somewhere in England, and I wade right in and bend my head and gulp down the cool fresh water.

I wake with a start, full of longing for that damp and rainy climate I grew up in. Chilly summer days. And green. Green everywhere.

It seems impossible now, that there is such a place. Inconceivable. Tears prick my eyes. Will I ever go home again?

'Hey, Zoey,' Riley calls from under her tarp. 'You want one of these?' She holds up a granola bar. 'You should keep your energy up.'

She tosses it over. I unwrap it and take a bite, but I feel too sick to eat. I make myself swallow what's in my mouth, then wrap up the rest and tuck it into my rucksack. I lie down again. My head is aching worse than ever and I'm absolutely desperate for a drink.

'I think I see them,' Riley exclaims in an excited voice.

I sit up and follow the direction of her finger, spotting tiny stick figures on the horizon.

'One of them is missing,' Sonoya says. 'There's only two.'

Fuck. I squint through the shimmering air into the distance. Sonoya's right. As they approach, painfully slowly, I see the missing person is Axel.

Oh God, what's happened to him?

'Where is he?' Riley runs up to meet them. 'Where's Axel?'

'Tripped on a rock and sprained his ankle.' Tamara grimaces. 'We had to leave him there.'

'What do you mean "leave him there"?' I ask, almost demented with anxiety. 'What else can possibly go wrong?'

'He's fine,' Finn assures us. 'We left him in some shade by a bluff. We reckon we've found the route back so we'll pick him up on the way.' He turns to study Maia. She barely seems to be aware of any of this, lying under the tarpaulin with her eyes closed, her face contorted with pain.

'How is she?' Finn asks Sonoya.

'Not good,' she whispers. 'We have to get her to hospital fast.'

'Can she walk?

Sonoya shakes her head.

'What are we going to do?' Riley wails. Her eyes are wild and her hair matted with sweat. 'We can't abandon her here.'

'Of course we're not going to abandon her,' I snap. I close my eyes for a second or two, thinking. 'The tarp,' I say. 'Is it strong enough to hold her weight?'

Finn studies it, assessing. 'Reckon so. But we'll need something at each end to carry it. Those tarp strings are too flimsy.'

Tamara glances around. 'Pack straps,' she says. 'If we cut them off and attach them to the holes on the tarp, they'll take her weight.

'Use mine,' I suggest. 'I'm out of water anyhow.'

'You can put anything you want in my pack,' Riley offers. She rolls up my sleeping bag and ties it onto the back of her own rucksack. 'We'll take it in turns to carry it,' she says, and I force myself to smile. I feel awful, worse by the moment. As if I can barely stand or walk, let alone lug a heavy rucksack in this heat.

Pull yourself together, I tell myself, helping Tamara sever the straps from my pack and tie them to one of the tarps. 'You two hold each end,' I say to Tamara and Finn. 'Riley, you test it out – you're about the same weight as Maia.'

Finn and Tamara pick up the tarp and lift the straps onto their shoulders. Riley climbs into the resulting hammock.

To my immense relief it holds. But for how long?

'You got any idea how far it is to the house?' Sonoya asks Tamara.

'About two miles to the point where we left Axel, then I reckon another four or so.'

I gaze at the pair of them. Six miles, possibly more, with Axel barely able to walk, and two people carrying Maia. *We'll never manage it*, says a panicky voice in my head. We all look on the point of collapse as it is, and the sun is still high in the sky.

'Maybe we should wait a few hours,' I suggest. 'Until it's cooler.'

Finn glances at Maia. 'I'm not sure we can, Zoey.' He doesn't say it, but it's obvious what he means; if we rest up even for an hour or two, Maia might not make it.

'Let's go then.' I pull on my socks and boots and heave myself upright, ignoring the pain in my feet.

Finn goes over to Maia. 'Hey.' He crouches, touching her shoulder. Her eyes open, but they barely seem to focus on him.

'We've found the route back,' Finn tells her. 'And we're going to carry you, okay? I need you to sit up so we can get the tarpaulin underneath.'

Maia nods, and pushes herself up. A second later she collapses with a cry. Sonoya and I rush forward to help, lifting her under each arm while Finn and Tamara slip the tarp beneath her. Sonoya pulls out her sleeping bag and uses it as a pillow.

Finn signals to Tamara, and they each pick up an end of the tarp. It takes the strain, but I can see the effort it's costing Finn. He's still wearing his fleece as protection against sunburn, but he looks really hot. Then I realise he's not wearing his hat.

'Where's your hat?' I ask as we get going.

'I gave it to Axel. He put his down somewhere and lost it.'

'Here, have mine.' I go to put it on his head as he carries the tarpaulin, but he shrugs it away. 'I'm fine, Zoey.'

'Take it,' I insist. 'You need it more than I do.'

I trail behind them, worrying how Finn and Tamara are managing, imagining how much it has already taken out of them to walk so far retracing our route, then come all the way back here to get us. And now they have to do it all again, this time carrying Maia. I glance at Riley and Sonoya. Neither of them looks strong enough to help. And Axel is out of the equation now.

I catch Finn's eye and offer a smile of encouragement, but he doesn't respond. Is he still angry with me? Or simply exhausted?

It doesn't matter, I decide. All that matters is we get out of this place alive.

We start the long slow trudge back in the direction we came. We can only walk as fast as Finn and Tamara can carry Maia. I'm stupidly grateful it's no faster. Each step is harder than the last. The pain in my feet is now dwarfed by the thump in my head as the sun beats down on my face.

What wouldn't I give for some of those painkillers in Rory's rucksack.

Two hours later, the small bluff where Axel is sitting finally comes into view. He waves as we approach, relief etched on his features. I realise how scary it must have been, left there alone. No certainty we'd ever return.

Axel catches sight of Maia, suspended on our makeshift stretcher. He heaves himself to his feet, bending to pick up a stick. He uses it to help keep his weight off his right leg and hops over.

'She okay?'

Sonoya shakes her head. Maia doesn't even open her eyes, let alone respond.

Oh hell. I'm feeling increasingly desperate. *How will we ever make it back to the Sanctuary? Axel's barely able to walk, and I'm not much better.*

'You sure you can manage?' Finn asks Axel.

'I'll have to jettison the backpack,' he says, 'but I should be okay if we go slowly.'

Tamara studies the terrain. 'I'm pretty sure if we hike over there, to that hill, we then pass around the other side and bear west.'

'A map and compass would have been good,' grumbles Riley. 'Not to mention a spare sat phone.'

'Maps are next to useless in terrain like this,' Tamara says calmly. 'There are so few markers to get your bearings. And you don't need a compass when you've got the sun.'

She sets off, studying the ground as we walk. 'Look!' She bends over a patch of earth to the left of us. 'Footprints.'

We go over and study them. Sure enough, there are boot marks in the dirt, toes pointing back the way we came. 'We can use these as a guide to get us home.' Tamara glances up at the sky. 'About six hours till sunset, I reckon. With any luck, we'll make it to the Sanctuary before nightfall.'

Thank God, I think. But my relief is short-lived. Moments later, the world goes black and I'm falling, falling, falling into the abyss.

I don't even feel myself hit the ground.

37

'Zoey? Can you hear me?'

Something touches my face. I swat it away.

'Zoey!' The voice is more insistent. 'Open your eyes!'

I force my lids apart to see Tamara and Sonoya crouching over me. Sonoya is holding a water bottle. Lifting my head, she pushes it to my lips.

'Drink,' she insists, her tone commanding.

I gulp down a few mouthfuls, then choke. I try to push myself up, but she stops me.

'Take a couple of minutes.' Her fingers press against the inside of my wrist while she looks at her watch.

'What happened?' I mumble.

'You fainted,' Finn says. 'You fell like a tree. Your head nearly hit a rock.'

'Pulse is fast,' Sonoya mutters, pressing her palm to my forehead.

'What's wrong?' I groan. 'Tell me.'

'Heat exhaustion. Have you had any other symptoms? Dizziness? Headache?'

I nod, wincing from the pain of moving my head. She takes my hand and pinches the skin, leaving a ridge that slowly softens to a hill, strangely reminiscent of the landscape surrounding us.

The test for dehydration, I recall Rory showing us. Then I remember he's dead. I try to cry, but there are no tears, just the dull ache in my head.

'Give her mine.' Finn hands Sonoya his water bottle.

'No, I—'

'Drink it, Zoey,' he insists. 'If you collapse again we can't carry you too.'

I do as he says, gulping the contents greedily. I could drink for ever. I could drink a whole sink full of water. A pond. A lake.

After a few minutes I feel a little better.

'We should go,' Sonoya says, checking my pulse again.

Finn gazes around him. 'Perhaps we could stay here,' he suggests to Tamara and Sonoya. 'Camp out for the night.' He bends down, placing my hat back on my head.

The therapist nods at Maia. 'We have to get home.'

'No, I mean I'll stay here with Zoey. You can return for us in the jeep.'

Sonoya looks at Tamara, uncertain.

'I'm fine.' I heave myself to my feet. 'I can walk. Let's go.' I set off in the direction of the others.

Finn and Sonoya catch me up. 'Zoey—' Finn says.

'I'm fine,' I repeat, glaring at him. It's not true. My head is thumping, and I feel sick, but I'm not going to be the person who delays us even a second longer. All I want in the world right now is to get back to the Sanctuary, and board that chopper the minute it arrives.

Though that might not be possible now, I realise. Rory's dead. The police will want to talk to us – who knows how long it will all take.

Then it hits me again.

One of us killed Rory.

One of the people I'm walking with this very moment picked up a knife and stabbed him in the belly.

The dreadful thought of it, the horror of it, spurs me on. One foot in front of the other, over and over, a mantra performed by my exhausted body. I feel like a zombie, a member of the walking dead; probably look the part too. I'm so tired and thirsty that every step is a torment. I want nothing more than to lie down in the dirt and let the desert swallow me up. Anything, but keep going.

I keep going.

'Oh my Lord, will you look at that!'

Riley is pointing. Not at the horizon, but up in the sky.

'Jesus.' Axel lets out a whistle.

I stare upwards. Out of nowhere the sky in the distance is filling with clouds. Huge grey rainclouds. There's a whiff of humidity too, the air hot, but moist.

'Monsoon,' Tamara says, resuming her long slow trudge across the desert. But something in the atmosphere has changed – literally. As the clouds roll ever closer, there's an electricity in the air. A charge of anticipation.

On we go. On and on, the sky growing preternaturally dark as the sun disappears behind the rolling bank of grey. Suddenly, a blinding flash illuminates the wilderness around us, followed by a long, slow rumble.

Thunder.

Another moment later Riley does a long low whoop that reminds me of Axel howling during the ceremony. 'We've made it!' she yells, punching the air. 'Look!'

I gaze ahead. Sure enough, about half a mile away, is the outline of the Sanctuary.

'We've made it!' Riley shouts up at the heavens. '*We're not going to fucking die!*'

The heavens answer with another flash of light, another deafening clap of thunder, then something touches my cheek. For an instant I have no idea what it is, until a second fat rain-drop hits my nose.

A few drops become many. Within moments it's raining hard, and a minute later it's a deluge, sinking into my hat, my hair, my skin, my clothes, until they too drip onto the thirsty ground. I gaze upwards, tears in my eyes, mouth open to let the rain into my throat. I'm crying and laughing, then Axel is hugging me, and we're both hugging Riley and crying and laughing and dancing together.

'Come on,' Finn yells back at us. 'We need to get inside.'

We hurry across the desert towards the house. As I reach the garden, I hobble to the tap and open the pivot, sticking my mouth underneath ready to take great long gulps of water.

'Steady.' Sonoya catches up with me. 'Don't overdo it. You'll screw up your electrolytes and make yourself ill if you drink too much at once.'

But all that comes out are a few drips.

'What on earth . . .?' Tamara's voice is barely audible under the sound of the rain hitting the tin roofs on the sheds. I straighten up, the brim of my hat buckling under the weight of the water hurling itself out of the sky, assuming she's talking about the dry tap. But she's staring over at the carport. We stand there, drenched, taking in what she's just seen.

The jeep has gone.

Sonoya breaks into a run, heading into the house. 'Mike,' I hear her yelling as I reach the front entrance. 'Mike, are you there?'

Silence.

She turns to us, bewildered, as we all crowd inside, Axel and Finn angling the makeshift stretcher through the door. 'There's no sign of him.'

'Let's get Maia into the clinic,' Tamara says, glancing at Sonoya. But she seems rooted to the spot. She stands there, dripping water onto the floor tiles, her face rigid with emotion. At first I don't recognise her expression, then the penny drops.

Fear, I realise. She looks terrified.

'Sonoya!' Tamara snaps. 'Come on.' She motions Finn and Axel to carry Maia into the clinic. I follow, watching as they ease her onto the exam couch. Maia's features are twisted with pain. Her cheeks are flushed and her hand so swollen now that the skin is ballooning around the edge of the improvised bandage.

Tamara switches on the light, but nothing happens. 'What the hell?' she swears under her breath.

'Probably the generator,' Finn says. 'That's why the water pump is off.'

'Could you go check? The keys are in the office.'

'I'll do it.' Finn turns to leave, Axel hobbling after him.

The rest of us stand there, gazing at Maia. Simpkins appears and twists through our legs, yowling for food.

'We need to call the emergency services.' Tamara pulls out her phone. 'I'll see if they can send out an air ambulance.'

And the police, I think, remembering Rory lying out there in the desert. The thought of him left alone like that makes me wretched.

Tamara tries to turn on her phone, then swears. 'Out of battery.'

Sonoya snaps out of her trance and retrieves her own. 'I've still got a bit left.' She hands it to Tamara.

'No signal,' Tamara says, gritting her teeth with frustration. 'Must be because the electricity is off – we've lost the satellite and signal booster. I'll call as soon as it's back.'

'It could be a wait.' Finn appears at the door. 'The office is locked. Do you know where there's a spare key?'

'Mike had one set, and Rory took the other,' Sonoya says, then groans.

'Don't tell me.' Finn grits his teeth, exasperated. 'They're in his backpack. Jesus Christ . . .'

'I'm sorry.' Sonoya sounds close to tears. 'I didn't think—'

'Give her a break, Finn,' Tamara snaps. 'She wasn't to know Mike would shut up shop and do a runner.'

I stare at the pair of them. Is that what's happened? Why on earth would Mike do that? And how? This place is only accessible by helicopter, isn't it?

'We should break the office door down,' Axel says.

'I already tried that,' Finn replies. 'It must be reinforced or something. It won't budge. You need a ram or something, but anything we could use is locked in the store sheds, and those doors are pretty secure too.'

'Mike might come back,' Axel says. 'We're not due here till tomorrow after all.'

Sonoya shakes her head again. 'I don't think so.'

'Why?' Finn asks. 'What's going on, Sonoya? Where is he?'

Her lips tighten but she doesn't reply.

Finn balls his fists in frustration. 'At some point, Sonoya, you're going to have to explain what the fuck is happening here.'

She inhales, nods. 'Let me make Maia comfortable first. And we need to work out how to get help.'

'I'll take the phone outside and see if I can pick up a signal somewhere,' Tamara says, scooping up the cat as she rushes out of the door.

We all gaze at Maia. She's lying there, eyes closed, her breathing inaudible.

'Can't you give her something?' I ask Sonoya. 'Some painkillers at least.'

328

She nods. Reaching inside her desk, she pulls out a little key, using it to open the medicine cabinet. She removes a packet of pills and turns on the tap to fill a glass with water.

Nothing comes out.

'Jesus!' Sonoya leans on the sink and closes her eyes.

'The pump's off,' Axel reminds her. 'I'll see if there's some in the kitchen.'

Riley flashes me an anxious look. I know exactly what she's thinking? *What the hell is going on here? And what are we going to do?*

'Here you go.' Axel returns with a bottle of water. Sonoya drops in a couple of soluble pills, stirring until they dissolve, while Finn and Axel help Maia to sit up. She opens her eyes and groans.

'Here, swallow this.'

'What is it?' Maia mumbles.

'Paracetamol and codeine,' Sonoya tells her. 'It'll ease the pain.'

Maia takes the glass with a shaking hand and gulps it down, pulling a face at the taste, then collapses back onto the couch. Sonoya finds the blood pressure cuff and puts it on her good arm. Watches it inflate and release, a knot of tension on her forehead.

'How is she?' I ask.

'Blood pressure is way too high,' the therapist mutters, returning to the cabinet. She picks out some antiseptic wipes and a sterile bandage pack. Slowly, carefully, she unwinds the tie-dye strips covering the wound.

Riley gasps. Maia's hand has ballooned to three times its normal size, and the skin has an alarming purple tinge. Sonoya inspects it carefully, then opens the antiseptic wipe and dabs it over the affected area, apologising when Maia winces and swears.

'No luck.' Tamara enters the clinic, her hair dripping wet again, her clothes soaked to the skin. 'And now your phone is out of charge as well.' She stops dead and stares at Maia's hand. Her expression says everything as she silently watches Sonoya cover it with a clean bandage.

'We have to get her help,' Tamara murmurs, rubbing her temples as she thinks. A moment later she disappears, returning with a black panel and lead. 'I remembered Rory kept a solar charger in his room – thankfully it was unlocked. I'll take it outside and try to charge my phone, then walk up to the nearest hill and see if I can get a signal up there.'

'But it's raining, and nearly sundown,' Finn points out. 'You won't get much in the way of charge till tomorrow.'

Tamara grimaces. 'Gotta be worth a try.' She hurries out of the clinic again.

Sonoya glances back at Maia, who appears to be dozing now the painkillers have kicked in. She turns her attention to me. 'How are you feeling, Zoey?'

'Head is killing me,' I admit.

She returns to the medicine cabinet and finds a couple more painkillers. Then gives me a packet of some sort of powder. 'Oral rehydration formula, you know, the stuff you had before. It'll help balance your electrolytes. Change out of those wet clothes and lie down. I don't want you keeling over with heat stroke.'

'Are you sure?' I ask, as she hands me the pills.

Sonoya nods. 'Let me know if you need more.'

'Will Maia be okay?' I whisper.

'I really hope so.'

38

I pour water from one of the gallon containers in the kitchen, and swallow the pills with the orange liquid made by the powder. Its sickly sweetness takes me straight back to the morning I woke up here, with no idea where I was.

It feels like months ago. Years.

I go to my room and strip off my wet clothes, digging fresh ones out of my cupboard. I'm so exhausted part of me wants to collapse on the bed, but I'm too agitated to rest.

Where the hell is Mike?

And why is Sonoya so certain he won't return?

Now the initial relief of making it back to the Sanctuary alive is wearing off, my mind returns to Rory. The most likely explanation is one of us killed him. We have no way to contact the police, and we're stuck in the middle of the desert, miles from help of any kind.

At least we have shelter now, and won't starve, or die of thirst, I think, remembering the rain tanks and all the food in the kitchen and supplies shed – we'll have to find a way to break in if we get desperate.

I put on the clean clothes, leaving my bare feet exposed so the air will dry the blisters, then hobble off in search of Finn. I find him with Axel and Riley in the lounge, sprawled across a sofa, his face red and sore from too much time in the sun. Someone has loaded the coffee table with cans of soda and various snacks from the kitchen. I grab a lemonade, then collapse into an armchair, taking in the scene.

Despite hats and sunblock, our skin is tinged with sunburn, and a fine layer of dust that nobody has been able to wash off yet – no showers, I guess, until the power is back. Axel has put on cargo shorts, his exposed ankle bandaged now, resting on the coffee table. Riley has changed her clothes too, but her hair is still wet from the rain.

We resemble refugees from a war zone, scared, exhausted. Or traumatised survivors of some natural disaster, stranded and waiting for help to arrive. No one speaks until Sonoya turns up, Tamara right behind her.

'Is Maia okay?' Axel asks.

Sonoya nods. 'She's sleeping for now. We need to get her to a hospital soon though.'

'Any luck with the solar charger?' I ask Tamara. I'm guessing not. A glance out of the window tells me we're close to sunset.

'I've put it out by the pool, where there's the most sun. At least it's stopped raining. I'll check it when it's properly dark.'

Finn drains the rest of his drink then sets the empty can on the table. 'We need to talk,' he says, eyeballing Sonoya as she sits down in an armchair. 'About what's going on here, and what we're going to do.'

'I don't know,' Sonoya replies.

'You don't know what's going on?' asks Riley. 'Or you don't know what to do about it?'

The atmosphere in the room shifts. A dam bursts, releasing a torrent of pent-up frustrations.

'Where's Mike?' Axel demands.

'Yeah, why isn't he here?' Riley adds. 'Why is the Sanctuary shut up like this?'

Sonoya stands. 'I haven't got time for—'

'Sit down!' Finn's tone is forceful. 'You owe us some

explanations, Sonoya. You too, Tamara. What happened to Alejandro? And who the hell killed Rory?'

'Don't ask me.' Tamara shrugs. 'I haven't got a clue.'

'Nor me,' says Sonoya feebly, but she sounds beaten, defeated by the onslaught of questions.

'*The fuck you don't!*' Finn leaps up, glaring at Sonoya with such undisguised animosity that I'm tempted to intervene.

But something holds me back. *Is this a cover?* I wonder. A clever way of deflecting attention from himself?

Because Finn and I both know he had a pretty clear motive for wanting Rory dead.

'Leave her alone, Finn.' Axel pushes himself upright. 'I'm not kidding,' he warns, when Finn doesn't move. 'I am too tired for this shit, okay?'

All of a sudden Sonoya drops her head into her hands, hiding her face. We all gape as her shoulders shake with the force of her tears. It's awful, disturbing even, to see someone usually so calm, so self-controlled, completely breaking down.

'This isn't helping.' Riley's voice is surprisingly restrained given everything that's happened today. 'We need to focus on how to get out of here.'

'And on Rory,' Axel adds, sitting down again. 'Why aren't we talking about who killed him? It strikes me it's no coincidence that we get back here and find the place deserted.'

I glance at Sonoya, but she still has her face hidden, unable to make eye contact with anyone.

'Who had a motive for killing Rory?' Axel cuts through the silence, his gaze travelling from one to the next. Of all of us, he seems the least affected by the day's catastrophic events, his eyes clear and his skin glowing with health.

Riley snorts. 'Well, you did. You loathed him. You told me you thought he was totally fake and you hated his guts.'

333

'That's true,' Axel says evenly. 'I did think that.'

'But you don't now?' I ask.

'No.'

'What the hell happened to you anyway?' Riley says. 'Ever since the ceremony you've been so fucking ... weird. Like you've had a personality transplant or something.'

'Don't you believe people can change?' There's no malice in Axel's expression, but Riley can only hold his gaze for a few moments before looking away.

'Maia has a motive,' she points out.

Everyone turns their attention to Riley. 'She was angry with Rory, the evening before the hike. I heard them arguing in Maia's room.'

'Rory was in Maia's room?' Sonoya frowns. Despite Maia's obvious distress earlier, when we found his body, Axel and Finn look equally aghast. Only Tamara and Riley seem unsurprised.

So they knew.

Tamara laughs. 'Oh come on, Sonoya. This can't be news, surely? Did Maia never mention their affair in one of your sessions?'

'Did you hear what they were arguing about?' Axel asks Riley.

She nods. 'Some of it, anyway.'

'And?' I try not to sound exasperated.

Riley chews her lip. 'Well, he was saying he wasn't sure what to do. That if he reported what he knew, it would be the end of everything, of all the good work they'd done here. He said this place had turned people's lives around, and that he completely believed in the Sanctuary and what it does. That was the gist of it, anyway. I felt kinda shitty eavesdropping so I walked away.'

'Why didn't you tell us this sooner?' Finn asks.

'None of my business.' Riley shrugs. 'Or yours.'

'I'd say it's very much all of our business now,' Finn retorts.

Riley pulls her sleeves over her scars. 'For what it's worth, I can't believe Maia would hurt Rory.' She sighs. 'She really likes him. Sure, Maia's a bitch, and sort of shallow, but she's still a real person. And Rory's a good guy – Maia could do a lot worse.' Her face falls. 'Could have done a lot worse, I mean.'

'How about you?' Tamara stares Riley down. 'You had a crush on Rory, didn't you? I've seen you, always hanging around him – admit it, that's why you were eavesdropping. How do we know you didn't kill him in a fit of jealous rage? I bet you hate Maia, don't you? I reckon you made up all this other stuff to cover up what you've done.'

Riley's mouth drops open. She looks as if Tamara just assaulted her.

'That's ridiculous,' Finn growls. 'Of course Riley didn't kill Rory. She's tiny.'

'Anybody with a knife can kill someone,' Axel points out. 'With a weapon, all bets are off.'

'What about you?' Riley turns to him. 'How do we know you didn't do it?'

'Go screw yourself,' Axel snaps. 'Anyone could have done it. Especially you, you fucking little weirdo.'

'And there he is.' Finn shakes his head. 'The old Axel reasserts himself. We knew you were in there somewhere.'

I stare at Finn, paralysed with indecision. If there's ever a time to point out his connection to Rory, it's now.

And yet I remain silent.

Riley starts crying, rocking backwards and forwards. 'It's all of us,' she screams. 'Don't you get that? We *all killed him.*'

'Oh well done.' Finn glares at Axel. 'Now you've set her off. Like this situation wasn't dire enough already.'

Axel heaves himself upright again, his whole body quivering with rage. He eyeballs Finn, as if making up his mind, then launches himself, landing a punch on Finn's jaw. Finn grabs him and pushes him back onto the sofa. 'This place,' Axel roars. 'This place is—'

'STOP IT!'

We all turn to see Sonoya has leapt to her feet. '*Stop it!*' she screams. 'I know, all right. I know who killed Rory.'

There's a moment of stunned silence as everyone gapes at Sonoya, who's shaking with suppressed emotion. 'It was Mike,' she stammers. 'Mike did it.'

'Mike?' Finn frowns. 'How? He wasn't even with us.'

Sonoya sinks back on her seat, rubbing her temples. 'I think he drove out to the campsite during the night.'

'But we didn't see any tyre tracks.' Finn rubs his jaw as he slumps back into a chair.

'You wouldn't,' Sonoya continues. 'Not if he drove out using another route. He could have taken the long way, bypassing the Chinita Hills.'

'But why?' Axel asks, perplexed. 'Why would Mike want to hurt Rory?'

Sonoya sits there, mute.

'I know why,' I say, gazing at her. 'He found out, didn't he? Rory discovered what you and Mike were doing.'

The therapist inhales, rubbing her tear-stained face and staring back at me.

'Are you going to tell them, or am I, Sonoya?'

She clears her throat. 'Rory discovered something, right before we left the Sanctuary. Something bad about the business.' Her voice falters. 'Really bad.'

I glance at Tamara, who is watching Sonoya carefully. She doesn't look surprised. She knows what's coming, I realise.

'I . . . oh God.' The therapist wrings her hands, trying to pluck up the courage to continue. 'I . . . we . . . did something very wrong.'

'Like?' Finn prompts.

'Blackmail,' says Tamara.

Sonoya turns and blinks at her. 'How do you know?'

Tamara snorts. 'You think I'm stupid, don't you? That I'm just this brainless flaky woman who makes macramé and chants mantras. You think I haven't been paying attention? Mike's computer – he's got his password taped to the inside of his drawer, for heaven's sake. I'm aware of everything that goes on in this place, including what a mess it's in financially. Plus I found some interesting payments into the Sanctuary bank accounts.'

Sonoya swallows again, her eyes fixed on Tamara.

'What the fuck?' Axel growls at Sonoya. 'What is she talking about?'

'I can't.' Sonoya squeezes her eyes shut, as if blocking us all out. 'I can't do this.'

'You have to,' Finn insists.

She opens her eyes and looks at him, then at each of us in turn. 'You must understand I had no choice. One of the clients persuaded Mike to make a series of investments in his stock market fund, and, well, we ended up losing a lot of money. We had to find a way to pay off our debts and keep the Sanctuary running so I . . .' She stops, covers her face again. 'So I came up with a way to persuade some of our wealthier clients to help us out.'

Riley and Axel stare at her in horror, things falling into place.

'You blackmailed them, didn't you?' I say to her. 'Recording the therapy sessions and using what people told you in confidence.'

'Jesus Christ.' Riley looks stunned. She's stopped crying now and is sitting there, wide-eyed with bewilderment.

Sonoya's expression is as abject as I've ever seen. 'I can't excuse it. I suppose we thought of ourselves like Robin Hood, robbing a few of the wealthier clients so that everyone might benefit. We honestly believed we were doing good.'

Finn's laugh is a bark. 'You have to be fucking kidding me.'

'I don't understand,' Axel cuts in, frowning. 'So you think Mike killed Rory to stop him, what, destroying the Sanctuary?'

The therapist nods. 'Rory told us right before the hike that he was leaving for good, and that he planned to report us to the police when he got back.'

'But how did Rory know?' Axel asks, his expression puzzled. 'Did he look on Mike's computer too?'

Sonoya shakes her head. 'He rang Ed, about Alejandro. Ed told him about the blackmail.'

'*So that's why Ed left?*' Riley stares at Sonoya with red swollen eyes. 'Because you blackmailed him?'

Sonoya doesn't respond. But she doesn't deny it either. Riley squats in her armchair, clearly shell-shocked.

'So where's Mike now?' I ask. 'Where could he go in that jeep anyway? I thought there was no road access from the Sanctuary.'

'There isn't,' Sonoya confirms. 'Not really. But there's a pass about fifty miles from here that you can just about get a vehicle through. It's risky though. If you get stuck and anything goes wrong with your sat phone, you're screwed.'

'Why not simply call in a chopper?' Finn frowns.

'Leaves a paper trail – not what you want if you're planning to disappear.'

'You think he's done a runner then?' I ask her.

Sonoya nods. 'We were going to talk to Rory after the hike, try to persuade him not to go to the police. But I guess Mike decided that was too much of a long shot.'

Nobody speaks for a minute or two, everyone trying to take in the enormity of what Sonoya has told us.

'What about Alejandro?' I turn back to her. 'Did Mike kill him as well? Ed told him about the blackmail too, didn't he?'

Another silence descends on the group. Axel and Riley both seem winded, horrified.

'Tell us,' Finn says. 'Tell us what happened.'

Sonoya inhales, comes to a decision. 'The night of the ceremony, Maia saw a body in the pool. She ran inside, told Mike, who calmed her down and sent her to her suite. He thought it was simply the medicine, the ayahuasca, but when Mike went out to investigate he found Alejandro had drowned.'

'So what are you saying?' I gasp. 'That it *was* an accident?'

'I think so.'

'But you didn't call the police, did you?' I say. 'You packed us off for that barbecue and made up the story about them taking Alejandro's body. But you actually buried him in the desert.'

A whimper from the opposite chair. I turn to see Axel bent right over, making a keening noise, his hands grasping the side of his head and pulling at his wispy blond hair.

'What the fuck, Axel?' Finn frowns.

'It was me . . .' he replies in a small voice. 'I think I did it.'

'You?' Riley rounds on him, her expression horrified. 'What do you mean?'

Axel sits up. Forces himself to meet her eyes. 'After I took that second dose, at the ceremony, it was a . . . a really weird time. I was having all these wild visions about being a coyote, then a warrior, and I ran out of the Top to immerse myself in the desert. Tamara came with me, minding me, and I went to sit by the pool, I had this urge to be close to water, but then I started freaking out and Alejandro turned up to calm me down and I . . . I pushed him. He fell in the water. And I ran away.'

I stare at him. Was *Axel* the person Maia said she saw in the bushes?

'Why?' Riley leaps up, her face full of rage and horror. '*Why didn't you help him?*'

'I thought he'd climb out,' Axel whimpered. 'I knew he'd be angry, so I ran, I ran like a coyote. Then later when I sobered up a bit I came back. Mike was there, but Alejandro had gone. I told Mike what I'd done and he convinced me none of it was real, that it was simply my mind playing tricks, so I assumed the whole thing had only happened in my head.'

'*And you believed him?*' Riley shouts, incredulous. 'Even when he told us Alejandro was dead?'

Axel gazes at her with a helpless expression. 'I was so confused. I couldn't really make sense of it.' He drops his gaze. 'I guess I didn't want to think about it.'

'And you,' Riley turns to Sonoya, her fists clenching, 'you knew all this?'

'I didn't know it was Axel,' Sonoya says quietly.

I find my voice. 'But there was another person there,' I say. 'Maia told me she saw someone disappear into the bushes, when she came across the body in the pool. Someone watched Alejandro drown.'

Riley stares at me. 'Why didn't you tell us this before?'

'We knew an accident like this would be the last straw for the Sanctuary—' Sonoya cuts in before I can say anything.

Finn shakes his head again. 'Christ, Sonoya, you're something else. I've gotta hand it to you, you've got this butter-wouldn't-melt routine down pat. No one would guess it's all fake.'

'What do you mean?' Riley asks him, her expression bewildered.

'Why don't you ask *Doctor* Kimura?' he replies, drawing out her title with a sarcastic lilt.

I narrow my eyes at him. 'I don't understand.' I glance at Sonoya, who's dropped her head, bracing herself for what's coming.

'Our esteemed medic and psychotherapist here got the job on a fake CV,' Finn mutters. 'Sonoya Kimura never finished medical school, did you?'

'I . . . I . . .'

'You mean you're not actually a doctor?' Tamara gazes at her, astonished.

Sonoya swallows. Doesn't speak.

'Are you actually a therapist?' Riley's eyes widen at her.

'I did the training, yes, but . . .' Sonoya stops dead. We all fall silent, listening.

Outside, in the gathering dusk, the unmistakable sound of a vehicle drawing into the carport.

'Who is it?' Riley looks around wildly as if one of us might know.

'It's Mike,' Sonoya whispers, fear etched deep on her face. 'He's back.'

39

Riley stares wide-eyed at Sonoya. 'Why do you think Mike's come back?'

'I don't know . . .' She stops again, biting her lip. She looks truly terrified.

She thinks Mike's come for her, I realise. If Mike wiped all the computer and network files before he left, Sonoya's the only witness to the crimes they've perpetrated. He must have guessed that she would crack, confess, after he killed Rory. That we'd return to the Sanctuary to get help.

But what does that mean for the rest of us? My heart begins to race. We're all witnesses now, aren't we?

What will Mike do about us?

Get a grip, Zoey, I tell myself fiercely. He can't kill everyone. I shoot a look at Finn, who's standing at the entrance to the lounge, listening.

Outside, the car door slams.

'I'll check that phone,' Tamara says urgently. 'I'll try to find a signal and call the police.' She disappears before anyone can stop her.

'Do you think he's dangerous?' Riley whispers. 'Do they have guns here?'

Finn shakes his head. 'The gun laws in Mexico are very restrictive.'

'Still, we know he's handy with a knife,' Axel says grimly.

'This is ridiculous.' Finn grits his teeth. 'There's one of him and five of us. We need to go out there and confront him.'

'But what if he's brought somebody with him?' Axel asks. 'Maybe he's paid people to help him clean up.'

'What, like roaming Mexican bandits?' Riley snorts.

'We have to help Tamara,' Sonoya mumbles, trembling, but doesn't move.

'Go and shut yourself in the clinic with Maia,' I tell her. 'You don't need a key to lock it from the inside, do you?'

'No, you can do it manually,' she confirms.

'Go on,' Finn urges. 'If Mike's back, you should stay out of his way.'

Sonoya doesn't need any more persuading. She hurries off towards the clinic.

'Right,' Finn gazes at the rest of us. 'We should split up. Riley and Axel, you go out to the veranda and check around the house. Zoey and I will take the outbuildings. We'll meet back in here if we don't find him.'

'Perhaps some of us should stay inside.' Riley looks uncertain. 'In case he comes in, looking for Sonoya.'

Finn considers this. 'Okay, you two stay here. Zoey and I will check outside.'

'And what do we do if he rocks up?' Axel asks. 'Reason with him?'

'We should have something to protect ourselves,' Riley agrees. 'All of us.'

'Knives,' Axel suggests. 'That's about our only option.'

'I'm not going to fucking *stab* someone!' Riley wails.

Finn turns to her. 'You got any better ideas? Mike's already killed Rory. He isn't going to waltz in here empty-handed, is he?' Finn goes off to the kitchen, returning with three small knives. The cheap kind with plastic handles, mainly used for peeling fruit and veg. 'They're all I could find, someone cleared out the big ones.'

'What . . .' I stutter. 'Why?'

'Who knows?' shrugs Finn, handing them out. 'Perhaps Mike took them. They were pretty decent – worth at least $100 a piece.'

Riley stares at Axel's paring knife with disbelief. 'What is he supposed to do with that? *Peel* him to death?'

'Just shut up and get going,' Finn says. 'Go check out the bedrooms.'

'We'll need a torch,' I say to him. 'It'll be dark out there now.'

Finn walks over to a window. 'The clouds have thinned and there's a little moonlight – we're better off not advertising our whereabouts with a flashlight.' He heads towards the front entrance.

Axel hovers in the doorway. 'You sure you guys will be okay?'

'Go,' Finn insists. 'We can handle ourselves.'

Finn and I creep out of the house. He's right. The rain clouds have largely retreated, leaving a few stragglers scudding across the sky, and the near full moon is bright enough to see roughly where we're going. We make our way towards the sheds. No sign of Mike, but the jeep is parked in the carport.

Finn heads straight for it, clutching the knife in his hand. I follow, reluctantly. The jeep seems to be empty, but what if someone is hiding on the rear seat?

Finn tries the driver-side door. It swings open and he peers inside.

'Anything?' I whisper.

He shakes his head. 'Only water and lots of spare fuel. And a couple of suitcases.'

I press my face to the window, the hairs prickling the back of my neck. There's something super creepy about the empty jeep.

'C'mon, let's check the supplies shed.' Finn sidles up to the door and tries the handle. Still locked. Together we walk around the building, heart in mouth. The moonlight bathes everything in its soft silvery light, creating dark shadows all around us. There's an eerie silence. Not even the cicadas are singing.

Where's Tamara? I wonder if the phone had enough charge, if she's managed to get a signal.

I pray she's succeeded. That the police and an ambulance crew are already on the way, that this nightmare might end soon.

'Nothing,' Finn whispers as we round the outside of the other shed and test the door. It doesn't budge. 'He's not here.'

'He may have locked himself inside.'

Finn shakes his head. 'Can't see why he would.'

We stand there, hesitating. Wondering what to do next.

'Do you really think he's come back for Sonoya?' I hiss.

'What other explanation is there?'

I picture Sonoya and Maia, holed up in the clinic. We have to find Mike before he can get to them. Because he's got keys, I realise – he can unlock the clinic door from the outside.

Oh shit.

A second later there's a loud crash. We both stop dead.

'What was that?' I ask Finn, unable to keep a tremor from my voice.

'Sounds like it came from the veranda.'

Finn runs back towards the house. I follow as fast as I can, but I'm still slow and sluggish from the ordeal in the desert. Then the moon disappears behind a cloud, and my foot catches on a lump of stone.

I hit the ground with a sickening thump, and lie there, stunned, desperately hoping I haven't injured anything. By the time I catch my breath and sit up again, I'm alone in the darkness.

An animal screeches somewhere out in the wilderness beyond the Sanctuary wall, making me jump and my heart race even faster.

Then silence.

I stand up carefully, testing each limb. I'm stiff and sore, but nothing seems to be broken. It's then that I hear another noise; not a crash like a few moments ago, but a low, soft moan.

A human noise.

I freeze, listening. Nothing for a moment or two, then it's there, again. A grunt of pain, somewhere to the left of me.

I retrace my steps, quietly, cautiously, peering into the blackness. 'You okay?' I say tentatively.

'Zoey?' My name in a gasp. From near the garden.

I'm there in seconds. By the bench overlooking the flower borders, lies a man, half sitting, half slumped against the seat.

Mike.

I take a step backwards, terrified, but then the cloud cover clears, and I spot a deep red mark blooming across his white shirt, see the way he's clasping his stomach. He raises his head to look at me, his face pale in the moonlight, a soft sheen of sweat on his skin.

'Mike.' I move towards him. 'Are you hurt?'

He gives a barely perceptible nod before keeling onto his side. I run up and crouch next to him. It doesn't take many moments to realise what's wrong.

He's been stabbed. In the stomach, in almost exactly the same spot as Rory.

'I'll call for help.' I grasp his hand, about to shout for Finn and Axel.

'No,' Mike rasps, barely able to speak. 'No . . . don't.'

'Why?' I lower my head so I can hear him. His breathing sounds slow, laboured. 'We thought you'd gone. Done a runner.'

'The pass was blocked,' Mike grunts. 'Flash floods.'

'Can you get up?' I ask him. 'I'll help you to the clinic. Sonoya's there with Maia.'

'Be careful, Zoey, she's crazy . . .' His face contorts in pain and his grip loosens.

'Mike,' I whimper, dropping his hand and shaking him. I peer into his eyes but they're closed. I put two fingers to his wrist, but I'm trembling so much I can't feel a pulse.

Is he dead – or has he just passed out?

Oh God. I close my eyes briefly, my mind stalled in panic. What do I do? Should I try and revive him, or run to Sonoya for help?

Think, Zoey. Think.

Be careful, she's crazy . . . My brain finally processes Mike's words. And that Sonoya must be wrong about Mike being Rory's killer.

Or she lied.

Fuck.

I push myself to my feet and run in the direction of the house. But as I reach the veranda I see a figure over by the pool. 'Hey, Zoey!' Tamara waves.

'Mike,' I wheeze, running towards her. 'Sonoya stabbed him. We have to find the others and stop her.'

'Sonoya?' Tamara frowns at me in the moonlight. 'Are you kidding?'

I shake my head, glancing at the phone in Tamara's hand. 'Did you manage to get a signal?'

'I tried all around here. No joy.'

I want to collapse onto the ground and weep, but pull myself together. 'Come on,' I say urgently. 'We need to get to the others before Sonoya—'

'Before Sonoya destroys everything?' Tamara cuts in. 'Bit late for that.'

I stare at her. 'What do you mean?'

Tamara doesn't answer, just squints at me through the darkness. 'I like you, Zoey. As I said before, you remind me a lot of myself at your age.'

I frown at her. 'Thanks for the compliment, but we need—'

'You have . . . tenacity,' Tamara interrupts me again. 'Like a dog with a bone. Nothing scares you off, does it?'

I gaze at her, bewildered, and something falls into place as I recall what she said in the lounge, about having access to Mike's computer.

I know everything that goes on here.

Is that how she knew I had a brother? When Tamara caught me in Mike's office, I didn't have time to shut down my email account before I slammed the laptop shut. If she knew his password, she could have gone back into the office and read my messages. Some of the older ones from Dad mention Marcus and the rift between us.

Shit. Perhaps there was even some way she could tell I'd opened Ed's email to Mike. Through the browser history maybe.

'It's all ruined.' Tamara sighs, eyes glinting with tears. 'I gave up everything to work here. I sold up my house and my car, and left my son to come to the Sanctuary, because I believed in this place, in what we were doing, with all my heart.'

It was Tamara, I realise. She's been keeping tabs on me ever since she caught me in the office. It was Tamara who put that tarantula in my bed, and meddled with my shower, and sent me that text. She must have spotted the activity on Alejandro's phone via the Wi-Fi, and guessed it was me.

But why? Was she trying to scare me off?

Or was she actually trying to hurt me?

'They ruined it,' she hisses. 'Mike and Sonoya. They've ruined it all.' She's no longer looking at me, I notice, but back at the house. I turn to discover what's caught her attention.

At first sight, everything appears normal. Then I spot it. An odd, flickering light in the window, that initially I mistake for a candle. It takes my brain a few seconds to register the truth.

Not a candle.

Fire. *The Sanctuary is on fire.*

Shit. I grab Tamara's arm. 'Riley and Axel are in there, Maia and Sonoya too. We have to get them out.'

But Tamara won't budge. She seems mesmerised by the dance of the flames inside the house. Completely entranced.

'Come on,' I urge, but Tamara shakes her head, and suddenly I know why.

'It was you, wasn't it, that Maia saw in the bushes by the pool? You were with Axel that night, during the ceremony. You saw what he did, then let Alejandro drown, didn't you? Rather than have him jeopardise your precious Sanctuary.'

Tamara doesn't respond, still transfixed by the orange glow inside the house.

A moment later a shape runs towards us out of the darkness.

'Finn,' I gasp, with a surge of relief, but he barrels past me and grabs Tamara, trying to tackle her to the ground.

Then stops.

Stumbles.

As he falls, I see the knife in Tamara's hand. My mind freezes in horror.

This can't be happening.

None of this can be happening.

'Run, Zoey,' Finn gasps, clutching his side as he sinks to his knees. 'Warn the others—'

Tamara lunges at him, and he lifts an arm to fend her off. She'll kill him, I realise. He's no match for someone with a knife.

A demented, guttural roar rips through me, piercing the night as I charge at Tamara. I slam into her hard, knocking the wind right out of me, pitching us both sideways.

Black water swallows us, no pool lights to illuminate anything. I'm so dizzy, so disoriented I can't tell which way is up or down. Within seconds, my lungs are screaming for air as I flail around, frantically trying to reach the surface, panic filling every fibre of my being.

Relax, Zoey. Finn's voice in my head. *The water won't let you sink.*

I let myself go limp. Feel it push me upwards. I'm just breaking the surface and taking a desperate breath when a hand grabs my ankle. Water rushes into my lungs as I'm dragged down again. I try to fight, but the searing pain in my chest, in my head, is overwhelming.

Behind it, beyond it, a billowy calm envelops me as the darkness crushes in.

This is it, my last thought comes.

This is the end.

40

'Thank God!'

Sonoya's face hovers over mine as I come round, coughing convulsively, my body racked with pain. I'm on the patch of grass near the bushes, I realise, as she turns me on my side to bring up more water. My lungs are burning. Tears of anguish stream from my eyes.

'Finn!' I gasp, trying to get up, but Sonoya pushes me back down. 'He's okay, Zoey. He'll be fine.'

I stop fighting her. 'You sure?' I pant, unable to breathe normally.

'I just checked. He'll have a couple of scars, but the knife didn't hit anything important.'

'Tamara,' I croak. 'Is she . . .' I convulse with another fit of coughing. 'I think she stabbed Mike.'

'She's over there.' Sonoya points to the other side of the pool. I turn my head to see Tamara sitting on the ground, drenched, shoulders hunched, Riley and Axel standing over her.

No sign of that knife, thankfully.

Riley is wet, I notice, her long dark hair hanging in tendrils. Axel too, his shorts sodden, clinging to his legs.

'What happened?' I rasp, clearing water from my throat.

'We heard you yell and came as fast as we could,' Sonoya says. 'Riley leapt straight in and pulled you to the side.'

'*Riley?*'

351

'She's a pretty strong swimmer, it turns out. Axel jumped in too and tackled Tamara.'

It's then I remember the house. 'The fire.' I push myself up and gaze around wildly, but can't see the building from this angle. 'Did you get Maia out? Did you find Mike?'

Sonoya nods. 'Maia's safe in the Top.' She doesn't say anything about Mike.

I scramble to my feet and almost wish I hadn't. The Sanctuary is lost. A deep red glow emanating from its windows, flames licking at the veranda, aiming for the roof.

'Isn't there something we can do?' I whimper, suppressing the urge to cough. 'Shouldn't we try to put it out?'

Sonoya shakes her head. 'It's too late, Zoey.'

'But we can't simply stand here and watch it burn!'

No one answers. For the next few minutes, we all do exactly that. Watch that beautiful building brighten and blaze. I can feel the heat from here now, warm on my skin, making our faces glow.

'We need to get you out of those wet clothes,' Sonoya says. 'Before you freeze.'

She takes hold of my arm, and this time I let her pull me away.

The scene in the Top resembles the aftermath of a combat field. I stand there, shivering now, trying to take it all in. Maia is lying on an assortment of cushions, her face turned away. Finn is next to her, prostrate on the tarpaulin that covers the ground. Sonoya has bandaged his wounds using medical supplies Axel found in the storage shed, after locking Tamara in the generator unit. Thankfully he also found Mike's sat phone in the side pocket of the jeep.

On the other side of the tent, Riley is struggling out of her wet clothes and wrapping herself in a blanket.

No sign of Mike. I feel a wave of sadness. I guess they decided to leave his body for the police.

'Take off those clothes, Zoey.' Sonoya glances at me. I'm shaking from head to toe – more from shock than cold. I strip off, pulling a blanket around me, relieved to spot Simpkins curled up on a chair at the edge of the Top.

A moment later Axel is back from hunting down dry clothes. 'I can't get anywhere near the house,' he says dejectedly, 'but I got these.' He drops a pile of overalls he must have retrieved from one of the sheds. He looks at Finn. 'You all right, dude?'

'Never better,' Finn grunts.

'I'll go call again, make sure help is on the way.' But as Axel turns to leave, we hear the noise. Faint at first, but growing louder with every second. I pull on the overalls then join Riley and Axel at the entrance of the Top, staring up at the moonlit sky. Within a matter of seconds, headlights come into view.

'What on earth . . .?' Sonoya breathes, joining us. 'The air ambulance can't be here already.'

'Maybe someone spotted the fire from a plane,' Axel shifts his weight from his bad ankle, 'and alerted the emergency services before I did.'

'And they, what, sent a *helicopter?*' Riley frowns. 'How's that going to help with a fire?'

Nevertheless we start yelling and running, waving our arms to attract the pilot's attention, all gripped by the same fear that it might fly past. But within a minute, as the insect whine of the rotors increases to a steady roar, it becomes obvious the helicopter is looking for a safe place to land. It touches on a patch of bare earth a hundred yards or so from the Top.

We all watch, mesmerised, as two men climb out, ducking their heads, then pausing to stare at the burning building.

'Over here,' Axel yells, waving again. The taller of the men turns, breaking into a jog in our direction.

Suddenly Riley lets out a yelp and starts running towards him. She collides with the man, flinging her arms around his waist, wrapping him in a hug.

'Fuck me,' Axel breathes. 'It's Ed.' He bursts into laughter, a mix of incredulity and relief, as Ed approaches, Riley hanging on to his arm. His open, handsome face exudes friendly concern.

'What the hell happened?' He nods at the blaze in the distance. 'Have you called for help?'

'I did,' Axel says. 'Though there's nothing much they can do about a fire. Not out here.'

Ed glances about, his expression alarmed. 'Where are the others? Did you get everybody out?' He looks at Sonoya. 'Where's Mike?'

Sonoya shakes her head. 'Maia French is here, and she's hurt. Rattlesnake bite. You need to get her to the hospital. Finn too – he's got two knife wounds that need sutures.'

Ed's eyes widen, but he doesn't waste time with more questions. 'Where are they?'

Sonoya indicates the Top. Ed runs to the other man approaching our little group, and they both return to speak to the pilot. A couple of minutes later they're carrying Maia towards the helicopter, suspended in a blanket; behind them, Axel and Riley help Finn, his arm in a makeshift sling.

As he reaches the helicopter Finn stops, turns back.

Searching for me, I realise. I hurry towards him. He looks pale and shocked. Withdrawn. 'Get better,' I say, wanting to give him a hug but afraid I'll hurt him.

Finn nods. 'You too, Zoey.' His eyes linger. I sense there's something else he'd like to say, but there isn't time. 'Stay in touch,' he mumbles, then climbs into the helicopter.

Ed walks over to Sonoya. They talk for a few moments, then

she follows Finn inside, the pilot closing the door behind her. An instant later the rotors whirr into action and the chopper takes off again into the night.

There's a pain in my chest that has nothing to do with my water-damaged lungs. I watch the lights of the helicopter grow fainter, wondering if I'll ever see Finn again.

'Zoey?'

I turn to the other man who has stayed behind. Mid height, roughly my age. He's wearing a black bobble hat, and his tight clipped beard reminds me a little of Rory. I push away another pang of sadness, thinking of him still out there, all alone in the desert.

'You don't recognise me, do you?' the man says in an English accent, with a hint of a smile.

I frown, confused. *Why is he staring at me like that?*

'Should I?' I mumble. A wave of dizziness hits me, and I close my eyes until it passes. 'Sorry. Today has been . . . terrible.'

The man holds out a hand to steady me. A second later, Ed is by our side.

'I'm guessing you're Zoey.' He looks at the guy with the beard, then back to me. 'So, do you remember Jake?'

I turn and stare at the other man. It's difficult, what with us both being a dozen years older, and his hat, but I notice a bit of red fringe peaking out beneath. 'What's going on?' I stammer, trying to hold it together. Behind me the house is still blazing, and the crack and hiss of the flames is a terrible sound.

'Let's get you into the Top.' Ed takes my arm. 'You need to warm up. It'll be an hour, probably, before the helicopter returns and we can fly you the heck out of here. Meanwhile you look like you could do with some of this.'

He holds up his hand. There's a large Thermos in it. I'm praying it's full of something hot.

Ed helps me to the Top, sitting me on the cushions and wrapping me in more of the wool blankets kept for the ceremonies. He pours a steaming cup of coffee from the flask. I cradle my hands around it, waiting for it to cool enough to drink.

'Why are you here?' I say to Jake Harris as Ed disappears with Riley and Axel – presumably to check on Tamara. 'Or more to the point, why am I?'

Jake sighs. 'Yeah, I guess it's all rather confusing. To answer your first question, we were worried about you – all of you. After Ed spoke to Rory, and he found out about Alejandro, Ed finally told me what happened with Sonoya and Mike.' He gives me an inquiring look. 'You know about that?'

'Yes, I know about the blackmail,' I say, feeling increasingly uncomfortable. Is Jake here for some kind of showdown?

If so, who with? Sonoya – or me?

'Ed called up some of the people he'd met here to find out if they'd been blackmailed too, discovered a few others. So we both tried ringing the Sanctuary and couldn't get through. We kept calling, and when there was no answer we decided to hire a helicopter to come and check things out.'

'Okay,' I say warily, wondering why Jake Harris would have the slightest concern about my welfare. 'How about my second question – why did you intervene with the police and pay for me to come here? Was it some kind of weird revenge?'

'So you know about that too?'

I nod.

'How?'

'Finn Cooper found out. He told me.'

Jake closes his eyes for a moment. 'That must have been . . . baffling.'

'You don't say.' I raise an eyebrow at him.

'That's why I didn't want you to know, Zoey – I knew you wouldn't understand.'

'So explain it to me. When we spoke at Laura's funeral – the *only* occasion we ever met – you made it pretty clear you blamed me for what happened to your sister. What changed?'

'Time.' Jake sighs. 'Experience. Everything seems so simple, doesn't it, when you're that age? But as you get older, as inevitably you mess up your life – and other people's . . . you make mistakes, then make amends, and you realise things aren't so black and white.' He gazes at me. 'I'm truly sorry about what I said to you at Laura's funeral, Zoey. I was angry and I was grieving and you were there, so I took it all out on you – instead of your brother.'

'How did you know it was him?' it occurs to me to ask. 'Did Laura say anything?'

He shakes his head. 'I found her diary, after . . . afterwards. I didn't give you an opportunity to explain. Later, I realised it wasn't your fault—'

'Yes it was,' I say. 'I should have done something. I shouldn't have kept quiet.'

'It was your *brother*, Zoey. Your twin. And though he did a shitty thing, a really stupid, cruel thing, he was young too. And neither of you could have known what my sister . . . what Laura would do. It's all very well with hindsight, isn't it? All simple and straightforward, what we should and shouldn't have done. But we forget that when you're in it, in that moment, you can't see what will happen, what might be the consequences of your actions.'

I swallow, trying to clear my throat, then give in to an overwhelming rush of emotion. Dropping my head and crying and crying until there's nothing left to cry out. Jake conjures up a box of tissues and hands them to me, one by one.

'I'm sorry,' I sob, wiping my eyes. 'It's all been . . . much too much.'

'I can imagine.'

I blink at him, unable to focus through my tears. 'I mean, I'm grateful. Don't get me wrong, I'm very grateful.'

To my astonishment, Jake folds my hand in his, holding it firm. 'I did a lot of damage too, Zoey, after Laura died. Drinking too much, numbing out too much. Neglecting the people I claimed to love. I have many regrets. And the more they accumulated, the more I regretted how I treated you that day. It took a lot of guts and compassion to come to Laura's funeral – I'm sorry I couldn't see that at the time.'

We both sit there for a minute or so, letting the silence speak.

'But how did you know about what happened at the club in New York?' I ask eventually. 'Were you keeping tabs on me?'

He sighs. 'When I finally went to AA, to start dealing with my issues, one of the first things they encourage you to do is make amends. So I checked you out on social media, followed you from a fake account so you wouldn't know it was me. And I saw enough . . .' he stops.

'What?' I prompt.

'I saw things weren't going so well for you either. That your life had . . . I'm not sure how to put it . . . stalled. And I felt bad about that. Anyway, I kinda kept an eye on you. And I contacted your friend Franny, asked her to do me a favour.'

I frown. 'What sort of favour?'

'I asked that if you were ever in trouble, she'd call me.'

'So Fran called you?'

'As soon as you were arrested. I rang a law firm in New York, and they negotiated your release on condition you attended rehabilitation. And I sorted things out with Mr Havell.' Jake pulls a look of distaste. 'It didn't take much. Money is the only thing a man like that has any respect for.'

'And you chose to send me here? Because it had worked for you?'

'That's right – because it had worked for me.' He inhales, glancing around the Top. 'But I'm guessing this wasn't exactly the therapeutic experience I had in mind.'

I muster up something approaching a smile. 'Well, it's certainly been an experience.'

Jake gives me a sorrowful look. In the distance we hear the buzz of the helicopter returning. 'Come on.' He gets up, extending his hand. 'Let's get you the hell out of here.'

Epilogue

'Zoey!'

Mum's voice calls from the kitchen as the doorbell rings. 'Can you get it? It'll be Hermes or Amazon again. I'm in the middle of fixing the bloody dishwasher.'

I click save on my job application and go downstairs, seeing a dark shape visible through the stained-glass panels in the door. But the man standing on our porch in a smart black tailored suit and dark wool coat is most definitely not a delivery driver.

I blink at him, trying to process what's right in front of me.

'Your face is an absolute picture.' He grins. 'You look like a startled meercat.'

'Finn!' I stammer. 'What the fuck are you doing here?'

'Good to see you too, Zoey.' He looks past me and waves. I turn to find Mum wiping her hands on a tea towel, gazing at the two of us with undisguised curiosity. 'Hello, Mrs Baxter!' Finn calls.

'Zoey, for goodness' sake let the man in.' My mother's face breaks out into her politest social smile as she greets Finn in the hallway. 'Very pleased to meet you, Mr . . .?'

'Mr Finley Cooper, but please call me Finn.'

Mum's eyes widen at the mention of his name. I suppress a groan. Please God, I pray under my breath, please do not let her say anything crass about the gossip columns.

'I read all about your adventure in the desert,' my mother gushes, ushering him indoors. 'Though Zoey hasn't been very forthcoming.'

'I told you all about it, Mum,' I say in a weary voice that makes me sound about ten years old. 'Several times.'

My mother raises a conspiratorial eyebrow at Finn, then glances at her watch – too early, thankfully, to offer him supper.

'Come into the kitchen,' she says, trying to disguise how flustered I know she is. 'I've got some scones in the freezer, I could defrost a couple if you'd like. And a coffee? I guess you Americans don't drink tea.'

'That would be perfect, Mrs Baxter, but only if it's no bother. And I'd love a cup of tea, thank you.'

'For heaven's sake call me Jenny,' Mum says, busying herself with the kettle and teabags while Finn settles at the kitchen table, giving me an amused smile. I can't bring myself to return it. I'm so thrown by his sudden appearance on our doorstep, not to mention I'm still wearing my baggy sweat pants and one of Dan's old shirts.

He squints at me. 'You look . . . different.'

My mother gives me a quick once-over and comes to exactly the same conclusion. 'Go upstairs and pop some proper clothes on, Zoey.'

I don't argue. I turn tail and climb the stairs in several bounds, throwing open my wardrobe. Most of my decent clothes are still in Dan's apartment in New York, and there's nothing here that isn't years out of date. I flick through some old dresses, contemplate borrowing something of Mum's, then pull myself together.

It's just Finn, I remind myself. Finn, who's seen me hot and sweaty and ragged with exhaustion. Finn, who I last saw being loaded into that helicopter, along with Maia.

Finn, who I haven't heard from since – though I've been back in the UK for three months now.

What is he doing here? I wonder, stomach tightening with apprehension. And something else I can't quite put my finger on – a kind of desolation. I've spent those months coming to terms with what happened – and with the fact I most likely would never see him again; I've just about made peace with it all.

I peek over the bannisters as I come back downstairs, dressed in a pair of old jeans and a top Mum bought me a couple of birthdays ago. The incongruity of seeing Finn, in his dark suit and smart overcoat, his expensive polished leather shoes, sitting in our shabby and not-so-chic kitchen chatting to my mum is almost more than I can deal with.

'How are you?' My breezy tone sounds fake even to me. I sit at the table. Mum plonks a mug of tea in front of me and gives me a look of mingled pride and exasperation.

'Oh, you know,' Finn sounds equally cheery, 'getting back into the swing of things.'

'When were you released from hospital?' I ask, though of course I know – I've been reading the online gossip columns too.

'I was only there a week. Flesh wounds.'

'Terrible business.' Mum removes the scones from the micro-wave and piles them on a plate. God, what a cliché we are, I think, my stomach clenching in embarrassment.

So bloody provincial.

Finn smiles politely. 'It was . . . interesting.'

'I saw you in the papers,' Mum says. 'And that Maia French too.'

'Yeah, you can hardly open a magazine these days without seeing a headline like Maia French's Near-Death Snake Bite Drama.' I allow myself a teenage-style eye roll.

Finn laughs, and even my mother smiles. 'They've been call-ing round here, you know,' she says to him. 'The reporters. Though Zoey won't speak to any of them. I told her, she should sell her story, get a bit of money to go back to college with. But she won't listen.'

Finn raises a bemused eyebrow and I stare at the table, cheeks flushed with humiliation. 'I can do without my mugshot plastered all over *Heat* magazine,' I say to Mum, flashing her a look that screams *shut-the-fuck-up*.

'There was that piece in the *Daily Mail*,' she continues, oblivious. 'And you didn't even get paid. If you'd talked to them, you'd at least have something to show for it, Zoey.'

I grimace. Being door-stepped for several weeks after I got home was one of the more unnerving experiences of my life, even after the dramatic events at the Sanctuary. I glance at Finn, wondering how he's been coping with it – especially given what happened with his sister.

'Stony face, walk fast, say nothing,' Finn advises. 'And never read the shit they print about you.'

Suddenly I have a thousand questions. How is Finn, really? Is he using again? What has he been doing? Has he spoken to any of the others?

I've stayed in touch with Naomi and – weirdly – Riley, who's just been offered a book contract for her memoir. We've been messaging each other regularly on social media, a small impromptu support group of our own. But Finn isn't on Facebook, or anywhere else, it seems. And I didn't like to ask Jake if he had any way of contacting him. Despite what he said when we parted in the desert, it felt too . . . presumptuous. I didn't want to be that girl, the sad, silly, desperate acquaintance who lacks the dignity to move on.

'What are you doing here anyway?' I blurt, as Finn swallows his second scone. I can tell he's not hungry, that he's simply being polite for Mum's sake, and for some reason it makes my heart ache even more.

'Zoey!' Mum admonishes. 'That's a little rude.'

'It's fine, Jenny.' Finn smiles. 'I'm used to Zoey's bluntness.' He turns back to me. 'I'm here for a meeting in London, actually, so I thought I'd check in on you.'

'Okay,' I say. 'That's nice,' I add, as Mum catches my eye and glares at me.

'Wondered if you'd care to show me around a bit?' He drains the rest of his milky tea, his eyes never leaving my face.

'The house?' I ask, incredulous. 'It's not exactly very grand, but you're welcome to view our vintage avocado bathroom suite. It's been there since the eighties.'

'I hear Guildford has an impressive cathedral,' Finn smirks.

He's teasing me, I realise, and relax a little.

'You could take Finn to Stoke Park,' Mum suggests, wiping crumbs from the table. 'You might be in luck with the weather.'

I glance outside. Patches of blue sky just visible between the clouds.

'You sure?' I ask him. 'When do you have to be in London?'

'Any time,' he says casually.

'Okay then.' I get to my feet, grab my coat, my purse and my phone, stuffing them in my pocket. Finn follows me to the front door, shaking Mum's hand and doing his best impression of the polite American gentleman. Mum beams back at him, clearly smitten.

'Oh, Zoey,' she calls after me as we reach the gate, 'could you pick up a pack of dental floss from Boots if you're in town? And some Gavsicon.'

I head up Church Road, with Finn by my side, as fast as my legs will carry me. Which isn't very fast. Ever since the hike, and everything that happened afterwards, I've been weak and tired.

Delayed shock, my GP says. My body and mind occupied with processing the trauma.

Finn, however, doesn't appear the least affected by those last days in the desert. Did the police interview him too? I remember all too well those long hours in the station in Hermosillo, giving statements. If Finn flew direct to a hospital in the US, would he have been interviewed there? Perhaps that's another thing the super-rich avoid, their people behind the scenes pulling the right strings.

But I don't want to spend these few precious hours raking over that awful day; I'd rather forget all about it. 'Do you really want to go and see the cathedral?' I ask Finn instead.

'Would you recommend it?'

'Not especially.'

'Why don't we go to that park your mum mentioned?'

I lead him there. We wander through the Japanese garden, pausing by the model boating lake to watch the fish. Finn spots the children's playground and makes a beeline for the swings.

'They're for kids,' I say, glancing about for irate parents – thankfully there's no one much around, just a dad helping a toddler negotiate the climbing frame.

Finn shrugs. 'I'm a rule breaker.' He pats the swing next to him. 'Sit down.'

I sit. The seat is still damp with rain and it soaks into the back of my jeans. I conduct a quick internal scan, like the psychologist referred by my GP taught me. *Name your emotions, Zoey.*

Right now I'm scared and confused.

But mainly scared.

'Hey.' Finn squints at me. 'I know what's different – you've removed your piercings.'

I nod. 'I felt I'd kind of outgrown them. Plus they were annoying, to be honest – always getting infected.'

'I like it,' he says. 'Makes you look more . . .'

'Grown up?' I raise an eyebrow at him. 'About time, isn't it?' I take a deep breath. 'So why are you here?' I ask Finn again, in a tone that makes it clear I'm not up for a flippant response.

'I heard via Ed and Jake that you're looking for a job.'

A dip in my stomach that registers as disappointment. *Get real, Zoey*, I tell myself. *What did you expect? For him to come all this way and ask you to marry him?*

He's married already, I remind myself.

'Yeah, well, like you said out in the desert, I need to grow up – and get from under Mum's feet. And that means finding gainful employment.'

Finn looks embarrassed. 'I'm sorry I said that. I didn't mean—'

'You did, and you were right. But it turns out there isn't a huge demand for thirty-two-year-old screw-ups with nothing of note on their CV, so I might have to go back to college and train in IT or whatever.'

'I thought your ambition was to be a lawyer?'

I frown at Finn. 'How do you know that?'

'I was listening when you said it on the hike. For what it's worth, I reckon you'd be really good at it.'

'Well, like I told Axel, it takes years to train, with a massive student debt to boot. I've left it a bit late.'

'So you're not wedded to that then, as a career?'

I shake my head. 'Honestly, I'm not sure I'm cut out for it anyway. I'm over any sort of drama in my life.'

Finn studies me. I'd forgotten how he does that. Like an X-ray machine, peering right inside you. A human MRI scanner. I ask him a question I've been wanting to ask, ever since that terrible last evening at the Sanctuary.

'Finn, why didn't you tell me about Sonoya? You know, that stuff about her fake CV.'

He shrugs. 'She was doing you good, Zoey. Despite everything, Sonoya was a great therapist. I didn't want to ruin that for you.'

Will she get to practise again? I wonder. I'd heard she had the charges against her suspended, in return for being a witness for the prosecution in Tamara's upcoming trial.

I think about what I confessed to her, about Marcus and Laura, about my part in it all. And how telling Sonoya helped me tiptoe towards self-forgiveness, to accept I'm not defined by one bad decision.

I think, too, about telling Finn. Right here, right now. About how I know Jake, as well. But I don't want to spoil the moment. Don't want it to colour what may well be the last time we'll ever meet.

'Sonoya kept some files on you too,' I say. 'I should have told you before. But I guess they were destroyed in the fire.'

'Did you listen to them?' Finn looks at me.

I shake my head again. 'I didn't have a chance. The battery on the phone gave out.'

He falls into silence, watching a group of boys on the playing field kicking a football around in a half-arsed sort of way.

'Would you like to know, Zoey?' he says, after one of the boys somehow manages to miss an open goal. 'Do you want to hear all my dark and dirty secrets?'

I gaze back at him. Do I? I'm not sure. 'Some other time,' I say breezily, then cringe inside as I realise how that sounds.

Finn rocks gently on his swing, his expression thoughtful. 'Actually, I have a proposition.'

'An offer I can't refuse?' I quip.

'That's what I hope.'

'At your dad's company?' My curiosity is piqued.

Finn shakes his head. 'He offered me my old job back, but I'm done there.' I read about Finn's reconciliation with his father, after he came out of hospital. I was pleased that there'd been at least one decent outcome in the aftermath of the Sanctuary's destruction.

Or perhaps two. I've finally got back in contact with my own father, even had a conversation with him on the phone. And he's halfway to persuading both Marcus and me to meet. To try and put what happened behind us.

After all, if Jake can manage it, why can't I?

'What is it then?' I ask. 'This proposition.'

'Ed and I are starting a research foundation,' Finn says, 'looking into the use of psychedelics in addiction and other psychological disorders. We'll also be a kind of lobby group, with a view to changing the law and bringing products to market that are safe and tested, with predictable effects.'

I gaze at him, impressed. 'That's a great idea,' I say. 'Congratulations.'

'I'd like you to help us run it.'

A laugh explodes out of me. The boys turn and stare for a moment, then swing their attention back to their game.

'Why is that so funny?' Finn asks.

'I dunno.' I shrug. 'I thought perhaps you were going to offer me something secretarial, or maybe a job in the post room.'

Finn doesn't answer for a while. 'You don't rate yourself very highly, do you, Zoey?'

I squint at him.

'I mean, you saved my life, and probably a few others,' he says. 'You're brave and honest and fiercely intelligent, and only a little bit fucked-up.'

Stupid tears prick my eyes. 'I can't do it, Finn.'

He frowns. 'What, because of those charges? I thought Jake told you he sorted it. He paid off that guy Havell, and without a witness statement from him, the police have nothing.'

'No, it's not that.'

'So what's the problem then? You've got dual nationality so a visa shouldn't be an issue.'

I feel a surge of guilt that he came all this way, traipsing out to the Surrey suburbs for me to turn him down flat. 'Finn,' I say, 'it's just that . . . I don't think I can.' I falter. Am I really going to do this?

I take another deep breath and force myself on. 'I don't think I can be your colleague, I mean. Or your friend. Sorry.'

There's a long silence. I wait for Finn to glance at his watch, tell me he has a car waiting to take him back to London.

'Me neither,' he says eventually.

I swallow down another surge of disappointment. And the urge to get up and run is almost overwhelming, because suddenly this is more painful that I can bear.

Not over him at all, it seems.

Finn sighs, eyes still fixed on the boys' football game. 'I had a lot of time to think after I came out of hospital. About everything. What I wanted to do with my life, what my priorities were. And Verity and I had a long talk about our marriage, and it's clear that it's over – on both sides, I should add. We've filed for divorce.'

'Okay,' I say, not wanting to interrupt. I can see how hard this is for Finn, to come here and admit this stuff.

'The thing is, whatever else happened to me at the Sanctuary, despite all the madness, those ceremonies changed me. You were right, I went there with a heart full of anger and hatred, wanting revenge, but the ayahuasca showed me how futile it was, how Rory and I . . . we were locked in some kind of karmic battle . . .' He stops. Regroups. 'I can't really explain it, Zoey.

But the irony is, Rory did me a lot of good. And I could see that he was a decent man. He made mistakes. We all make mistakes.'

His words, so like Jake's, take me back to the Top, that night. When I assumed I'd never set eyes on Finn again.

'Have you?' I ask him. 'Since you left the Sanctuary, have you made any mistakes?'

'Have I fallen off the wagon, you mean? The answer's no. No, I haven't. I even refused antidepressants, after I got out of hospital. I wanted to face things exactly as they are.'

He turns and looks at me. 'How about you, Zoey? Have you been okay? You reckon you're ready to move on?'

I consider the nightmares I've had since leaving the desert. The panic attacks. The low-grade anxiety that haunts my waking hours. 'I think I came out of there a different person,' I admit. 'Not entirely in good ways.'

Finn gets up and stands in front of my swing. 'Please come back to the States with me. The job offer is simply an excuse, though I happen to believe you'll be an asset wherever you end up. But more than that, I miss you, Zoey. I miss your . . . what's that word you Brits use? Spunkiness.'

I blink at him again, not believing what I'm hearing and trying not to cry. Every time I considered contacting Finn – which was about twenty times a day – I pictured those old photos I'd trawled through on the internet, Finn with one glamorous woman after another, including that actress from the HBO hit series.

Could he seriously be interested in me?

Finn reaches out and takes my hand. I'm well aware how odd we must look, a scruffy girl in deeply unfashionable jeans, and a smartly dressed guy in a designer suit and overcoat, holding hands by the children's swings. The picture amuses me so much I giggle.

'Zoey, I lay in that hospital bed and a whole procession of people came to see me, but every time there was a knock on the door, I realised I was hoping it was you.'

I lose the battle with my tears. Finn doesn't comment, simply pulls a handkerchief out of his coat pocket and hands it to me. I gaze at it. Fresh starched cotton, with a little FC embroidered in the corner.

'This is ridiculous,' I say, laughing and crying at the same time. 'Who uses handkerchiefs any more?'

Finn laughs too. 'Friend of mine sells them. He says reusable tissues are the next big thing.'

I dab my eyes carefully. 'If I said yes,' I ask, handing it back to him. 'What happens if it doesn't work out?'

Finn stuffs the hankie in his coat pocket. 'As they say in recovery, Zoey, one day at a time. No need to get ahead of ourselves, is there?'

I gaze up at him. He's right. Where will I ever be if I always expect to fail?

Time to stop playing it safe, Zoey.

Time to stop running, and actually get in the game.

'Fancy a drink?' Finn extends a hand. 'Something non-alcoholic, that is. As long as it's not milky tea.'

That makes me smile. As does the thought of Mum's face, when I go home later and tell her the news. Finn and I walk through the park, hand in hand, past the boys kicking the ball and hurling casual insults at one another, then head up towards the chemist on the high street.

Acknowledgements

Many thanks for everyone who helped me with this book, especially my ever-patient family – I promise I'll get around to some housework and cooking one of these days. Right after I've finished this next chapter . . .

Thank you too to my agents Mark 'Stan' Stanton and Julie Fergusson, editor Jo Dickinson, along with Sorcha Rose, Jenny Platt, Melis Dagoglu, Charlotte Webb, and all the hard-working team at Hodder.

As ever, I'm indebted to all my lovely writer pals on Facebook, but particularly Caroline Green, Julie-Ann Corrigan and Catherine Cooper for beta reading – thank you so much! As always, particular thanks to Marie Adams for keeping me afloat in the stormy seas of writing – and life in general.

Finally, a special mention for Alex Skinner, who loved the last one. Hope you enjoy this one too, Alex!

Emma

Enjoyed *The Sanctuary*?
Don't miss Emma Haughton's first novel!

'A superlative locked-room mystery' *Sunday Times*

'Tense, thrilling and unpredictable' ALLIE REYNOLDS

Out now in paperback, ebook and audio.